
The envelope arrived. Inside was a check for a hundred pounds and a list of five names. There was no letter. Not even a note.

Helen tore them all up: the envelope, the check, the list. And flushed them down the toilet.

She waited for a phone call, but none came. After a week she called his flat. The number was no longer in service.

He had flown out of her life, leaving her nothing to remember him by but a bracelet and a baby.

SUSAN BOWDEN

Returning

HarperPaperbacks
A Division of HarperCollinsPublishers

This is a work of fiction. The characters, incidents, and
dialogues are products of the author's imagination and are not
to be construed as real. Any resemblance to actual events or
persons, living or dead, is entirely coincidental.

HarperPaperbacks   *A Division of* HarperCollins*Publishers*
                 10 East 53rd Street, New York, N.Y. 10022

Cover photograph by Herman Estevez

First printing: July 1993

Printed in the United States of America

HarperPaperbacks, HarperMonogram, and colophon are
trademarks of HarperCollins*Publishers*

❖ 10 9 8 7 6 5 4 3 2 1

For Eileen Fallon, my ever-supportive agent, who fanned the flame and kept it burning. Without Eileen, this story might never have been told.

I years had been from home,
And now, before the door,
I dared not open, lest a face
I never saw before

Stare vacant into mine
And ask my business there.
My business,—just a life I left,
Was such still dwelling there?

—Emily Dickinson
"Returning"

1

The telephone rang just as Helen Lawrence was about to scrape the mound of finely chopped onion into the casserole. At the first ring, her heartbeat increased its pace. She set down the chopping knife.

"I'll get it," she said quickly to David, but she was too late.

David crashed down the chair he had tilted against the wall and bolted across the kitchen to answer on the third ring. "Probably be for me," he said over his shoulder to his mother. "Hallo? Oh hi, Aunt Ann, how are you?"

Helen's heartbeat slowed down. Ann phoned from Toronto every year on this date.

"Tell her I'm just washing my hands," she mouthed at David as he chatted away to his godmother. He nodded.

Drying her hands on a kitchen towel, Helen stood beside David, waiting to speak to Ann.

"Okay. Bye." He handed the receiver to her and then resumed his seat, picking up the sports section of the *Winnipeg Free Press*.

"Are you all right?" Ann's voice, still very English after almost thirty years in Canada, sounded anxious.

"I'm fine."

"I suppose you can't say much with David there."

"That's right."

"I just wondered how you were, with it being May the twenty-first, you know."

"Yes, I know." Helen's hands felt damp again. "I'm just fine. Getting ready for a dinner party."

"Good. Keep yourself occupied."

Silence stretched between them.

"How's the job search going?" Helen asked at last.

"Not that hot. No one seems to want old-fashioned secretaries with only shorthand and typing anymore."

"You'll have to take a computer course."

"I'm already looking into that."

"How's the new apartment? Are you and Eric settling in okay?"

"It's fine." Another awkward pause. "Well, old girl," Ann said, "I'd better go and let you get on with your dinner party. Hang in there. Remember, as Scarlett O'Hara said, tomorrow's another day."

"Right. You're a darling to call, Annie. I'll phone you back tomorrow and we can have a long chat."

"Right. Do that. When Bruce and David are out. Bye."

"Bye, Ann." Helen set down the receiver and switched on the answering machine.

"I'm expecting some calls," David said.

Helen ignored him.

"You okay?" David asked. "You look as if you'd like to take a stick to the phone and beat it to death."

"I would. You know how I hate the telephone."

"It's an obsession with you. Really, it is. Something bad must've happened in your past and you got the news by—"

"Haven't you got an essay or something to write?"

David grinned at her. "Almost twenty-one and still my mother's telling me to do my homework."

"I don't care what you do, but I'd like my kitchen to myself so I can prepare this dinner."

David put his arms around her waist. "I could help."

"Thanks, love, but I'm better on my own." She squeezed his hands and then ducked away from him.

"What did Ann want, anyway?"

"Oh, just to chat, really. I told her I'd call her back tomorrow when I had more time."

"It's amazing, isn't it, you and Aunt Ann emigrating to Canada all those years ago, and you're still friends?"

"What's so amazing about it?"

"Well, for one thing, you're in Winnipeg and she's in Toronto, over a thousand miles away. And for another, much as I like Aunt Ann, she doesn't seem your type. I can imagine her being one of those jolly Girl Scout leaders."

Helen smiled. "Girl Guides? Yes, she was. Actually, I was a guide, too."

"Somehow I can't imagine you in guides, Mom."

"I left when I was fifteen."

A week after her fifteenth birthday, to be exact. She had at last summoned up the courage to tell her mother. There'd been a terrible row, but, for the first time in her life, she had won.

"I hated it," she told David. "All that regimentation and camp songs and drill." She shuddered.

"You're too ethereal to be a Girl Guide."

"Too what? Get out." Laughing, Helen swatted him with the kitchen towel. "I wish I were ethereal. Unfortunately, I like cooking and eating food too much."

She was still slim, but her hips had rounded in the past years. Her grandmother would have been pleased to see her now. "You're far too thin for your height," she used to say when Helen was seventeen. "We'll have to fatten you up."

Helen began slicing tomatoes with tense, staccato movements.

Cooking usually relaxed her, but not today.

David hoisted himself up on the countertop. "What are you making?"

"At the moment, I'm *trying* to prepare the sauce for the lamb. I've already made the rolls and sherry trifle. And we're having smoked salmon to start. Nice and easy."

"Sounds good. I suppose I'm not invited." David grinned at her, but his eyes didn't quite meet hers.

"I thought you had a rehearsal tonight. Besides, you'd be bored to tears," Helen said lightly. "It's just Bill Trueman and Gordon McKenzie and their wives."

"Yo! Another fun evening devoted entirely to the scintillating topic of . . . the law. Lucky you, Mom."

Helen sighed and began sorting through the drawer for the corkscrew. "Open that for me, will you? And don't drink it," she added as he tilted the bottle to his lips.

"Is Karen attending this legal bash?" David deftly opened the bottle and handed it to her.

"No, she's not."

"But she was asked."

Helen stirred the wine into the simmering onions, breathing in the pungent aroma. She didn't look at David.

"It's okay, Mom. Don't let it get to you. I don't mind if Dad wants my sister, but not me, here for dinner— even though Karen doesn't live here anymore. After all, she is that wonder of wonders—a lawyer."

Helen pushed him off the counter. "Oh, for heaven's sake, David, go away and leave me alone. I told you already, I need the kitchen to myself."

She hated to hear that bitter note behind his joking. Nowadays it was like open warfare when Bruce and David were home at the same time.

"Okay, okay. I'll be downstairs. And you're right, I do have a rehearsal tonight," he shouted as he loped down the basement stairs two at a time. A moment later the heavy beat of some rock band drummed through the house.

She could wring David's neck. All that nonsense about the dinner when he knew very well he wouldn't be in anyway. All the same, he did have a point. If Karen was invited, then he should have been, too.

If only . . . God, how she hated those words. If only David had been interested in law. If only his father would give him the chance to try theatre arts for just one year. If only Karen wouldn't gloat about how well she was doing in her first year of practice.

If only Bruce hadn't wanted to have his partners to dinner today, of all days.

Helen stood staring out the window, the heaviness about her heart lifting a little at the sight of the lilacs that had bloomed just a few days ago. The last patch of snow had melted only the week before.

After twenty-nine years of living in the Canadian prairies, she still marveled at the sudden onset of spring after the long, cold winters. Sometimes summer followed so closely that when the lilacs burst into delicate mauve flowers, tulips and daffodils were still blooming.

The image of her grandmother's garden at Lansdowne House swung into her mind: the standard roses between banks of lavender and hedges of box, the high wall of red brick . . .

No, she mustn't allow herself to think of the house or Petersham or anywhere in England. Not today.

She tuned the radio to CBC stereo, hoping that "RSVP" would drown out the monotonous beat of David's music—and her melancholy.

They were playing Butterworth's "Banks of Green Willow." She switched it off. Just a few bars of that was guaranteed to make her miserably homesick.

She opened the cassette case on the counter and chose a tape of Respighi's "Birds," to celebrate the return of the Canada geese. A few weeks ago she had heard their honking and seen their V-shaped flight formation. Now the young birds were hatching, a sure sign that winter was truly over.

As the familiar soaring and swooping of the strings burst from the tape player, Helen went to the refrigerator and took out the packet of lamb cutlets.

In a few hours Bruce would be on his way home. Instead of going up to bed and pulling the bedclothes over her head, which was what she felt like doing, she must finish preparing the meal, set the table, make sure the bathrooms were clean, and get dressed.

Please God, give me the strength to get through this day just one more time, she prayed.

Bruce Lawrence walked across the underground garage to his black New Yorker and unlocked the doors. He threw his briefcase in the back and slid onto the driver's seat, grunting as he loosened his tie.

God, what a day! Would he ever get this merger with Burrell, Stein worked out? Some new problem seemed to crop up every day. Today it had been time-sharing for the women lawyers with children. It sure had been easier in the old days, when women like Helen stayed home.

Helen had sounded strained on the phone. That wasn't like her. She was so well organized that dinner parties rarely fazed her. Perhaps she'd had a fight with David.

"That damned kid," he muttered. "It's time he got his act together."

As he merged into the lane to cross the St. James Bridge, Bruce smiled wryly to himself. Not quite the right expression to use in the circumstances. All this garbage about wanting to be an actor. What sort of career was that for his only son?

His hands tightened on the steering wheel. God alone knew where his son got his acting talent from. No one in his family had ever had any theatrical aspirations. Nor in Helen's, as far as he knew. But then, having been orphaned since childhood, she rarely spoke about her family.

Although Bruce was cool now, his neck was tight with tension again. He drew in a deep breath. He'd have a drink and a quick shower before the others arrived for dinner.

One thing was for sure, you could always rely on Helen to serve a good meal. He was intensely proud of her cooking and her skills as a hostess. She was also still a beautiful woman, moving with that unconscious grace that had first attracted him to her all those years ago in Toronto. "I'm a lucky guy," he told himself.

But if he was so lucky, why the hell did he feel so empty inside, as if the zest had gone out of his life?

2

Table set, long-stemmed wineglasses polished, the tray with the Bodum coffeemaker and the Rosenthal demitasse cups on the sideboard.

"Don't touch anything," Helen warned David as he hovered over the cheese and crackers.

"I'm starving."

"I've put some of the casserole in a dish in the oven for you and I'll cut you a bit of the Stilton cheese."

She had managed to grab a quick shower and was now dressed in her Laura Ashley blue cotton, which was perfect for this heat.

"There's French bread as well." She'd picked up some baguettes that morning from the bakery in St. Boniface.

"Here's your father," she said when she heard the whir and clunk of the garage door.

"So?"

She gave David one of her icy looks, but he pretended not to see it and kept on eating.

Helen had hoped David would be gone by the time Bruce came home. She dreaded the fights between them. Raised voices made her feel sick.

She was slivering almonds over the green beans when Bruce came in. "Hi, darling." She turned to him, offering her face for the ritual kiss. "How was your day?"

"Not that great. Yours?"

"Just fine," she said brightly.

"You sure? I thought you sounded a bit odd on the phone."

Helen's heart sank. If he could hear it in her voice, what would he see in her face?

"Odd?" She shook her head. "Nothing wrong, except the usual panic to get everything done on time. And it's hot in this kitchen, even with the air-conditioning."

"Hi, Dad." David turned from the kitchen sink, where he was filling up a glass with water.

Bruce's gaze ran over the cut-off shorts and ragged T-shirt. "Hi. Are you eating dinner with us tonight?"

"Sure am."

"Not dressed like that, you're not."

"You want me to put on my three-piece suit?"

"Don't be a smart-ass. If you want to eat with us, dress properly or forget it."

"I will if you ask me nicely, Dad."

Something in his father's expression warned David to stop right there.

"For heaven's sake, Bruce, can't you tell when David's having you on?" Helen said, close to screaming point. "He's already had his dinner. He's got a rehearsal tonight."

Bruce glared at David, who shrugged and then stomped off, muttering something about people who couldn't take a joke. Helen winced as he slammed his bedroom door.

Bruce's face was grim. "I was going to have a drink, but I think I'll take a shower first, if there's time."

"They're not coming until seven-thirty. You've got plenty of time." She looked up into his face, noticing how tired he looked. "Don't let Dave get to you, Bruce."

"He doesn't get to me. I just don't like guys who goof off from work and yet think they're smarter than me."

"He only does it because he can't talk any other way to you. You won't listen to anything he has to say."

Usually Bruce would have been annoyed at her for taking David's side, but tonight he looked just plain dispirited, as if he didn't have the energy to argue. "I don't need this, Helen. I've had a tough enough day at work without getting this hassle at home."

Eager to calm him down, not to have the entire evening go wrong, Helen patted his arm. "Go and have that shower. It'll make you feel much better."

He grunted and turned to go upstairs.

She finished preparing the vegetables and then checked off all she had done on the list she had made. While the coffee beans were grinding, she completed the fresh fruit salad with a topping of strawberries. The sensual colors of food gave her immense pleasure. For a moment she lost herself in contemplating the acid green of the sliced kiwis, the rich gold of the cantaloupe.

Then she turned to look at the phone.

Still five and a half hours to go before the twenty-first of May was over. Would this year be the one?

Don't be such an idiot, she told herself. As if the date made any difference after all this time.

But, however irrational it might be, she had grown used to thinking that if it ever happened, it would happen on this date. It was the same each year: the feeling of feverish excitement mixed with mortal dread.

What if the phone were to ring during dinner? The thought sent chills over her. She would have to leave on the answering machine, even though Bruce hated it.

She closed her eyes for a moment, leaning against the counter of the island in the center of the kitchen.

Dear God, why can't I forget, after all this time?

"Anything wrong, Mom?"

She started at the sound of David's voice. "Hey, don't let Dad get you down."

She turned and put her hand up to his face, the

cheek slightly rough against her fingers. "I do wish you'd try not to fight him all the time."

"I put on a shirt, didn't I?" he said, his green-gray eyes—her eyes—smiling at her.

He had. A casual cotton shirt, crumpled but clean.

"And I'm not even eating with you."

"You want me to iron it for you? I've got time."

"No, Mom." His voice was firm. "It's just fine as it is." He went over to the counter to take a strawberry off the top of the fruit salad.

"Leave that alone," she ordered. David grinned at her. "If you want to make yourself useful, take these nuts into the living room for me."

"Yes, ma'am." Saluting, David took the bowl from her.

Helen put the vegetable dishes in the warming drawer.

"How about a quick drink now?" Bruce appeared in the doorway. "I'm going to have a gin and tonic. Would you like one? Or a sherry?"

"A sherry, please. You were quick."

"Needed to be. By the way, I told the others not to dress up as it's so warm. Hope that's okay."

"Of course it is."

Bruce had changed from his suit into beige cotton pants and an open-necked shirt. She gave him a quick smile.

Although he now had to fight the inevitable middle-aged weight problem, Bruce was still a remarkably good-looking man, tall and muscular, his dark brown hair only lightly touched with gray. Helen had first been attracted to his coffee-colored eyes, bright with intelligence and humor.

"Everything's organized," she said, turning from him to avoid meeting those searching eyes. "David helped a bit."

"Wasn't he at class today?"

"I don't think he had one," she said lightly. "David knows what he's doing, Bruce."

"Does he? I'm glad you think so. I've—"

"Bruce . . ." Helen drew in a deep breath and released it slowly, fighting the panic that was building inside her. "Let's go and have that drink, or I won't have time."

The flush of anger faded from his face.

David was in the family room, one long leg thrown over the arm of the old maple rocking chair Helen had refinished. He was staring out the window, but she could tell from his expression that his thoughts went far beyond the lawn and flowers he was gazing at.

"David cut the lawn today," she told Bruce as he carried in the drinks from the basement bar.

"Great." He set her Tío Pepe down on the coffee table. "Thanks, Dave. You want a beer?"

It was a gesture of reconciliation, as had been the lawn cutting. They were like two dancers locked in some ancient, ritual dance: one step forward, two steps back.

David flashed his winning smile. "Thanks, Dad."

Bruce fetched a beer from the refrigerator and set it down before David.

And the phone rang.

Helen leaped up. "I'll take it in the kitchen," she shouted from the hall. "I've got to check the lamb."

She rushed to the kitchen phone, praying that David wouldn't pick up the receiver in the family room.

"Hallo?"

"Mother, it's me." It was Karen. "Are you eating?"

"No, not yet."

"Good. I won't keep you. I just want to ask Dad something."

"I'll get him. How's everything?"

"Fine."

Helen sensed that was all she'd get out of Karen. She was in one of her brisk, businesslike moods that made her mother feel utterly inconsequential. "I'll get Dad for you."

"Thanks, Mother. See you at the cottage on Sunday."

"Unless you have something else more important to do." Helen couldn't help the slight edge of sarcasm.

"Don't be silly, Mother."

"Will John be coming with you?"

"No." Karen's tone said "Mind your own business."

"Have you two split up?"

Karen answered with a grunt.

"Oh, I am sorry. I really liked John. What happened?"

"I don't have time to explain now. Put on Dad, would you, please?"

"Bruce, it's Karen for you," Helen called. She put the receiver on the counter and went to check the lamb braising in its rosemary-and-tomato sauce in the oven.

As she opened the oven door the pungent smell of rosemary swept her back to her grandmother's old-fashioned kitchen, with its gleaming black Aga cooker in the tiled alcove and the large, scrubbed-elm table.

She slammed the oven door shut. This was definitely not the time to be dwelling on bygone memories.

Damn Karen! Why did she have to phone now and add to her tension? She hated to feel hot and flustered, but that was exactly how Karen always made her feel. To Karen her mother was a dinosaur, a relic from another age.

What with her volunteer work at the International Centre, where she helped new immigrants learn English; taping books for the Blind Institute; and looking after the house *and* the garden, because Bruce didn't have the time, Helen's days were filled to bursting point.

Yet her daughter considered her—and women like her, who chose to stay home—irrelevant. "Kept women," Karen had once called them, scathingly.

Which was also Magda Trueman's attitude, Helen thought much later as they were sitting around the table, drinking coffee and liqueurs.

Magda was a tall, slim blonde, her long hair coiled around her perfectly shaped head. She was Bill Trueman's second wife and twelve years younger than he was.

Magda had sold real estate until the market had ground to a halt. Last year she had bought a women's clothing boutique in Osborne Village, the trendy area of Winnipeg, which, so she was telling them, was highly successful.

"You should think of getting involved in something like that, Helen," she said. "It would give you some interest outside the house."

"I'm useless when it comes to selling anything." Helen tried to hide her resentment at the implication that her voluntary work was unimportant. "I can't even sell raffle tickets. I always end up buying the entire book myself."

"Besides," said Joan McKenzie, jumping to her defense, "I think Helen works harder than most women our age."

Magda smiled. "Oh, yes, but that's volunteer work. If you're efficient, you should be paid, is my motto."

The phone rang. Saved by the bell, Helen thought. She had been about to say something to Magda she would regret later.

"Shall I get it?" Bruce said impatiently, pushing back his chair.

"No, no. It's okay. I've put the answering machine on. I'll check it later."

"I wish you wouldn't put that thing on. I'm expecting a call from Peter Engel. Even though we're installing them in all the new offices, I hate those damned machines."

Everyone murmured agreement, except Magda. "Oh, Bruce, they're invaluable for business. Mine saves me from all those annoying little calls from women friends who just want to chat." She smoothed the coil of golden hair, her crimson nails glinting in the candlelight.

"Check it out now, darling, would you?" Bruce asked Helen quietly.

She glanced at her watch. Ten-fifteen. Still a little less than two hours to go, here in Canada. But in England it was after four o'clock the next morning. The morning of the twenty-second.

Surely by now she was safe.

For the first time today the constriction in her chest eased, so that she could breathe freely again. Yet, at the same time, she felt tears of disappointment stinging the backs of her eyes.

She got up. "More dessert for anyone?"

"I couldn't eat another bite. That trifle was incredible." Bill Trueman patted his ample stomach.

"Just a little too rich for my liking," said his wife, smiling sweetly.

"That's why I made the fruit salad as well." Helen's smile was even sweeter. "I'll take the trifle away, then. David will eat it when he gets back from rehearsal."

Damn. The words were out before she could stop them. Immediately everyone was talking about David and the summer show at Rainbow Stage.

Helen slipped out before she could become embroiled in yet another defense of David.

She slid the kitchen door shut and put the trifle into the fridge. The kitchen was a mess, with dirty plates and casseroles and pots piled high in the sink and on the countertops. She'd do it all later, when everyone had gone home. It would give her time to think.

Her hand hovered over the answering machine. Then she clicked it on to the message replay.

"Hallo. This is Elaine Isaacs. Could Bruce please call me before the ballet board meeting? He has my number."

Helen scribbled a note. As she was sticking it on the fridge door with a magnet, the long beep sounded.

Helen was surprised. She thought there had been only one call since Karen had phoned earlier. It must have been when she was out in the garden, picking mint for the potatoes.

After a moment of hesitation, during which Helen could swear she could hear the caller breathing, the voice of a young woman came on the line, distorted slightly by the machine. She spoke with the new accent of the English southerner, rather like Princess Diana. Certainly not the cultivated Oxbridge accent Miss Lovell, Helen's old elocution mistress, would have preferred.

"I'm not sure I have the right number," said the voice. "I'm looking for Mrs. Helen Lawrence. She used to be Helen Barstow, who lived in Petersham, Surrey." Another pause. Then hurriedly, knowing the machine could cut her off: "This is Emma Turner. Please, would you call me at—" A moment of hesitation. "No, I'll call again. I'm phoning from England, of course. I expect you'll have realized that." A nervous giggle, almost childlike. Then, "I do hope I have the right Helen Lawrence," and the line went dead.

Helen stood in the center of the kitchen, staring at the answering machine. She was acutely aware of the blood pounding in her ears, the whir of the refrigerator, the tap dripping onto the pile of plates in the sink.

From the dining room came the sound of Magda Trueman's high-pitched laugh.

Helen touched the machine as it began to go into old messages. Her fingers moved back and forth, stroking its plastic surface, noticing it needed dusting.

She wanted desperately to play the message back again. To hear again the voice she had longed—and dreaded—to hear for so many years.

"Emma," she whispered.

The kitchen door slid back. "I do hope you're not tackling the dishes all by yourself," Joan McKenzie said.

Helen stared at her.

Joan frowned. "Are you okay, Helen?"

Helen wondered how plump and placid Joan would

react if she were to say, "I'm fine, Joan. Just had a call from the illegitimate daughter I gave up for adoption thirty years ago."

The machine was still issuing old messages. Helen turned it off. She would have to erase the tape.

No, she couldn't do that. She would take it out and hide it.

Joan came right into the kitchen. "Are you sure you're feeling okay? You're as white as a sheet."

Helen licked her lips. She tried to speak, but at first nothing would come. Taking a deep breath, she released it slowly. "I'm fine. Just a giddy spell, that's all. Must be the heat in here. I forgot to turn the oven off."

"Or our age," Joan said wryly. "I hope you're on hormones. I'd be a basket case without them. Come on in and sit down. Magda and I will do the dishes."

Their eyes met, and Joan smiled. "I know, I know. That, you'd like to see. Okay, then *I'll* do the dishes."

Helen pulled herself together. "You certainly will not. I'm going to leave them until the morning."

"Promise?"

Helen nodded.

"It was a wonderful meal, Helen. As always. I don't know how you do it."

Helen herself wondered the same thing as she was saying good-bye to everyone an hour later. Just getting through the past hour without falling apart had been quite an ordeal.

Yet at the same time she was longing to play back the tape, to hear again the voice of her firstborn daughter.

Joan McKenzie hugged her. "Look after yourself, Helen. You still look very pale. Promise me you won't do those dishes tonight."

Bruce put his arm around Helen. "I promise you she won't."

Helen tensed as she felt his hand squeeze her waist.

The door closed behind them. Helen felt light-headed

with relief to see them go at last. But she still had Bruce to deal with. He was in a great mood now, relaxed and good-humored.

Good in one way, not so good in another.

"Let's have a nightcap." He ran his hand up and down her back. "That was a terrific meal, darling. God, I'm a lucky man to have married such a fantastic cook."

She escaped from his arm. "Is that all I am, a fantastic cook?"

It was the wrong thing to say, considering his mood. His eyes darkened. "Let's forget the nightcap. I'll show you what else I think you're fantastic at."

She turned from him. "I must just clear the dining room table."

"Can't you leave it until the morning?"

She was already busy, gathering up glasses and plates from the table. "I won't be more than five minutes," she said, her back turned to him.

"Okay. I'll go on up." He came behind her and kissed the back of her neck. "Make it quick."

As soon as she heard him open and close the bedroom door, Helen darted to the kitchen. She took the tape from the answering machine and looked around, trying to think of the safest place to hide it.

The bedroom door opened again, and Bruce padded into the bathroom.

She hurriedly opened the cupboard under the sink and stuffed the tape right at the back, behind the cans of oven cleaner and furniture polish.

She whisked the rest of the stuff off the dining room table and stacked it any old way in the kitchen. Her heart was pounding so fast, she felt she was about to explode.

It was half-past eleven. God was punishing her by making sure she would suffer right up to midnight.

When she went upstairs Bruce was already in his favorite pajamas, the maroon ones. He came to her side of the room as she was undressing and put his arms around her, to draw her to him. "God, I'm a lucky man."

Helen's body resisted him. You wouldn't think that if you knew the truth about me, she thought.

"What's wrong?" he asked softly. "You've been tense all evening."

She could smell the wine on his breath. Normally she wouldn't have found that unpleasant. Tonight it made her feel nauseated.

She pulled away from him. "I'm just tired. It was a long evening. I thought they'd never go."

"Do you want a little time? How about a brandy first?"

He had taken it for granted that because he wanted to make love, so did she. Any other night she would have relaxed and just gone along with it, but she couldn't. Not tonight. Not after that call.

"If you don't mind, Bruce, I think I'd rather just go to bed and sleep." She turned away, to avoid seeing the hurt in his eyes at her rejection.

In the silence, she could imagine him trying to decide on the best strategy to employ. He put his hands on her shoulders and kissed her left ear. "You looked so beautiful tonight. Just like you did when I first saw you in the Royal York in Toronto, all those years ago."

Oh, God, Bruce, please don't talk about the past. If only he knew how guilty he made her feel. She turned and smiled a bright smile up at him. "You still say the nicest things, Bruce Lawrence. How can I resist you?"

He kissed her, and her mouth responded. Just a few minutes. Then she'd have time to work things out.

She relaxed against him and put her arms around his waist, turned on by the solid warmth of his body, the gentleness of his large hands.

Later, when Bruce had turned on his side and fallen asleep, Helen lay awake, her mind jumping.

What was she going to do? Now that Emma had her

number, she would keep calling. What if David or Bruce answered the phone the next time?

Should she tell Bruce?

Her entire body went rigid at the thought. What a relief that would be! But of course she couldn't. Bruce would never be able to forgive her for not telling him the truth from the outset. He was a stickler for the truth. He would accuse her of marrying him under false pretenses. All their friends would find out. She could just imagine the scorn on Magda Trueman's face—and on Bruce's mother's and sisters'. And Karen's disbelief. And David's.

No, whatever happened, she must keep it a secret. Thank God for the vast distance between Canada and England. At least Emma wouldn't be turning up on the doorstep tomorrow. That would be a disaster.

Or would it? As she thought of meeting the child she'd lost, Helen was aware of a nudge of warmth in a corner of her mind. Slowly it spread throughout her body. Her muscles began to relax. Her brain ceased its turmoil. And there stole over her such a sense of joy that she was amazed by it.

Her daughter was alive and seeking her birth mother.

Tomorrow she would have to face the pain of reality, but tonight she would take pleasure in the fact that the child she had abandoned did not hate her, as she had imagined she would. On the contrary, she cared enough to phone across thousands of miles to find her.

Warm tears filled her eyes, spilling onto the pillow. "Emma, my darling Emma," she whispered. Cradling the pillow in her arms, she closed her eyes, the memory of her lost daughter's voice filling her mind.

3

As the days passed, Emma's call began to resemble a remote dream. The telephone became less a symbol of her anxiety and sadness and more the nuisance it usually was. So much so that when she got home from her CNIB taping on Thursday morning, the ringing of the phone as she unlocked the door was just an annoyance. She threw down her bag and ran into the kitchen to pick up the receiver.

"Hallo."

"Hallo."

Immediately Helen recognized the seashell echo of an overseas call. The kitchen spun around her. "Who is this?" she asked.

"I—I'm so sorry to bother you again. This is Emma Turner. I called last week and left a message on your answering machine. Perhaps you didn't get it."

A pause, then Helen said, "Yes, I got it."

"Oh." Silence, followed by a shuddering breath. "Then you'll know that I'm looking for a Mrs. Helen Lawrence, who used to be Helen Barstow."

Helen hesitated. One hand gripped the receiver, the other picked up the yellow pen to draw mindless, swirling patterns on her notepad. "That is my name, at least, it was my name."

"Oh." Then a repeated "Oh," this time with an outrush of breath that denoted the girl's excitement. "Then I think you must be my mother."

Helen dug the pen into the notepad, pressing it so hard that it ripped the paper.

"Are you still there, Mrs. Lawrence?" said the girl.

"Yes, I'm still here. What makes you think I'm your mother?" Helen despised the coolness in her own voice.

"My father—that is, my adoptive father—told me your name. He says you know him. Richard Turner."

"And Richard told you I was your mother."

"Yes. I was told years ago that I was adopted, of course, but my mother—my adoptive mother, that is— got so upset when I asked questions about who my parents were that I promised not to ask again until I was older."

"You've waited a long time."

"Yes, I know. Far too long, really. When Daddy told me your name I had intended to phone you last year, but I put it off when Mummy became very ill."

"Is she better now?"

"She died six months ago."

The terse statement hit Helen like a physical blow. "Oh, no. I am so very sorry to hear that," she said, her voice gentle. "And so now you're looking for your—" She searched for the right word. "For your real mother."

"For my birth mother. That's what they call them— birth mothers."

"I see." Helen swallowed hard. "Well . . . you've found her." Strange phenomenon: her breasts were aching, as they had ached when she had first given birth to Emma.

A long pause. Then Emma said, "I can't tell you how happy that makes me."

Helen felt like laughing and crying at the same time. Then she felt as cold as an ice sculpture in February.

"I would like to see you," the girl said eagerly.

Oh, God, what I'd give to see you, my darling girl. "I don't think that's possible, really," Helen said, trying to remain calm. "You live in England. I live in Canada."

"I can fly out. Or, if you prefer, you could fly over here." Emma's enthusiasm was unquenchable.

"I'm sorry. I—I don't think it would be a good idea."

"You mean you don't want to meet me."

Suddenly the voice was that of a mature young woman, not a girl, a voice that strongly reminded Helen of Karen. All these years she had thought of Emma as a baby, a young child, but in fact she was an adult woman of thirty.

"Of course I want to meet you, but it just isn't possible. When I came to Canada, I put everything that had happened behind me. I began an entirely new life. Don't you understand how upset my family would be, knowing I've kept this a secret from them all these years? Richard had no right to tell you my name. He promised me he wouldn't."

"Yes, he told me that. But I pestered him about it, until he caved in."

"Why?" Helen asked. "Weren't you happy?" Please, God, don't let her tell me she was abused. Please, God, let her have had a happier childhood than mine, at least.

"Yes, I was very happy. You needn't worry about that. I just have to *know*. Surely you can understand that."

"Yes, of course I can. But you must understand that your longing to know could ruin my life. As I keep telling you, my husband knows nothing about my past. He knows nothing about you. Neither do my children."

"You mean I have half sisters or brothers?" Thousands of miles couldn't muffle Emma's excitement. "Which? What are their names?"

"That's nothing to do with you. You must—"

"I beg your pardon. It *is* something to do with me. They are my flesh and blood. As you are." Emma was angry now. Angry and upset.

"You must forget about me, Emma." Helen was pleading with her.

Since that terrible morning when the Turners had taken Emma from her, not one day had passed that she hadn't thought of her. Now she was denying her daughter—and herself—the chance of being reunited.

"I see," Emma said out of the silence. "I am sorry to have troubled you like this." Her voice was controlled. Helen could only guess at the effort she must be making to hide her feelings.

"I know how disappointed you must be," Helen told her softly. "But it really is best . . . for both of us. You have your family, I have mine."

"I just thought you might want to see me, that was all," Emma said. "Even if it was just the once. I wanted to see what my mother looks like. And then there are things like medical background. I have nothing."

Nothing. The word echoed down the line.

And if I succumb to my longing to see you, thought Helen, then I, too, shall probably have nothing.

"I'll send you any medical details I can think of," she said after a pause.

"You'll write to me, then?" Hope lifted Emma's voice.

"I'll send you the medical information."

"And my father's?"

Helen went cold. "I know nothing about your father's medical background."

"My *real* father, I mean."

"That's what I mean. Nothing."

"Daddy won't tell me who he is. My father, I mean."

Thank God for that, at least. If only Richard had had the sense to keep *her* name and whereabouts a secret, she and Emma wouldn't be going through this agony now.

"Did you love him?" Emma asked.

"I must go now. My son is due in at any moment from university."

"So I do have a half brother. Now I know that, at least. What's his name?"

"No more, Emma, please." Helen was dizzy with tension. Her blouse was sticking to her body. Her hair clung in wet tendrils on her forehead and at the nape of her neck.

"Just answer this one question and I shall hang up. Please, *please*. Did you love my real father?"

Helen was startled by the question. She closed her eyes, trying to conjure up his face. "Yes, I loved him." The words came from her in a whisper. "He was my first true love."

Somehow the poetic phrase was right for the love she had felt for Emma's father.

Helen heard Emma clear her throat. Then she said, "Thank you. At least now I know I wasn't the result of rape or—or something like that."

"Heavens, no." Helen was shocked. "I'll try to put some—some details in with the background information I send you. Then you must put all of this out of your mind and get on with your life."

"That's the trouble. My life seems to have been put on hold. Somehow finding my parents seems to have completely taken over. I felt that I couldn't get on with the rest of my life, couldn't even have children of my own, until I found my real parents."

Oh, God, my poor child, thought Helen. "Please, Emma, please don't let this become an obsession," she begged her. "Just keep telling yourself that Richard and Mary Turner are . . . were your parents." Motherly advice for an abandoned daughter.

"But they weren't, were they? Not my real parents. Much as I love them both, I must find my roots, where I come from. There are so many questions I wanted to ask you." Emma's words tumbled out. "About my grandparents, for instance, and—"

Prolonging this any further would be unbearable for both of them. "I'm terribly sorry, but I must go."

"Yes, yes, of course. Thank you for listening to me, at least. Oh, I almost forgot to give you my address. It's Flat Fifty-seven, Hazelton Court, Richmond, Surrey."

"Postal code?"

"TW nine something. TW nine's enough. My phone number is—"

"I won't need your phone number."

"No, I suppose you won't. I seem to have really upset you. I shouldn't have called. I put it off until my birthday, thinking it might be a big birthday surprise for both of us! It was on my birthdays that I thought of you most."

Tears spilled down Helen's cheeks, making watery blotches on her shopping list. "Oh, Emma, I know," she whispered, not loud enough for her daughter to hear.

"I kept telling myself that it mightn't work out, but I had to try. I waited until Daddy was asleep, but even then I kept putting it off. That's why I didn't phone until early the following morning."

"What will you do now?" Helen asked after an awkward pause. The dispirited tone of Emma's voice worried her.

"I'm going to search for my real father. Don't worry, I won't ask you any more about him. I'm sure I can get some more information out of Daddy."

Oh, God. Surely, in the circumstances, Richard would never tell her who her real father was.

"I don't think that's a good idea at all," she said at last. "Please try to forget what's in the past and get on with your life, Emma."

Emma said nothing.

"I really must go now," Helen said in desperation. "Good-bye, Emma. Take good care of yourself."

"Good-bye. You won't forget to write . . . to send . . . the things . . . you know."

"I won't forget. But then you must forget all about me, all right? It really is better that way. Good-bye."

For a moment Helen pressed the receiver against her cheek, knowing that Emma was still hanging on at the other end. Then, slowly and very carefully, she set it down.

4

The click followed by the buzz of the dial tone felt like the blow of an ax to Emma. She had prepared herself for rejection, but no amount of preparation could have readied her for this feeling of emptiness.

She was numb. Her fingers set down the receiver in its cradle, but they felt neither its solidity nor its form. Her body sat motionless on the office chair in the small studio-office. She felt as if she were in one of those dreams where your feet are trapped in thick, cloying treacle and you can't get out.

Since she was a teenager, the thought of speaking to her birth mother, of meeting her, getting to know her, had grown and grown until it had taken over her life, feeding off her like some strange creature in a science fiction novel.

When she was eighteen, her father had told her the bare minimum: her birth mother's first name and age and the fact that she had emigrated to Canada, that was all. "I promised her that I would never tell you who she was," he told her. "As it is, I'm breaking that promise."

Emma had thought it strange that he said "*I* promised her," not "We promised her."

"Don't talk about this to Mummy," he warned her,

"or she'll think you're not happy. After all, in her eyes she is your mother."

"Of course she's my mother. I'll never think of her as anything else," Emma told him vehemently. "If only you'd both understand that this doesn't mean I don't love you. You've been the most wonderful parents possible."

How many times in the past few years had she said that to her father? But the knowledge that her mother would be deeply hurt if she knew she was looking for her real mother had forced her to give up the idea of searching.

It wasn't until her mother died that her father had told her that Helen was married to Bruce Lawrence, a Winnipeg lawyer. The rest had been easy.

Emma sat with her head in her hands, staring down at the sketch she had made of the drawing room of Pendleton Manor and yet not seeing it.

Her real mother didn't want to meet her. She didn't want her to write or phone . . . ever. "Forget all about me," she'd said.

Her mother had coldly rejected her.

Why am I so surprised? Emma asked herself. After all, it wasn't the first time, was it? Her mother had rejected her as a baby, too.

"Working late, Emma?"

Emma started. She hadn't heard the door open. Alan Grenville, one of the senior partners, stood in the doorway. "Sorry. I didn't mean to scare you. I did knock first."

She tried to stand up, but somehow her feet became entwined in the leg of her drafting stool and she stumbled.

He started forward, but she managed to catch hold of the edge of the desk to save herself from falling. "Are you okay?" He had never seen the usually efficient and sunny-tempered Emma Turner so flustered.

Her chin trembled. She drew in a shuddering sob and, to his horror, let out a wailing, "No, I'm not."

For a moment he hadn't a clue what to do. He could search for some other female who might still be around to deal with it, but it seemed a bit cavalier just to walk out and leave her. Besides, it just wasn't like Emma. It must be something pretty serious for her to break down this way.

She stood, bent over her desk, her heavy red-gold hair swinging forward to hide her face. Only by the convulsive movement of her shoulders could he tell that she was weeping.

The time passed agonizingly slowly. Should he leave her? Should he speak? Then she lifted her head.

"So sorry," she whispered, trying to smile. "Stupid of me." She opened her drawer and dragged out a handful of tissues from the box. He rather liked the way she scrubbed at her tearstained face and streaked mascara instead of dabbing at it genteelly, as many women would have done.

"What can I do to help?" he asked. "Just tell me. Would you like me to phone someone for you or see if Jenny or Pauline are still here?"

Emma shook her head. "I'll be fine. You've been very kind." She gave him a sheepish grin. "Most men would have run a mile."

His eyebrows lifted. "I like to think I'm not most men."

He watched her as she pressed powder on her blotched face and applied lipstick the color of deep apricot to her lips. Apart from her obvious distress and her embarrassment at weeping before him, her movements were graceful, precise.

Emma Turner had been employed by their architectural partnership for more than a year now. Yet, although she was extremely pleasant on the eye and extraordinarily efficient, Alan had never thought of her as anything but a talented interior designer. He must be slipping.

Or perhaps his white-hot affair with Nadia had blinded

him to all other attractive women. It could be that he was more perceptive now that that fire had died.

"Are you hungry?" he asked Emma suddenly.

"I don't think so."

"Well, I damned well am. Why not join me for dinner? You can eat or just watch me eating, talk or not talk, whichever you prefer."

She shook her head. "There's no need—"

"If you think I'm going to leave you here, alone, you're dead wrong." He strode to the small closet. "This your coat?" He took out the bronze silk-gabardine raincoat. She nodded. He held it up by the collar. "Good. Put it on and let's go."

Still numb, Emma did as she was told. She shivered as his hands touched the nape of her neck. Any other time she would have been thrilled at the thought of having dinner with Alan Grenville. Tonight, unfortunately, the experience was wasted on her.

But she was extremely grateful to him for making it possible for her to postpone returning home. Her father always knew when something was troubling her. She hated the thought of having to give him an explanation tonight.

As they went downstairs, Alan took her elbow, as if he were afraid she might fall down the steps. "I think somewhere quietly luxurious is indicated," he said as they walked to the garage near the river where he parked his car. "Not bright and trendy. A comfortable, old-fashioned hotel dining room, perhaps?"

Emma gave him a faint smile and nodded. She didn't really care. She just didn't want to be left alone.

She climbed into his new, dark gray BMW, relaxing gratefully on the comfortable leather seat.

"Like the new car?" Alan asked.

"I think I preferred the old bright red one. More snazzy."

He turned to grin at her. "Ah, but this fits my new

traditional image better, don't you think? Lord Barrington of Pendleton Manor might deem Zinnober red to be too flashy for his architect."

He drove well, his hands firm on the wheel. She had driven with him before, of course. Usually they talked about work. Today she was grateful for his silence.

"The Connaught Hotel," was all he said as he pulled up before the famous but decidedly unflashy hotel in Mayfair. "I think the Connaught dining room is just what we need tonight."

Emma had never before been to the Connaught; far too rich for her salary. But as she entered the foyer of the old hotel, with its glowing wood and soft carpeting, she felt the tension slide from her.

Somehow it was easy in these surroundings of comfort and quiet elegance to tell Alan all about the phone call.

The meal itself was simple and soothing: a cocktail of deliciously ripe avocado, cream of tomato soup, lamb cutlets, and fruit salad with cream.

Afterward, sitting back in the burgundy velvet chair in the lounge, swirling the golden cognac in a balloon glass, she found it hard to remember actually eating any of it.

"That was a wonderful meal."

"You didn't eat much."

"No, I was too busy talking."

"Feel better now?" Alan asked.

Emma met his gaze. He had brown eyes, which contrasted interestingly with his corn gold hair. Usually one would have expected blue eyes with fair hair. "Yes, I do. It helps to be able to talk about it to someone who's not involved, if you know what I mean."

He nodded. "No emotional baggage."

"Do you often eat here?"

"God, no. I keep it for very special occasions only. Or when a client is paying. Americans love the Connaught. It's so very English."

Emma looked around, too numb to think of anything else to say. The room, with its wine-colored chairs and sofas of fern green damask, was very relaxing. Across the room, a gregarious American was offering cigars to his companions.

"Please smoke, if you want to," Emma said to Alan. "I quite like the smell of cigars, as long as they're not being smoked on a plane or in my own room."

"Thank you, no." Alan flashed a smile at her. "Do men usually ask to smoke cigars in your room?"

A rush of warmth spread from Emma's neck to her face. What the hell was wrong with her, blushing like a thirteen-year-old schoolgirl? "If they do, they don't get asked back."

She waited for some follow-up remark, but none came. She took another sip of coffee and then sat the cup down in its saucer. "What should I do, Alan?" His name somehow sounded comforting on her lips. "Should I give the whole thing up? Forget it all and get on with my life, as she—my mother—told me to do?"

"Why don't you discuss it with your father?"

"He won't talk about it. Says it's up to me, keep him out of it."

"That sounds as if he doesn't really approve of your contacting her."

Emma picked up one of the petits fours, sinking her teeth into the strawberry dipped in dark chocolate, and didn't reply until she had finished it.

"I would have said so, too, except that I get the strangest feeling that while he's discouraging me, part of him is saying, 'Go for it.' Does that make sense?"

"Perhaps. It could be that he knows you won't settle down, get on with your life, until you're reunited with your mother."

"Yes, that could be it." She sighed. "You've been so understanding. I've been an absolute bore about all this, I know. I am sorry."

"Don't be. I'm glad I was able to help." He shrugged. "Not that I've done much."

"You've been a willing ear. You saved me from chucking myself out the office window."

"They don't open. You would have had to jump through the glass. Very messy. Would have given the firm a rotten image."

Emma chuckled. "And you've made me laugh. That's something I thought I'd never be able to do again, after she . . . my mother . . . hung up on me."

"I suppose you have to think of her side of it. Here she is, a middle-aged woman, married to some prosperous lawyer. She's probably on the boards of all the women's groups. Feeling secure and comfortable. And along you come, out of the blue, after thirty years. Must have given her a hell of a shock."

Emma blinked at him. "You make her sound awful."

"You have to face the fact that she might *be* awful. That you and she could have absolutely nothing in common."

She dug the spoon in and out of the brown sugar crystals. "I faced that fact long ago. I came to the decision that whether or not I liked her didn't matter. What matters is knowing what she was like, where she came from. Where *I* come from. Most especially, why she gave me up."

"So even if she's one of those North American committee queens, you would still want to meet her."

Emma nodded. "I'd be disappointed, of course, but I must know." She met his gaze, biting her lip. "God, Alan, I *have* to know." She was close to tears again.

He moved his left hand to brush her fingers. "You look all in. No more thinking about it tonight. Have you had enough coffee?"

Emma gave him a wan smile. "Yes."

"Good. I'll get the bill and then I'll see you home."

"There's no need to see me home. I can get the tube." Emma glanced at her watch. Quarter to ten.

They had been here nearly three hours. "I wish I could kill some more time," she said without thinking.

"Why?"

"That sounds awful, doesn't it? As if that's all I've been doing this evening, killing time." She met his eyes. "I can never thank you enough for your kindness."

"I asked you why you want to kill more time."

"Because I don't want to face my father tonight."

"But you said that he didn't want to discuss anything about this with you."

"Perhaps not, but he'll still be up when I get home and he'll want to talk about my day, his day. Now that my mother's gone, he's desperately lonely. He waits up for me, whatever time I come home."

Alan glanced at the bill the waiter had brought him and slid his credit card into the leather folder. "Which puts a lot of pressure on you."

"I'm not complaining," she said hurriedly.

"Of course you're not. But tonight you don't need any added pressure, right?"

Emma nodded.

"Then why don't you come home with me?"

The question was asked so lightly, with just the right inflection not to startle her, that she wondered if she had grasped his meaning correctly.

"With you?"

"Yes. As you know, I have a flat on the Thames in the Docklands development."

Disappointment flooded over her. She should have guessed that his kindness, the elegant meal, the cognacs, all had a price. How naive she had been. She knew all about the end of his affair with the fabulous Nadia Perrin, she of the drawling, sexy voice that television viewers and theatergoers loved so much.

Now Alan Grenville was between women, and here was Emma Turner, emotionally vulnerable and seemingly ripe for the picking. Gloom descended upon her.

That was all she needed. She loved her job with Parmenter and Grenville. It might not be easy to find another job in the field of classical and restoration work.

Whether she accepted or rejected Alan's offer, Emma was deeply concerned that it would affect her position as an associate in the interior design team.

She stood up. "Thank you for the offer, but I think I'll go home."

"Okay." His face was devoid of expression.

As he held her coat for her in the foyer, she could sense his tension. Too damn bad. She might have been happy to go to bed with him on another occasion, when she was capable of weighing the pros and cons, of deciding whether he was the right man to be her first lover, but his timing was decidedly off this evening.

She realized, as they walked silently to the door, that the wave of depression engulfing her like a gray, damp cloud was a result of acute disappointment.

As they waited for the doorman to bring the car, neither of them spoke.

"Would you take me to Green Park tube station, please?" Emma said when Alan started the car.

"Has anyone told you that you have a transparent face?" he asked her.

"No." Her hands gripped her bag tightly in her lap.

"Perhaps it's only tonight, when you're feeling so unhappy, that you can't hide your feelings."

So now he felt that because she had confided in him he had the right to analyze her. "Perhaps."

"I wasn't asking you to go to bed with me, Emma. I was offering you a place of refuge for the night."

He was very close to her, but he made no move to touch her, not even to take her hand. In a perverse way, she wished he would. She had a longing to be held, to feel the warmth of another person's body against hers.

To hell with her job. She'd been a fool to turn down his offer. At least she wouldn't have had to be alone tonight.

"I'm sorry. I'm afraid things aren't making too much sense for me at the moment. I'm very tired."

"I know. Let me take you home, at least. Your home, I mean. I'll drive you back to Richmond."

"No." She turned to face him. "I'll come home with you, if the offer still stands."

The streetlight illuminated his face. He was frowning. "Are you sure?"

"Yes. I don't want to go home yet."

"Right."

She was grateful to him for not arguing.

As they drove, Alan entertained her by telling her about some of the work he had done before he decided to join Desmond Parmenter. Then he fell silent, sensing she wasn't in the mood for talking.

Emma had taken a boat trip down the Thames to Greenwich two summers ago, mainly to see the new dockside development from the river. It had been astounding to see the changes wrought in the widest reaches of the Thames. Modern glass structures of varying heights—in particular, the vast Canary Wharf—had replaced the derelict wharves and warehouses that had been the London settings in several of Dickens's novels.

Alan's flat was a penthouse in a three-story building that seemed to consist entirely of glass, with steel struts. Emma knew that Alan had been the architect for the building. That was before he had made the big changeover to a classical, traditional style, which included the restoration of old buildings.

She wasn't sure if Alan's change had been motivated by revulsion at the ugliness of many of the new buildings in London or an astute sense of business. There was no doubt that Prince Charles's war against what he called "monstrous carbuncles" was gaining many converts.

She could see little from the narrow street outside. But when they entered the flat and Alan switched on the lights, they revealed a large room of simple, almost classic lines, with golden teak furniture and a large, curving sofa of cream leather. Plump cushions of tangerine, yellow, and green added color and warmth.

"Not quite my current style, is it?" he remarked as Emma stood looking about her.

"Perhaps not, but I like it."

"I'm thinking of selling it, but the Docklands market is rotten at present. I don't think the flat suits my new classical image. Besides, it's too far from Chelsea."

He took her coat and hung it up for her. "Make yourself comfortable." But Emma was making for the sliding door that led to a terrace the length of the main room.

"I'll open it for you." He unsnibbed the lock and slid back the window. The river breeze gusted in, cool and fresh, ruffling her hair.

She stepped out. To her right shone the lights that outlined Tower Bridge. There were lights everywhere: on tugboats and wherries, on glass buildings lining the south side of the river . . .

As she leaned forward, her arms on the railing, a pleasure boat chugged by, laughter and blaring rock music coming from it in waves of sound.

She heard Alan come up behind her and turned to him eagerly. "It's wonderful. I can't believe it. All this . . ." Her arms waved in an attempt to take it all in. "I don't think I'd ever sleep, if I lived here."

"It quietens down once the pleasure boats have docked for the night. Anyway, you get used to it. Like living by a railway line."

"Or on a flight path."

"Would you like a drink?" he asked.

"What I would love is a cup of tea. Or do you think that's too prosaic a request for such a spectacular setting?"

"I think it's a great idea. I'll join you, except I'll make mine a coffee."

She stood outside for a little longer and then went in to join him in the kitchen. "Can I help?"

He had taken off his jacket and tie and looked very comfortable and informal in his open-necked striped shirt and wide, crimson braces.

"Biscuits?" He indicated the tin.

Her heart jumped when she saw the name on the tin: Barstow's Biscuits. "What kind are they?"

"Have a look." The kettle boiled, emitting a whistle that rivaled the ships' horns from the river.

Emma carried the biscuit tin into the main room and set it down on the oval glass-and-teak coffee table, before sinking onto the huge sofa. Then, deciding that she might as well relax completely, she kicked off her shoes and tucked her feet under her.

Alan came in with the tea tray and set it down on the table. He sat down, hands behind his head, studying her. "You make my home look quite different," he said at last.

"You mean I don't treat it with the deference it deserves. I'm sorry, sir." With an expression of mock humility, Emma swung her feet down and sat primly, her hands folded in her lap.

"Drink your tea," she was told.

She helped herself to one of the crunchy oat-ginger biscuits. "Do you mind if I dunk it in my tea? I promise not to drop it on your lovely white leather sofa."

He laughed out loud. "Go ahead. And it's not white. As an interior designer, you should know that nothing is ever just plain 'white.' It's Devonshire cream—or so the interior designer told me."

"Touché." She grinned at him. "Tell me about this place."

He did so with enthusiasm, telling her how he had been tempted to sell it before he had moved in when he saw how commercial the entire river development was becoming. "But the thought of living on the Thames, at the very heart of London, won me over."

He made her laugh with stories of bungled deliveries

and carpets that had been laid with the pile in the wrong direction. All the disasters they both knew happened but hoped wouldn't.

By now she was so tired she could only nod and smile in response.

Eventually she must have dropped off, for she heard his voice coming at her as if he were at the other end of a long tunnel. "Time for bed."

Emma roused herself. "I must phone my father first. I'll tell him I'm staying with a friend."

Their eyes met. Alan's expression was noncommittal. "Here's the phone." He put the portable phone on the table.

When she had made the call, she sat for a little while, just staring into space. Then she felt herself almost lifted from the sofa and the comforting feel of Alan's arm about her waist. They walked down a corridor.

"Here you are. Towels on the bed. Bathroom's through that door."

"I don't think I have the strength to wash."

"Then don't bother. Need anything else?"

She stood close to him, swaying with exhaustion. His face blurred before her. "Just . . . would you mind holding me for a moment?"

He gave her a frowning look, then said, "Wait there." The next thing she knew was the wetness of a warm facecloth on her face, followed by the soft roughness of a towel.

"Take off your blouse and skirt and put this on," Alan said, holding out a black silk dressing gown, and left the room again.

Emma did as she was told. She was like a robot, programmed to do its master's bidding.

Alan came back and took off his shoes. "Lie down," he said, pulling back the bedclothes. She did so. The feel of a pillow beneath her heavy head was bliss.

Then came the weight of his body beside her. But,

when she reached out for him, she found that he was lying on top of the bedclothes.

She fell asleep with the weight and warmth of his arm about her and the feathery feeling of his breath on her hair.

5

Helen was exhausted by Emma's call. She sat staring at the phone for several minutes and then dragged herself up the carpeted stairs to the large master bedroom. "Master bedroom"—what a strange, archaic term. The bedroom of the master of the house.

She looked around her, at the king-size bed with its peach-and-beige appliquéd cover and the matching curtains. Hardly a man's room, really.

When they had moved into this architect-designed house ten years ago, Bruce had given her a free hand to decorate as she pleased. At the time she had been delighted with the fabrics she had chosen, but today she was looking at it all through new eyes, and the colors seemed insipid, drab, lacking in character.

Rather like me, she thought.

She walked across the room to draw the curtains against the brightness outside, her feet sinking into the deep-piled carpet. The feeling added to her sense of unreality. The windows were shut tight, the hum of the air-conditioning drowning out the occasional sound of a car engine or a dog barking. No laughter and screams of young children playing in the streets nowadays. They were all in day care.

Thank God she'd had those happy days at home with her two in their smaller house in River Heights. Nine o'clock in the morning, all the doors had opened and the children tumbled out to play in the sandboxes or, in the winter, to make angels or forts in the deep snow in their backyards.

What sort of childhood had Emma's been? Had she been as happy as Karen and David? Or had the Turners packed her off to some all-girls' boarding school at the tender age of eight or nine? She sincerely hoped not.

It would be evening in England now. What would Emma have done after she had put down the phone? Had she a husband or lover to turn to in her distress? Someone she could tell that the mother who had given birth to her had rejected her yet again?

Helen dragged back the bedclothes. Without even bothering to take off her skirt, she lay down on the bed, switching on the electric blanket to high.

She was shivering violently, her teeth chattering together. What a strange world they lived in. It was sweltering outside, but they kept the electric blanket on their bed in case the air-conditioning made it too cold.

She could control the atmosphere they lived in, but there was little else in her life she was able to control.

She lay there for a long time, her mind spinning. Just two telephone calls had both fulfilled her dearest dream and realized her worst nightmare.

She had spoken to her firstborn child. But that child wanted to meet her, to come back into her life.

What did her daughter look like? Helen wondered. *Whom* did she look like?

He was my first true love, she had told Emma. She closed her eyes, striving to conjure up his face, but nothing came. Easy enough to get up and find an old picture of him, of course, but she was looking for something more than a flat, black-and-white glossy photograph or a face in a yellowed newspaper. She was searching for the essence of the man who had entered her life like a shining comet, when she was only seventeen, and changed its direction forever.

The spring of 1960 was the most exciting time Helen Barstow had experienced in her entire life. She and her best friend, Ann Sturgis, had finished their training at secretarial college in March. After answering an advertisement in the *Richmond and Twickenham Times,* Helen had found her first job, as a clerk-typist in Milbourne and Blanchard, a local solicitor's office in Richmond. She was earning the immense sum of seven pounds a week.

"You won't get very far on that," her mother had told her with one of her sniffs. "You realize you will have to pay me at least half of that for your meals and upkeep. And why Richmond? It will take you an hour to get there by bus from Ealing every day."

"Not that long, Mother," Helen said. She was a coward, as always, postponing what she knew would cause a major row.

"You should have looked for a position nearer home, to save money on fares. I'm sure you would have been able to find something in Ealing—or Chiswick."

"I hate Chiswick. I hate Ealing even more."

Surprised at this outburst, her mother looked up from her knitting. She was working on one of her seemingly endless gray cardigans. Gray like herself, thought Helen. Gray like this dreary vicarage, like their lives. Her mother's thin lips pursed together. "You should be grateful to have a roof over your head. Think of—"

Helen jumped up from her chair. "For once I'm not going to think of any orphans or refugees or starving children in Africa. I'm thinking of *me!*"

Her mother stared at her, openmouthed, as if she were convinced her daughter had gone quite mad.

"Gran has asked me to come and live with her and

Aunt Hilary in Petersham," Helen told her, "and I've said I will."

"You had no right to do so without first consulting your father and me. Besides, it is out of the question. Your grandmother and aunt don't need the worry of a young person living in that big house."

Helen clenched her hands into fists at her sides. Her mother always had the power to reduce her to tears. This time she refused to give her the pleasure of seeing her cry. "I intend to be a help to them, not a worry."

"You have never been anything but a worry to us. Why should that change because you are living with your grandmother?"

"Because I shall be happy with them, that's why."

"Your father will not permit this."

But, for once, her mother was wrong. Helen never did find out exactly what had passed between her father and grandmother. All she knew was that by the end of April she had moved to the red-brick Georgian house near Richmond Park that had always spelled home to her.

Lansdowne House had been the home of the Dunsmores of Petersham, a family of comfortable but by no means wealthy estate, for most of the nineteenth century. It was not as large as many of the other Georgian houses in Richmond and Petersham, having only five bedrooms, a drawing room, dining room, breakfast room, a scullery, and a large kitchen—the warmest room in the house—with the housekeeper's private room beside it. The maid's room was in the attic, but, as they had no maid, it was used as a box room for suitcases and piles of old magazines and two huge trunks filled with old clothes smelling of mothballs that Helen had loved to dress up in when she was younger.

The entire house was a delightful combination of shabby elegance and comfort. A place to be lived in, not just to look at.

It had not been lived in by Dunsmores for the first

decade of the twentieth century. The family money had dwindled, its disappearance hastened by an elder son who had gambled away most of what was left. The house had to be sold to pay his debts.

After many years it was bought by her new husband as a wedding present for Amelia Dunsmore, who had disgraced herself and her family by falling in love with— and insisting on marrying—a common cake and biscuit manufacturer named John Barstow, who spoke with a strong Yorkshire accent.

Amelia Dunsmore Barstow was Helen's grandmother. Her husband had died many years before, leaving her with two children, Geoffrey and Hilary, together with a fairly large interest in Barstow's Biscuits that kept her and her unmarried daughter in reasonable comfort in their home.

Helen's room had a window seat that overlooked the back garden. This had always been her favorite place in the house. The plump cushions were covered with the same pink-rosed chintz as the curtains.

She'd loved to curl up in the window seat with *The Scarlet Pimpernel* or an Alexandre Dumas historical. But *Jane Eyre* was her absolute favorite. Jane, too, loved to draw the curtains of the window seat about her and read.

By the time Helen was fifteen, her youthful imagination conjured up the perfect romantic male as a composite of the heroes from her favorite books. He would be considerably older than she, of course, and with a past, like Mr. Rochester. Tall and gallant, with a sense of humor, like Sir Percy Blakeney. Most of all, he would be a man of experience and sophistication.

Reality came in a far different guise, of course. Reality was boys with clammy hands and bad breath and spots, who tried to grope her breasts when the lights were turned out at the few awful mixed parties she had been to.

Helen had always thought of herself as plain and strange-looking, with her pale skin and long, straight auburn hair. Her mother had always insisted that she wear it in neat plaits pulled back so tightly from her face that her skin felt stretched and her head ached.

Her grandmother told her she was beautiful.

"For the love of heaven, child, let your hair hang loose," she told Helen once she had moved permanently into Lansdowne House. "God gave you beautiful hair, so let's see it. Cut it if you wish, but stop hiding it."

So, daringly, Helen untied her hair and brushed it until it shone like the copper pans in her grandmother's kitchen, and kept it tidy with a black velvet headband.

The effect was amazing. The first morning she wore her hair loose to work, a man on the 65 bus to Richmond offered her his seat. And in the office, old Mr. Blanchard's eyes goggled when he saw her and he slopped his tea on his desk and young Mr. Turner raised his eyebrows at her and said, "Very nice, Miss Barstow."

Only Miss Price, Mr. Blanchard's elderly secretary, disapproved. "That hairstyle is not appropriate for this office, Miss Barstow."

Unfortunately for Miss Price, her remark was overheard by Mr. Turner.

"Nonsense, Miss Price. I was only just saying to Mr. Blanchard how Miss Barstow has really brightened up our dusty old office."

So Helen's hair stayed as it was, but she gained a new enemy in Miss Price.

Everyone was talking about Princess Margaret's romance with a handsome photographer and her coming wedding, but far more exciting to Helen was the letter she received one morning in late April from the Thames Drama Club.

Ever since her father had taken her to see Richard Burton in *Hamlet* at the Old Vic, all virile vitality, Helen had been stage-struck. Her favorite magazines were now *Theatre World* and *Plays and Players*, which were piled up in glossy stacks in her room.

For a while Emma dreamed of being an actress, of

going to drama school, but her mother soon put an end to that idea.

"You may have a little talent, but the theater is far too precarious a career for a girl."

Helen wasn't sure if she meant precarious monetarily or morally. Probably both. Whatever her meaning, the outcome had been the same: no theater school for Helen.

So, instead, she'd joined the local amateur dramatic society, one of the best in England.

The big show of the year was their open-air production in Richmond Park in the last week of July. This year it was to be *A Midsummer Night's Dream*.

Although they had told Helen she was rather young, at seventeen, to be a full member, once she had auditioned no one mentioned her age again.

Now she held in her hands a long envelope bearing the blue-printed name and address of the Thames Drama Club. She would have preferred to run to her room and open it in private, but her aunt waved her back to the breakfast table. "Finish your porridge first. It's getting cold. Then open your letter. Prolong the delicious anticipation."

Sometimes Helen was convinced that Aunt Hilary herself had once harbored theatrical aspirations.

She choked down her almost cold porridge and then took up her knife and slowly slit open the envelope.

The letter was short. Just five typed lines, signed by the producer, Raymond Beresford.

> *Dear Helen,*
> *I am pleased to inform you that your audition for us last Tuesday was successful. We would like you to play the part of Titania in the upcoming production of AMND. The first read-through will be at 7.30 on Monday, May 9th.*
> *See you there, Raymond Beresford.*

"Is it bad news or good?" her aunt snapped impatiently.

Helen looked up from her third reading. "I can't believe it," she whispered. "I'm going to play Titania."

"Splendid," said her aunt, her gray eyes bright behind her steel-rimmed glasses. "Go up and tell your grandmother. Quickly now or you'll miss your bus."

"Is she awake?"

"Edith took her breakfast up half an hour ago."

Edith was their housekeeper-cum-maid-cum-cook, who ruled the household with a will of iron.

She lived with three formidable women, Helen thought as she passed Edith in the hall and was told to "Mind you bring 'Er Ladyship's tray down with you." Edith always called Helen's grandmother "'Er Ladyship."

"I got a part in the play," Helen shouted in reply as she dashed up the stairs to the large and sunny front bedroom that was her grandmother's.

Edith's voice came sailing up after her. "Good for you. I knew you'd do it. Don't you forget that tray."

As she knocked on the paneled door, Helen smiled. Their confidence in her abilities had been contagious. "No such thing as can't," had been her grandmother's terse comment when Helen had said she couldn't possibly audition for any major roles as she was too young and inexperienced. "You are beautiful. You have talent. Go for it."

And she had.

"Come in," called her grandmother.

Helen went in. Her grandmother was a tiny figure in the large, curtained bed. She was almost hidden by the several plump pillows behind her and the mahogany tray that lay across her knees.

"Morning, Gran." Helen bent to kiss her papery cheek. She smelled of baby powder and Helena Rubinstein's Apple Blossom. "I must rush or I'll be late. I just wanted to tell you I got the part of Titania in the play. See?"

Her grandmother took the letter from her. "Titania,

eh? Yes, I should think you would make a perfect fairy queen. Well done, Helen. Are you pleased?"

Helen beamed at her. "Pleased isn't the word. I know I tried for the other parts, but it was Titania I really wanted." She bent down again, this time to fling her arms about her grandmother's neck. "It's all thanks to you, Gran. I never would have done it without you egging me on."

Her grandmother patted her arm, her faded blue eyes suspiciously damp. "It's well deserved. You're a good girl. Now get along and take this tray with you. And tell Edith if she makes me pale toast again, I shall give her notice."

Helen picked up the heavy tray, carefully balancing the white china teapot with pink rosebuds in the center. "Tonight we shall have to start coaching you with your lines," her grandmother said when she reached the door.

This was obviously going to be a venture for the entire household.

The next two months rushed by, filled with work during the day and rehearsals almost every evening. Ann Sturgis saw so little of Helen that she joined the drama club herself and worked as an assistant stage manager, just so they could spend a little time together.

After rehearsals most of the company would troop to Tony's Espresso Bar. There they drank strong, sweet coffee, ate apple strudel with dollops of whipped cream, and gossiped about the theatrical world that obsessed all of them.

The current scandal was the front-page news of the breakup of the Oliviers' marriage.

"Have you seen him in *Rhinoceros* yet?"

"No, but Ian and I have tickets." This from Helen's Oberon, Peter Young, who was tall and very handsome but a little aloof. He and Ian, who was the choreographer of the show, were best friends, apparently, always arriving and leaving together. They also fought a lot. She had never realized that two men would argue like that, one vicious and biting, the other pleading and cajoling. Their quarrels reminded Helen in a weird way of her mother and father.

Although she had hoped her parents would be excited about the news of her part in the play, they had reacted in exactly the way she had expected. Her father had lifted his lackluster eyes from his book for a moment to congratulate her, then spoiled it by saying, "I do hope all these rehearsals won't affect your work, my dear. Remember, you owe your first loyalty to your employers."

Helen wondered if he might not have been a little more enthusiastic if her mother hadn't been there. But then, she and her father were rarely permitted to be alone together. Consequently, on those occasions that they had a few minutes by themselves, they were like strangers, nervously making small talk. Her mother's reappearance usually came as an obvious relief to her father.

Her mother had said that Helen must be careful not to mix socially with these people.

But even her parents couldn't dampen her excitement. During those hectic weeks, Helen learned to move gracefully, to hold her head up confidently, to pitch her voice far across the church hall in which they rehearsed.

"Don't forget, this will be in the open air," Raymond reminded her. "You could also be fighting against a wind, so direct your voice to the farthest point."

On the dress rehearsal night, which was a disaster—a good omen, they all said afterward—she was given tips on makeup: how to blend numbers five and nine greasepaint sticks together to create a glowing complexion; how to make her eyes look bigger; how to redefine her cheekbones.

"Not that *you* need that," said the woman playing Hermia, who was definitely on the plump side. Helen caught the older woman's expression in the mirror and for the first time experienced the uncomfortable feeling of another woman's jealousy.

Uncomfortable, yet at the same time exciting.

Helen had taken a week of her holidays for the show, so that she could sleep in in the mornings and rest during the day. But she awoke early on the morning of the first performance with that horrible sensation in the pit of her stomach that she used to get when she was sitting exams.

Her sleep had been plagued with dreams of standing center stage in front of the altar of St. Matthew's, her father's church, and discovering that she had no clothes on.

Somehow, with the help of everyone in the house, she got through the day. At five-fifteen, resigned to her fate, she left to catch the 65 bus into Richmond.

By six o'clock she was swept up in the excitement and chaos in the little encampment of tents behind the stage. She dressed in her skimpy costume of semitransparent green gauze and decided that it was a good thing her parents weren't coming until later in the week. That would give her time to get used to the idea of revealing so much of herself to them—and to the large audience that was filling the sloping lawn above the natural auditorium.

By ten o'clock it was all over. The audience was drifting away. It hadn't rained. She had remembered every word of her part. Peter had hugged her and told her she'd been "absolutely marvelous, darling." She felt flushed and exhilarated. Having told her she was just perfect and beautiful and that they had heard every word, her grandmother and aunt and Edith had gone home. Someone thrust a glass of champagne into her hand. Someone else told her to get out of her costume before she died of the cold.

She was hurrying back to the women's tent when a man's voice stopped her. "Excuse me."

She turned around, the evening breeze lifting the gauzy

costume, riffling her hair. The lanterns hanging from the trees swung back and forth, creating moving shadows.

The man was of medium height, with dark hair, which he wore rather long so that it curled a little over his ears. He was probably Peter's age, she thought, in his mid- or late twenties. He glanced at his program and said, "Helen Barstow?" and then looked at her with a strange, penetrating gaze that disconcerted her.

"Yes, I'm Helen Barstow." Was he a reporter? she wondered. There were critics at the opening night, she knew.

She shivered.

"Thoughtless of me. You must be perished with the cold. Here, put my coat on." He swung his tweed jacket off his shoulders and had it around hers before she could say a word. The jacket was still warm from his body and smelled of cigarette smoke and men's cologne.

It was the most romantic thing that had ever happened to her.

"Now you will be cold," she said, looking up at his face. It was vaguely familiar, but she couldn't think where she had seen him before.

He took her arm, his white shirt gleaming in the shadowy darkness. "Is this your first part?" he asked. He had a resonant voice, pitched low, but his words were very distinct.

"Yes," she said eagerly.

"I thought so. Very amateurish."

She was bitterly disappointed. Anger made her bold. "This is, after all, an amateur company. And I thought I did jolly well, for my first major part."

"Jolly well," he repeated sarcastically, aping her youthful voice. His hand tightened on her arm. "Miss Barstow, I may tell you that 'jolly well' is not good enough for a person of your considerable, if decidedly raw, talent. You have a luminous quality that made you stand out from your fellow crowd of amateurs tonight."

She stared at him, her eyes wide. "You must be joking. Besides, I don't even know who you are."

"No, I am not joking. And I am Julian Holbrooke."

Helen gasped. "Of course. I thought I knew you. I saw your Cassio at the Old Vic."

"Good for you," he said. "You had better get dressed or everyone will have gone."

She had visions of him taking back his coat and melting away into the darkness, never to be seen again.

"Thank you."

"For what?"

"For what you said . . . about me."

"It was the truth," he said impatiently. She sensed that he was anxious to leave. "I suppose you're going on to some first-night party."

"Yes. Would you like to come?" she asked, surprised at her own daring.

"God, no." He leaned over her to reach into his jacket pocket. "Give me your address, will you?"

Bemused, she did so. He wrote it down in a little black notebook, which he then slipped back into his pocket.

She stood awkwardly, not knowing what to do or say.

He came closer to take her face between his cold hands, his head blotting out the light, and bent to kiss her on the lips. She made no move, remaining as still as one of the marble statues in the park grotto.

"I mean to make you a star, Helen Barstow," he said, and, snatching the coat from her shoulders, walked away.

6

Having an affair and keeping it a secret was impossible in Winnipeg. If you had grown up there, you couldn't go downtown to shop in The Bay or Portage Place without meeting half a dozen people you knew. And although there were several intimate little restaurants in the city, you were bound to see someone across the dining room who knew you—friends of your parents or a colleague with his wife.

Karen Lawrence had never had to worry before about encountering people she knew when she went out on a date, but in early July she had begun an affair with a married man, a partner in Danzinger, Shawarsky.

After only one month she was tired of having to cook meals in her apartment and wished that once, just once, they could go out for dinner together.

Michael Pascal was attractive. Eight years older than she, lean, athletic . . . but she wasn't in love with him. In fact, she had been too busy during law school and her articling year to find the time to fall in love with anyone. But now that she had achieved her primary goal—a position in Drybrough & Gregg, one of the top law firms in town—she was beginning to feel that there should be more than just law in her life.

Although Karen would never admit it to anyone, least of all her mother, since she had moved into her apartment she had been desperately lonely. She missed the comforts of home: the good meals, the conversation and advice over a cup of tea or a drink when she got home from a tough day, the atmosphere of order and relaxation.

Michael never stayed the night with her, of course. He always had to return to his wife after his evening "working on a case." But at least he was someone with whom Karen could share the occasional meal, a little bitchy gossip about the legal community . . . or an hour in bed.

Michael was also safe. He expected no commitment on her part. His work, like hers, was all important.

Of course, Karen, too, preferred it that way. It meant that she didn't have to consider the future, make choices, decide between having babies or not having them. She saw women lawyers juggling babies and their career. That was not for her, thank you very much.

By taking Michael as a lover, Karen assured herself, she was having the best of both worlds.

On a hot night in August, Michael stepped out onto the balcony to gaze at the lights of the city, the dark ribbon of the Assiniboine River spread out below them. "Shall we sit out here?" Karen asked from behind him.

"No, no. Just looking at the view." He quickly came back inside, sliding the glass door shut against the heat, and stood, leaning his back against it. "I don't quite know how to say this," he began.

Oh, God, he's going to end it, Karen thought. She smiled brightly. "Then just say it."

"Okay, I will. Sam Heppner told me he saw your father in Amici's last week with a younger woman."

Karen smiled to hide her relief. "So? A business lunch with one of the lawyers in the firm."

"She wasn't a lawyer, Sam said. And it was dinner, not lunch."

Karen turned to pour herself another glass of Chardonnay. "Perhaps it was my mother. She can look quite young and attractive when she wants to."

"Sam knows your mother. It wasn't her."

A little shiver of fear ran up Karen's spine. She swung around, almost splashing the wine on her white carpet. "What in hell am I supposed to do about it? Challenge my father because he has dinner with a woman?"

"Just thought you should know, that's all. Probably nothing to it."

"Probably not," she said pointedly, "considering they ate out in public under the awful glare of the Winnipeg legal community searchlight."

Michael looked at his watch. "Time I went, I think."

Damn, there was the evening shot, at eight-fifteen. Nothing left to fill the rest of it but work or a rerun of an episode of "L.A. Law."

"Sorry," Michael said. "I shouldn't have told you."

"Yes, you should. If there's anything to worry about, I'd rather hear it from you. Strange thing is, it's Mother I've been worrying about, not Dad. She's been terribly jumpy lately, which isn't like her."

"Perhaps it's all connected."

"Perhaps it is." Karen chewed on her lip. That was all she needed, parental problems. All about her were people splitting up after three or five or twenty-five years of marriage. She had always felt that her parents' marriage was the one stable thing in an unstable world. Perhaps infidelity was catching.

When she had shut the door behind Michael, she decided she'd have to work out some way of speaking to her father without actually challenging him.

"Is there something wrong with Mother?" Karen asked when she and her father met for a quick lunch together a few days later.

He looked up from his steak sandwich. "Wrong? How do you mean?"

Karen toyed with her salad. She wasn't enjoying it that much, but she had put on two pounds in the past few weeks. All those "special" dinners she'd had to cook. She was large-boned like her father and had to watch her weight.

"I can't really put a finger on it. She just seemed sort of distant when we were at the lake last weekend."

"Your mother's always a little distant nowadays."

"No, not distant in her usual, absentminded way. As if something really important were worrying her." Karen looked directly at her father. "Is there something, Dad?"

"Not that I know of. She did say she didn't want to spend any time at the cottage this summer, other than the weekends with me. A pain in the butt. It means we have to drag down groceries every weekend."

"Why doesn't she want to go?"

"Something to do with that immigrant woman from Chile she's helping to learn English." He emitted a sound between a grunt and a sigh. "Why can't she just work on committees like other women?"

Karen had to smile. "Because she's not like other women." She gazed into her black coffee. This conversation was getting them nowhere. She could ask him, of course, but somehow she couldn't bring herself to do it. He was her father, strong and reliable. To ask him outright would upset the balance between them. Perhaps permanently.

She would have to tackle her mother instead.

"Do you think she might be ill?" her father asked suddenly, having ordered the bill. "She had her annual checkup at the end of June. Perhaps they found something in her mammogram and she doesn't want to tell us."

The thought had also occurred to Karen. It could be an explanation for the gray, drawn look on her mother's face. God, not that.

"I don't think so, Dad," she said hurriedly, seeing the

hint of panic in her father's eyes. "I'm sure she would have told you about something serious like that."

"You're probably right." He didn't look entirely convinced. He rubbed his fingers across his forehead. "Hell, I don't need this worry with all the hassle over the merger."

Karen leaned forward, wishing she'd kept her mouth shut. "Tell you what, I've got a free afternoon on Thursday." And a million things to catch up on, dammit. "I'll take Mother out for a good lunch and we'll go clothes shopping. We haven't done that for ages."

"I wish you would. It's hard to get her to buy new things. She keeps telling me she has plenty in the closet."

"Well, that's what we'll do." She smiled at him. "Come on, Dad. I'm sure there's nothing wrong. She's probably just worrying about David's future."

Her father's face darkened. "Aren't we all?"

Helen was surprised by Karen's call. Apart from a few weekends at the lake and the occasional family dinner at home, she had seen very little of her since she had moved into her apartment.

Now, this call out of the blue, suggesting a "long, leisurely lunch with wine at Le Beaujolais" and something about looking for new clothes. It hadn't been clear whom the clothes were for, but Helen guessed that they were for her.

It had all sounded most suspicious. They were worried about her, obviously. Over the past few weeks she had tried very hard to be her usual bright, calm self, but it wasn't working. She thought she had played the role quite well outwardly—while inside she was falling apart—but it appeared she had fooled no one.

She was living in a dream world that revolved around that damned telephone . . . and the mailbox. Only now, instead of dreading another phone call, she longed to hear Emma's voice again.

The letter she had begun writing that same evening in May had started out as one page, containing nothing but cold facts about her medical background. Soon it had grown to four pages, each line more warm and intimate than the last.

She had torn that letter up, of course. The one she had finally sent was just a little warmer than the first had been.

On Thursday morning she had her hair done and put on an old favorite, the pale green linen dress she had bought five years ago at Holt Renfrew. Might as well make the best of it, she thought. Today she was to play the role of the contented, middle-aged mother with not a worry in her head, going off to spend a rare afternoon with her daughter, a bright lawyer with glowing prospects.

A formidable daughter, who had inherited her father's ability to stick only to what was relevant to the topic of discussion. Once Karen was on track, it was hard to get her off.

Helen felt physically ill at the thought of the long day ahead of her. A possible six hours of being probed by her daughter to discover what was troubling her. It would take all her resources to keep up the pretense that there was absolutely nothing wrong.

As she was about to leave, David came wandering down, dressed in his pajama shorts, his hair on end. "Hi, Mom, got any waffles?" he said, opening the freezer door.

"In there. At the side." She was just about to find them for him, then stopped herself.

He got the waffles out and then turned to look at her. "Hey, you look great. Going somewhere?"

"Thought I'd dig over the vegetable plot."

David laughed. She liked to hear him laugh. He had been a different person since he'd been given the part with Rainbow Stage. He was even going to all his summer classes. And, despite Bruce's warning that this damned show would certainly put an end to his chances of getting those extra courses he needed for third year, he'd been getting good marks.

"Seriously, Mom. Where are you going?"

"Out for lunch with Karen."

"Yo! Heavy-duty stuff."

Their eyes met. "Has she said anything to you . . . about me?" Helen asked him.

"Karen? We hardly ever speak to each other. Why?"

"I think she's worried about something and wants to discuss it."

"Worried about herself, do you mean? Or you?" David turned away to put two waffles into the toaster.

"Me?" Helen's smile froze on her face as he glanced over his shoulder at her.

"Yes, you. Something's getting to you, I can tell. You want to talk about it? I won't tell Dad—or Karen."

For one wild, suspended moment she considered pouring it all out to him. David would understand. He was not judgmental like Bruce and Karen. She might even get some sound advice from him.

Don't be stupid, she told herself. David had enough worries on his mind without adding his mother's to them.

"Nothing's wrong with me," she said with a bright smile. "Except Karen's going to be mad if I'm late. I must go." She hugged him and walked to the door.

David began to pour maple syrup over his waffles. "Have a good time," he said without looking up.

She was ten minutes late when she arrived at the restaurant in St. Boniface, the French quarter of Winnipeg, but Karen kissed her cheek and said nothing about the time. A bad sign.

Although the pâté maison was delicious, Helen found it almost impossible to swallow. Remember, you haven't a care in the world, she kept telling herself.

They touched on trifling matters at first. Wasn't it great at the lake last weekend? Did you hear that the Hudsons were retiring to Victoria?

Over pan-fried pickerel they talked about the aboriginal intervention in the constitutional talks. Then Helen asked Karen about work.

It surely wasn't her imagination that Karen seemed particularly relieved to get onto a subject she could control. She launched into a prolonged and legally detailed description of a complicated litigation case she was researching for the senior partner of her firm.

Lawyers always seemed to think that people outside the profession must not only understand but also be fascinated by the legal jargon and convoluted processes of the law. Helen was used to this with Bruce. Asking questions only got you in deeper. Better to nod and be genuinely interested in those facts you could comprehend.

With the desserts and coffee came silence, which Karen hurriedly filled up with questions about a holiday next winter. Hawaii, Arizona?

"Your father says he's too busy to go away."

Karen leaned across her fresh strawberry *gâteau.* "Try to persuade him to get away, Mother. He's looking tired. You both could do with a longer break."

Helen steeled herself. Here it comes. But Karen was still talking about possible holiday venues. "What about California for a few weeks? Or London in springtime? You really enjoyed that theater trip to London two years ago."

London. Helen's mouth twitched into a strained smile. "Yes, we did. But it wasn't that restful."

"Maybe you could take a couple of weeks and hire a car. Tour around England. I know you haven't any close relatives there anymore, apart from your aunt. But there must be cousins or other relatives of some sort. Wouldn't it be great to go and find some of them?"

"After thirty years? No. If there is anyone left, they wouldn't even know who I was."

Karen frowned. "It's hard to imagine, really—being an orphan and not having any family—apart from the aunt who sends you the flower seeds and cards at Christmas."

"You are my family," Helen said vehemently. "You and David and your father. That's enough for me."

Careful now. She must be more careful. Her voice was getting a hysterical edge to it.

"I still think you should plan a longer trip this year," Karen insisted. "Somewhere really romantic."

"Thank you for your concern, darling, but there's time enough. Here's you, talking about winter holidays and it's still only August." Helen pushed aside her half-eaten *gâteau*. "Now, to change the subject, what's all this about clothes shopping? I have a closet full of clothes. After all, what do I need for the lake and slopping around the garden?"

"You need some more suitable, up-to-date things."

"Suitable for what?"

Karen slammed her dessert fork onto her plate. "Suitable for the wife of a prominent lawyer. Honestly, Mother, you're impossible. You're attractive. You still have a good figure. You need . . . brightening up, that's all."

Helen gave her a mock bow across the table. "Thank you for these kind words—I think."

Karen glared at her. "You know what I mean. I know you have some good clothes, but most of them are about ten years old. Dad wants you to buy some new things, and that's what we're going to do. We'll start with Holt Renfrew and then go on to some of those boutiques on Academy Road. Or how about Magda's store in Osborne Village?"

Helen shrank from the thought of Magda Trueman trying to "brighten her up." It was time to put an end to this. "You should know by now that I don't like clothes shopping, Karen. It doesn't turn me on in the least."

"I still think—"

"No. We shall end up fighting, and I don't want that to happen. Let's just relax and enjoy our time together. It's such a long time since we just chatted."

"If that's what you want." Without realizing she was doing it, Karen looked at her watch.

Thinking of all that charged time she's wasting, thought Helen. "Do you have to get back to the office?"

"No, no. I took the afternoon off." Karen gave her a tight little smile. "I thought we were going shopping."

"Now you're making me feel guilty." Helen hesitated. Maybe she was being paranoid. Maybe Karen had something worrying *her* and wanted to discuss it. If that were so, surely she should give her the opportunity. "Tell you what, why don't we go back to your apartment? It would be heaven just to sit out on the balcony and bask in the sun."

"You could do that all the time if you stayed at the cottage in the summer," Karen pointed out.

"Has your father been complaining about that again? Anyone would think he was having an affair, he's so keen on packing me off—" Karen's stricken expression stopped Helen midsentence. "What is it? What's wrong?"

Karen bent to search beneath her chair for her leather bag, which was the size of a small briefcase. "Nothing, Mother," she said when she sat up again, her face flushed. "There's nothing wrong. That's a great idea, going back to the apartment, I mean. I'll just get the bill."

"My treat," said Helen.

"No. You and Dad paid the bills for years. Now it's my turn to treat you."

"Thank you, darling. It was delicious. I don't think I'll be able to eat again today after all that good food."

As they drove back over the bridge to Karen's apartment, Helen felt cold and slightly sick. Was that what was worrying Karen? she wondered. That her father's having an affair? The legal community in Winnipeg was a small, close-knit one. It was likely that Karen would hear news like that long before Helen did.

Throughout their marriage, Bruce had been her rock. Now Helen felt as if her world were built on shifting sand and was slipping sideways at an alarming rate.

"Must pop into the bathroom for a minute," she told Karen when they reached the apartment.

Should she broach the subject herself or just leave it alone? she wondered as she closed the door in Karen's scarlet-and-black bathroom. She stared into the mirror and saw a white-faced woman, her lipstick eaten off. She tried to see herself as Bruce saw her every morning and night.

"Good bone structure." It was as if Julian were right there in the bathroom with her. A fine sweat broke out on her forehead as she remembered how he had taken her face in his long-fingered hand and examined it.

She thrust the memory away. To her, Julian Holbrooke was as good as dead, and no amount of stifled memories or news items in newspapers and magazines would resurrect him.

She went back to her critical examination. Her green-gray eyes were still large and quite striking, but the tinted bifocals she had started wearing two years ago hid their color and expression a little. She was a bit heavier beneath her chin, and her neck bore a few fine lines. Her figure was not bad. She had put on some weight, of course, and like everyone else was always struggling to get it off.

She certainly couldn't call herself exciting. Nothing compared to some of those women in their twenties, who wore figure-hugging stirrup pants or miniskirts. (Hadn't they said that women would never have to wear those wretched things again?)

But she knew in her heart that it wasn't how she looked that might have turned Bruce to another woman. It was the fact that they had drifted apart over the years: he, to immerse himself in his work; she, to lose herself in their home and the volunteer work that gave her the only true satisfaction in her life.

Bruce had always been a good lover. It was as if he became another man in bed, tender and patient, wanting to please her, his aggression stripped away with his dark gray suit. But recently—since Emma's first call, to be exact—she had found herself cold to his lovemaking.

Their entire life was boring, monotonous. Everything planned. Nothing spontaneous.

"Are you all right, Mother?" Karen called.

Helen started guiltily. "Coming." She ran the water to wash her hands, reached for the hand cream . . . and saw the golden bottle of Obsession for Men on the shelf.

The flash of heat she had felt when she'd thought of Julian now turned to an icy cold.

She was being ridiculous. Perhaps Karen preferred to use a man's cologne. Helen herself found the spicy fragrances far more attractive than the floral scents for women. But the more likely explanation was that a man was visiting her daughter here in her apartment, sleeping with her.

Why should she be shocked? She surely didn't expect her daughter to live a celibate life at her age.

It was the fact that she was keeping it a secret that bothered Helen. Karen was the sort of woman who delighted in shocking her mother. She would think nothing of saying she was living with a man. But this man wasn't living with her.

There were no other signs of masculine occupancy.

Perhaps they liked their own individual space.

Perhaps he was married.

Karen rattled the doorknob. "Tea's ready."

Helen dried her hands. It wasn't any of her business, Karen would say. But it was impossible to undo all those years of caring and mothering. She had carried this child, like her other daughter, within her body for nine months, held her hand as she took her first steps, stuck Band-Aids on her skinned knees, attended innumerable school plays and freezing skating competitions, encouraged her aspirations, and mourned her failures. And now what her daughter did was none of her business?

She opened the door. Karen was standing out in the hall. "Whose cologne?" Helen jerked her head at the bottle.

Karen's eyes widened. "A friend." Her lips tightened into a thin line. "Keep out, Mother," her expression said.

"Is he nice?"

"Very. Let's go and have that tea before it gets cold."

Helen followed her into the living room. "Are you in love with him?"

"No, Mother, I am not."

"Then he's not someone you would want to bring to the lake or home?"

"For you and Dad to inspect, you mean?" Karen slammed the teapot down on the tray. "Get real, Mother. Those days are long gone." There was a hard edge to her voice.

Helen sat down and smoothed out the skirt of her dress, which had creased in the heat. "I suppose they have. It's sometimes hard to adjust."

"You live in the dark ages, Mother." Karen's voice was harsh now. "You're so out of it, you can't even see what's going on beneath your nose. I didn't want to tell you this, but someone saw Dad in Amici's with a woman last week."

Helen's heart pounded. "Really?" she said calmly. "I thought something was bothering you. Now I know what it is."

"I didn't want to tell you," Karen muttered.

Helen bent to pick up the milk jug. "Is it skim?"

"Two percent. Is that okay?"

"Of course." Helen poured a little milk into her cup and added tea. "You're worried that your father is having an affair, is that it?"

"Is he? He's at a very dangerous age, you know. But you don't seem at all surprised."

"I'm not. Of course he's not having an affair. He told

me he was having dinner with a client from out of town last week."

Karen met her eyes and then looked away. "Sorry, Mom. That was stupid of me."

"Not at all. Far better to tell me than to be worrying yourself sick about it."

"You're right. You can't believe what a relief it is to hear that you knew all about it." Karen sat back on the couch and thrust her fingers through her short, brown hair. "Now that's over, let me tell you all about this conference I'm going to in Quebec in September."

That night Karen allowed herself the luxury of a good cry. Her mother had been lying when she'd said she knew about the dinner at Amici's, she was sure. But at least she had been able to warn her. Although what good that did, she had no idea.

Her mother had always been unflappable, invincible. The sort of mother you came to with your problems when you were a kid. Not later, though. Not when you were grown up. She had almost told her about Michael when she'd asked about the bottle in the bathroom. It would have been a relief to tell her. To ask her advice.

But her mother wouldn't understand. She was too perfect, cocooned in her suburban life-style, her horizons a well-cut lawn and the local Safeway grocery store. She was too innocent of the real ways of the world, the cut and thrust, the selfishness, the dirty tactics.

She was like Snow White in her glass case. Let in the polluted air and she might crumble to dust.

Her mother must be kept exactly as she was, with her beautiful English voice and her full peasant skirts and her archaic vision of the world.

From now on, Karen decided, she would keep her worries to herself.

7

The letter from Emma arrived the second week of September.

At first Helen set it aside on the kitchen table. She sorted through the collection of bills and this week's copy of *Maclean's* magazine and useless flyers. Her heart was thumping so hard that she felt dizzy with it.

Eventually she couldn't put it off any longer. She sat down, pushed aside the dirty breakfast dishes, and opened the letter, her hands shaking.

There were two pages, folded separately, marked with a large *1* and *2*. Helen unfolded number one.

> *Dear Helen,*
> *(Please excuse my calling you "Helen," but I can't bear to call you "Mrs. Lawrence." It sounds so cold. And I know you wouldn't want me to call you "Mother" or "Mum" or anything like that!)*
>
> *I can't begin to describe how wonderful it was for me to receive my very first letter from my birth mother. I put off writing to thank you because you told me to forget you. Also, I know how worried*

you are about your husband and family finding out. But I can't forget you. Your letter is under my pillow. Each night I fall asleep with my hand touching it. (It's getting awfully creased!)

I'd like to write pages and pages to you, but I know you don't want me to, so I won't. Thank you for all the information about childhood diseases, etc. Nothing major, thank heavens. You didn't say what your parents died of. I take it that it was just the usual illnesses of old age. There are so many other questions I want to ask you. And so much I want to tell you about me.

You don't even know that I'm an interior designer in an architectural partnership. Parmenter, Grenville Associates. The two architects are Desmond Parmenter and Alan Grenville, and we have some draftsmen—one's a draftswoman, actually—and three interior designers. I'm the most junior associate. Our offices are in Chelsea, near the river. We specialize in classical design and the restoration of old buildings. Desmond Parmenter is brilliant but rather weird.

Well, I'm waffling on. Daddy says I do that! By the way, I told him I had phoned you. At first he pursed his lips up—very solicitorish. Asked me if you were angry at him for telling me who you were. But afterwards he seemed really excited and made me repeat all we had said to each other over and over. He was sort of crying and smiling at the same time. Very strange. For a moment I thought he might actually have been my father. But I know he would have told me if he was.

So the hunt is still on. Daddy clams up and gets furious when I ask him about my father. So I will have to do the detective work by myself. Don't worry. When I find my father I won't tell him where you are, I promise.

I'll try not to write again, but there's so much else I want to ask you and tell you.

I love you.

          Your daughter, Emma.

P.S. Thought you'd like a photo of me.

After a second reading, Helen stared at the letter, her fingers smoothing out the two creases where it had been folded. Then she laid her head down on the table, beside the marmalade jar. Leaning her forehead on her arm, she rocked her head from side to side, her despair issuing from her in a great wail that went on and on.

When she came to her senses several minutes later, she felt deeply ashamed. *Your conduct is disgusting, uncivilized,* an inner voice told her.

She went to the sink, doused a paper towel in cold water, and pressed it on her eyes. She scrubbed her face, the paper rough on her delicate skin.

"Oh, God, what am I going to do?" she whispered.

She stared out at the rich colors in the garden. The crackerjack marigolds had not yet been nipped by frost. Their brilliant yellow and orange blooms overwhelmed the more subtle bronze and gold of the fall chrysanthemums. The leaves of the maple tree were beginning to turn russet red.

How beautiful it was, that world outside.

The photograph. She hadn't even looked at it. Helen unfolded the second sheet of paper, to reveal the photo of a girl gathering up an armful of leaves from the ground, laughing into the camera. She wore jeans and a dark green sweatshirt, the color setting off the rich red gold of her shoulder-length hair.

Red hair. Emma had red hair, like her mother.

Helen felt she was falling apart, exploding into a million pieces.

She had been taking Valium just to get her through

the day until she could take a sleeping pill at night. Yet still she fell into the black abyss of despair at some time each day.

The nights were worse. Around three o'clock every morning she would wake with her heart pounding and her brain seething with unrelated thoughts and consider if it would be safe to take another Valium.

But no amount of Valium could conceal the unmistakable fact that Emma had inherited her red hair.

Emma was her child, flesh of her flesh. She existed, she breathed, she still loved the mother who had rejected her not once, but twice. Denying her the right to speak to her, to know her, to hold her, to be comforted by her.

"What am I going to do?" she asked the dishwasher, the black microwave oven, the almond stove and fridge.

The inanimate objects, symbols of her material wealth, gave her no answer.

Ann. She must call Ann. Helen's hands shook so hard that it took her two tries before she could press the right buttons for Ann's number in Toronto.

"Please, dear God, let her be in," Helen whispered.

The answer came on the fifth ring. "Hallo?"

"Ann. It's me. Helen."

"Hi there. How are you doing?"

"I'm fine. How about you?"

The ritualistic words of greeting were out before Helen could stop them. A great sob welled up in her chest. "No, I'm not fine," she wailed down the phone. "Oh, Ann, I think I'm going crazy."

"Hold on a minute. I have to turn the radio off." A pause. Then, "What's happened?"

Helen took a deep breath. "A letter from Emma."

"Ah. You thought she'd write, didn't you? No one else saw the letter, did they?"

"Oh no, it's nothing like that. I just don't know what to do. I seem to be falling to pieces."

"I still think you should tell Bruce."

"I know you do. But I can't, Ann. I just can't. Especially now."

"What do you mean, especially now?"

Helen hesitated. Somehow telling Ann her suspicions about Bruce would make them more real. Besides, she had her pride. "This merger is causing him a lot of headaches."

"Are you saying a merger is more important than your life, your health?"

"Oh, Ann. You make it sound so easy. How can I tell Bruce that I'm not me at all? That the woman he married all those years ago was spoiled goods with an illegitimate baby?"

"For God's sake, Helen, you sound just like your mother."

"That's all I need, to be like my mother."

"I didn't say you were like her, I said you sound like her when you spout rubbish like 'spoiled goods.'"

"What am I going to do? You should read Emma's letter. She says she keeps my letter under her pillow."

"Poor girl. You already know what I think. I keep telling you. You should face up to Bruce, tell him about Emma. Then you and Emma can write and phone each other as much as you like. You could even fly over for a visit, or bring her here. After all, you can afford it."

Helen was surprised to hear the tinge of bitterness in Ann's voice. It wasn't like her. "You don't understand the repercussions of telling Bruce. He . . ." She hesitated. "He might want to leave me."

"I doubt it. You look after him too well."

"But what would I do if he asked for a separation?"

"You'd manage. Thousands of women do."

Panic swamped Helen. If Ann wasn't on her side, she was utterly alone. "Could I come and spend a few days with you? I think it might help me if we could talk. Talking on the phone isn't the same."

The silence seemed to stretch on for hours.

Helen flushed with embarrassment. "I'm sorry. It's probably not a good time. I shouldn't—"

"Don't be daft. Any time's a good time for old friends like us."

Ann's hearty tone didn't deceive Helen. For some reason, she didn't want her to come to Toronto.

"Is something wrong? I've been so busy telling you all my troubles these past weeks, we've hardly talked at all about you. Are you okay, Ann—and Eric?"

"I'm fine," Ann said briskly. "The only reason I hesitated is that I haven't much room in this place, but we'll manage. Book your flight and let me know when you're coming."

"I don't think—"

"It's been ages since we spent any time together. And it'll do you good to have a change. Give you a new outlook on life. No more arguing, Helen Barstow. Just do it."

Helen had to smile. "Aye-aye, Captain."

"That's more like it. Phone me when you know when you're coming. And, Helen . . ."

"Yes?"

"Hang in there. It will all work out, you know."

Helen had grave doubts about that. When Bruce eventually came home that evening—having phoned yet again to say he was working late and not to bother with a meal for him—she was tempted to blurt out the truth.

"Bruce, can you give me a few minutes?" she asked him when they had finished watching the news in the family room.

Look at me! she felt like screaming. Can't you see what's happening to me? Or don't you care anymore?

No, this was not a good time. The fear of his reaction, the thought of having to leave the security of her home, living on her own, finding a job . . . stopped her.

"I'm going to visit Ann in Toronto for a few days."

He turned to her, frowning. "Ann?"

"Yes, Ann. Ann Carlson. My best friend. Remember?"

"No need for sarcasm." He clicked off the television. "What caused this sudden decision?"

"I need a break. We haven't been away for ages."

"You could have had a break all summer if you'd gone to the lake."

Helen sighed. "Oh, Bruce, not that again. You know how I feel about wilderness and wild animals. . . . Besides, it's a change I need. And it's two years since I saw Ann."

Bruce took off his glasses and rubbed his eyes. "It's a bad time."

"It's always a bad time with you. You never like me going away on my own. It might mean you would have to look after yourself for a change." Her voice rose. "I have to get away. I have to."

Bruce moved over to sit beside her on the couch. "Darling, you're shaking." His voice and expression were genuinely concerned.

Now. Tell him now.

He put his arm around her, drawing her head onto his shoulder. "That's better. Tell me what's bothering you."

His shoulder and arm were strong, solid beneath her head. She felt secure here, with the even thump of his heart against her cheek.

This might be a good time after all.

She opened her mouth to speak . . . and closed it again as he said, "I'm really worried about you. You haven't been yourself at all lately. First thing tomorrow I want you to make an appointment to see the doctor."

She twisted her shaking hands together in her lap. "I'll try. But he may not be able to fit me in."

"Tell his office they have to fit you in. There must be something he can give you to help make you feel better. I need you back to your old self for the merger party, you know. It's only a month away, you realize."

She was suddenly cold, as if someone had opened the front door and let in the September night air. Slowly she released herself from his arm. She sat up straight and smoothed her hair.

"I shall be fine for the merger party. Especially if I get a little time away by myself. Don't worry, Bruce. I'll make sure to fill the freezer with special meals before I go. So you won't have to cook for yourself and David."

Or you could get your mistress—whoever she is—to cook for you, she was tempted to say.

He put his hand on her arm. Her muscles tensed at his touch. "What would you say if I asked you not to go away?" he asked. "Not now, at least."

Something deep in his eyes sought to connect with hers, but she looked down at her hands, twisting the diamond-and-sapphire engagement ring round her finger. "I must go now, not later. I've already told Ann I'm coming."

He turned away to take some papers from his briefcase.

Helen got up. "I'll leave you to your work," she said, and went out, closing the door behind her.

Bruce remained seated on the couch, his hands dangling between his knees.

Did she know?

Surely not. He'd been very careful not to meet Carla Remillard in public, at least not since that first dinner when they had been nothing more to each other than lawyer and client.

So careful that Carla was becoming impatient. "I am tired of eating Chinese food from plastic containers at 'ome," she told him, her dark eyes bright with anger, "or 'aving to cook for you." Carla was one Frenchwoman who didn't like to cook.

She was also tired of his refusal to go to bed with her. She found it insulting that he resisted her when she herself was so eager to sleep with him. "Imagine, you, a big lawyer, afraid of your cold English wife," she taunted him.

How could he explain to her that he had never before been unfaithful to Helen? That to go to bed with another woman would betray the wife he had loved for so many years yet seemed to have lost somewhere along the way?

If only Carla knew how difficult it was to resist her. Just the very thought of her heavy-breasted body, her sleek black hair, the scent of her, excited him now to the point of discomfort.

He stood up.

Would Helen still be awake?

"Christ!" He picked up the copy of the merger report and flung it across the room.

What sort of man would go to his wife and ask her to make love because he was aroused by thoughts of the woman he was seeing on the sly?

Besides, Helen would say she was too tired. After all, he thought bitterly, that was what she'd been saying for weeks now.

Of one thing he was certain: if Helen went away to Toronto, he would find it very difficult to continue to resist Carla Remillard.

8

"*It is kind of you* to drive me to the airport," Helen told Karen as they pulled away from the house. Her mind was busy checking off the long list: meals in the freezer, garden cleanup arranged, library books returned . . .

"I hope you know what you're doing, Mother."

"What on earth is that supposed to mean?"

Karen raised her eyebrows but didn't answer.

"Honestly, I've never seen such a fuss, just because I'm going away for a few days. David telling me he'll be leaving all his washing until I come home; and your father—"

"David's a lazy slob. You've spoiled him."

"I've spoiled you all," Helen said acidly. "Your father's the worst one. Like a bear with a sore head because he has to look after himself for a few days."

"Don't worry about him. He'll probably eat at the Manitoba Club every night."

Helen sincerely hoped he would, but she doubted it. When she had gathered up his white shirts to take them to the laundry yesterday, a waft of some exotic perfume had come from them. Certainly not her Ombre Rose. Probably Poison.

She couldn't think about that now. Nor could she worry about how Bruce and David would get along. "They'll just have to manage without me."

"Who will?"

Helen started. "Oh, I was just thinking aloud. About Bruce and David being left alone together."

Karen bit back the retort that it must be nice to have such tiny troubles to worry about. She couldn't believe that her mother would leave home at a time when something was going on between Dad and this "other woman."

There had been another sighting of the two of them together. Michael had even managed to find out who the woman was: a divorcée called Carla Remillard. Apparently she had changed her name from Charlotte to Carla when she had become a fashion model years ago. Now she was an executive of a women's fashions manufacturing company.

Sounded dangerous. An attractive divorcée who had been a model, and apparently at least ten years younger than her father. Extremely dangerous.

Yet here was her mother flying off for a week in Toronto, as if nothing were wrong. Surely she couldn't be that naive, thought Karen, not after I warned her.

Her hands tightened on the steering wheel. "Mother," she began, then hesitated.

"Do you realize it's more than two years since I was last in Toronto?" Her mother turned to her, her eyes bright. "I am so excited about seeing Ann again."

Karen let out a sigh. To hell with it. She was not her mother's keeper. "You must be. I hope you have a wonderful time."

Perhaps this little holiday will do her good, Karen thought. If her mother came back rejuvenated, it might improve her marriage. God, she hoped so. She couldn't bear the thought of her parents separating.

"David thinks you might have been overdoing things

lately," Karen said casually, glancing sideways at her mother.

"How could I, of all people, possibly overdo things? A housewife with no job?"

"No need for sarcasm. I know how much you do, with all your voluntary activities. David's worried about you."

"He doesn't need to be. Actually, I'm worried about him. He seems really down now that he's back full-time at university again." Helen sighed. "He was a different person this summer. He had such a great time doing the Rainbow Stage shows. Now he's short-tempered and miserable again."

"You're changing the subject, Mother. We were talking about you, remember?"

"I'm fine. It's just my age."

"Garbage. If it is the start of menopause, there's no need to go through all those miseries nowadays, not with hormone replacement easily available. Even you can't be that old-fashioned." Out of the corner of her eye, she saw her mother smile an enigmatic smile.

"No, dear." Helen looked out the side window. "How's Michael?"

Karen shot her a startled look. "How the hell did you know about Michael?"

"Your father told me. I asked him if he knew you were having an affair. He said he was embarrassed to speak to you about it. He's worried about you, Karen. People are talking. And he doesn't like Michael Pascal."

"Well, you can tell Dad it's none of his bloody business." Karen slammed on the brakes as the car in front came to a halt at the lights.

"Careful, darling. Keep your mind on the driving."

"Damn the driving. What else did Dad say?"

"Why don't you ask him yourself?"

"I wouldn't dream of discussing my private affairs with my father."

"A rather unfortunate choice of words."

Karen glared at her mother.

Helen pretended not to see. "Don't forget the speed limit's thirty kilometers an hour in the airport zone."

Karen eased her foot off the gas pedal. "I like Michael. We have a good time together."

"He's also married."

Karen felt chilled by the ice in her mother's voice. "Oh, Mother, you're so—"

"Old-fashioned? Come on, Karen. Even these days it's not acceptable to sleep with a man who's still cohabiting with his wife."

"If it wasn't me, it would be someone else. So where's the harm?"

"The harm is that you are our daughter, and we mind very much that our daughter is sleeping with a married man."

Karen came perilously near to saying something about glass houses or casting the first stone, but she didn't want to send her mother off to Toronto with even more worries on her mind. "I'm an adult, living away from home," she said through tight lips, "and what I do is my business only."

"I've said my piece. Just remember that as a new and very junior member of a prestigious law firm you are expected to conform to certain rules of society."

Karen drew the car up to the airport entrance and then sat, her face and body stiff with anger.

"Oh, darling." Helen put an arm around her daughter's unyielding shoulders. "It had to be said sometime. I just wish it hadn't come up now."

"I'll help you with your bag," was all Karen said. She drew away and got out of the car.

"Thanks, darling. But don't bother to come in with me. I can manage. It saves you having to park the car."

As Karen opened the trunk, Helen sat still for a moment, her eyes closed. Dear God, what lousy timing.

The exhilaration she had felt at the thought of

spending a week in different surroundings, being able to talk with Ann, seeped away, leaving her feeling depressed again.

It was a relief to say good-bye to Karen, who stood stiff as a lamp standard, not returning her mother's hug. Helen waited for Karen to get back into the car. As she turned to wave she felt a deep sadness when she saw that the car was already pulling away.

It was an easy flight. The plane arrived dead on time, two hours and fifteen minutes after takeoff. As soon as she had collected her bag and swung it onto the cart, she pushed her way through the crowd of people.

The automatic doors opened . . . and there was Ann, baring her large teeth in a laugh.

"Ann Sturgis is far too common for you," her mother used to say. "I don't like you spending time with her."

Ann Sturgis, now Ann Carlson, was the best and most loyal friend anyone could ever have had.

Helen threw her arms around Ann's sturdy body and hugged her tight. "Oh, Ann. It's so wonderful to see you again."

"Hold on, hold on, you idiot. It's great to see you, too, but it's nothing to cry about."

Helen rubbed her eyes with a tissue. "You're right. It's something to be happy about. Oh, God, Ann, I've longed for this so much. Just to be with you again. We've got so much to talk about, poor Eric will never get a word in. How's he doing, by the way?"

"Eric?" Ann was striding along so fast with the cart that Helen almost had to break into a run to keep up with her. "He's okay."

Ann was silent after that, until they reached her battered old Toyota in the car park. "Still the same old car," Helen said, and immediately wished she hadn't.

"That's right. Long may she reign. Do you want to go on the 401 or along the lakeshore, so you can see the city?"

"Lakeshore, if it's not too much out of the way."

As they were driving along the busy highway beside Lake Ontario, it seemed to Helen that she was doing all the talking. Ann was restrained, preoccupied.

"You're very quiet," Helen said at last.

"Roads are busy."

They were, of course. Helen always found it difficult to adjust to the fast pace of life in Toronto. A two-hour plane ride was all that divided the slow, prairie pace of Winnipeg from the frenzy of thousands of cars hurtling side by side in all directions.

It was always a shock to the system.

"I don't know how you can drive here. I'd be terrified."

"You get used to it, I suppose. No alternative if you want to get about."

To her right, Helen caught the occasional glimpse of the shimmering waters of Lake Ontario between the buildings that lined the lakeshore.

"Whereabouts is Bellerby Road?" she asked when, to her relief, they turned off the highway and drove up Spadina.

Ann kept her eyes on the road. "Off St. Clair West. Remember when we ate in a little Italian restaurant last time you were here? We bought some prosciutto in one of the stores along St. Clair."

"Oh, right." Helen recalled European-style grocery stores, with stalls outside displaying shiny aubergines and big, ripe Roma tomatoes. "I don't remember any apartment blocks in that area."

"I'm not in an apartment block. I'm on the top floor of an old house that's been converted into four apartments."

"I see." Helen really didn't see at all. Why hadn't Ann told her this before?

"Toronto's not like Winnipeg, you know," Ann said belligerently. "It's bloody expensive to live in."

Feeling uncomfortable, Helen decided to keep quiet.

As Ann drove along St. Clair West, trying to avoid the streetcar lines in the road, Helen turned her head to look out the window. Her eyes saw the red-brick buildings that always made her think of England, the little stores with their display stalls that reminded her of Europe, but her mind was on Ann's strange mood.

Usually so open and direct, Ann seemed morose and reluctant to talk. Should she ask her outright what was wrong? Because there definitely *was* something wrong.

"Here we are."

Helen blinked. She hadn't even noticed that Ann had turned off St. Clair and driven down a narrow side street.

They had drawn up outside an old house with a sagging porch, brown paint peeling off the woodwork.

Ann clapped her hands on the steering wheel. "Well, old dear. This is it. Your palace for a week."

Her light tone hid acute embarrassment.

"Anywhere you are is great for me," Helen replied. "Let's get in. I'm dying for a cup of tea."

The large maple trees along the narrow street had begun to shed their leaves. "Beautiful trees," Helen said as Ann opened the car trunk.

"They're a damned nuisance, dropping their leaves all over the place. Then they get tramped inside."

For the first time for quite a while, Helen smiled. "Come on, Ann. It can't be so bad that you hate trees."

She was appalled to see Ann's eyes fill with tears. "You don't know the half of it." She led the way up the three sloping steps to the porch.

When Ann opened first the screen door and then the inner door, an overpowering smell of cats and cabbage hit Helen. The stairs had once been painted, but the paint had worn off and they were down to bare board, coated with dust.

"I keep sweeping them, but . . ." Ann shrugged and bent to pick up Helen's case again.

They paused on the first landing to get their breath. The nasal sound of some country and western singer wailing her anguish issued from behind one of the two doors.

"Let me carry the case now," Helen said.

"No way. I'm used to these stairs. You're not."

Ann lugged the suitcase up another flight of even narrower stairs, banging it against the wall as she went.

By the time they reached the top, Helen was fighting for breath.

"We're here at last," Ann said. She turned the key and opened the door.

The door opened into a tiny, cluttered living room with one small window, high on the wall. The room was crammed with a few pieces of furniture. A small beige couch stood beneath the window, its bland color brightened by two cushions with tapestry covers in an oriental pattern that Helen recognized as Ann's handiwork. In front of the couch was a small coffee table covered with one of Ann's beautiful hand-embroidered cloths. A bookcase of unvarnished wood stood against the far wall.

All that divided the living room from the minuscule kitchenette was a square table with two kitchen chairs drawn into it.

"Now, aren't you sorry you didn't bring Bruce with you? He'd have loved it here, wouldn't he?" Ann kept her face averted from Helen. "I've put you in the bedroom."

"I'm not taking your room from you," Helen protested. "Where are you and Eric going to sleep?"

"I'm going to sleep on the sofa bed, here in the living room." For the first time since they'd come into the apartment, Ann looked directly at Helen. "As for Eric, I don't know or care where he's sleeping. He and I separated in the spring."

Helen stared at her, horrified. "Oh, no, Annie. Why on earth didn't you tell me?"

"Because it's a long, sordid story and you had enough on your plate without worrying about me."

Helen put her arm around Ann's waist, but she moved away awkwardly. "Must put the kettle on. Sit down," she said over her shoulder as she went into the kitchenette.

It consisted of an old stove, a refrigerator with a loud hum, and a small sink with one cupboard on the wall above it. "If you need it, the bathroom's just round the corner," Ann told Helen as she reached for cups and saucers.

Helen grasped at the opportunity to escape. "Yes, I do. Thanks." She hesitated. "Then we'll talk."

Once inside the bathroom, she locked the door and glanced at herself in the tarnished mirror over the sink. She'd come to Toronto for comfort and advice, but now, for the first time ever, it seemed that Ann needed her help. Why on earth hadn't Ann told her about Eric on the phone? Helen wondered as she washed her hands.

She asked Ann the same question a few minutes later, over strong tea and biscuits.

"I thought you had enough to worry you, that's why," Ann replied, her mouth full of ginger biscuit.

"You've always been there for me," Helen told her. "Why wouldn't you share this with me?" Although she was trying not to show it, she was deeply hurt.

"I don't know, really. Somehow I always think of you as being sort of fragile, not able to handle these things. Besides, you've suffered enough in your life without worrying about my sordid little problems."

Helen reached out a tentative hand to touch Ann's. This time Ann did not draw away. They squeezed hands for a moment, and then Helen sat back on the small couch. "Tell me what's happened. All of it, mind."

Ann took another biscuit and dunked it in her tea. "It's not that complicated, really. Eric and I haven't been getting along for years now. Since long before

Peter was married and moved to the States. Last year Eric—" She rubbed her mouth with one of the little hand-embroidered napkins. "His firm found that he'd been embezzling money from them systematically for several years."

"Oh, no."

"To avoid the scandal and bad publicity, they said they wouldn't press charges if Eric paid the money back. We had to sell everything we had, the house, the car, furniture . . . everything."

"Does Peter know?"

"Yes. He's helping me a bit. Keeping my head just above water, bless him. It's not easy, when he's just starting out, after all those years at university. You know what it's like."

"Yes, it isn't easy." Helen wondered whether Karen would help her as Ann's son was doing. Possibly. She wasn't sure. David would, if he had the money.

"Peter won't even talk to his dad. It was the last straw when we found out he had another woman."

Helen went cold.

Ann's smile was bitter. "That was part of the reason he did it. Stole the money, I mean. For her. Well, she's got what she deserves now. Eric moved in with her and she's having to keep him for a change."

"Do you miss him?"

"I miss having a man around. I don't miss Eric himself. He was a bastard. This woman wasn't the first."

Helen didn't know what to say. Somehow she'd always thought that Ann could be in control of everything. To learn that she couldn't—and wasn't—was frightening.

"It's a bugger, isn't it?" Ann held out her hand. "Give me your cup. I'll pour you another one."

"That'll be my third."

"That's okay," Ann said. "We'll move on to the booze later."

Helen never knew what made her say it; perhaps because she wanted to show Ann she was not alone, perhaps because this was the time for truth, but as she took back the cup of tea from her, she said, "I think Bruce is having an affair."

"Bruce?" Ann's voice rose in a hoot of disbelief. "Never."

Helen nodded. "I don't know how far it's gone, but Karen's heard about it. I told Karen the woman was a client and I knew all about it, but of course I didn't."

"I just can't believe it of Bruce. He's too . . ." Ann shrugged, searching for the right word. "Too upright. Besides, he adores you, Helen. Always has done."

"Not anymore, it seems. I've become so taken up with this thing about Emma that I'm never there for him."

"Mentally, you mean? Or in bed as well?"

Helen flushed. "Both."

"That's bad."

"I know it is, but I can't help it." Helen was shaking now. "I just can't bear him to touch me. It's hard to explain, but it's more that I feel I'm dirty, that he shouldn't be touching me, that if he knew about . . . about my past he'd be disgusted by me."

"That bitch of a mother of yours has a sin to answer for. Several of them. Forget the dirty bit, Helen. You went to bed with a man before you were married. So, big deal! You thought Julian was perfect. He seduced you. Then he left you to rot when you became pregnant. How does that make you the evil one, I'd like to know?"

Helen twisted her napkin into something resembling a rope. "I shouldn't have done it. Oh, God, Ann, how often do I lie awake, saying 'If only I hadn't slept with Julian. If only I hadn't been so stupid.'"

"What about asking, 'If only Julian had been more careful'? It's in the past. Forget it."

Helen slammed her cup onto the table. "How can I

forget it, when Emma is phoning and writing to me? Not only that, but think how guilty I feel now when I realize that, but for me, you wouldn't have married Eric Carlson?"

"How so?"

"Because if I hadn't slept with Julian and got pregnant and had Emma, neither of us would be in Canada, would we?"

"Of course we would. We often talked about going to Australia or the States or Canada when we were kids."

"Yes, but it was because I was so depressed after Emma was born that you suggested we come to Canada. I'm the one to blame for it all."

"Oh, for God's sake, Helen, cut it out. Honestly, I've never known you to be as bad as this. Use the napkin," Ann snapped as Helen scrabbled in her bag for a tissue.

Helen blew her nose. "I know. I've even had to take tranquilizers and sleeping pills to keep going."

"Well, you're not taking them here. We might get drunk every night, but we certainly won't fill ourselves with those bloody chemicals male doctors give us to cover up the pain men cause."

Helen managed to smile. "You sound like one of those rampant feminists."

Ann grinned. "I do, don't I? I think I'm about to join their cause. Did you have any Valium today?"

"No. Why?"

"Because I've got a bottle of brandy and we're going to have a shot of it." She got up and opened the cupboard beneath the kitchen sink.

"In the middle of the afternoon?"

Ann gave a roar of laughter. "You're priceless, Helen. After all these years you still sound like a vicar's daughter."

"Well, that's exactly what I am," Helen said indignantly.

"And it shows, love, it shows. If you don't mind my saying so, your father was hardly the ideal Christian, was he? Turning his back on his only child when she was pregnant. God, talk about Victorian melodrama."

"It wasn't exactly like that."

"Almost." Ann took out two glasses and polished them with a dish towel.

"I don't want to talk about it."

"Of course you don't. You never did. Sweep it under the carpet. Pretend it never happened. That's your motto. And that's why you're in the fix you're in today, isn't it? Here, drink this down."

Ann set a brandy glass with at least two inches of brandy in it before her.

Helen picked up the glass and took a sip. Then a gulp. The spirit sent fire down her throat, fire that warmed and eventually relaxed her. She leaned forward. "We've got all the time in the world to talk about me. What about you, Ann? What are you going to do now?"

"Keep on trying to find a job, for starters. I'm doing some home typing, but that doesn't pay enough for food, never mind rent."

"If I were to ask you what you would most like to do right now, what would you say?"

"Get drunk."

"No, be serious. Would you want to go to the States, be near Peter?"

"Not really. He's got his own life to live now. Besides, getting into the States is like getting into the kingdom of heaven. I don't have the right qualifications." Ann's dark eyes brightened. "If we're talking about fantasies now, the thing I'd really want to do is go home."

"Back to England?"

"Yes. Back to Richmond. I know Mum and Dad aren't there anymore, but it's where my heart is. Always has been." Ann laughed a brittle laugh. "Wouldn't it be great if I could hitch a ride on a time capsule and go back to those swinging sixties in London? Just think of all the fun we missed by leaving before they really began. Only I can't, can I?"

"Oh, Ann. You make me feel so awful," Helen whispered.

"For what? I've loved Canada. It's been a great adventure in a great country. I don't regret it at all. But much as I love it, there's nothing for me here anymore. Now that I've lost my nice home and all the comforts, including a husband in my bed, I feel empty somehow. I'm forty-nine and I've got absolutely nothing to show for a life of hard work. I just want to go home." Ann smiled a twisted smile.

"I'll treat you to a holiday in England," Helen said. "Stay as long as you like. They say that soon gets the homesickness out of your system. You've told me yourself that Britain's a different place now."

"Thanks, love. But then I'd still have to come back. I couldn't bear that. It may have changed, but the older I get, the more I want to go back to England. I've just never settled in like you have."

"I'm not sure I have, really. I get homesick, too, you know."

"Of course you do. I should think that all emigrants do at some time or other, even the ones who come here to escape persecution of some sort."

"But I never wanted to go back," Helen said vehemently. "Never."

Ann leaned forward to pour more brandy into their glasses. "Of course you didn't. That's understandable, I suppose. But it's festering inside you still, isn't it? Your auntie Hilary and your gran and your mother and—"

Helen held up both hands to ward her off. "I don't even want to think about them."

"That's the difference, you see?" Ann said sadly. "I've never stopped thinking about home."

"What's keeping you from going back, then?"

"Money. That's what. See?" Ann's voice was bitter.

"I've become a real Torontonian, thinking only of money."

"I've already said I'd pay your fare."

"Thanks, Helen. I'd take you up on your offer, honestly I would. But if I go back, it would be for good. And I'd want to live in or near Richmond, where all the old happy memories are. Do you know what that would cost?"

"I've no idea." Helen wished Ann would stop talking about Richmond. It made her feel ill.

"It's one of the most prestigious areas, within easy reach of the City, which means prices have gone sky-high. I couldn't afford a room there, never mind a house or a flat."

"I wish I could buy you a place," Helen whispered, staring at her brandy glass. "I owe it to you—and more."

"Don't be so daft. You've got nothing but Bruce's money. Even if he had that sort of money floating around to spare, which I know he doesn't, it's not yours to give."

Helen could understand the reasons for Ann's bitterness now. But despite her reassurances, she still felt responsible for Ann's fate.

Ann scraped back her chair. "Don't look so down, ducky. Let's forget all this for now. I've booked a table at the local pizzeria. We're going out on the town to celebrate being together again."

"I'm paying," Helen said.

"You're damned right you are. Otherwise we're not eating. In fact, you're paying for this entire week. I hope you've got lots of plastic."

"Tons," Helen replied, entering into Ann's suddenly carefree mood. "We're going to have a great time, and Bruce can pay for the lot."

"That's the spirit."

Neither of them spoke about their main worries again that evening. But when Helen lay in Ann's bed late that night, her mind whirling from too much wine, for the first time in weeks she worried about someone else's troubles rather than her own.

What was to become of Ann? She couldn't bear to think of her trapped in this shabby place—or somewhere like it—for the rest of her life. She could give her money, offer to pay for a computer course, but there was only so much Ann would take from her. Helen knew that from the past.

It was all her fault. If only she had never met Julian. If only she hadn't slept with him.

How different their lives might have been had Julian Holbrooke not come back into her life after that first meeting.

9

A *Midsummer Night's Dream* was over; the tents taken down. When Helen returned to the park the following Sunday it was as if the show had never happened. The rows of green deck chairs had been taken away, the gouges in the smooth green lawn the only proof they had ever been there.

The birds sang in the great oaks and chestnuts surrounding the natural stage, but Helen felt no joy at their singing, nor at the warmth of the August sun on her back. Her short burst of fame was over. What was even worse, she would never see Julian Holbrooke again. Every night she had sought for his face in the audience, but he hadn't returned for another performance.

Now she would be trapped forever in the mundane, boring world of typing and making tea and watching the nine o'clock news on the BBC every night.

All the excitement in her life had gone.

But when she walked into the office on Monday morning, she was greeted by a chorus of voices.

"Good morning, Miss Star."

"Can I have your autograph?"

"Are you quite sure you want to sully your hands by working in our humble office?" The last from Mr. Turner, who stood at the open door of his office, smiling broadly. His smile faded as he saw Helen's bewilderment. "Don't tell me you haven't seen it yet."

Helen shook her head. "I don't know what you're talking about."

"There's a picture of you in the paper."

"In the local paper, you mean?"

"No, a national one. The *Evening Standard,* no less." Mr. Turner held out the newspaper he had in his hand. It was folded into four. As Helen looked down at the page, she saw a large photograph of herself as Titania. Oh, Lord, she thought as she saw how inadequately the thin gauze covered her chest. Her parents would be absolutely horrified.

Then she saw the headline: FUTURE STAR SHINES IN SHAKESPEARE PLAY.

"Gosh," she said.

"Is that all you can say—'Gosh'?"

She looked up into Mr. Turner's amused eyes. "I don't know why they'd put me in. Mine was only a small part."

"But you were terrific," said Jimmy Watts, the junior clerk.

"You certainly were," agreed Mrs. Pelham, Mr. Turner's secretary.

Miss Price said nothing. Her baleful glance over the top of her steel-rimmed spectacles spoke for her. She turned away and marched into Mr. Blanchard's office, her stiff back—from the mauve crepe blouse tucked into the thick gray wool skirt down to her old-fashioned buttoned shoes—eloquent of her severe disapproval. The door slammed behind her, its frosted-glass window shivering.

"Oh, dear," Helen said. "I don't think Miss Price is very happy with me."

"Don't you worry about Miss Price." Richard Turner smiled at her. He held out his hand for the paper.

Reluctantly Helen gave it to him.

"Don't you have a copy?" he asked.

"No. I knew nothing about it."

He hesitated for a moment, then handed it back to her. "Here, take mine."

"No, no. I'm sure I can find another copy."

There was some strange sort of embarrassment between them that she couldn't understand. Mr. Turner's cheeks were slightly pink. "I was rather hoping to keep it for the firm scrapbook," he explained.

"Then please do." She looked away. The expression in his eye made her feel uncomfortable.

"I've got a copy at home," Jimmy said, his voice making them both start. "Bought it for the racing results," he added with a grin. "I'll bring it back after lunch."

Once that was settled, everyone got back to work. To Helen's relief, nothing more was said about the photograph.

Nothing, that was, until the telephone rang later that afternoon. Jimmy picked it up. "It's for you," he told her.

Unfortunately, Miss Price had come out from her office to search for something in the filing cabinet. "Personal calls are not permitted, Miss Barstow."

"Yes, Miss Price. It—it may be a client, of course."

"Asking for you? Surely not."

"No, I suppose not. I'm sorry. I'll make sure it doesn't happen again, Miss Price."

Her apology was received with a grunt.

Helen took off her pearl earring and picked up the receiver. "Hallo?"

"Did you see the Saturday *Standard*?"

"To whom am I speaking?" she asked in her best office style, but she knew exactly who it was. Her heart beat so fast that she could barely breathe.

"Julian Holbrooke," he said impatiently. "Did you see the picture?"

"Yes. I saw it this morning. It was quite a surprise." Her voice sounded insipid, inane, in her ears.

"It was good, though, wasn't it?" His voice sounded a little warmer. "I thought you'd be pleased."

"Did you arrange for it to go in the paper?" Miss Price was huffing behind her, but the rush of happiness Helen felt insulated her against ten Miss Prices.

"Of course. Who else? I told you I'd make you a star, didn't I?"

Helen pressed the receiver against her ear. "Thank you," she said softly. "Thank you so much."

"My pleasure."

"Miss Barstow." Miss Price moved into her line of vision. With one peremptory finger she indicated that Helen should put the phone down.

"I'm so sorry, Mr. Holbrooke, I must go."

"Dragons in the office, eh?"

Helen smiled at the secret joke between them. "Yes."

"Right-ho. Glad you saw the picture. We'll see what else we can do. I'll call you again. Bye for now."

Before she had time to reply she heard the click of the phone and the harsh dial tone.

August moved into September. Helen had marked the day of the call with a red cross in her diary. Five weeks had passed since she had spoken to Julian Holbrooke. She was beginning to think she would never see or hear from him again. And she had no idea where she could find him.

By the end of the second week in September she had sunk into a numb despair. On Friday evening she sat on her window seat, staring out at the incessant rain that fell upon the growing pile of fallen leaves, listening to Rachmaninoff.

Downstairs, the phone rang. "Phone call for you, Helen," Edith shouted from below.

Helen scrambled to her feet. She grabbed a washcloth from the porcelain sink in the corner of the room, rubbed her eyes with it, and then ran downstairs.

Edith held out the phone to her. "It's a man." Her voice carried a mixture of disapproval and excitement.

"Thank you, Edith." Helen covered the mouthpiece until Edith had retreated reluctantly into the kitchen.

It would be Johnny or Alec from the drama club, she told herself. They were doing *The Rivals* in November, and she was one of the assistant stage managers.

She put the receiver to her ear. "Hallo?"

"I was about to hang up."

Oh, God! It was him.

Helen leaned her back against the wall and closed her eyes. "I'm sorry, Mr. Holbrooke. I was upstairs."

"Ah, you recognized me this time. Julian, please, not Mr. Holbrooke. What are you doing?"

"Doing?"

"Yes. Have I interrupted something important?"

Laughter gathered in her throat. No, I was only crying my heart out over you. "I was just listening to some music."

"What?"

"I said I was—"

"I heard what you said. What were you listening to?"

"Rachmaninoff," she murmured, her cheeks flaming. It was a good thing he couldn't see her.

"Ah, you were in a romantic mood. Glad to hear it. Look, no point in wasting money on this call. I'm at a friend's house in Richmond. Thought you might like to take a run and have a drink somewhere."

Drive with him in his car? Alone or with friends? "Aren't you working tonight?" she asked, stalling for time.

"No. We're into rehearsals at the moment. I leave for a two-month tour of Australia and New Zealand in a fortnight. I wanted to see you before I went."

Her hesitation was blown away. "I'd love to come for

a drink with you. I'm—I'm not dressed for going out, though. How long will you be?"

"Depends where you are, exactly."

"Take the Petersham road from Richmond. Our road is on the right, just before the common. We're near the end."

"I know it. I'll be there in . . . let's say half an hour. Okay?"

"Yes, that's fine. Thank you very much."

He laughed. "You're a funny girl."

"Why funny?"

"Thanking me. I'm supposed to thank you, not the other way about."

"Oh." She'd done the wrong thing. He'd think her naive, unsophisticated—a child.

"Don't worry," he said softly. "I like you the way you are."

Her face grew warm. It was as if he had read her thoughts over the telephone.

"See you in half an hour," he said, and put the phone down.

By the time he rang the doorbell, she was in an absolute frenzy. First of all, her grandmother and Aunt Hilary had subjected her to an interrogation about this stranger she was meeting. Her assurance that he was a famous actor did nothing to reassure them. Far from it.

"They are the worst," declared Aunt Hilary. "You can read about their immorality in all the newspapers. Look at that Laurence Olivier and Vivien Leigh!"

Aunt Hilary smuggled the *Daily Mirror* and even, on occasion, the *News of the World*, into the house. The last time Helen had caught her reading the *Daily Mirror*, Aunt Hilary had insisted she bought it because it had the best pictures of the Queen's new baby, Prince Andrew.

Helen was close to tears. "You sound just like Mother," she accused them.

"We don't like your going out with a strange man in

his car without knowing anything about him," her grandmother told her firmly. "Especially as he might be drinking as well. I shall tell this Mr. Holbrooke so when I see him. After all, you are only seventeen and we are your guardians."

"If you are going to tell him that," Helen said in a low, throbbing voice, "then you may just tell him I'm sick and in my bed. I will not be humiliated."

"Hoity-toity, girl." Her grandmother banged her stick on the floor. "I have no intention of humiliating you. We'll have him in for a sherry—"

"Oh, no, Gran."

"We shall invite your Mr. Holbrooke in for a sherry and then decide."

"You can't—"

"No more arguments. He comes in and meets us like a gentleman, or you don't go out with him. Take your choice."

Helen looked at her watch in a panic. She had only fifteen minutes to get changed and put on her makeup. "I can't meet him like this. It's too late. He'll be here in less than a quarter of an hour."

Aunt Hilary set down her knitting and got up from the chair by the fireplace. "Get on with you. I'll set up a tray for the sherry and some of Edith's macaroons. Take your time. We'll entertain Mr. Holbrooke until you're ready."

It was the last thing Helen wanted.

"My Apple Blossom perfume is on my dressing table," her grandmother said. "You may use some of it."

Helen sighed. "Thank you, Gran." She plodded up the carpeted stairs. They would spoil everything. This would be the first—and last—time Julian took her out. If, in fact, they permitted him to take her out.

She felt like defying them, throwing on her coat and running down the street to intercept him before he got to the house, but she couldn't do that. They were too good to her. Besides, if they turned her out, she would have to return to her parents in Ealing.

Nothing could be as bad as that.

Frantically she washed and then changed into her best underwear, the lovely slip and knickers of pale green matte satin edged with lace that Aunt Hilary had given her for Christmas. Somehow there had never been an occasion important enough for her to wear them. Until now.

Not that he would see them, of course, she thought, her face warming at the very idea. But *she* would know she was wearing them.

Carefully she applied the rose-beige pancake makeup, then the pale coral lipstick, finishing with a light smear of silver-green eye shadow and a little mascara.

Was it too much? she wondered, peering anxiously at her reflection in the dressing table mirror. The fine-boned face, framed by a curtain of straight auburn hair, smiled back at her. No. She looked quite good, actually.

What to wear? She flung open the door of the mahogany wardrobe and peered inside. Nothing looked right. Sensible tweed skirts. "Good" jumpers and cardigans. One or two Sunday-best dresses and a pale blue evening dress with shoestring straps.

Nothing suitable for a "run in the car and a drink" with a professional actor.

Eventually, in desperation, Helen decided on one of her favorite dresses, a classic tartan wool with a pleated skirt and white Peter Pan collar and cuffs. It was far too schoolgirlish, but it would have to do.

A spritz of perfume from her grandmother's pink bottle, and then she drew the dress carefully over her head.

The doorbell rang. Helen froze, the dress half on, half off. He was here. Too late now for her to intercept him in the hall.

She dragged the dress down. Fingers trembling, she maneuvered the back zipper up and then hurriedly brushed her hair, anchoring it with a black velvet Alice band.

She gave one last glance at herself in the mirror before picking up her black patent handbag. The quicker she rescued him, the better.

But when she entered the drawing room, Julian didn't seem to be in need of rescuing. In fact, she heard his laugh just before she turned the brass doorknob.

He stood up when she came in. He was dressed in a blazer and dark gray trousers. He wore a cravat, not a tie, with his white shirt, like someone in a Noel Coward play. "Hallo there." His smile crinkled the skin at the corners of his eyes.

"Hallo." She stood awkwardly in the doorway, wondering if she should sit down or get him out of there immediately.

"Come and have a sherry, Helen," her grandmother said, deciding for her.

As she sat on the edge of the sofa beside Julian, Helen saw that he had a crystal tumbler before him. He must have passed the first test, then, for her grandmother to have offered him whiskey instead of sherry.

As she sat down, Julian casually extended his arm along the back of the sofa. "I've been admiring your beautiful home," he told her. "You never told me you lived in such a wonderful historic house, Helen."

He spoke as if they were old friends.

Her grandmother replied for her. "Oh, I don't know about its being historic. I'm not sure anyone famous has lived here. Someone once told me the fireplaces and some of the ceilings might be by Robert Adam, but I've never bothered to verify it." She waved a nonchalant hand at the fireplace, its once white molded plasterwork stained with smoke from almost two centuries of fires.

Julian got up to examine the fireplace more carefully and then looked up at the plaster ceiling. "It's marvelous."

Helen had been afraid he might be bored, but there was no doubting the tone of sincerity in his voice.

"Would you like to see the dining room?" her grandmother asked him. "It has rather an interesting ceiling. A trifle ornate for my taste, but one grows used to it."

"I should be delighted to see it, if it's not too much trouble."

"Not at all." As her grandmother rose from her chair, Julian went to assist her. "Thank you, Mr. Holbrooke." Leaning on his arm, she led the way across the chilly hallway and into the dining room.

Behind them, Helen gritted her teeth. At this rate it would soon be too late to go out. But, in a way, she was glad to have their departure postponed. She was afraid she wouldn't know what to say to him when they were alone.

She looked up at the familiar ceiling, with its painted medallions, the colors and ornate gilt molding also stained and darkened with smoke. "It needs cleaning," Aunt Hilary said severely.

"Yes, I suppose it does," agreed her mother. "But I'm used to it as it is. I am not sure I'd like to have all those gaudy cherubims glaring down at me while I eat."

To Helen, all the ceilings and fireplaces and ornate railings were just part of the old house she loved. She took them as much for granted as she did the cold tiled floor in the scullery or the gas geyser in the bathroom that wheezed and gurgled before spitting out hot water into the rust-stained bath.

She looked at her watch. "It's getting late."

Her grandmother smiled at her. "So it is. It's a little late to be driving out into the country, I'm afraid." She looked a question at Julian.

"Oh, I think we'll stay somewhere close at hand. What time would you like Helen home?"

Amelia Barstow beamed at him. "It's Saturday tomorrow, so ten-thirty would do very nicely."

Helen bit her lip. The pubs didn't close until eleven on Fridays. She opened her mouth to protest, only to catch Julian's imperceptible little shake of the head.

"Ten-thirty it is." He flashed a smile at Helen. "Miss Barstow, your carriage awaits."

She went to fetch her camel wool coat from the little room that served as a downstairs lavatory and cloakroom.

The coat was taken from her. As he helped her on with it, Julian squeezed her shoulders. She turned to him to murmur her thanks. It was the first time this evening that she had looked at him directly. She had forgotten—or maybe she hadn't been able to see before, in the darkness of the park—how intensely blue his eyes were. They seemed to bore right through her forehead and read her thoughts.

Outside, the rain had become a chill drizzle. They turned to wave to her grandmother and Aunt Hilary, who stood in the doorway to watch them go. The light from the hall shone through the fanlight above them.

He had a small sports car, an MG or a Triumph, she wasn't sure which. The canvas roof was up to shelter them from the rain. He held the door for her as she clambered in rather inelegantly. She wasn't used to cars, most especially this sort, where you had to sit almost on the ground.

"Comfortable?" he asked when he got in.

"Very." She watched his profile as he started the car. "I'm sorry about all that."

"What?"

"My grandmother and aunt . . . and everything. They live in the past, I'm afraid."

"I thought they were delightful." He turned to her. "Don't be ashamed of them, Helen."

She blushed. "I'm not," she protested. "I love them both very much. I just thought you might find all that talk about the house boring."

"Not at all. I love old houses. One day when I'm rich I mean to have a beautiful house of my own." He smiled at her. "So relax. I wasn't at all bored by your family."

He drove down the avenue and out onto the Ham

road. "By the way, don't you have a mother and father?"

"Yes, of course I do. They live in Ealing. My father's a vicar."

"But you don't live with them."

"I found a job in a solicitor's office in Richmond. It was easier to live here, with my grandmother and aunt."

"And you're happier with them."

She clasped her hands tightly in her lap. "How did you know that?"

"It was obvious. Your voice became pinched when you spoke of your parents and Ealing. As an actor, one learns to notice these things about people. You will find that out for yourself. Were you very unhappy with them?"

"Yes. Very unhappy. Mainly because of my mother." She was surprised to hear herself speak so openly of her parents. Until now, Ann had been the only person with whom she'd been able to share her feelings about them.

He squeezed her hand. "Poor little thing." As they turned the dangerous corner on Petersham Road, he took his hand away to change gear.

"I had intended to take you out to Shepperton, but it's a bit late now. Why don't we have a drink in the Dysart Arms and just talk?"

Helen was disappointed. She had hoped for a long drive, sitting close beside him in the little car, breathing in its masculine aroma of leather and tobacco. "That's fine."

He glanced at her. "I promise I'll take you somewhere special when I get back from Australia. We'll have dinner by the river somewhere. The Compleat Angler or the French Horn. Would you like that?"

"I'd love it," she said lightly.

The saloon bar in the pub was packed with people, many of them standing crushed together at the long bar.

"There's a table in the corner," Julian shouted to her. "What do you want to drink? Sherry, Babycham?"

Helen hesitated.

"Hurry up or we'll lose the table."

"I'll have a lemonade, thank you."

She pushed her way through the crowd to the little table and sat down on the solitary chair beside it. The table was littered with dirty glasses and several empty Smith's Crisps packets.

"Sorry, love. Soon have that cleared for you." A woman with her hair tied neatly in a red scarf gathered up the glasses and whisked the table with a damp cloth.

The room was noisy and smelled strongly of beer. But otherwise it was not at all the den of iniquity Helen had once thought pubs were. She smiled to herself.

"You're looking very pleased with yourself." Julian set down his pint glass of beer and her lemonade. He turned to the people at another table and, with his charming smile, took a chair for himself.

"I was just thinking how happy everyone looks."

"Not everyone. See that old chap in the corner."

Helen looked around and saw an old man in a grubby raincoat, with two glasses in front of him.

To her amazement, when she turned back, she saw the morose expression on the man's face duplicated on Julian's.

She clapped her hands together and gave a delighted laugh, so that people turned, smiling, to look at her.

"Oh, gosh," she whispered, "everyone's staring at me."

He put his elbows on the table and took her chin in his hand. "They're thinking what a beautiful couple we are."

To Helen's consternation, he leaned forward and kissed her, right there, with all those people watching!

"Oh, Julian, you mustn't."

He sat back and laughed. "Oh, but when you look at me with those great, beautiful, sea green eyes of yours full of innocence, I must." He leaned forward again.

"You are as exciting to me as uncharted waters are to an explorer," he said softly.

She had no idea what he meant, but it sounded wonderfully poetic.

People kept coming in through the glass doors, but no one seemed to be leaving. The room was thick with smoke now, and her eyes were smarting from it. She finished her drink.

"How about a sherry this time?"

She hesitated. That would be against the law; she wasn't eighteen yet. Then she said, "Yes, please."

When Julian came back, he set down two glasses before her, one of lemonade, one of sherry. "One for thirst and one for the effect, m'dear," he said with a broad leer, like Robert Newton playing Long John Silver.

She laughed. She was feeling more and more relaxed with him. He told her entertaining stories about the theater and about famous people like Richard Burton and Michael Redgrave. She could have listened forever to his amber voice.

A man lurched against the table as he made his way to the gentlemen's.

Julian frowned. "It's too busy in here. Drink up, that's a good girl." Then, seeing the disappointment on her face, "It's all right, I'm not taking you home yet. Cinderella has another hour to go." He drank down his beer and stubbed out his cigarette. "Ready?"

Helen gulped down the rest of her sherry and nodded. When she got into the car, she felt warm inside and out. She couldn't bear the thought of leaving him.

"There's a little lane down to the river just around the corner from here," he said. "It'll be nice and quiet. We'll go and sit there and talk."

When they reached the dimly lit lane, another car was there, but its occupants were too preoccupied with each other, their heads close, to notice them.

Julian drove past the car and parked. They were so

near to the river that Helen could hear the noise of lapping water through the slightly open window.

For a long time they sat, shoulders touching, talking. They talked about Helen's chances of getting into professional theater. "You must get accepted by one of the drama schools," Julian told her. "The sooner the better."

Helen discovered that he had begun acting when he was at Oxford, but she learned very little else about him. Actually, she found herself doing most of the talking. Julian asked her numerous questions about her school, her family, her aspirations. Never before had she shared so much of her hopes and fears, her inner self, with anyone.

An owl hooted in the tree above them, startling her. She turned, to find Julian's face very close to hers. His arm went around her shoulders, drawing her as close as he could, with the gearbox between them. His lips pressed down on hers.

Helen closed her eyes. His mouth was gentle at first, then more searching. She lifted her hands to the nape of his neck, feeling his hair crisp beneath her fingers.

"Helen, my sweet Helen," he murmured against her mouth. His kisses made her feel all soft and melting and open to him. His hand moved beneath her coat. She gasped as it brushed against her breasts, his fingers moving gently, so gently, back and forth and around. She pressed closer to him, arching her body, unaware of anything but her need to feel his warmth against hers.

"Damn this bloody gearbox!"

His words and sudden movement away from her crashed in on her with the force of a blow.

She looked at him, stunned. He ran his hands through his hair. "Sorry, my sweet. I didn't mean to startle you. I just wanted to get closer to you, that's all."

"That's how I felt," she whispered.

She heard the rasp of his lighter and its flame lit the darkness. "You look like a woman who's been soundly kissed," Julian told her.

She touched her lips. "I'll put some lipstick on."

The light went out. "In a moment." He reached for her again.

A few minutes later he drew away. "Now you should put on your lipstick and powder your nose. I'm going to get a breath of fresh air for a moment."

"I'll come with you."

"No, you stay there," he said harshly. "I'll be back in five minutes."

He sounded angry. Perhaps he was disappointed with her or disgusted. She opened her compact and peered into it, trying to see by the faint light of the lamppost by the river.

When he returned, he looked tired and cold. She put a tentative hand on his arm, his blazer damp beneath her fingers. "You're not angry with me, are you?"

"Angry? Why should I be?"

"I don't know," she said miserably.

"Helen . . ." He stopped to light a cigarette and blew smoke out the window before turning to her. "Promise me you won't let anyone else touch you the way I did."

"Of course not. You know I—"

He placed two fingers on her mouth. "Just promise me that you'll keep yourself for me. I can't bear the thought of some scrubby schoolboy . . ."

She drew away from him. "How can you even think of such a thing? You're the first man ever to—to touch me like that."

"Good. I know I'm going to be away for some time, but I promise you I'll be back. We have your theatrical future to think about." He took her face in one hand. "But most of all I'm asking you to save yourself for me. I want to be the first, the only, man in your life."

10

Helen didn't see Julian again until two days before Christmas.

She had hoped for at least a postcard from Australia. Then, when she knew he must be back in England again, she prayed for a letter from him.

Each morning brought her nothing but disappointment.

On the day before Christmas Eve the office was to close an hour early for a little Christmas party.

She wasn't at all in the mood for a party, but she dressed in her best ivory crepe de Chine blouse and her full black velvet skirt. She didn't put on the emerald velvet headband until they had finished work and locked the outer door, in case Miss Price considered the color too bright.

She could see from Mr. Turner's appreciative lift of the eyebrows that he, at least, thought she looked nice.

"Let me get you a drink, Helen. What'll it be, shandy, sweet sherry?"

"Sherry, please, Mr. Turner."

His wife appeared at his side. "And a piece of Christmas cake, Miss Barstow?" Mrs. Turner had baked a large Christmas cake and iced it with marzipan and gleaming white royal icing, topped with marzipan holly leaves and berries.

Having sliced several pieces, she set the cake on a desk. "Are you enjoying working with Milbourne and Blanchard, Miss Barstow?"

Helen made a suitable response and, for a few minutes, was trapped in conversation with her.

She had met Mr. Turner's wife a few times before, of course. She knew from typing personal documents for Mr. Turner that Mary Turner was only twenty-six. Yet her plump figure and sedate manner made her seem much older. Her father was a doctor who lived in Devonshire. He had come into the office once, a hearty countryman dressed in heavy tweeds.

Today, Mrs. Turner was wearing an ill-fitting pale blue dress of draped wool jersey that emphasized her matronly figure. As she spoke to Helen, she fingered the two strands of pearls about her neck in a nervous little gesture that was unlike her. She had always seemed friendly. Now the tiny smile about her lips did not extend to her cornflower blue eyes. As Helen looked into them, she felt chilled.

In her rather depressed mood, the thought that Richard Turner's wife now disliked her for some inexplicable reason brought a lump to her throat.

She was about to escape to the ladies' room when the doorbell rang.

"I'll get it," yelled Jimmy, who had been celebrating freely since the party began.

"No, Mr. Watts," Miss Price said in a freezing tone. "You are not in a fit state to see clients at the moment."

"Shall I go, Miss Price?" Helen asked.

But Richard Turner was already in the corridor. Helen heard his voice and then another voice that set her heart pounding.

"I wonder if I might see Miss Barstow for a moment."

Helen felt as if everyone were looking at her. "It's a friend," she murmured.

She hurried across the room, but Mr. Turner was already ushering Julian in. "Come and have a drink," he said. His eyes met Helen's, a slight question in them.

Julian smiled at Helen. His face was tanned, making him look even more handsome than usual. "I seem to have arrived at exactly the right moment," he remarked to the room at large, and everyone smiled or laughed. His energy seemed to bring instant life to the dull party.

Helen found it impossible to hide her delight at seeing him. She tucked her hand in his arm and turned to face the expectant faces in the office. "I'd like to introduce Julian Holbrooke, the famous actor," she announced.

She beamed up at him, not caring that she was showing him and the entire office exactly how she felt about him. Today he was hers, and she was proud of it.

Julian held up his hands in a gesture of modesty. "An actor, maybe, but famous? Alas, not yet."

But his smile, and the fact that his hand had closed over hers when she had released his arm, told her that he was not at all embarrassed by her introduction.

For the rest of the afternoon he shone like the star he was, charming everyone, even Miss Price. Helen stood by, bursting with pride yet also longing to be alone with him.

"How long have you known Mr. Holbrooke?"

She turned to find Richard Turner at her side. "Since the summer. He saw me in the play."

"Ah, I see. Have your grandmother and aunt met him?"

Helen was annoyed at the slight inflection of disapproval in his voice. She liked Mr. Turner, but she didn't like him behaving like an uncle. "Of course they have," she snapped.

Mr. Turner's eyes were serious behind his horn-rimmed glasses. "You'll say that it's none of my business, Helen, but you will be careful, won't you? Holbrooke is obviously far older than you, and—"

"Now, what are you two talking about so seriously in the corner?" Mary Turner's overbright voice broke in on them. "Not work, I trust."

Richard Turner shook his head. "Of course not." He smiled his slow, attractive smile at Helen, apparently unaware of the sharp glance his wife was darting at her.

Later, when Helen was crossing Richmond Green with Julian to get to his car, he said, "You didn't tell me Turner was a young man."

"I don't think of him as young, really. He's married and very settled in his ways." Helen laughed. "Not a bit like you."

Julian glanced at her as if he were about to reply, but thought better of it. His arm slid about her waist and they strode across the green, matching steps.

Helen glowed with happiness. She wanted to be with him forever, but for now she was content to take whatever time he would give her.

During the next few months, she was delighted to find that Julian seemed to want to be with her a great deal more than before. As well as theater, he took her to art galleries and the opera and ballet. "The cultural education and civilization of Helen Barstow," he called it. And he talked about arranging an audition for her with John Fernald at RADA or perhaps finding work for her at Q Theatre.

She saw *Fidelio* from the grand tier at Covent Garden, *Swan Lake* from the gods. . . . Where they sat usually depended upon whether or not Julian could get free tickets.

They ate bacon and eggs cooked in individual iron skillets at Lyons' Corner House or the finest spaghetti and chicken cacciatore at Gennaro's in Soho, depending upon the state of Julian's bank balance.

The door to a world of riotous color and sensual sounds and sights had been flung open to Helen.

And Julian was her guide.

She knew herself to be a different person. It was as if she had been dead all her life and had suddenly come alive. She talked nonstop, bombarding Julian with myriad questions. Bought new clothes: a pimento-and-black Mondrian shift, its skirt hem daringly way above her knees; a lime-green A-line dress trimmed with huge pink buttons. And Julian ordered her to throw out all her poppit beads and bought her chunky bright earrings and bangles instead.

Although Helen relished the times they spent together, she often worried about Julian's coolness to her. Ever since she had complained about him touching her too intimately the evening after the Christmas party, he hardly touched her at all. His infrequent, brotherly kisses left her feeling frustrated. She was afraid that he might be seeing someone else.

"You do care about me still, don't you? You think I'm attractive?" she asked him plaintively as they walked hand in hand in the gardens of Ham House. She had to be so careful not to mention love or anything permanent like that. Julian was ambitious. He didn't want to be tied down.

Julian turned his dark head from the contemplation of the beautifully symmetrical red-brick building. "Of course I do. What on earth made you ask?"

Her foot in its open leather sandal scuffed the gravel. "It's just that you don't seem to want to touch me anymore."

He released her hand and surveyed her. Then he laughed. "Women! You're either complaining that I touch you too much or not enough."

Helen murmured something about a happy medium.

His eyes darkened. "If you haven't discovered by now that I'm not a 'happy medium' type of person, then you know nothing about me at all. At present, I prefer to keep sex out of our relationship. We're working on filling up the empty vessel of your mind, not your body."

She had no idea what to say to this.

"We'll get to the other part later," he said, hugging her against him for an all-too-brief moment.

After that, she noticed a subtle change in him. When they said good night, his kisses were more passionate, but quickly over, leaving her breathless and aching for more. Frequently he would brush a hand against her breast or thigh but never let it linger. His fingers seared her flesh with darts of sweet pain through the layers of clothing.

Her desire to be closer to him flamed at the least little touch. When he kissed her, he was the one to draw back first. When he touched her, she boldly covered his hand with hers to prevent him from moving it away.

"Little girls shouldn't play with fire," he told her abruptly one hot night in July as they sat in the car.

She felt like crying. "I just want to be alone with you, Julian."

He smiled a slow smile and raised his eyebrows. "Miss Barstow is becoming a woman at last."

"Of course I'm a woman," she said indignantly. "I'm eighteen."

The mention of her age seemed to trouble him. She wished she hadn't reminded him of the eight years between them.

"Eighteen's just a child," he said shortly.

"I'm not a child anymore," she protested. "I was when I first met you a year ago. But not anymore."

He looked at her, the brilliant eyes searching hers. "I do believe you're right. Is it really a year?"

"A year on July the twenty-third."

He continued to study her face. Yet Helen had the feeling that he was also looking at something beyond it.

Eventually he said, "Then we must do something very special to celebrate that first meeting."

The "something special" was dinner at an exotic little restaurant in Soho. Her grandmother gave her the money for a new outfit for the occasion. She bought it in a July sale: a short, strapless dress of iridescent green shot silk that rustled seductively as she walked. It made her feel sophisticated and sexy. Around her shoulders she wore the black mohair stole that Aunt Hilary had knitted for her.

Normally she came up to London on the tube or train to meet him, but this time he drove down to Petersham.

"It's a special evening, Mrs. Barstow," he explained to her grandmother, elegantly crossing one black-clad leg over the other. "We're having dinner and then going dancing."

"Which means Helen will be late home, I suppose? So long as I know that she's with you, Julian, I shan't worry."

It hadn't taken long for her grandmother to progress to calling him by his first name. But to Aunt Hilary he was still "Mr. Holbrooke."

As he drank his whiskey and chatted with her grandmother about the film he was hoping to make, Helen gazed at him, thinking how wonderful he looked in his dinner jacket and pleated white evening shirt.

He looked up and gave her a secret wink, his mouth quirking into a smile for her alone.

The restaurant was small, one side of the main room lined with tiny booths for two people only. They were shown to one of them, the green velvet curtains looped back to allow them to enter.

"How romantic," Helen breathed when the waiter had gone to fetch their drinks. "I love it."

"I told you tonight was going to be special."

At the end of the meal, when they were drinking thick Turkish coffee and nibbling on pink-and-lemon Turkish delight, the waiter closed the curtains and they were enclosed in a sweet-scented sanctum.

"May I join you?" Julian slipped onto the narrow seat beside her and drew her close. It had been a very long time since he had kissed her so thoroughly. Even without the sherry and wine and Benedictine she would have succumbed willingly. Their effect merely removed any lingering inhibitions she might have had about being kissed so ardently in a public place.

Besides, no one could see them.

By the time the waiter had discreetly slipped the bill between the gap in the curtains, the last thing she felt like was going dancing.

Julian counted out pound notes and then turned to her. "You have exquisite shoulders," he said. "They gleam like ivory in the candlelight."

She was tempted to make some retort about their being too bony but bit it back. Julian had long since cured her of responding to his praise with self-deprecation, by comparing her to Uriah Heep, telling her to read *David Copperfield* again to see what he meant.

He lifted her hair with one hand and kissed her bare shoulders with slow kisses that made her breasts ache.

She ran her hand down his cheek, her fingers tracing the shape of his ear.

He looked at her. "Do you want to go dancing?"

She shook her head.

He let out a long sigh, as if he had solved some difficult problem, and got up. "Let's go back to my flat."

He had never taken her to his place in Kensington before. It consisted of only two rooms and a tiny kitchen at the top of a Victorian house. He shared the bathroom on the next floor with another flat.

The furniture in the lounge was shabby: the small sofa covered in a slipcover of shiny cretonne, the faded curtains inadequately covering the tall windows.

As Helen looked around her, she felt a sense of disappointment. These commonplace surroundings definitely were not the right setting for Julian Holbrooke.

"Pretty shabby, eh?" he said.

She turned quickly, anxious not to seem critical. "I think it's very cozy."

"I do have a couple of treasures," he said defensively.

He drew her to a corner of the room to show her a beautiful rosewood revolving bookstand, its rich surface gleaming as if he polished it regularly. Above it hung a small picture of a voluptuous nude woman.

"That's a Renoir lithograph," Julian said proudly.

"It's lovely."

"My one ambition is to be so rich that I can surround myself with beautiful things like these, only better." He was breathing hard, his eyes looking at her yet beyond her. "And nothing's going to stop me."

Helen shivered.

He seemed to come back to her. "Poor darling, are you cold? Sit down. I'll turn on the fire." As she sat on the sofa, he bent to switch on the electric fire. "There, that's better." He went behind her, to lift the mohair stole from her shoulders, but she clutched at it.

"Still cold?"

She wasn't really cold. The stole was the last piece of armor between them.

She was like two people, one observing the other. This is Helen alone with Julian for the first time in his flat. This is Helen sitting down on Julian's sofa.

He sat beside her, sliding his arm around her shoulders. Suddenly everything was all right again.

"I was afraid, not cold," she whispered against his scratchy shirtfront.

He took her face between his hands. "You've nothing to fear from me. I am at your command. We can stay here or go out, or I can take you home. You're in control."

She wanted to believe him, but she knew that she wasn't in control anymore. The other Helen, the one whose body ached to be held by him, was the one in control.

"You're so beautiful, so beautiful," Julian whispered, drawing the stole from her. His hands were on her shoulders and then, remarkably easy with the strapless dress, encircling her breasts.

Some time later he guided her into the bedroom and

they lay down. The eiderdown and blankets cocooned them like the velvet curtains at the restaurant. The sheets and pillow smelled of Julian. She was surrounded by Julian, caressed by Julian, kissed in all her most intimate places by Julian. He was her joy, her delight, her lover.

She abandoned and opened herself utterly to Julian.

At some point she was aware of sharp pain, but he gathered her so tightly in his arms at that very moment and then cried out his joy at the pleasure she gave him, muffling his cry in her hair, that it was as nothing.

Later she was overcome with disappointment that she had felt no pleasure herself. Tears welled up, sliding down her cheeks.

"What is it, darling?" Julian leaned on his elbow to look down on her. "Why are you crying?"

Helen sniffed. "I'm just being stupid."

"Of course you're not. Tell me what's wrong?"

"I—I thought it would be . . . more—"

"More pleasurable for you?" he asked gently. He cradled her in his arms. "It will be, I promise you that, my darling." His mouth curved in an infinitely tender smile. "You've waited all these years before making love, be patient for just a little while longer." He kissed her on the mouth and eyes and cheeks, and then her mouth again. "Will it help if I tell you what immense pleasure you gave me?"

"I don't see how. I'm not very good—"

He stopped her mouth with another kiss. "You are very good," he said, emphasizing each word with a kiss. "And I consider it a great privilege that you chose me to be your first lover."

His loving assurances and infinite gentleness dispelled the concern that she might not be normal. "Next time will be for you," he told her.

She was secretly relieved to think that there would be a next time. So much for all her mother's warnings about men using and then discarding you, she thought triumphantly.

11

All that week, typing in the office, helping Edith with the breakfast, cutting lettuces and pulling radishes in the garden with Aunt Hilary, Helen wondered if anyone saw a difference in her. She had become a woman. She was loved. Yet no one seemed to have noticed it. How strange, how very strange, when she herself felt so different.

"Did you have a good time last night?" her grandmother had asked the next morning.

"Very nice, thank you, Gran," Helen had said, seemingly preoccupied with spreading marmalade on her toast.

"Good, good." Her grandmother had turned back to the *Times*.

It had been that easy.

Ann was the only one to notice a difference in her. As they were walking back to Ann's house in Halford Road after a rare evening together, she said, "I hope you're being careful with your Julian."

Ann had met Julian in May, at a performance of *Henry V*, in which Helen was playing the French princess. As she had suspected, Ann and Julian had absolutely nothing in common and were coldly polite to each other.

"Careful?"

"Yes, careful. Don't look so innocent. It's me, Ann, your friend, remember? I'm not saying you have slept with him. You'd be a fool if you did. But he must have asked you to by now, surely. I can't imagine someone like the great Julian Holbrooke not trying it on."

"I—it's none of your business."

"I'm just warning you to be careful. If you do want to sleep with him, be sure to pay a visit to the Family Planning Clinic first."

They stood outside Ann's house, the dusty privet hedge at their backs.

Helen smiled. "I love him so much, Annie. You wouldn't believe how wonderful he is to me."

Ann didn't return the smile. "You've been to bed with him already, haven't you?"

"Been to bed" sounded crass, common. It hardly described being made love to by Julian.

"For God's sake, watch it, Helen," Ann said.

"He loves me." Helen fingered the gold bracelet Julian had given her for her eighteenth birthday. A single golden charm dangled from it: a star. "I told you I was going to make you a star," Julian had reminded her as he'd clasped it around her wrist.

"Of course he loves you," Ann said sarcastically. "They always say that."

Helen bent her head, pretending to be doing up the clasp on the bracelet. "Julian said he'd—he'd look after everything."

Ann gave a short laugh and pushed open the wrought-iron gate, scraping it along the flagstone path. "Where have I heard that one before?"

Helen looked at her watch. "It's getting late. I don't think I'll come in after all."

"Oh, come on, Hel. Don't get angry with me. Mum's made your favorite caraway-seed cake. She says she hasn't seen you for ages." Ann took her arm and dragged her inside the gate. "I promise I won't say another word."

Ann kept her promise, but her warning remained with Helen, subtly tainting her anticipation of the next meeting with Julian.

Maybe she should go to the clinic. But how could she? She remembered talking about it when she was in the upper fifth at school. One of the girls had said you had to be engaged to go there. They asked you all sorts of questions, like when were you getting married. Ann had said that was all a cover-up. You just had to buy a cheap ring at Woolworth's, pretend you were engaged, and everyone was happy.

Helen hadn't even met Julian at the time of that conversation, of course. It must have been at least two years ago. Maybe things had changed since then. But still the very thought of marching into some strange clinic, with everyone's eyes on her, having to say she was there to get some form of birth control, even though she wasn't married, made her go hot all over.

No, she would leave it all to Julian. He was experienced and would look after her.

Oddly enough, she was far more nervous the second time they made love. Somehow it was less spontaneous and certainly far less romantic. Julian met her at the South Kensington tube station on Sunday afternoon and took her back to his flat right away.

In the daylight the flat looked even shabbier than she had remembered. Although Julian was very tidy, the carpet was worn down to string in places, and his many books were stacked on bare boards, supported by bricks.

It had all seemed so romantic the last time, in the candlelit darkness, through the haze of wine and liqueurs. Now it looked just a little sordid.

Although Julian was tender and passionate, she felt

rather uncomfortable at the idea of getting into bed with him in the afternoon, with the sun shining through the unlined brown curtains.

"Relax, darling," he said.

Eventually, beneath the magic of his hands and lips, she did.

When they had finished and she had told him how wonderful it had been, he lay on his back smoking a cigarette. She lay beside him, staring up at the ceiling. In the corner, above the bed, was a large spider's web and, slowly descending from it, a spider.

"Let's get dressed and go out for tea," Julian suggested. "Sorry I have that poetry reading tonight."

"Can't I come?"

"Sorry, my sweet. It's by invitation only."

And you wouldn't ask for an invitation for me, she wanted to say, but didn't.

"I'll have time to drive you home beforehand, though," he said, seeing her disappointment. "We'll have a slap-up tea with scones and cream cakes."

He was like a grown-up placating a sulking child. How she wished she were more like Ann, able to speak her mind. But even if she were, how could she risk driving him away?

So she smiled and said that would be wonderful and how happy she was to be able to spend some of his precious time with him.

And inside she despised herself for it.

The splendid tea and a short walk along the river dispelled some of her gloom.

"I love you so much, Julian," she said to him later as they sat in the car outside her house.

Surely now that they had slept together twice she could speak of love.

"You are very special to me." He kissed her gently.

"Won't you come in for a moment? Gran always enjoys seeing you."

He glanced at his watch. "All right. But just for a minute, mind."

Her grandmother was sitting on a deck chair in the garden, wearing her cartwheel straw hat tied beneath her chin with a broad pink ribbon.

"Ah, Julian," she said, her faded blue eyes lighting up as he approached. "How lovely to see you again."

He sat down beside her, regretfully declining her offer of tea but replying to her questions about his work as if he had all the time in the world to speak to her.

Watching him, Helen thought that it was no wonder Gran liked him so much. Not only did he treat her like a human being, rather than an old woman with nothing to contribute to life, he also flirted with her as if she were eighteen. Her cheeks were growing pink at whatever he was saying.

"Ah, Julian. I fear you are a flatterer," she said with a delighted giggle. "But I love it."

"Your grandmother's a delightful person," he said later as Helen walked down the pathway with him to the car. "You're a lucky girl to be able to live in such a beautiful house." His gaze swept over the lovely old house, with its rose-brick walls and white-sashed windows.

"It is beautiful, isn't it? I hate to think what will happen to it when Gran dies."

Julian gave her a sharp look. "Surely it will stay in the family."

"I'm not sure. Gran hasn't much capital left. My father has very little money. There are the family shares in the old Barstow firm, that's all, and they won't sell those."

"I thought—" He broke off, his face very pale. "You surprise me," he said lightly. "Strange to think of people with such a fine house not having money."

"Oh, I expect there are lots of people in the same boat. I just loathe the idea of it having to be sold to someone outside the family, though."

"I suppose so," he murmured. He pushed back his shirtsleeve to look at his watch. "Must be going." He kissed her on the cheek. "Bye, my sweet."

His abrupt leavetaking startled her. "When will I see you again?" she asked as he got into the car.

"I'll call you."

Before she could say more, he had revved up the engine and was gone.

He did call her eventually, to say that he was flying to Los Angeles for a screen test. She found it hard to share in his excitement.

Her period was ten days late.

"I need to see you, Julian. I must see you before you go." She didn't want to tell him now. It might be nothing. But the thought of him being thousands of miles when she might be pregnant horrified her.

"You don't sound very pleased for me. I thought you'd be thrilled to think of me making a Hollywood film."

"Of course I am. But I must see you before you go."

"Can't. I leave first thing Tuesday. I've got all the arrangements to make. Thank God the play closed last week or I'd have lost this chance."

"I'll come and help you pack," she said in desperation.

"It's already done. No, my sweet. I get back a week Wednesday. I'll call you then. Okay? Be good."

This can't be happening to me, she thought, the dial tone buzzing in her ear. Please God, don't let me be pregnant, she prayed as she slowly went upstairs.

Surely she couldn't be pregnant after sleeping with Julian only twice? Surely you had to sleep regularly with someone to get pregnant? It must be some change in hormones after you went with a man that was causing her to be late.

She had tried hot baths. At least, as hot as she could get the wretched old gas geyser to go. Her skin had turned scarlet, but still nothing had happened.

She had even smuggled in a half bottle of gin and

actually drunk glasses of it neat while she was in the bath, hoping that the combination of the two would have the right effect. All it did was make her violently ill.

And now Julian had left England.

Of course he would marry her when she told him. If, that is, she was truly going to have his baby. But she dreaded the thought of his anger at having to settle down with a wife and family before he had planned to do so.

He might even have to give up this film in Hollywood.

No, she would never expect him to give up any chance of furthering his career for her and their baby. He had too brilliant a future for that. She would make a comfortable little home for him, so that he would look forward to returning to it whenever he went away.

As the days went by, these dreams of their married life together were her only source of comfort.

So successful had the trip to Hollywood been that it was five weeks later before Julian flew home.

At least, that was the explanation he gave Helen for not having called her. As she had phoned the flat in Kensington several times, with no reply, she saw no reason not to believe him.

It had been the most nerve-racking few weeks she had spent in her entire life.

There was no longer any doubt that she was pregnant. She had at last plucked up courage and taken the bus down to the Family Planning Clinic. There, after she had been examined, she left a urine sample. Next day, in her lunch hour, she returned to be told that she was, indeed, pregnant. Her baby would be born around the middle of May.

All the way to Kensington, she practiced in her head the best way to tell him.

Julian, our love has created a child. Too mushy.

Julian, I'm pregnant. Too direct.

When she reached the flat, she was soaked from a

sudden downpour of rain. Julian kissed her lightly on the mouth and fetched her a towel to dry her hair, but he seemed preoccupied.

She was so overwhelmed at seeing him that she almost blurted out the news right away. But, knowing this was going to be a momentous occasion for both of them, she held back.

"Are we going out to eat?" she asked him. "I'm starving."

"I'll put on some spaghetti." He uncorked a bottle of Chianti and poured out two glassfuls. "I want to talk to you before we eat." He looked tired.

"I think you've lost weight. Did you eat properly in Hollywood?"

He sighed and ran his hand through his hair. "It was very hectic. Work all day, party all night."

She sat down on the cane chair and stripped off her sodden stockings. "I'm dying to hear all about it."

He offered her the glass of wine. She looked up from drying her legs and feet. "No thanks, I don't really fancy wine. I wouldn't mind another kiss, though."

He looked at her, through her, as if he hadn't heard what she said. She got up and came behind him to put her arms around his neck. Carrying his child within her made her feel more powerful, as if she were more in control.

"I must put on the water." He eased away from her and went into the tiny kitchen, with its two-ring stove and small refrigerator.

He was different. Something must have happened in America. Yet he had told her on the phone that it had been a successful trip.

This wasn't going the way she had planned at all. She no longer wanted to wait to tell him her news. But how could she tell this man she was carrying his baby, when he was staring, stone-faced, at the pot of water that bubbled on the stove?

She touched his arm. "Julian, I have something very special to tell you."

He turned his eyes on her. She recoiled when she saw his bleak expression. "You heard from the Q Theatre?" he asked, turning away to tear open the packet of spaghetti.

"No, not yet. And I don't care anymore about the blasted Q or any other theater. Julian, will you please look at me!" she cried, tugging at his sleeve.

"Before you tell me anything, Helen, there's something I have to tell you." He set down the open packet. "I wanted to wait until later, but you will insist on talking now."

"It can wait. Me first."

"No, it can't wait." His hand clenched on the spaghetti, and she heard the brittle sticks snap in his grasp. "Go in there," he said, turning and shoving her ahead of him, so that she hit her elbow on the door frame.

"Julian, what on earth's wrong with you? You're scaring me." Tears started in her eyes. "Please don't be like this, not tonight especially. Please." She held up her clasped hands to him.

"Cut the histrionics, for Christ's sake, Helen. You're making this very difficult for me."

She was making it difficult for *him?* She almost laughed out loud. She stumbled to a chair and sat down, terror mounting in her throat.

He stood by the window, half looking out, so that she could not see his face properly. "It's finished, Helen. Kaput. We're over. Do you understand? I'd like to put it more gently, but there's no gentle way of saying it."

She stared at him, eyes wide. "I don't understand what you mean." She picked at the skin around her thumb.

"I should have thought it was quite clear. I can't put it more clearly than that, surely."

She stared at him blankly, as if he were speaking Swahili.

"For God's sake, Helen. Don't make this more difficult for me by acting dumb. I am not going out with you anymore." He overenunciated the words, spitting them out at her like slow bullets.

"I'm pregnant, Julian."

He stared at her uncomprehendingly at first. Then he said, "Christ in heaven, that's all I need."

She tried to hold back the tears—Julian hated tears—but couldn't stop them.

He went on his knees before her, gathering her in his arms. It's all right, she thought, burying her face in his woolen jersey. Julian will make it all right.

"Are you sure?" he asked, sitting back on his heels.

"Yes. I went to a clinic and they said so. The baby will be born next May. I've been out of my mind waiting for you to come home."

"Poor Helen. Poor girl. It must have been awful for you." He sprang up to pace about the room. "Have you told anyone else yet, your grandmother, your mother?"

"No."

"That was sensible. They need never know."

"How on earth can I keep it from them?"

"I'll make all the arrangements. You can tell them you're going away for a weekend with your girlfriend. What's her name? Ann. Ann Sturgis, right?"

"Aren't they bound to notice before the baby's born?"

He let out an exasperated sigh. "I'm talking about an abortion, Helen."

Her mouth fell open in horror. "Abortion? You mean, killing the baby? But—but that's illegal."

"Don't worry about that. There are plenty of ways of getting around the law, so long as you're willing to pay."

"Pay?" Her mind was all cloudy, full of echoes, as if he were talking to her from the other end of a long, fog-filled tunnel.

He knelt in front of her again, taking her hands in his. "It's all right. I'll look after the money side of it, I promise. In fact, I'll make all the arrangements."

Now it was sinking in. Rage welled up inside her, but

she was too numb to articulate it. "I thought . . . I hoped you'd marry me. I thought you would want to. You are the baby's father."

"Marry you?" He stood up and crossed the room, to set some distance between them. "I'm not ready for marriage, my sweet, nor for fatherhood, I'm afraid. I'm flying back to Hollywood next week. I just came home to close up this place and pack everything away. I'm going to star in some historical epic. We'll be shooting for at least six months. That's what I was going to tell you, before you hit me with this bombshell."

"Let me get this straight. You will arrange for an abortion for me, but you won't marry me."

"Right first go."

"Then what's to become of me?" she whispered.

"I've already told you. I'll make all the arrangements before I leave. It's as easy as one, two, three."

Helen felt icy cold. He spoke as if it had happened before. "You promised me you would look after . . . that side of it. I trusted you."

He turned on her. "It's a bit late to be worrying about that now, isn't it? Besides, you were just as eager as I was, so there's no use crying rape, either."

"I wouldn't dream of doing so." She wanted to run to him, cling to him, beg him to marry her, to save her from disgrace. Instead she began to draw on her still wet stockings, shrinking from their clamminess on her bare legs.

He watched her. "Come on, darling. Don't take it so badly. It'll be over before you know it. Then you can get on with your life, become the great actress you're destined to be. Don't waste that wonderful talent, sweetheart," he pleaded. "I'll write letters for you before I go, make some calls about auditions."

She stood up, slipping her feet into her damp shoes. "No, Julian. I refuse to go to some horrible woman and have our baby ripped out."

"You mean you won't have the abortion? You must be mad." He stared at her, his eyes darkening. "Don't expect a penny from—"

"I expect nothing from you, Julian." Helen picked up her coat.

He darted across the room and grabbed her arms. "Hold on, now. You're not thinking rationally, my pet."

"I think I am. For the first time in ages."

He released her to fetch his wallet from his tweed jacket. "You'll soon change your mind, when you think of the alternative. Take this for now. I'll find some names and send them to you." He stuffed notes into her unresponsive hand. She couldn't tell if they were one- or five-pound notes.

Screwing them up, she let them fall to the floor. "Don't bother. I won't have an abortion. It's not just that it's against my beliefs. I love you. This is our baby. I refuse to destroy it. I'm going to keep it."

"And expect me to pay for you and it, I suppose." His handsome face turned ugly. "Blackmail. Marry me or else."

"I told you before, I expect nothing from you." She walked to the door. "Have a good time in Hollywood, Julian. I wish you a successful life."

All the way down the two flights of stairs, she hoped to hear the sound of his footsteps running after her. But when she went down the outer steps and looked up at the window, he was standing there, looking down.

He raised his hand a little way and then let it drop.

She raised hers in an automatic response and then set off in the driving rain to walk to the tube station.

12

Two days later the envelope addressed to her arrived. Inside was a check for a hundred pounds and a list of five names. There was no letter. Not even a note.

She tore them all up: the envelope, the check, the list. Into tiny pieces. And flushed them down the toilet.

She waited for a phone call, but none came. After a week she called his flat. The number had been cut off.

Julian Holbrooke had flown out of her life, leaving her with nothing to remember him by but a bracelet and a baby.

She explained her red, swollen eyes by telling her grandmother and Aunt Hilary the truth: that Julian had gone to Hollywood to make a film and she had no idea when he would be back in England.

Her grandmother said, "Poor Helen. He was such a charming man. Never mind, darling, you'll go out with many men before you meet the right one for you."

Aunt Hilary said, "Good riddance to him, I say. He was too old for you. Choose a boy your own age next time."

If she had been going to tell Aunt Hilary about the baby at any time, it should have been then.

Helen sleepwalked through her work, wondering how on earth she was going to cope with the next seven months, never mind the rest of her life. At the same time, she mourned the loss of the man she had loved . . . *not wisely but too well.* Shakespeare's words summed it up exactly.

Each night she cried for Julian, smothering her weeping in her pillow, her sorrow mixed with fury at his cruel desertion.

There were times when she told herself she had been too hasty in rejecting an illegal abortion. After all, if she had one, everything would be back to normal in a couple of days. Without the baby she could get on with her life, go to a drama school, become a professional actress.

With the baby, however, all doors were closed to her. But the new tenderness in her breasts and the slight queasiness in the mornings told her that Julian's child was growing within her. She could not destroy it.

Her first and most difficult decision was that she must leave Lansdowne House. She could just imagine the faces of Colonel and Mrs. Rawsthorne in the large Queen Anne mansion down the road if they saw her slinking about Petersham with a huge stomach and no wedding ring.

She could not, would not, burden her grandmother and aunt with this shame. Not after all they had done for her.

But how could she manage on her own? Her wages would barely cover the cost of food and a single bed-sitter, never mind the expenses of a baby. And how could she work once the baby was born? Besides, no landlady would let an unmarried woman with a baby live in her house.

But to whom could she turn? Her mother? She felt sick at the thought.

Her father, then. After all, he was a clergyman. Surely he must have dealt with this problem before. But telling her father meant telling her mother, also.

She was so weary and listless, so depressed, that she couldn't find the energy to make decisions.

She decided not to tell anyone for now. It would be

two months before she began to show. That would give her time to think, to make plans.

She visited her parents. Her mother was suffering from a bad bout of flu. The perfect excuse.

"You're looking awful, Mother. You should be in bed."

Her mother turned resentful eyes on her. "You know very well there's far too much for me to do in this big house and in the parish to be able to take to my bed."

"I wish you would do so," said her husband with a sigh. "The doctor's warned you it could turn to pneumonia."

Helen said a silent prayer of thanks for God's intervention.

By the end of the visit it was all arranged. She would move back to Ealing to help her mother. Temporarily, of course, she assured her aunt and grandmother later.

"I should hope so," Aunt Hilary said. "Don't let that woman get her talons into you or you'll end up miserable and ugly, like me."

"You're not miserable or ugly." Blinking back tears, Helen hugged her angular aunt.

"Hold on, now. You're not going away forever, you know. Just until your mother gets well."

Her grandmother said the same thing. "If I have to come to that frightful house myself and drag you away, I shall," she warned.

"You won't have to. I promise I'll come and see you every weekend. As soon as Mother's better, I'll be back."

Helen hated lying to them. Once they knew, they probably would never forgive her. No one would. Life would never again be the same for her.

She left some of her favorite things in her room: her books and records and her stuffed teddy bear and panda, so that her aunt and grandmother would think she was coming back to live with them.

Of course, she never would.

"I'll just go and say good-bye to Edith," she said, having hugged them both.

Edith was making pastry for an apple pie for dinner that night. She gave Helen a floury hug. "Mind you don't stay one moment more than you must," she warned. "We need you here. It does us three old women good to have a pretty young girl here to brighten us up."

Helen had a sudden image of her baby in Edith's plump arms. She turned away abruptly. "See you soon." She left by the kitchen door, unable to bear any more good-byes.

She went out into the back garden, down the brick path, across the dewy lawn. There had been a sharp frost the night before, and the nip of approaching winter was in the air.

For a few minutes she stood in the shelter of the trees, listening to the sounds of autumn: the rustle of dry leaves and the rasping caw of the crows wheeling about the sky. She shivered in the chill October air. Drawing her coat more tightly about her, she left the orchard.

As she walked back, she paused to drink in this rear view of the house that had stood here for two hundred years. Solid, dependable, it looked back at her, its white-rimmed windows like benign but reproachful eyes.

She probably would return, in the next few weeks, anyway, but she would never live here again. As she gazed with love on the house, the words from a poem she had read in one of her father's religious books sprang to her mind: *Farewell house, and farewell home!*

The blare of the car horn told her that her father was waiting for her. She took the side path to the front of the house, past the greenhouse and the wooden toolshed. A quick last wave to her grandmother and aunt and Edith, who were standing on the front step, a casual "See you next week," and it was over.

She had counted upon another two months at least before her pregnancy would be noticed. Within two weeks of her having left Petersham, however, Ann had guessed.

"I'm going to make a dress just like Audrey Hepburn's," Ann said after they had seen a late afternoon showing of *Breakfast at Tiffany's*.

Ann's sturdy, capable hands could perform magic with a needle, whereas Helen, who had long, slim fingers, was useless at sewing even a simple hem.

She felt a surge of envy at the thought that Ann could wear all the new brief, bright shifts, while she would have to hide her body in loose sacks for several months.

"How about a curry?" Ann suggested.

Helen closed her eyes at the mere suggestion of curry. The slight queasiness in the mornings was turning to nausea that struck at all times of the day.

They turned down the little side street by the cinema. "What's wrong with you, Hel? You used to love curry."

"I just don't fancy it, that's all."

"No need to shout at me. You're so touchy recently. I can't say a thing without getting my head bitten off."

Helen turned away and began to march down the road. Ann ran after her and grabbed her arm, pulling her around. "What's the matter with you? You've been acting really peculiar lately. I can't make you out—" Her mouth dropped open. "Oh, no. Don't tell me."

Tears were rolling down Helen's cheeks now. She couldn't stop them. Thank heavens it was dark. She dragged a handkerchief from her coat pocket and turned away to dry her eyes and blow her nose.

Ann rubbed her hand up and down her back. "Is it a baby, Hel? Is that it?"

Helen nodded.

"That bloody swine. I knew he'd do it to you."

"You can't put all the blame on Julian," Helen said between gulping sobs.

"I certainly can. He should have looked after you, selfish bugger. Is he going to marry you?"

Helen shook her head. "He's gone to Hollywood."

"I know he has. That doesn't stop him from marrying you, does it?"

Helen faced Ann. "He's going to be there for several months. He's in a big, epic film that will take ages to make. He wanted me to have an abortion. Gave me a hundred pounds and a list of places where I could get it done."

"Big of him!"

"I tore up the list and the check."

"More fool you. It's probably all you'll ever see from him."

"I don't want anything from him. I can manage by myself."

Ann looked appalled. "How? Do your parents know?"

"Not yet. I'm going to wait a month or so before I tell my father."

"I wish you luck. My mum would kill me if I got pregnant."

Helen shivered. "Somehow I don't think she would, you know," she said, thinking of Ann's loud, plump mother. Mrs. Sturgis had always been quick with her hands. They administered slaps and consoling hugs in equal measure.

"Well, just you remember that I'm here for you. Anything I can do to help, you just ask."

Helen squeezed Ann's hand. "Thanks, Annie. You don't know how much it means to have someone to share this with."

They walked slowly down the dark road, arms linked.

"What about your job?" Ann asked.

"I suppose I'll have to leave as soon as I begin to show." Helen's face grew warm. "I'd hate anyone in the firm to know. I'll have to invent some lie about another job."

She could foresee weeks, months, even years, of lying.

Three weeks later, nausea overcame her at the

breakfast table. It was as bad as the seasickness she'd had on a channel steamer going to France.

She just made it to the bathroom.

As she crouched over the toilet bowl, Helen heard her mother's footsteps approaching down the hall. When she came out, her mother was standing outside the door.

"Are you ill?"

"I think it must be flu."

Her mother put a cold hand on her forehead. "No temperature." Her eyes narrowed. "You and your father were guzzling that box of Black Magic chocolates last night."

"Of course. That's probably it."

Her mother walked past her into the bathroom, wrinkling her nose. "I hope you cleaned up after yourself."

"Of course I did."

No more was said. But it served as a warning to Helen that she must speak to her father within the week.

"Forgive me for asking, Miss Barstow," Mr. Turner said later the same morning, "but are you feeling all right? You're as white as a ghost."

She conjured up a smile. "I must have forgotten to put on some rouge this morning. That's the trouble with us redheads, we have such white skin."

"It's not just your color. You've been looking unwell for several days."

She looked down at her shorthand book. "I think I may be getting the flu."

"Then you should be at home, resting." He closed up the file on his desk. "Come along. I'll drive you home."

Helen was horrified. "I couldn't possibly—"

"You're living in Ealing now, aren't you? I've been putting off seeing an elderly client in Acton for ages. She wants to change her will, but she's housebound. This will be a good chance to get it off my mind."

"I can't take the day off with Mrs. Pelham away."

He was adamant. "We can manage. You look as if you're about to collapse. A couple of days in a nice, warm bed and you'll be fine."

It was a seductive thought. But she knew, if her mother was home, she would have to go through another inquisition before she'd be able to go to bed.

To her relief, when they arrived in Ealing, Mr. Turner did not accept her invitation to come in. He surveyed the gloomy, Victorian-Gothic vicarage as if he had misgivings at leaving her there. Then, warning her not to come back to work until she was fully recovered, he drove away.

The garage was empty, its doors open. This was her father's day off, so it was likely that her mother had taken the Austin to go shopping.

Her father was in his study working on his sermon for the first Sunday in Advent. When she put her head around the door, he looked startled.

"My dear Helen. What are you doing home so early?"

"I wasn't feeling well."

"Ah yes, your mother said something about influenza this morning."

He looked down at his papers and books, eager to get back to his sermon.

She pushed the door open farther and went in. The familiar smell of coal smoke and old books assailed her. The study was bitterly cold. He had turned on only one bar of the electric fire, compensating for the lack of heat by wearing a cardigan under his old tweed jacket, the one with worn leather patches on the elbows.

Although it was a Monday, he wore his white clerical collar. He always wore it, even on holiday. Helen once said she was surprised he didn't wear it with his pajamas to bed. Her father had smiled, but her mother had not been amused.

Helen swallowed a lump that was like a rock at the base of her throat. "Daddy, I need to speak to you."

Reluctantly he laid down his fountain pen and screwed the top of the bottle of Waterman's blue-black ink. "What is it, my dear?"

She shut the door behind her. His eyes fixed upon it, as if he were a prisoner wishing to escape. "It's freezing in here," she said. "Could we sit by the fire?"

"Yes, yes. You mustn't catch cold." Casting a wistful look at his desk, he got up to switch on the second bar of the fire, then sat down on his favorite stuffed leather armchair. Helen sat across from him.

Folding his hands, he peered at her over the top of his glasses. "Now, what is the problem?"

She did not answer him instantly but sat picking at the threadbare arms of her chair. Her heart pounded like a piston engine in her chest.

"I'm afraid I'm going to have a baby," she said when the silence had been stretched to breaking point.

He stared at her, eyes wide behind his metal-rimmed glasses. "That is impossible, Helen. You must be mistaken."

How typical of him. Denial of any problem that might affect him personally. "I wish I were, but I'm not. I've been to a clinic and they've confirmed the pregnancy."

He shook his head in disbelief and then slumped down in the chair. "How could you do such a thing, Helen?"

"Sleep with a man, you mean, or have a baby?"

"This is not a time for flippancy, girl. Who is the father?" He held up a thin hand before she could answer. "No need to tell me. That actor, I suppose." He seemed to shrink farther into the depths of his chair. "I knew we should never have permitted you to live with Hilary and Mother. They are to blame for this."

Helen jumped up. "How can they possibly be to blame for my pregnancy?" She pounded her chest. "I am to blame. Not Gran and Aunt Hilary. I was the one who slept with Julian, not them."

He flinched visibly. "He is the most to blame, of course. An older man seducing a young, inexperienced girl. He will marry you, of course."

A coldness crept over Helen. She went to stand by the net-curtained bay window. "No, Father. I don't think he will. He's gone to America to make a film."

He ran a hand through his thinning sandy hair. "But he must marry you." His voice rose in his distress. "He must be made to do so. Otherwise what will become of you?"

"He wants me to have an abortion."

Her father looked shocked. "Abortion is not only the murder of an unborn child, it is also a criminal act."

"I know that," she said impatiently. "But there are ways to get around the legal part."

He closed his eyes for a moment. "I can't believe what I am hearing. And from my own daughter. What have we done to deserve this? What in the name of heaven is your mother going to say?"

"She'll be furious with me. That's why I wanted to speak to you first."

He took off his glasses to polish them on the front of his drooping cardigan. "This is a matter between a girl and her mother. You should have spoken to her first."

"I was afraid to speak to her first. I thought as you were a clergyman you would understand. You must have heard this same story from other people."

"That's as may be. Never did I expect to hear it from the lips of my own daughter. How could you do this to your mother? She has had a hard enough life as it is, without her only child disgracing her, disgracing us both."

The front door opened and shut. The heels of her mother's leather brogues clicked across the linoleum floor of the hallway.

"I'm home," she called.

As Helen's father levered himself out of his chair, Helen darted across the room to clutch at his arm. "I'm afraid to tell Mother. Will you tell her for me, Daddy? Please."

He shook off her hand, his eyes widening in horror. "Never. You must tell your mother yourself."

"Tell me what?"

Helen spun around to see her mother standing in the doorway, still holding her wicker shopping basket. "Tell me what?" she repeated. "What is the matter, Helen? Why are you home at this time?"

When neither of them answered, she set her basket on the floor and pulled off her drab felt hat, placing it neatly on top of the basket. "Geoffrey, will you kindly tell me what is going on?"

He looked at Helen and away again. "You must ask Helen," he said, crossing the room to set a distance between him and his daughter.

Helen's heart sank. She faced her mother, alone.

"Helen?"

Helen squared her shoulders. "I'm going to have a baby, Mother," she said defiantly. "The father is Julian Holbrooke, and he won't marry me."

Her mother's face flushed red first. Then the color drained from it, leaving it blotchy. She sank down on the Windsor chair near the door. "I don't believe you," she whispered.

Helen was afraid. Never before had she seen her usually unemotional mother so shaken. She stepped forward. "I'm sorry, Mummy. I didn't mean to put it so bluntly, but there was no easy way to tell you."

Please be a mother for once and help me, she begged her silently. I'm so afraid. I don't know what to do.

"You little slut." Her mother sprang up and struck her hard across the face. "You—you whore of Babylon!"

The shock of the blow and her mother's attack sent Helen staggering back against the corner of the bookcase.

"Now, now, Jane dear," her father muttered. "Violence will not help matters."

His ineffectual intervention only served to draw his wife's wrath upon him. "You know who is to blame for this, don't you?" she spat at him. "Your sister and mother, that's who. This would never have happened if Helen had lived here, with us, as she should have done. They've let her have her own way about everything, exerting no discipline whatsoever."

"For heaven's sake, Mother, I'll be nineteen in a few months. You speak as if I were twelve."

Her mother glared at her. "There's a wild streak in the Dunsmore family, and our daughter has inherited it, to our great shame."

"All I've inherited is the red hair," Helen shouted. "So has Father. Does that make him wild as well?"

"Helen." Her father's voice cut through Helen's near hysteria. "This is no time to be playing with words. What are we to do, Jane?" he said, appealing to his wife.

"You must write to this Julian person and demand that he marry Helen or you will have him arrested for . . . for ravishing your daughter."

"But he didn't ravish me," Helen said in a cool voice.

"I don't want to hear any more from you. Your father and I are discussing what is to be done about you."

"You talk about me as if I were a thing, not a person."

"You are not yet legally an adult. We are responsible for you."

Helen held out her hands, her mouth quivering. "Then please help me. I don't know what to do. I've been so afraid to tell you both."

She longed for both of them, one of them, to take her in their arms, to pat and stroke and kiss her and say, "There, there, it's going to be all right," but neither of them moved.

"As well you might be. Do you realize the shame

if this were to come out? The vicar of the parish of St. Matthew's with a pregnant, unwed daughter?"

A wave of nausea washed over Helen. "I don't feel very well."

"Now, now," said her father. "This has been a terrible shock. We are all upset at the moment. Let us try to remain calm and assess the situation."

"What is there to assess? Helen is pregnant. The father of her child is thousands of miles away, in America."

The floor shifted beneath Helen's feet. She grasped the back of the chair. "Please. I must go and lie down."

"She cannot remain here, in the vicarage, Geoffrey. Think of the disgrace. She must be sent away to a home, somewhere far from here where no one knows her. Then, when the child is born, we can put it up for adoption."

"No, no, no." Helen pushed her face close to her mother's. "If I had wanted to give this baby up, I would have had an abortion. That's what Julian wanted. But I love Julian. I want his baby. I won't give it up."

"Is that your last word?" said her mother, her voice dangerously soft.

"Yes. I intend to keep my baby."

"Then, madam, you may march upstairs to your room and pack your case and leave here today. We'll have no illegitimate babies in this house."

Their eyes clashed. Helen appealed to her father. "Daddy, what am I to do?"

He passed a hand across his face in a gesture of weariness. "You must do as your mother says. Be sensible, child. It is the best way."

"To have to go away all by myself, when I need my family, and then to give up my child? That's the best way?"

"Your mother thinks so."

"But you, Daddy," she pleaded, "what do you think? What would you advise me to do?"

He went to his desk, taking his fountain pen from his pocket. "I would advise you to do what your mother says." He adjusted his papers and opened one of the books, signifying his desire to get back to his work.

"Do your grandmother or your aunt know about this?" her mother demanded.

"No. I don't want them to know."

"Those are the first sensible words I've heard from you." Her mother gave her an awkward pat on the shoulder. "We'll speak about this later, when I've had time to discuss it with your father."

Her head swimming, Helen went upstairs, too sick to argue. She could hear their voices rising and falling below. Poor Father, she thought as she dragged herself onto her hard, narrow bed, he wasn't going to be allowed to get back to his sermon.

One thing was certain: she could not remain in this house. She would rather run away and be alone than have her mother organize her life for her. She was too weary now to work out a plan, but she was determined to keep her baby and to make her own decisions about the future.

She dragged the eiderdown over herself, closed her eyes, and fell into an exhausted sleep.

The ringing of the telephone woke Helen. Somehow it sounded strange. Long rings with pauses between instead of two short rings at intervals. She opened her eyes and blinked.

On the plain white wall opposite the bed was a framed tapestry of a deer surrounded by red-hued trees and a National Ballet of Canada poster of dancers Karen Kain and Frank Augustyn.

The violent pounding of her heart slowly subsided. Relief swept over her. She was in Ann's apartment. This was Toronto, Canada, in the nineties, not Ealing, England, in the sixties.

Her head ached. It had been quite a night. She peered at her watch but had to fumble for her glasses and put them on before she could see the time: ten-sixteen.

She could hear the murmur of Ann's voice, still on the phone. She waited until she had finished and then dragged on her dressing gown and went out into the living room.

"Morning," Ann said. "Help yourself to tea. There's some digestives in the tin. I've got to go to the bathroom."

"Thanks." Helen got the feeling Ann was in a bad mood. Probably a hangover from last night.

She poured herself some tea into a Queen Elizabeth Silver Jubilee mug. She hated drinking from mugs but didn't want to go rooting around for a cup and saucer.

"You're never going to guess who was on the phone," Ann said when she came out of the bathroom. She stood by the sink, dragging a hand through her tousled gray hair.

"Do I know her—or him?"

"You sure as hell do."

Something in Ann's expression set Helen's heart racing again. "Was it Bruce? Is something wrong at home?"

"No. It wasn't Bruce. It was Emma."

"Emma! You mean *my* Emma?"

"The very same."

"How on earth did she know I was here?" Helen's hand jumped to her throat. "Oh, my God. Don't tell me she called home. I wrote a note to her asking her not to contact me there again as I was going away."

"I don't know how she got this number. But it was her father she was trying to track down, not her mother. She said she'd found out that I was one of your best friends. 'Did you know I've been in touch with my birth mother?' she asked me. I said I did. Then she said that she was now searching for her birth father. Could I help her?"

"Oh, God. What did you tell her?"

"I told her she'd be better getting on with her life, but if she persisted in searching for her father, she must find out his name from someone other than me."

Ann was angry, Helen could tell. Her face was stiff.

"I'm so sorry to have you dragged into this. You've got enough worries without having mine on top."

Ann drained down her tea and set her mug down sharply. "You're right there, old pal."

Helen faced her across the counter. "This can't go on, can it? I've got to do something about it. But what?"

"You could start by telling Bruce."

"No. That comes absolutely last, not first. If I can deal with this without having to tell Bruce, I will. He'd never forgive me for having deceived him all these years."

"Well, you'd better do something pretty quick," Ann said. "If Emma has been able to trace me, here in Toronto, think how easy it will be for her to find people from the drama club."

Helen felt cold. "You're right."

"People who won't have any reason not to tell her who your boyfriend was. And don't tell me they won't remember, either, with Julian so famous now."

"I dreamed all night about Julian," Helen whispered. "Ann, I can't bear the thought of Emma discovering who he is, of finding out what sort of man her real father is."

"There's not a thing you can do about it. It's only a matter of time now."

13

Emma stared out her studio window at Chelsea Embankment and the River Thames beyond it. It was a cloudy day, although not actually raining, the wind blowing the fallen leaves in sudden gusts along the street.

The reasons for her dejection lay not in the signs of approaching winter, but in what she saw as the present failure of her personal life. She had found her birth mother, only to be totally rejected by her. She still hadn't succeeded in tracking down her birth father. And although they remained friendly, her relationship with Alan Grenville was still purely a professional one and likely to remain that way.

"Studying the colors of autumn?"

Startled, she turned to find Alan standing in the doorway. "Sorry," he said, "I should have knocked first."

"No, no. I was just thinking about winter coming."

"A melancholy thought. I was wondering if you'd finished the Symington House sketches?"

Emma picked up a large portfolio from her desk. "Yes, all done. They're just preliminary, of course." She smiled. "I'd welcome any suggestions."

"If they're anything like your usual work, I'm sure

they'll be great." He was about to leave, then turned back. "Any further developments in the quest?"

Was he just being polite, or was he really interested? She knew it had become an obsession with her, but . . . "I don't want to bore you with my stupid problems." She looked down at her desk, rolling a carbon pencil back and forth across its surface.

"If I was bored, I wouldn't have asked," he said quietly. "What's new?" He set the portfolio against the wall and perched his tall frame on her drafting stool.

She told him about the call to Toronto.

"How did you track the number down?"

"I phoned Winnipeg, knowing she wasn't there. She'd warned me not to call while she was away. I got David Lawrence, her son. My half brother. He sounded very nice."

"Did you tell him who you were?"

"No, but it was so exciting to talk to someone who was my own flesh and blood, I was terribly tempted to tell him I was his sister."

"But you didn't."

"No." Emma looked down at her hands. "It has to come from her, my mother. It's just that she's so terrified her family will turn against her, I doubt she'll ever do it."

"I'm sorry," Alan said. "Family relationships can be hell, can't they?"

His tone was light, but there was some deeper feeling behind the remark, Emma was sure. "I'm the one who should be sorry. You must be wishing you'd never brought up the subject."

"Not at all. I know how this woman's rejection has hurt you."

Their eyes met, held. Then Alan slipped down from the stool to pick up the portfolio.

The memory of that night at Alan's flat hovered embarrassingly between them. Although Emma remembered it in every detail, the fact that Alan never mentioned it was a sure sign that he wished it had never happened.

Not that anything of significance had happened, of course. At least, not from a sexual point of view. But now, whenever she and Alan were together, Emma was acutely aware of that tender, compassionate side of his nature, which he kept well hidden most of the time beneath a flippant, man-of-the-world exterior.

"Ah, there you are. The very two people I wanted to see."

The arrival of the flamboyant senior partner, Desmond Parmenter, on the scene came just at the right time. Today he was wearing his black cloak with the red silk lining, a white silk scarf thrown nonchalantly about his neck, his curled, dyed-black hair glistening with pomade.

"I am right in thinking that Francesca is away, am I not?" he asked Emma.

"Yes. On maternity leave," she replied.

He shook his head, clicking his tongue. "You women, you will insist on having babies, won't you?"

Realizing that this was supposed to be a joke, Emma smiled.

"What are you both doing this coming weekend?"

Emma glanced at Alan.

"Would you be free for an urgent assignment?" Desmond Parmenter asked impatiently when neither of them replied to his first question.

"I'd prefer another time," Alan said. "I have plans for this weekend."

"Unfortunately, it has to be this weekend. Sir Julian is planning to be back in London on Monday. He has particularly requested that I or my partner meet with him for a consultation this weekend."

"Sir Julian?" Alan asked. "You mean Julian Holbrooke? Didn't you do extensive work on his house a few years ago?"

"That is correct. Marsden Court." Desmond turned to Emma. "A glorious Jacobean house in the Cotswolds," he explained. "Apparently Sir Julian wishes to convert a barn to guest apartments and add a conservatory to the house."

Alan raised his eyebrows. "A Jacobean conservatory?"

"Yes, quite. I am not at all certain that that will work. In any event, I cannot meet with him this weekend. I am committed to the Japanese client and his castle in Scotland. I don't want to say no to Holbrooke, if I can help it."

"Sounds like an interesting project," Alan said.

"I thought you'd think so." Desmond seemed to be taking Alan's acquiescence for granted. "You'll need someone to take notes and offer ideas for the interior design work. Can you work with Emma? Is she good enough?"

Emma grinned. She was used to the senior partner's bluntness.

"Oh, she's definitely good enough," Alan said, smiling at her with such warmth that her heart lurched. "The only thing is, she hasn't said yet if she would be available."

"Yes, I think I could be. I can change my plans."

She didn't want them to think she had just an empty weekend stretching before her, because she hadn't. But she and Tony had an understanding that work always came first.

"Excellent. You will find all the details of the previous work in the Marsden Court portfolio. Once you've taken a look at it, I'll have a chat with you about it, Alan, before I leave for Scotland."

"Fine. I'll take it home with me tonight."

Desmond gave Emma a little bow. "My eternal thanks, my dear, for giving up your weekend to the demands of your grateful employer. No doubt I will be the cause of abject despair for some handsome beau, who had hoped to spend the weekend with the fair Emma."

"Tony will understand," Emma said with an enigmatic smile. "He's a busy barrister and often has to work at weekends himself." Besides, we're just good friends, not lovers, she wanted to add for Alan's benefit, but didn't.

"Excellent, excellent," Desmond enthused, rubbing his hands together. "By the bye, Emma, apart from Mrs. Pennington, the formidable housekeeper, Marsden Court is a bachelor establishment at present, Sir Julian's second wife having divorced him several years ago. I trust that will not disturb you?"

Emma met Alan's amused glance and had to fight to keep a straight face. Desmond could be extraordinarily old-fashioned at times. "No, not at all. After all, I will have Alan there to protect me."

"Of course you will," Desmond said quite seriously. "Then that is all settled. Good, good. I shall speak to you tomorrow, then, Alan."

Before Alan could do more than nod his head, Desmond had sailed from the room.

Emma and Alan exchanged smiles. "I must remember to pack my sword and matched pistols," Alan said, "to protect you from the horde of bachelors bent on ravishment. Seriously, though, you don't have to cancel your weekend plans. I can manage on my own."

She wasn't sure if he was saying he didn't want her to go with him or not, but she was thinking professionally, not personally, when she said, "This could prove to be a very important commission for me. I'd like to do it."

"Great. Then I'll leave your Symington House sketches here for now. The Marsden Court stuff will take up my entire evening, I should think. I'll let you have them tomorrow. Tonight you can go home and bone up on Jacobean conservatories," he said with a grin, and was gone.

Emma wondered how his latest flame would take the news that she would not be seeing him for an entire weekend. Knowing Alan, she should be used to it by now. As with Tony, his work always came first.

Much as she was attracted to Alan Grenville, Emma was not at all blind to what she saw as the main drawback about him. Personal commitments seemed to figure extremely low on the list of important matters in his life. His relationships with women blew hot and cold, and she had never heard him mention one member of his family. For all anyone knew, Alan might well be an orphan without siblings or even cousins.

Although she loved her work, family was extremely important to her, especially now.

Before she left to go home that evening, Emma gathered up several books to take home with her. She wanted to be fully primed for tomorrow.

Several years ago, when her mother had first been diagnosed as having multiple sclerosis, Emma and her parents had moved from their house into a large flat in a block on Richmond Hill. When she had started her first job, Emma had hoped to move into her own place, but by then her mother had become an invalid. And it would be cruel to leave her father by himself in that large flat so soon after her mother's death.

When she opened the front door, she was greeted by the smell of liver and bacon. Her father was usually home first and had the meal all prepared by the time she got in.

Richard Turner was in the kitchen, standing over the stove, when he heard Emma come into the hall. He had taken off his suit jacket and was wearing his favorite apron, the olive-green vinyl one with Harrods Food Halls printed on it, over his waistcoat.

"Hallo, darling," he said when she came into the kitchen. "How was your day?"

She went to kiss him. "Marvelous. Absolutely marvelous. I've got the chance of an important new commission. One that could give me some international publicity. At least I hope so. Depends on the client, I suppose. He may say he's never heard of me and demand someone else."

"Nonsense. Whoever the client is, he'll be impressed with your talent and snap you up. It all sounds very exciting." Richard wiped his hands on a dish towel. "Let's have a drink to celebrate this commission. I want to hear all about it. Go on into the lounge, and I'll make up some gin and tonics."

His enthusiasm was caused more by Emma's excitement than by the commission itself. She had been so despondent over the past few months, because of Helen's rejection, that he had been extremely worried about her.

He blamed himself entirely. He should never have told Emma who her real mother was. Not only had it caused her a great deal of subsequent anguish, but he had also broken the promise he had made to Helen at the time of Emma's birth, that he would never divulge her name to her child.

The trouble was, he thought as he opened the bottle of tonic and poured it over the gin and ice, he could understand both sides: Emma's desire to find her birth mother and Helen's desire to keep her past a secret. Except that her rejection of her daughter didn't fit at all with the bright, gentle girl he had known thirty years ago.

Obviously time and circumstances had hardened and changed the Helen Barstow he had known.

He took off his glasses, passing his hand wearily over his eyes. Then, having stared blindly at the cuckoo clock on the wall for a moment, he replaced his glasses and carried the drinks through to the lounge.

"Now," he said when he had given Emma the drink, "let's hear all about this fabulous commission."

She sat on the footstool, beaming at him, her hair a

bright halo around her face. "Well, I suppose 'commission' is a slight exaggeration. Desmond Parmenter wants Alan to visit a valuable client this weekend. As Francesca is on pregnancy leave, I am to go with him, to advise on the interior work." She leaned forward. "If I play my cards right, there's a good chance I could get the interior work for myself."

"Marvelous. Of course you'll get it."

"It would be the making of my career if I did. You'll never guess who this client is."

"No, I won't. How could I?"

"Julian Holbrooke. Sir Julian Holbrooke. Isn't that amazing? He has a wonderful Jacobean mansion called Marsden Court and . . ."

She went babbling on, but Richard heard nothing more of what she said. God Almighty! Why, why, why? he wanted to shout. Of all the homes in England, of all the famous people, she had to be sent to that swine Julian Holbrooke.

Would he be there? Of course he would. Emma was saying so at this very moment, that this was the only time the famous actor-producer could meet with his architect and designer.

Richard's hands clenched so tightly around his glass, he felt he could crush it.

Emma suddenly stopped midsentence. "What's wrong, Daddy? You look as if you've seen the proverbial ghost."

Richard pulled himself together. "Sorry, darling. I've just remembered I didn't turn down the liver. Hang on a minute and I'll see to it."

"Liver! You haven't said a word about what I've been telling you, and now you're worried about the liver." She was smiling, but he knew she was hurt at his strange lack of enthusiasm.

"It's wonderful news," he said mechanically. "Hang on, I'll be right back."

He took his glass through to the kitchen with him and poured himself another, much stiffer, gin. He just had to get out of the room before he gave the game away.

Should he tell her now that Julian Holbrooke was her father? The thought of that twice divorced devil getting his fangs into his darling Emma, maybe using his wealth and fame to alienate her from her adoptive father, enraged him. He threw some more cubes of ice into his glass, splashing gin on the kitchen counter.

Then reason took over. Surely there was little chance of the subject of Emma's adoption coming up in professional conversation. In fact, Holbrooke had never known that he had a daughter. As far as he was concerned, Helen had probably had an abortion.

He was such a swine that he had never even bothered to find out what had happened to Helen. She had told Richard that herself in Devon, when she was only a few weeks away from giving birth. "Julian never wrote to me or tried to find me when he returned from Hollywood," she told him, her eyes brimming with tears. "I only knew he was back from reading it in some newspaper."

Of course, to be fair, Julian hadn't known where she was. No one had, apart from himself and Mary—and Helen's best friend, Ann Sturgis.

When she was four months pregnant, they had spirited her away to Ilfracombe in north Devon. She had written two notes: one to her grandmother, one to her parents, saying that she was being well looked after but preferred that they not know where she was. Richard had posted the notes for her in London so that they wouldn't have a Devonshire postmark.

No, there was little chance of Julian knowing who Emma was. And the entire thing was far too much of a coincidence for Emma to have an inkling that he was her father. Certainly they didn't resemble each other at all, apart from that seemingly boundless energy that both of them had in common.

Richard recalled that first encounter with Holbrooke, at the Christmas office party, which had suddenly livened up when he had made his entrance, damn him!

"What on earth are you doing, standing there in the middle of the kitchen, muttering to yourself?"

Hearing Emma's voice, Richard pulled himself together. "Cursing myself for almost burning the liver."

Emma went over to inspect it. "Looks fine to me." She put her arms around her father. "You're getting like a fussy old woman about your cooking," she teased him.

He hugged her back, looking down into her lively face. "You're right. Forgive me, sweetie. I really am very excited about your new project. Sir Julian will be delighted with you, I'm certain. How could he fail to be? You're a very talented young woman. Don't you ever forget that." He kissed her on the nose. "Now, I really must serve up this dinner of ours, or it will be absolutely inedible."

"I'll go and lay the table." Emma took out side plates from the cupboard and went into the dining room.

Richard went to the stove, congratulating himself on the seeming ease with which he had spoken Holbrooke's name. If he were to tell Emma what he knew about her father, she would be devastated. After finding and then being rejected by her mother, she was particularly vulnerable. To learn that her father had vilely seduced and then deserted Helen might cause a depression.

No. Far better to leave well alone and pray to God that the subject of adoption would not be raised at Marsden Court this coming weekend.

14

Helen flew home to Winnipeg from Toronto on Friday. As she came down the airport escalator, she caught sight of Bruce standing at the edge of the waiting crowd.

Part of her was happy to see him. But she also felt a desire to hide herself in the corner of a taxi and not have to speak to anyone.

Bruce put his arm around her and kissed her. "Have a good time?"

"Just great," Helen replied, determined to give him the reply he expected.

"I've missed you," he said, but when he spoke his eyes didn't meet hers. He was pretending to check the luggage carousel for her bag.

"How's David? And Karen?"

"Let's talk about them later. We'll get your bag first." He strode away to the edge of the carousel.

Helen felt as if she were about to enter a minefield.

The wind was cool as they crossed the street to get to the car park. "It feels a bit colder here than in Toronto."

"We've had some more rain. Still very little frost, fortunately. Not bad weather, really."

Bruce strode ahead of her, carrying her heavy case as easily as if it were a small tote bag.

"How's the merger going?" she asked as she settled onto the front seat. How comfortable the leather seats of the New Yorker were in comparison with the split vinyl ones in Ann's dilapidated Toyota.

The thought swamped her with guilt.

Bruce turned on the ignition and drove the car out of the car park. "All sewn up, apart from a few odds and ends."

"That must be a tremendous relief, darling," Helen said, trying hard to seem enthusiastic.

"Damned right. Sorry if I've been a bit of a grouch recently."

"That's okay. I understand."

"It's been a swine to get organized. Forty-three lawyers to shuffle around: partners, associates, all wanting their share of the pot, the senior partners arguing about who should get the corner offices. Not to mention all the headaches with the staff." He gave her a smiling grimace. "You know the sort of thing."

She smiled back, relieved to feel the tension between them ease. "It's been a big strain for you, I know."

"And once the merger party is over, we start work on the move to the new offices. Wait till you see them, Helen." He was suddenly revitalized, his entire body registering excitement. "Ceiling-to-floor windows, blue-and-gold marble in the reception areas, an entire computer section. I'll take you over next week, when they've finished the floors."

But Helen wasn't thinking about the new offices, however wonderful they might be. She had put the merger party completely out of her mind while she was in Toronto. Now just the thought of it filled her with panic. Less than two weeks away and all the final preparations to be made.

Her determination to make immediate plans to fly to

Britain leached away. This merger had been in the works for two years. It meant a great deal to Bruce to have it all go smoothly. She owed him that, at least. Once the party was over, she would come to a decision about Emma.

The trees along Forest Boulevard were almost bare of their leaves. Several people were out raking their lawns, piling the leaves into large plastic bags. Although the weather was beautiful at present, those who lived on the prairies knew that snow could come at any time. If it came in October, it could be a long-drawn-out winter.

Helen shivered involuntarily. It wasn't the intense cold of Manitoba winters she hated. After all, for most of the time the cold was tempered with brilliant blue skies and sunshine. It was the length of the winters: five, sometimes six, months of bitterly cold weather. You couldn't safely set out your bedding plants until the end of May. Then the first frosts came again in September to turn the marigolds black. Summers were usually hot, filled with sunshine and fast lush growth, but over far too quickly.

Like her time with Julian.

"You're very quiet," Bruce said as they turned into their street.

Startled, Helen gave him a fleeting smile. "I was just thinking about winter."

"That's a long way off."

"It snowed in October last year."

"That was last year. Press the garage opener, will you?"

As they pulled into the driveway, Helen looked up at the Colonial-style house. The gleaming white paintwork, the spacious lawns and mature evergreens, lifted her spirits. She always loved coming home.

Maybe everything was going to work out after all. "It's good to be home," she said as they drove into the garage, with its familiar smells of pine logs and gasoline. Strange how you took things for granted until you went away. When you returned, everything seemed fresh yet comfortingly familiar. "Is David home?"

Bruce switched off the ignition. "Don't know." When he went to get her bag from the trunk, he mumbled something else she couldn't catch.

"What?"

"I said he's been staying with a friend for the last few days." Bruce slammed down the trunk lid and strode ahead of her into the back hall.

Helen closed her eyes for a moment, the flutter of nerves back again. "Why?"

Bruce set the suitcase at the foot of the stairs. "I'll put the kettle on for a cup of tea for you."

Helen grabbed at his arm. "Why did David move out, Bruce?"

"How should I know? He's been goofing off, coming in at all hours, skipping classes. When I told him to smarten up, he said he'd stay with some friend until you came home."

"Which friend?"

"That fellow with the long hair, Phil something or other." Bruce went into the kitchen and handed her the kettle.

"Phil Hebert, you mean. I like Phil. He's got a great sense of humor."

"The kid's a long-haired dropout. And his father drives a truck."

Helen swung around, her hand on the faucet. "What's wrong with that?"

Bruce sighed. "God, Helen, why do you always have to be on the opposite side to me about everything?"

Helen felt like saying, "Because you're a middle-class macho bigot and snob." But that wouldn't have been true, either. Bruce was far too complex a person to be summed up in one derogatory sentence. "I don't mean to be. It just bothers me when you put down people because of their jobs."

"I don't. I just prefer my son to mix with—"

"People his own class? Honestly, Bruce, you're worse than the Brits. I thought Canada was supposed to be a classless society? That's what I like most about it. Yet here's my own husband—"

"Let's not fight the moment you're back. Want a drink?"

"No thanks. Tea's enough. Then I'll phone David and Karen."

"I thought we'd get Chinese food in for dinner, okay?"

"Perfect. Just what I fancy." She set the teapot down to brew for a moment and went to him. "It's great to be home, darling."

His arms went around her, crushing her against him so tightly that her ribs ached. "Great to have you home," he murmured against her hair.

He released her abruptly, turning to fetch the tonic for his gin, but she thought she caught a glint of moisture in his eyes.

She knew that there was another side to Bruce that he kept well hidden. The tender, gentle side that had nursed her when she'd had pneumonia in 1971. The man who reacted with tears and generous checks to pictures of starving children on the CBC news. Or whose passion for the ballet and hard work on the Royal Winnipeg Ballet board were camouflaged by his assertion that "everyone should do his bit for the good of the community."

Poor Bruce. He was a product of his generation and upbringing, programmed to work until he dropped and to despise those who stopped to smell the flowers.

But now she was concerned that the rift between them was caused by far more than their differing vision of the world about them. Bruce's eyes continued to avoid hers, and there was a new edginess about him that disturbed her. Either he was feeling guilty, or the affair—if it was an affair—wasn't over yet.

As soon as she had finished her tea, she pressed Phil's number and asked for David.

"Hi there, I'm home," she said lightly when David came on the line.

"Hi, Mom. Have a good time in Toronto?"

"Great. Are you coming over?"

Silence. Then, "Phil and I are working on his set design for the Gas Station Theatre. I'll come over in the morning, okay?"

When Dad's not there, he meant.

"Okay, see you then." Helen tried not to sound as disappointed as she felt. "I'll make some orange coffee cake." It felt strange making an appointment to see your own son. "You won't sleep in, will you?"

"No way. Looking forward to hearing all about your trip."

"Don't you have classes in the morning?" The words were out before she could bite them back. Damn, damn, damn. She was as bad as Bruce.

"That's my business."

She could hear Bruce's voice in her head. *Not while I'm paying your tuition fees it isn't.*

"Sorry, Mom, but you and Dad have got to quit treating me like a twelve-year-old."

Helen swallowed the usual rejoinder about him acting his age. It was like an old, cracked record, repeating itself endlessly.

"See you tomorrow, then."

"I'll be by around eleven. Gotta go now."

She phoned Karen, but her machine was on. She left a message, but Karen didn't call her back.

That night Helen lay beside Bruce in the king-size bed, listening to the sounds of suburban Winnipeg. No heavy hum of Toronto traffic, rattle of streetcars, or wailing of sirens. Just the sighing of the wind in the trees and the occasional car passing by.

Normally she would have felt at peace, but home no longer signified tranquillity. No more could she use it as a haven in which to hide from the outside world. It never had been so, really. You could switch off the pictures of starving children by pressing a button, set up the answering machine to intercept calls, but the problems still existed.

She clasped her hands in the ritual of night prayers. *God bless Mummy and Daddy, Granny and Auntie Hilary and Edith.* The words rose like vapor in her mind.

All these years she had sought to escape the past, but now it was closing in on her, invading her dreams and her waking thoughts. It was like one of those nightmares, where you run on the spot with leaden feet, a monster at your heels.

Only by turning and confronting the monster would she be able to save herself.

It took her a long time to get to sleep, but once she did, she slept through the entire night. She was awakened just after nine the next morning by the telephone. She leaped out of bed, her heart racing.

"Did I wake you?" said Karen. "Sorry about that. I figured you'd be up by now."

"No, I wasn't, but that's fine. I should be up anyway. Your father must have cooked his own breakfast. How are you, darling? Had a good week?"

"Busy. How was Toronto—and Ann?"

"Both—" She had been about to say "great," but Ann certainly wasn't great. "Fine. Ann sends her love. When shall I see you?"

"I'll come over for Sunday lunch, if that's okay. I'm working late tonight."

With Michael Pascal? Helen wanted to ask, but didn't. She hadn't enough energy to solve her own problems, never mind Karen's. "Sunday's fine. Oh, Karen, while I'm speaking to you, can you tell me anything about David? Did he and your father have a row or something?"

She could sense Karen's hesitation. "Not anything more than usual, as far as I know. David was being his pain-in-the-neck self and just got fed up with Dad getting at him, I suppose. I don't think it's anything to worry about. He'll probably move back in now that you're home again."

"He's coming over this morning." For a brief moment she thought of asking Karen's advice about how to deal with David, then discarded the idea.

"You're too soft on him, Mother. Dad's right, you know. All this garbage about acting is just an excuse to get out of working."

"Thank you for that insight, Karen. I think David's old enough to decide things for himself, don't you?"

"I doubt it." More hesitation. "While you're on the phone, I think there's something else you should know."

"It will have to wait, I'm afraid. I have to go to the bathroom." That was true, but not quite so urgently as her tone indicated. "Bye, darling. See you Sunday."

It occurred to her later that so far her conversations with her family had been on two levels: banal clichés on the surface, with all that was important left unsaid below. Rather like a Samuel Beckett play.

She sincerely hoped that with David, at least, she could have an intelligent, straightforward discussion, without all the undercurrents.

She was not to be disappointed.

"Let's put it this way, Mom—you act as a buffer between Dad and me. When you're not here, we just can't stand the sight of one another." David reached for another slice of the warm coffee cake.

"I think that's exaggerating a little, don't you?"

"Not at all," David said through a mouthful of cake. "We don't see eye to eye on anything important. Dad wants me in a pin-striped suit, carrying a briefcase for the rest of my life. I'd rather die than end up like him."

"There are worse fates," Helen said dryly.

David sprang up from his chair, to pace about the kitchen like a caged cougar. "You should have heard him, Mom. He was more excited than I've ever seen him before. Why? Because he's going to have the largest office, with mahogany-paneled walls and lights that come up out of the floor at the press of a switch on his frigging control panel. All this, with kids lining up at the soup kitchens every day. And I'm talking about here in Winnipeg, not in Somalia or somewhere like that. It's obscene, that's what it is."

Helen gave her son a half smile, wanting to applaud and shake him at the same time. "And I suppose you told him that when he told you about the plans for the new offices?"

"I sure did. If I didn't tell him, no one else in the family would. Karen thinks it's all marvelous. 'It's going to be one of the finest law firms in Canada. You should be proud of Dad,' is all she can say."

"And so you should be. Your father's worked extremely hard to build up the firm. When he started out, it was just a small firm with shabby offices in an old block. I can imagine his disappointment when he told you all about the plans and you told him exactly what you thought about them."

David looked sheepish. "I don't think Grandpa would have liked these new offices, either. I mean, all the computers and technical stuff is neat, but . . ."

Their eyes met. Helen couldn't help smiling. "You're right. I can just see him telling poor Bruce that it's not the way law was practiced in his day." The smile faded. "Had it ever occurred to you that the grandpa who took you fishing at the lake might have been a pretty tough father, expecting a lot of his son, too?"

David turned away to rinse his mug in the sink. "Could be, I guess."

"I liked your grandfather very much. We got along

really well. But he was always at your dad, telling him how he should run the firm, even when he'd retired from it. I think, even now, your father still hears him in his head."

"What's that got to do with me trying for theater?"

"I don't know. I'm not a psychologist. You took first-year psych. What do you think it means?"

"That he's repeating a pattern he learned from his own father?"

Helen nodded.

"That he's scared for me, I guess."

"Right. You won't understand that part of it until you have kids for yourself." Helen felt tears behind her eyes. "We're both scared for you. We know how ruthless the world can be. We want to protect you, to arm you with the weapons to make it out there in the modern jungle. One of the best weapons is education. That's why your father—"

"I know that's why. But he's got to learn to let go. He can't keep controlling me all my life." His eyes blazed. "Don't you see, Mom? Dad loves being a lawyer, and not just because of the money he makes. That's great for him. But how would he like it if his father had forced him to be a scientist or a computer analyst? He would have hated it, wouldn't he?"

"Why don't you tell him all this."

"Because he doesn't let me get a word in. Tells me I'm a smart-ass and don't respect my elders. Jeez, Mom, all that crap about respect went out with the dark ages. He should respect my wishes, my needs."

Helen was tired. She'd wanted straightforward discussion. Now she was tired of it. She shoved aside her coffee cup. "Sit down, David. No, not on the counter. Here, in front of me, so I can see you."

Surprised, David sat down at the table. "What are you going to do about it?" she asked him.

"What do you mean?"

"What I say. You want to go into the theater. That means years of training, possibly with nothing at the end of it. A little talent isn't enough, you know. A few amateur parts, a walk-on at the Theatre Centre, they mean absolutely nothing in the international world of professional theater."

"How would you know?" David was stung by her derisive tone. "What do you know about professional theater, other than buying season tickets for Manitoba Theatre Centre?"

She leaned forward, her temper rising. "Frankly, I don't think you want it enough. What have you done to discover what's out there for aspiring actors? How many theaters have you applied to, bugged, so that they have to give you a job just to get you off their backs? What about the National Theatre auditions? Could you manage on your own if your dad cut off the money supply? Would you *want* to manage without his support? Or is this all a dream to get out of university, to avoid a bit of hard work? I'll tell you, David, you'd find working in the theater a darn sight harder than university."

She could hardly believe the words that were spewing out of her mouth, nor the vicious tone in which they were spoken.

David looked at her as if she'd gone mad.

"Don't look so surprised," she said. "I should have said all this a long time ago. It might have avoided a lot of strain in this house. Perhaps the reason your father isn't willing to support you in your desire to go into theater is that he doesn't think you've got the guts or the perseverance to make it."

When she saw David's stunned expression, she felt like crying. She wanted to fold him in her arms and hug him tight against her. But she didn't. The words she had spoken might be unfair, considering they were dredged up from her own eighteen-year-old self, but they wouldn't kill him. And they might just prick him into some action.

"Is that what you think?" he asked her, his face white, "that I haven't got the guts to make it in theater?"

"I don't know. All I do know is that the theater is even more demanding than the law. You have to be willing to give up everything for your acting—relationships, a normal home life, family, comfort. It has to burn in you with such passion that none of these matter as much as acting up on that stage or in the film or television studio."

That was the way it had been with Julian, she realized suddenly. That was why he had abandoned her. Only in Julian's case, acting wasn't enough. He'd also wanted fame and all the rewards that fame brought.

Although she would never be able to forgive him for his cruelty, for the first time in thirty years she began to understand the state of Julian's mind when he had abandoned her and gone to Hollywood.

15

Emma and Alan left after lunch on Friday, so that they could avoid the heavy commuter traffic on the M40. As they sped along the motorway, Emma settled back and sighed.

Alan glanced at her. "Tired?"

"No. Not at all. Just end-of-the-week relaxation." She had the feeling that, one way or another, this weekend would decide what her relationship with Alan was going to be in the future. She couldn't continue silently holding a torch for a man who thought of her solely as a talented interior designer.

They talked mainly about the commission. Alan agreed with Emma that turning the tithe barn into guest quarters was going to be easier than building a conservatory that would blend with a Jacobean house.

"It's been done, of course, but I wouldn't want to spoil the symmetry of the main building."

Emma sat thinking for a while. Then she asked, "Do you think there's the slightest chance of my getting the interior design work? I mean, as the chief designer."

"A pretty good chance, I should think, particularly with Francesca away and Paul working with Desmond in Scotland. It will depend on your ideas. And on how well you hit it off with the client. As you know, when it comes to interior work, rapport with your client is essential."

"Of course." Emma's mind was racing. In more ways than one, this could be the most crucial weekend of her life.

After they had passed Oxford and joined the A40, they lapsed into a companionable silence, listening to a Haydn cello concerto on the compact disc player.

We even have the same taste in music, Emma thought. Damn it, why couldn't he be interested in her as a woman as well as a colleague!

"No wonder Sir Julian chose this place," Alan said as they turned off the A40 a few miles past Burford. "Very convenient for town."

It certainly was. The fast M40 from London to Oxford, and then the A40 for another seventeen miles, a short drive along a lane lined with a hedge of hawthorn and blackberry, and they were there, in front of the wrought-iron security gates and high stone wall that surrounded the grounds.

Marsden Court lay in a slight valley sheltered by gently rolling hills, but all they could see of the house at present were its numerous stone chimneys.

Emma was out of the car before Alan had opened his door. "I'll do it," she shouted, eager to experience the countryside as soon as possible. Scuffing through the fallen leaves, she walked up to the gates and pressed the speaker button. "Alan Grenville and Emma Turner from Parmenter, Grenville," she announced.

"Thank you," said a voice through the speaker.

Before she could get back into the car, a uniformed security guard appeared at the gate, restraining a fierce-looking Doberman that dragged at its chain.

Although the gate separated them, Emma shrank back. She was a little afraid of all dogs, particularly Dobermans with bared fangs dripping saliva.

"Don't worry, miss. He won't hurt you," the guard

said in the patronizing tone all dog lovers adopted when speaking to those who didn't share their devotion.

Alan got out of the car. "Is he going to let us in?"

"Just need your identification, sir, that's all. Then we'll open the gate for you."

Emma was happy to retreat to the car as Alan showed the guard his business card.

He got back into the car, the gates swung open, and they were inside, driving down a lane lined with horse chestnut trees, their branches still bearing yellow leaves.

"Tight security," Alan remarked.

"I suppose Sir Julian needs it. The high price of fame. Theater, films. He must be worth millions."

"Not to mention the television ads. I doubt he's worth that many millions, though. Not with taxes the way they were until Maggie became prime minister. But he must be pretty damn wealthy to be able to live in a place like this."

They came upon the house suddenly, just around the bend of the driveway. "Oh, Alan," Emma breathed.

He said nothing but drew the car to a halt a little way from the house and switched off the ignition.

They sat, separate yet united in their silent appreciation of the beautiful house before them, its creamy stone turned to mellow gold by the twilight and setting sun.

Part Elizabethan, part Jacobean, with asymmetrical gables and a great bay window. Emma's professional eye took in and assessed the obvious, only to reject it in favor of a far more subjective analysis.

"It's the most beautiful house I have ever seen." She turned to Alan and caught his slight frown. "Sorry, that's not a very professional response, is it?"

He smiled. "I'm not expecting an instant assessment before we're even out of the car. And, yes, it *is* beautiful." He started up the engine again, easing the BMW to the foot of the flight of stone steps that led up to the house.

A dark-haired man dressed in jeans and a black turtleneck sweater came down the steps to meet them.

"Not the butler, I think," Alan said from the corner of his mouth.

As the man approached the car, Emma saw that he was young, possibly her own age or even younger. "Not the great Sir Julian, either," she whispered.

Alan opened the window. The man leaned down to speak to him. "Hallo there. Come on in. Someone will park your car in the garage. I'll help you in with your bags." He went around to the other side of the car to open the door for Emma. "Hi." He held out his hand. "I'm Martin Holbrooke."

She shook hands with him. "Emma Turner, Mr. Grenville's—"

"Alan's," Alan said from behind the open trunk.

Emma grinned. "Alan's associate."

Alan slammed the trunk shut. He put out his hand to Martin Holbrooke. "Hallo. I'm Alan Grenville."

Martin shook hands with him and then picked up Emma's case to lead the way up the steps.

"Sorry. It's rather heavy," she said. "I couldn't decide whether to bring just an overnighter or not. I know it's supposed to be a working weekend, but I wasn't sure if we'd be trekking through muddy fields in wellingtons, behind beaters—or whatever you call them—or dressing up in the evenings. The suitcase and mountains of clothes won out."

Damn. She was talking too much. She always did when she was nervous.

Martin laughed. "The wellies would come in useful when we look at the barn," he said, turning to wait for them in the entranceway. "But as my father's not a hunting man, there aren't any beaters. He does like to dress fairly formally in the evening, though, so you probably did just the right thing in bringing the case."

"Oh, good. Sorry about the weight."

"Not at all. It's not heavy." Martin set down the suitcase in the hall. "My father's expecting you, of course. Come and meet him first. Then I'll show you your rooms." He led them down the hall. "When did you leave London?"

"Before three," Alan replied.

"Good. The M40 can be hell if you leave at five."

Emma barely heard this interchange. She was too taken up with gazing around her at the central hall, with its dark paneled walls, long narrow windows, and minstrel's gallery.

"This was the original Elizabethan hall," Martin said, seeing her interest. "The rest of the house was developed around it. It's a bit of a hodgepodge, I'm afraid. Not exactly a stately home, but for an old house it's remarkably comfortable, and my father loves it."

"And you?" The question was out before Emma could stop it.

His rather thin mouth twisted into a wry grimace. He paused in front of one of the larger doors off the hall, his hand on the brass latch. "At times, I suppose you could call it a love-hate relationship. I'm the estate manager, the agent. I love the place when I have it to myself, which is much of the time, thank God."

Behind Martin, Emma met Alan's eyes and hastily looked away. She had obviously caught Martin Holbrooke on a sore point. As he opened the door and stood aside to let them in, she was relieved to see that he appeared totally unruffled.

Emma had expected the room to be filled with people. Wasn't that usual for country houses at the weekend? But the room contained only one man, who rose from the leather armchair by the fire to greet them.

She recognized Sir Julian immediately. His was one of the most famous faces in England. But she was surprised to see that he was only a few inches taller than she was. All his films—even the time she had seen him in live theater, as Coriolanus—had given her the impression of great height.

In fact, she was disappointed. Although his dark hair was graying at the sides, he was still handsome, a hint of sexual arrogance in the aquiline nose, the winged eyebrows. But, otherwise, he appeared quite ordinary. Dressed in corduroy trousers and a thick-knit cardigan of burgundy red, he could have been your average squire of the manor.

A look of surprise had come over his face when he saw her. Perhaps he had expected someone older. Then Martin Holbrooke introduced them, and Sir Julian spoke.

"Welcome to Marsden Court, Miss Turner." The voice was warm and resonant, like a cello. His hand clasped hers in a firm handshake that sent a jolt of energy through her. "Did you have a good journey?" Although the question was addressed to both of them, Sir Julian was looking only at her.

Emma let Alan answer, but she was aware of Julian Holbrooke's intent gaze still upon her as she sat down by the fire. She was used to men finding her attractive, but Sir Julian's constant glances at her as he exchanged pleasantries with Alan were disconcerting. Downright rude, really. She pointedly turned away to look about the room.

Shelves lined with books, dark oak paneling, the darkness alleviated by the light carpeting and the ivory and eau-de-nil striped fabric on the sofa. The room had a comfortable, lived-in look, enhanced by the presence of an old spaniel spread out on the hearth.

"So, does my library meet with your approval, Miss Turner?" Sir Julian asked, drawing her back to the conversation. He flashed a smile at her. She had the feeling he was challenging her to meet his gaze, that her deliberate avoidance both amused and puzzled him.

"Very much so. I don't think there's anything I'd

want to change." She smiled back at Sir Julian but was surprised to see his smile fade in response. Was her dislike that obvious?

"Drinks for the weary travelers, I think, Martin," he said to his son, an edge to his voice.

"Good idea," Martin said, and strolled to the drinks table, which was laid out with a tray of glasses and filled decanters. "What can I get you, Miss Turner?"

"Would you think me a pain if I asked for a cup of tea? And please call me Emma."

"Emma it is. And tea it shall be." Martin started for the door.

"Ring the bell for Mrs. Pennington. Ring the—"

But Martin, ignoring his father, left the room.

"I am sorry to be such a nuisance," Emma said to Sir Julian. "We didn't have time to stop for tea on the way."

"My fault, I'm afraid," Alan said. "Once I'm driving, I hate to have to stop."

"I am the same way. What car do you drive?"

The conversation moved to cars and their respective mileage until Martin reappeared, bearing a large tea tray. He was followed by a stout woman in a navy blue silk dress with a white lace collar.

"Couldn't get you just a cup of tea, I'm afraid," Martin said, grinning at Emma. "This is Mrs. Pennington, our housekeeper and general majordomo."

"Cup of tea! More like a mug, if you had your way, Mr. Martin. Cup of tea! I should think not, indeed." She spoke with a pleasant country accent, the vowels broadened. "Tea at Marsden Court will be served properly, with freshly made scones and cakes."

Sir Julian's fingers tapped impatiently on the back of his chair. "And a bell should be used to summon you, I think you will agree, Mrs. Pennington."

"Quite right, Sir Julian. You should have rung the bell, Mr. Martin."

"Not me," Martin said good-naturedly. "Not while I've got two good legs to carry me to the kitchen."

Emma was beginning to wish she'd never mentioned tea.

As he was passing by her chair, having handed Alan the whiskey he had asked for, Martin bent down. "There's an automatic tea-making machine in your room."

She grinned at him. "I'll remember that next time."

She looked up to find Sir Julian's eyes upon them. Even from across the hearth, she caught their brilliance. She knew, from his films, that his eyes were arresting, but it was the intensity of his gaze, that smoldering look, that disturbed her.

She lifted her chin. That was all she needed, to be pursued all weekend by a sixty-year-old actor who probably wouldn't take no for an answer. Not much chance of rapport with one's client here!

For a while they talked about the restoration of Marsden Court. "Desmond Parmenter did a marvelous job with it," Sir Julian said. "You should have seen it when I bought it. Absolutely falling down, wasn't it, Martin?"

"I hardly remember. I was away at university at the time. I just remember workmen all over the place whenever I came home and never being sure where I was going to sleep."

When, at last, they began talking about the proposed new plans, Emma entered the conversation, at the same time managing to put away a scone with thick cream and homemade strawberry jam and a slice of lemon sponge cake, washed down with three cups of tea.

When they reached a welcome pause in the conversation, she stood up. "If you'll excuse me, I'd like to freshen up." She turned to Martin. "I take it we change for dinner." She glanced down at her rust-brown wool pants.

"Father prefers that we do."

Sir Julian sprang to his feet. He was far more agile than her father was. But then her father's life had been, of necessity, far more sedentary than Sir Julian's. No doubt all that horseback riding and fencing had kept him supple.

"If Martin had his way, Miss Turner, we'd slop around in jeans all the time," he said dryly. "But please feel free to dress as you please. What you have on at the moment is most attractive." His smile shut out the other two men, as if he and she were the only people in the room.

"Perhaps we should wait until we've seen the barn before we change," Alan suggested.

"Yes, that's a good idea." Like Alan, Emma was eager to get on with work. That was why they were here, after all.

Sir Julian waved the long-fingered hands that reminded Emma of an El Greco grandee. "No, no. It's almost dark outside. Wait until tomorrow. Let us spend a relaxed evening, getting to know one another."

Alan gave him a tight smile. "As you wish, Sir Julian. I thought we might make a preliminary examination tonight." He glanced at the drawn curtains. "But, as you say, it is getting dark. Perhaps we could discuss it over dinner. You could tell us exactly what you have in mind."

"And you will promptly tell me that it is impossible." Sir Julian laughed. "At least, if you will forgive me for saying so, you will be easier to deal with than Desmond Parmenter. He wouldn't even listen to what I had to say."

Alan's smile was a little more natural this time. "But you are pleased with what he did."

"Immensely." Sir Julian looked about him. "How could I be otherwise? It is a beautiful house, is it not?" His expression was that of a deeply enamored lover.

It was Emma who answered this rhetorical question. "It is. I must admit I was concerned that the interior couldn't possibly match the exterior, but it does."

Sir Julian turned eagerly to her. "I am particularly pleased that *you* approve of it, Miss Turner."

This really was a bit much, considering they had met only a short while ago. Embarrassed and annoyed by his effusive attention, particularly in front of Alan, she turned to Martin Holbrooke.

But Sir Julian was at her elbow, so close she caught the potent aroma of his cologne. "Mrs. Pennington shall take you to your room, Miss Turner," he said before she could say anything. "Take your time. We don't dine until eight." He looked at the gold watch on his thin wrist. "So, shall we say, seven-thirty for cocktails?"

She nodded. "Seven-thirty it is," she said briskly, striving to establish herself as a businesswoman rather than an object to be admired for its appearance, like one of the delicate porcelain bowls on his shelves.

He took her hand. She could have sworn he was about to kiss it, had she not turned it to grip his in a handshake. His eyes were on her face again, in that intense, almost wistful look she had caught several times since she had arrived. Then he turned away and strode down the hall, lithe as a man half his age.

Martin raised his eyebrows. "My father's really taken to you," he told Emma. "Haven't seen him quite so smitten for a long time."

Emma grimaced. "Oh, dear."

"Can't say I blame him," Alan said.

Emma was acutely embarrassed. It was the sort of comment men felt they must make, but coming from Alan, it didn't ring true, especially as she could tell he was puzzled by her unfriendly response to Sir Julian. "Would you show us our rooms, Martin? We don't really need to bother Mrs. Pennington."

He sighed. "Sorry about that. The older he gets, the

more old-fashioned he becomes. Mind you, a lot of it is playing the lord of the manor. It's his favorite role. He's not half as bad when he's away from here."

He led the way up the wide, oak-paneled staircase. Their bags stood on the landing. "Your rooms are next to each other."

"Thanks," Alan said. "Is it permissible for us to, ah, enter each other's rooms—strictly for conference purposes, of course—or does an alarm bell summon Mrs. Pennington from her parlor if we do?"

Emma frowned at Alan. Was he deliberately trying to imply that they were more than business colleagues or just trying to warn Martin Holbrooke off? Whichever it was, she didn't appreciate it. She was perfectly capable of protecting herself.

Too capable.

Alan met her scowl with his own dark look. "In fact, I'd like a word with you, Emma, if you don't mind."

"If you don't mind, I'd like a moment to go to the loo first."

Martin looked from one to the other of them. "Well, I'll leave you, then. You can toss a coin for the bedrooms. One's the blue room, the other's the green. Both have their own bathroom, so it's merely a color preference."

"Thanks," she and Alan said in unison.

"If you need anything, just ring. Or you can find me or Mrs. Pennington downstairs somewhere."

Emma picked up her case.

"Shall I carry it into your room?" Martin asked her.

"No thanks. I can manage."

"Okay." She liked the fact that he didn't argue with her. "Try to make yourselves at home." Martin grinned at her. "You'll be glad to hear the lord of the manor act eases off after a while."

As soon as Martin had gone back downstairs, Emma picked up her case and went into the room nearest her. It was delightful, light and airy, with jade-green-and-cream covers and curtains. "I get the green room," she announced.

"I want to talk to you," Alan said.

"I know you do. Give me ten minutes." Without waiting for a reply, she shut the door on him.

If the case hadn't been so heavy, she would have slung it across the room. She had been here less than an hour, yet already everything seemed to be going wrong.

She went into the bathroom, which was old-fashioned but well fitted, with all the comforts a bathroom should have: deep bathtub, mahogany toilet seat, piles of big, fluffy towels, a heated towel rail, an overhead heater. Really, Desmond and Francesca had done a superb job with the house. She had seen the before-and-after pictures. The house had been in an appalling condition before they began.

When she went back into the bedroom, she felt a little calmer. She just had time to brush her hair and dash on some lipstick before Alan knocked on the door.

"Come in," she shouted. "It's not locked."

He came in. "Nice room. Smaller than mine."

She sat down on the edge of the bed. "That's only right, considering you're the boss."

He stood in the center of the room, his height making it seem even smaller. "What's the matter with you?"

"What do you mean?"

"I've never seen you like this before. I thought you liked the place at first, but you've been on edge ever since we came into the house."

She looked away, running her fingers over the raised design of green-and-gold leaves and flowers on the duvet cover. "Probably end-of-the-week blahs."

"Well, you'd better snap out of it or you won't get this commission. Sir Julian might be smitten with you, but you certainly don't like him . . . and it shows all too clearly."

"He gives me the creeps."

"For God's sake, Emma, don't throw this chance away because of some whim."

"I'm sorry. But haven't you noticed how he leers at me? Every time I look at him, I find him watching me."

Alan sighed. "You're a beautiful woman. Why shouldn't the man look at you if he wants to?"

"He's old enough to be my father."

Alan didn't try to hide his impatience. "So what? That doesn't mean he can't look, does it?"

"You don't understand. It's impossible to explain. He just makes me feel extremely uncomfortable."

"Sometimes I think I'll never understand women nowadays. They complain if you don't look at them. And they complain if you *do*."

"It's the way he looks at me, that's all." Emma wished she had kept her mouth shut.

"You should be flattered. He's still a very handsome man. He can probably have his pick of any woman he wants."

"Would you like me to sleep with your precious Sir Julian, just so he will give me the commission?"

Alan just looked at her, shaking his head slowly. Emma suddenly felt very tired. Damn, damn, damn. This was so unlike her. She was screwing everything up. "I'm sorry, Alan. That was a really stupid thing to say." She ran her fingers through her hair. "I'll be fine once I've showered and changed, I promise."

He came to her then, sat down on the bed beside her and put his arm around her shoulders. She tried not to tense up at the unexpectedness of it. "This adoption thing is really getting to you, isn't it?"

"I suppose it is." She summoned up a smile but looked away when she saw how close his face was to hers. "I promise to make nice to Sir Julian from now on."

"Not too nice. Sleeping with famous actors isn't part of your job description."

Nor, apparently, with the boss, she was tempted to add. She'd missed her chance that night at his flat. One move from her was all it had needed, but virginal Emma couldn't make that move. She stood up. "I'm going to have a long, hot shower."

"Wish you luck. These old houses are notorious for their showers—or lack of them."

But the shower was more than adequate. By the time she had dried herself and sprayed on some Ysatis, she was feeling a thousand times better, ready to fend off a dozen aging actors in the most charming manner.

She was tempted to put on her denim skirt, just to annoy Sir Julian, but she had Alan to think of—and her job. So she put on one of her favorite dresses, a simple short-skirted black velvet with puffed sleeves and a scalloped, low-cut neckline. A mixture of innocence and sexiness, it was a wonderful foil for her red-gold hair and golden skin. Just right for Alan. Not so good for Sir Julian.

And Martin Holbrooke? Until now, she hadn't considered Martin as a possible admirer. He was attractive, in an informal, laid-back way, but she had seen him more as an ally, a possible friend. She was sure they would laugh at the same jokes. Certainly he seemed to share her dislike of the pretentious.

Once she had dressed, she knocked on Alan's door, but there was no reply. Assuming he had gone down already, she went to the staircase.

To her annoyance, Sir Julian was waiting for her, alone, at the foot of the stairs.

She had to admit he looked magnificent. The evening jacket of burgundy velvet set off his dark good looks perfectly. It was too bad that the old costume movies were no longer popular. He would have been wonderful in the swashbuckling Stewart Granger roles.

"Forgive me for waylaying you, Miss Turner, but I have an apology to make, and I wanted to do it while we were alone."

"An apology, Sir Julian? For what?"

"For making an ass of myself earlier, staring at you.

You must have been thinking I was behaving like a bloody idiot." He flashed his charming smile at her.

"Not at all. Why should I?"

"You're not a very good liar, you know."

She was about to give him a heated answer, when their eyes met. Unless he was employing his unique acting ability, she saw no artifice there, only wry amusement.

"Admit it. You were very annoyed, weren't you? I haven't been a keen observer of people all these years for nothing, you know. Actors are dangerous people. Like writers, they are always observing the actions of others, even when they themselves are emotionally involved. It's a despicable trait."

"Oh, all right," Emma said, "I will admit it, then. The way you kept looking at me did make me feel uncomfortable. I mean, it's very flattering to think you might find me attractive, but—"

His mouth quirked into a smile. "Is it, Miss Turner? An old man like me?"

Now he really was flirting with her, but in an open, fun way that both of them could enjoy.

"Yes, Sir Julian. You may be old enough to be my father, but you are definitely an attractive man."

She found, to her surprise, that she really meant it.

"Now we're both beginning to talk in clichés. And I regret that my explanation for staring at you is also something of a cliché. Simply put, you reminded me very strongly of a woman—a girl, really—I once loved."

"In your youth?" she asked, half teasing.

"A long time ago, certainly. Seeing you was quite a shock. She had red hair, too, you see."

She saw now that he was utterly serious. "I'm sorry," she said. "What happened to her?"

"I went to Hollywood."

She waited for more, but he was silent. It sounded something like *The Student Prince*. Actor meets red-haired waitress. Actor goes to Hollywood. End of love affair.

"But what happened to her?"

He looked at her as if she were someone he had never seen before. "Who?"

"Your red-haired love?"

"I have no idea. When I came home, she had gone away. I never saw her again."

"How very sad, but also very romantic. Like all the best love stories."

"And like all the best love stories, ours didn't last very long, I'm afraid. But your resemblance to her was quite a shock. For a moment, I thought it was her walking into my library." He took her hand in his. "Tell me I'm forgiven."

She drew her hand away gently. "Of course you're forgiven."

"We'd better go in or your Mr. Grenville will think I'm attempting to seduce you."

"I very much doubt it," she said dryly. "He told me off earlier for behaving so badly to you."

"Did he? Did he really?" He looked delighted at the thought. "We could play a wonderful little game on him and Martin, couldn't we? I could continue to be a leering devil and you could get nastier and nastier with me. What fun we could have with them!"

"It might be fun for you, but I have my job to think of, remember? So kindly behave."

Was this really the same man she had disliked so much? Here she was, telling the great Sir Julian Holbrooke, star of stage and screen, to behave, and he was beaming delightedly at her.

"What a spoilsport! All right. I promise to behave. After all, I must keep my interior designer happy, mustn't I?"

Her heart skipped a beat. "I should hope so. Otherwise

I shall decorate your guest quarters with chrome and yellow-and-purple plastic."

"Perish the thought. Talking about perish, you must be perished yourself, standing out here in this drafty hall. Come on in and have a drink. Then we'll start all over again, and this time we shall get to know each other properly."

16

The following morning, Emma awoke with the pulsing excitement that signaled the anticipation of something special. She jumped out of bed and padded to the window, drawing back the curtains.

The leaded casement window overlooked the gardens at the rear. Immediately below her was a flagged terrace, with steps leading down to the lawn and rose garden. Everything was dormant now, the bushes wet with the dew that sparkled in the pale gold sunlight, but her imagination conjured up a vision of the standard roses and floribundas in full bloom, filling the air with their sweet scent.

She smiled to herself. Really, she was in a strangely buoyant mood. It was a long time since she had felt quite so positive about life. On a day like this, surely anything—and everything—was possible.

She heard voices and saw Alan's fair head and Martin Holbrooke's dark one below her. She pushed the window open wider. "Hi! Is it as warm as it looks out there?"

They smiled up at her. "Good morning," Martin said.

"You'll need a sweater or jacket," Alan said. His hair shone in the sunlight.

"Hang on. I'll be down in a couple of minutes."

Not waiting for their reply, she ran into the bathroom, washed, brushed her teeth, ran back into the room, scrabbled in her case for clean underwear, a pair of jeans, her bulky mohair sweater, a pair of trainers, and dragged them all on. A dash of lipstick, and she was ready.

When she reached the terrace, she found Alan leaning against the wrought-iron railing, hands deep in the pockets of his brown leather jacket.

"Good morning again," he said.

"It's more than good. It's a glorious morning." Emma lifted her hair from her neck and felt the autumn breeze cool against the back of her neck.

"If you like it this cold. Personally, I prefer it a little warmer." Alan sounded disgruntled, which wasn't like him.

"Shall we take a look at the barn?" she suggested, knowing that work would soon put him in a good mood.

"I had already made that suggestion to Martin, but—"

"My father gave strict instructions that nothing should be seen or discussed until he is present," Martin explained with a rueful grin.

"Oh, dear." She gave him a sympathetic smile.

"It's okay, you know," he said quietly. "Nine months out of twelve I get to run the place the way I want. Anyway, I can't say I blame him. These are important additions to the estate. Not to be gone into lightly."

"If at all," Alan said from the lawn, having gone down the steps to study the rear view of the house.

"Alan's worried that a conservatory would spoil the line of the house," Emma explained to Martin.

"Ah, I see. Well, we'd better not even discuss it until my father's down. He's not usually an early riser. Why don't we go in and have some breakfast first?"

"I was hoping for a short walk before breakfast."

"Why don't you and Alan go for a walk? I'll meet you in the breakfast parlor in fifteen minutes. Okay?"

"Fine," Alan said. He muttered something beneath his breath as Martin went into the house.

"Pardon?" Emma said, coming down the steps.

"Nothing. You like it here, don't you?"

She looked at him, astonished at the question. "Of course I do, don't you?"

He started off across the dewy lawn. "Not really," he said over his shoulder. "I suppose I'm an urban type. I find the country house atmosphere a trifle precious, like one of those Frederic Lonsdale's plays on the telly, if you know what I mean."

Emma broke into a little run to catch up with him. "If you mean Sir Julian, I thought he really mellowed last night after dinner, didn't you?"

"You mean *you* mellowed towards him. What happened to make you change your mind about him?"

"Your warning, for one. Besides, I really want this commission, Alan. The publicity would be fantastic. I'd do anything to get it." She met his eyes. "Well, almost anything," she added with a laugh.

As they strode across the lawn and into the little copse beyond it, she wanted to tuck her hand into his arm. It was a heavenly autumn morning, the air filled with the scent of woodsmoke. In a clearing, a gardener was piling branches onto a bonfire that glowed red, sending its fragrant smoke into the air. From the branch of a sycamore tree, a thrush trilled its piercing song.

Had Alan been relaxed, Emma would have been utterly content. But he was not. She could feel his tension, as if it were steel wire surrounding him. Strange that a man who loved old buildings should feel uneasy in such a beautiful place.

Alan halted and turned back to survey the house.

"Holbrooke was right when he called it a hodgepodge," he said. "Bits added on here and there, three gables on one side, two the other. Oriel window on the left, bay on the right. But, by God, it's beautiful."

"I thought you didn't like it."

"The house is superb. It's the inmates I'm not so keen on."

"Sir Julian, you mean."

"Sir Julian and the 'incredibly efficient' Mrs. Pennington," he said, aping Martin's public school accent, "and the altogether amiable Martin Holbrooke."

"I like Martin."

"Good for you." He was about to add something but decided against it.

"It sounds to me as if you need some food," she said. "Let's go in for breakfast."

He smiled at her. "I am a bad-tempered bastard this morning, aren't I? Sorry about that. Don't mean to be."

To Emma's delight, he took her hand and drew it through his arm, pressing it against his side, and they strolled in companionable silence back to the house.

The breakfast parlor was easy to find, just to the left of the terrace entrance: a sunny room, well lit by three large windows.

Sir Julian was already seated at the head of the table.

"Before you complain about these windows being inappropriate for this house," was his greeting when they went in, "I must assure you that they were added long before I bought the house. Despite Parmenter's advice, I decided to keep them. If there is any sun to be had in England, I want it shining on me whilst I eat my breakfast."

Seeing the rays of sunlight slanting across the table, striking the silver chafing dishes on the sideboard, Emma was inclined to agree with him. "I can't say I blame you."

Alan remained by the doorway. "I trust we haven't kept you waiting, Sir Julian."

To Emma's ears, his words sounded stilted, far too formal, particularly at breakfast time.

"Not at all. Come in, come in. Help yourself to

whatever you please." Sir Julian leaned forward to ring the bell that stood on the table. Almost immediately, a maid dressed in black dress and white apron came in.

"Yes, sir?"

"Fresh tea and coffee, Jenny. And where is Mr. Martin?"

"He was in the study when I saw him last, but—"

"I'm here." Martin strolled in. "Morning, Father. You're up at the crack of dawn today." To Emma's surprise, he bent to kiss his father's cheek.

"At least I'm here to greet our guests."

As Martin made no reply to his father's rebuke, Emma spoke for him. "Martin was showing us the grounds earlier."

Sir Julian frowned. "Not the barn, I trust."

Again Emma sprang to Martin's defense. "No. He said you'd prefer to show us that yourself."

"Good, good. I want to talk about it before we go to see it. Help yourself to breakfast, Miss Turner. Or are you one of these women who don't eat breakfast?"

"Not a bit. I like the works."

He waved his hand at the sideboard. "Well, my dear, there you have the works. Porridge, the best Scottish kippers, scrambled eggs . . . you name it, we've got it," he said, lapsing into the cockney accent of a London barrow boy, "or if we 'aven't, we can cook up whatever you want."

"I'm going to start with some muesli," Emma said, laughing. She turned to Alan, who was hovering between table and sideboard, his face stiff. "What about you, Alan?"

"Unlike everyone else, it seems, I'm not a breakfast eater."

"You're not alone," Martin said. "I can't stand the thought of porridge and kippers first thing in the morning, however well cooked. Must be all those ghastly breakfasts at Winchester."

He dragged a ladder-backed chair from the table and

sat down. "Make yourself comfortable." He nodded to
the chair beside his. "Jenny's bringing fresh coffee. I can
recommend the croissants. How about a newspaper?"
He nodded at the pile of papers on a side table.

"Times, Telegraph, Independent?" Sir Julian asked.

"The *Independent,* I think," Alan replied. "If it's
available." He stood awkwardly by the chair and then
went to fetch the newspaper from the pile.

"I always order in extra copies when I have guests
staying," Sir Julian said. "There's nothing worse than
having to wait for someone to finish your chosen paper.
How about you, Miss Turner? What would you like to
read?"

"I don't mind. Whatever's available."

As they settled down to their various breakfasts, reading the morning papers, Emma felt very much at home.
She smiled to herself at the thought that in most English
homes, from a semidetached in Kilburn to Buckingham
Palace, this was the way most people began their day,
especially at the weekend.

Sir Julian broke the silence. "There's something
about Richard Reid's new civic offices in Epping in
today's *Times.* What's your opinion of his work,
Grenville?"

Alan relaxed visibly. It was as if Sir Julian's question
had put him back on his own turf. Emma buttered
another piece of crisp toast and spread it with thick-cut
marmalade, content to listen to Alan's lucid and infor-
mative answers to Sir Julian's questions.

She was not at all surprised by Alan's ability to make
what could be a difficult subject accessible to the layman.
What did surprise her was Sir Julian's knowledge of
architecture. He moved easily from the classical
architect Quinlan Terry to postmodernist Terry Farrell's
Charing Cross and back again.

"And what is the interior designer's opinion of the
famous—and fashionable—Quinlan Terry?" he asked her.

"I think his Richmond development is marvelous," she said, her mouth still full of toast. She swallowed it down and took a gulp of tea. "He's resurrected the lovely Georgian part of the town in an area that was an utter mess. But, on the other hand—"

"Richmond." Sir Julian set down his cup slowly. "It's a very long time since I was there."

"Emma lives in Richmond," Alan explained.

Sir Julian turned his blue eyes on Emma. "You live in Richmond?"

"Yes, we have a flat on Richmond Hill, actually."

"We?"

"My father and I." How strangely he was looking at her, as if she were transparent. "My father is a solicitor," she felt compelled, for some reason, to explain.

"A solicitor." His slender fingers drummed on the polished table. "What is his name?"

"Richard Turner."

The fingers ceased their drumming. "Richard Turner."

Martin noisily folded up his copy of the *Guardian*. "Well, I think it's time we—"

"Be silent," his father barked.

Martin grimaced. "Sorry I spoke. I didn't think Emma would feel like an interrogation over breakfast."

Sir Julian's tongue darted out to moisten his lips. "I have an important reason for asking."

"I don't mind," Emma said, giving Martin a reassuring smile. She was mesmerized by Sir Julian's face, with its El Greco cheekbones and bright blue eyes.

"Your father has his offices in Richmond, I gather?"

"Yes. Near Richmond Green."

Sir Julian released a small sigh. "Ah, yes. The Green. And . . . your mother?"

"My mother died almost a year ago."

"For God's sake, Father."

Sir Julian ignored Martin. His eyes were fixed on Emma's, as if she were the only other person in the room. "Forgive me, Miss Turner, but what was your mother's name?"

"Mary. Mary Turner."

Another small sigh. This time one of relief, it seemed, for he gave her a flickering smile.

His hand reached out to pick up the bell.

"Actually, she was my adoptive mother."

The bell was in his hand, its clapper already tinkling against the side, although he had not yet rung it. Slowly he set it down again.

"You were adopted?"

Now it was Alan's turn to intercede. "I am sure that Sir Julian would agree that it's not necessary for you to answer such personal questions, Emma."

Sir Julian spoke only to her. "I beg you, Miss Turner. Your answers to my questions are of vital importance to me. Perhaps, even, to you."

"Forgive me, Sir Julian," Alan said, "but I really cannot see how Emma's personal life is any of your concern."

"I agree," Martin said. "In fact, I'd call it bloody rude."

Sir Julian totally ignored them. "I would like to speak alone with you," he said to her.

Emma felt very cold, yet at the same time she could feel her face flaming, as it did when she was under stress. She got up and went to Alan. "Give us a few minutes alone together," she said quietly. "I don't mind, really I don't."

"Are you absolutely sure? Because you don't need—"

"Absolutely."

Sir Julian was already on his feet. Without another word he led the way from the breakfast room into the library.

He motioned to her to sit down but began speaking even before she had done so. "You say you were adopted. Have you any idea who your true parents were?"

"Not until recently. I knew I was adopted, of course, but whenever I asked questions about my birth parents, my mother got so upset I just dropped the subject. You see, she was ill with multiple sclerosis for a long time. It wasn't until last year, when she died, that I felt free to ask my father who my true parents were."

"And he told you?"

"He told me my birth mother's name and where she was. He absolutely refused to tell me who my father was."

"Your birth mother. May I ask who she was?"

"Helen. Helen Lawrence now, but her maiden name was Barstow. She lived in—"

"Petersham. She lived in Petersham. Lansdowne House." The words came in a whisper, so that she could barely hear them above the crackle of the fire and the old spaniel's snoring.

Their eyes met . . . and held. She did not ask him how he knew where Helen Barstow had lived. It was enough for her that he knew.

His eyes filled with tears. "She went away without telling me where she had gone. I searched everywhere for her. I never knew . . ."

She did not go to him. It was all too much like a dream to be real. Soon she would wake up and find herself in her own bed in her room at Richmond. She longed for her father. He would make everything real again.

Sir Julian took out a white linen handkerchief and blew his nose. "I know it's almost impossibly coincidental, but I believe you are my daughter." He flashed her an embarrassed smile. "If I read this in a play script, I would say, 'What balls!' and toss it aside as being far too melodramatic for words."

He waited for her reaction, but she was too numb to give him any.

"Have you nothing to say to me?" he asked sadly.

"A million questions are tearing around in my brain. The only one I can think of is, How can you be sure?"

"Very well. I shall respond by asking *you* questions. First of all, when were you born?"

"May the twenty-first, 1962."

He thought for a moment. "Yes, that fits exactly. We, ah, slept together in August 1961."

"Only once?" she asked, surprised.

"Twice, actually. I went away to Hollywood after that."

"Leaving her pregnant? My poor mother."

"I knew nothing about it. About you, I mean. I thought—" He stopped, apparently embarrassed.

"She wouldn't tell me who you were."

"Who wouldn't?"

"My mother. My birth mother. Helen."

He sprang up from his chair. "Christ in heaven. You mean she's alive? You've spoken to her, to Helen?"

"A few times. Why shouldn't she be alive? She's not that old, after all. About forty-nine, I think my—my father said she was." She hesitated, suddenly aware of the different relationship she now shared with this stranger who stood across the hearth from her. "She lives in Canada now."

"You have never met her, then?"

"No." Emma looked into the fire. "Nor am I ever likely to, either. She doesn't want to meet me."

"What the devil do you mean, she doesn't want to meet you?"

"What I say." For the first time in this strange conversation, Emma felt tears stinging her eyes. "My call upset her. I think she's terrified of her husband finding out about her having had me before they were married."

"Bloody hell." Eyes bright with anger, he paced up and down the length of the library, then came to a halt in front of Emma. "You mean to tell me that you telephoned her in Canada, said you were her daughter, and she told you to get lost?"

She managed a faint smile. "Not exactly in those words. She was quite kind. I could tell how upset she was. At first I felt sorry for her, but then . . ." Emma shrugged.

"I find this impossible to believe. It doesn't sound like the Helen I knew at all."

"People change over the years. Circumstances change them. She has a new life, a husband, grown-up children now. She never told them about me. Acknowledging me would cause her a great deal of pain and embarrassment, I suppose."

He came to her then. Sank on his knees before her. Gently took her face in one hand and turned it to his. His face wavered as she looked at him through eyes brimming with tears.

"Her rejection has hurt you deeply, hasn't it?"

She nodded, her tears splashing onto his hand.

He pulled the wine-colored handkerchief from his blazer pocket. "This one's clean," he said, smiling. With infinite gentleness he mopped her face and eyes. When he had finished, he took both her hands tightly in his. "Darling Emma, I promise I shan't reject you. I shall be happy to tell the world that I have a beautiful daughter."

But I already have a father, she felt like crying out.

He released her hands and stood up. "The first thing I am going to do is phone Helen. She must face up to her responsibilities as your true mother."

Now Emma sprang up. "No, no, you mustn't phone her. I promised I wouldn't bother her again."

He picked up the phone. "Do you know the number?"

She knew it by heart, of course. "I don't think we should do this. Her husband could be home."

"That's too bad. She should have been kinder to you when you called her the first time." Then, seeing her patent anxiety, "Don't worry, darling. I'll be the soul of tact. But she has to face up to reality, you must agree with me there. She has to acknowledge her firstborn child. What is the number?"

Emma told him.

"Good." He took out his gold pen from his blazer pocket and wrote it down in the leather telephone book. "Come here, beside me." She went to stand by him, looking down at the boldly written *Helen*, underlined three times in thick, black strokes.

He looked down at the name. "I don't think I shall ever be able to forgive her for not telling me about you," he said softly.

17

Helen was asleep when the telephone rang in the bedroom. The noise shocked her awake. As she jumped out of bed, she glanced at the clock. Who on earth would be calling her at three-thirty in the morning?

She got the phone on the third ring. "Hallo?" She spoke in a whisper, hoping to avoid waking Bruce, who was stirring, groaning something about "damned phone."

"Hallo. Is this Helen?" demanded a male voice.

Her face flamed. She held the receiver away, staring at it, tempted to yank the cord from the wall. But there were three extensions in the house. If he rang again . . .

"Hallo, hallo," the voice shouted.

She put the receiver to her ear. "I have to go to another phone," she said in a loud whisper. Glancing at Bruce, she saw that he had fallen asleep again. Thank God for that, at least.

She began to shiver and couldn't stop. Uncontrollable shaking that made her teeth click together. She grabbed the sweater she had worn yesterday and dragged it on. Then she ran downstairs and picked up the telephone in the den, her heart beating so frantically she could barely breathe.

"Where the devil is she?" the voice was saying to someone else.

"I'm here," Helen said. "Do you realize the time?"

"I do now. I didn't when I first called. Sorry about that, but it wouldn't have stopped me anyway. You know who this is?"

Of course she did. How could she mistake those peremptory tones for anyone but Julian?

"All I know is that you have woken me and my husband up at three-thirty in the morning."

"Emma is here with me," he said, totally ignoring what she had said.

"Emma?" she repeated as if she had never heard the name before.

"Yes, Emma. For Christ's sake, Helen, stop playing games. This is too important for that. Why the hell didn't you tell me I had a daughter? All these years and you never let me know. And don't tell me you didn't know how to get in touch with me, either. Anyone connected with the theater could have told you."

The furious tirade crashed down the line.

"I didn't tell you because I didn't think you'd be interested."

"Didn't think I'd be interested in my own child? Jesus Christ, Helen. To have a child, abandon her to strangers, and then callously forget all about her, without even telling her father? *You're* the one who wasn't interested, not me. You just plain didn't care."

Something exploded in Helen's head. "*I* didn't care? You bloody hypocrite!" she screamed. "You bloody, bloody hypocrite! It was you who told me to have an abortion. You who abandoned me, left me pregnant and alone, to waltz off to Hollywood, never even trying to find out what had happened to me when you got back. As far as you were concerned, I no longer existed."

"You must be crazy. What about the letter I wrote?"

"Nice try, Julian. You never wrote me one letter. All that time, when I was so alone, I never heard from you."

The den door swung open. Bruce stood in the doorway

in rumpled pajamas. "What the hell is going on? I could hear you shouting all the way up in the bedroom."

Her mind scrabbled for some plausible explanation. "It's my aunt," she hissed at him. "She's very ill."

"So? Why the yelling?"

"Just a minute, Bruce. I'll explain in a minute." She put the receiver to her ear. "I'll make arrangements to come over as soon as possible, Mrs. Harvey."

To her intense relief, Julian understood. "Your husband there?"

"Yes, that's right. I'll call you back tomorrow evening, I mean this evening, your time." She pretended to be listening. "Yes, I realize you didn't understand about the time difference. Sorry I was upset, but it was a shock to be woken up at this time and with bad news."

"I see that you haven't lost your dramatic ability," Julian said, amusement in his voice.

Damn him. How could he possibly find anything amusing in this situation? "I shall be in touch. Good-bye."

She put the phone back on the shelf and stood up. "Sorry I woke you, darling. That was my aunt's housekeeper, Mrs. Harvey. She's stone deaf. That's why I had to shout."

"Sounded like an almighty row from where I was."

Feeling her legs giving way, she hastily sat down again, this time on her own chair. "She was rather snarly about my never having been to see my aunt."

"I've often wondered about that myself. You wouldn't even go and see her when we went to London."

"We never got on, really. She was always a bit of a shrew. Disapproved of everything I did as a teenager. You know the sort." *Forgive me, darling Aunt Hilary.*

Bruce walked over and sat down on his leather chair, which made a *whoosh*ing sound as his large frame settled onto it. "What's all this about going over?"

"Aunt Hilary's very sick. I shall have to go to England, Bruce."

"When?"

"As soon as I can get a booking. I know it'll be expensive, but she's my only relative. I have to go."

"You mean you're going now?" he said incredulously.

"As soon as possible." She avoided looking at him. "The doctor told Mrs. Harvey she may not last very long."

"But what about the merger party?"

Oh, God, the damned merger party. Helen moistened her lips. "I'm very much afraid I won't be there."

"Won't be there?" Bruce exploded. "You and Margery Burrell are the two main hostesses. Wives of the most senior partners of the two firms. You'll have to be there."

Helen lifted her head. "I'm sorry, Bruce. I can't be. You'll have to manage without me or postpone it."

"Postpone it?" His face was scarlet with anger. "How the hell can we postpone it? We've been working on this thing for two years. And now you talk of buggering off to England just because some aunt you don't even like is ill."

"She's my only family. I must go."

"I don't damn well believe this. I'm going to get a drink." Bruce went downstairs to the basement bar.

She couldn't believe it, either. All that had happened since the telephone rang had a sense of the surreal to it.

Even now, facing up to Bruce's anger, she felt apart, remote. She had to admit that his anger was justified, considering how important the merger was to him. The high point of his career. It wasn't that she didn't care. She did. But there were other, even more important things to do now. It was time for her to deal with all the unfinished business of her life. Julian, Aunt Hilary . . . Emma. Especially Emma.

Bruce came back into the den, carrying a glass containing what looked like a double measure of Scotch.

"A bit late—or early, isn't it?" she remarked.

"It'll help me to sleep. That is, if you intend us to get any more sleep tonight."

"Of course. Why don't you go back to bed now?"

"What about you?"

"I don't think I could sleep a wink after that call. Besides, I've a lot of plans to make."

He sat down. "You really mean to go, don't you?"

"I really do. I'm truly sorry that it has come at such a rotten time, darling."

He ran his hand through his hair. "I can't believe this. It's just not like you." He looked bewildered.

She came to him and knelt in front of him, her hands on his knees. "You mean it's just not like me to put myself first. You're right, it's not. But, believe me, Bruce, I would never forgive myself if I didn't do this."

He looked down at her, his expression that of a little boy denied a visit to the circus. "You may change your mind in the morning," he said hopefully.

"No, Bruce, I shan't. I'm going to phone the travel agent in the morning and book my flight. I promise I'll go the cheapest way possible. Probably through Minneapolis and then some cheap charter flight from New York."

"For God's sake, who cares about the cost?" His eyes locked with hers. "What if I told you not to go?"

"Told me?"

His angry expression wavered beneath her bright, dangerous smile and turned to hurt. "Told you, asked you, what the hell's the difference? You're really letting me down, you know."

"I don't mean to. It's just that I have to do this, Bruce. It's extremely important to me."

"Obviously more important than I am."

It wasn't safe to reply to that. Bruce had always been important to her. She could remember the early years when they had laughed a lot and life with him had been exciting. He had always been there for her, solid, caring, and reliable. Until fairly recently, anyway.

God knew what was going on now between him and

this other woman. Was Emma—and the past—more important to her than Bruce? Yes. At this moment, she was. She had given most of her life to Bruce and their family. Only nine months to Emma. It was time for Emma to come first, for a change.

"You're determined to go, then," Bruce said.

"Yes." She got up, levering herself by leaning on his knees. "I am truly sorry." She bent down to kiss him. "Why don't you try to get some sleep? I'm going to make myself a cup of tea."

She left him sitting there contemplating the glass of Scotch in his hand, and went into the kitchen.

He followed her, still holding his glass. Then he set it down on the countertop and put his arm around her shoulders. "I'm sorry about your aunt."

She turned within his arm to lay her head against his chest. "Thank you. And I'm terribly sorry about the party, Bruce. You know I wouldn't do this unless I felt I must, don't you?"

He nodded. For a moment they stood together. Then the kettle boiled.

"I'm going to bed," Bruce said, releasing her. "I've got a heavy schedule tomorrow." He glanced at the kitchen clock and groaned. "Today. It's nearly four o'clock."

"Go on, get back to bed. What time shall I wake you?"

"Seven-thirty. No later than that." He laid his hand against her cheek. "Sure you won't come back to bed, too? You look as if you could do with some more sleep yourself."

"No. Not yet, anyway. My brain's buzzing. I'll feel better once I make a list of all I have to do."

He shuffled off to bed, leaving the unfinished glass of Scotch behind him.

Helen poured boiling water into the teapot and took three wheatmeal biscuits from the biscuit tin.

As she carried the tray of tea and biscuits into the den, she tried to concentrate on Emma, but her mind kept returning to the sickening confrontation with Julian.

Her heart lurched. "Oh, my God, I forgot to get his phone number or address." That meant Julian or Emma would have to call back again.

Thank God Bruce went into the office Saturday mornings!

The telephone rang only twice that morning. Each time she expected to hear Julian's voice at the other end of the line. By noon she was a bundle of nerves, but at least she had everything arranged.

When she had spoken to Julian she had been so upset that she had forgotten it was the weekend. The travel agent wouldn't be open until Monday. But she had managed to make a booking with Air Canada for a flight to London leaving next Tuesday. That would give her time to get organized, but not enough time to rethink her decision to fly to England.

When the expected call at last came, it was Emma, not Julian, on the line. Her tone was reserved, almost frosty. "You rang off before he—we could give you the phone number."

"I was too upset to think straight. Besides, my husband was standing right beside me."

"I'm sorry you were woken in the middle of the night. I tried to tell him, but he—"

"That's all right."

The awkwardness between them was worse than ever. Maybe she was making a huge mistake by flying over.

"He was very upset, too," Emma said. "Julian, I mean."

"So I gathered. More angry than upset, I thought."

"He said he had no idea you'd had a child."

Helen realized then that Emma had heard only Julian's side of the telephone conversation. No wonder she sounded frosty.

"Emma, I'm flying over on Tuesday, arriving

Wednesday morning. I'll explain everything when we get together."

Emma gasped. "You really are coming? We thought you were just saying that for your husband's sake."

"No. It's time I came." Helen hesitated. "I owe you that . . . and much, much more."

"Have you told your husband?"

"No. There's no need for him to know. He thinks I'm going to visit my aunt."

"I see. Have you really got an aunt?"

"Yes, I have." Helen paused, her mind turning over. "Where shall I meet you?"

"Well, he—Sir Julian wanted me to stay here, at Marsden Court, for a few days, but I have too much work to do. I suppose we could meet—"

"Look, Emma," Helen said urgently. "Although I'm dying to see you, I want to be fresh when we meet for the first time, if you know what I mean. I want everything to be just right for us. I think I really will go and visit my aunt in Petersham, stay with her for a couple of days to get over jet lag. Then we can decide where and when we'll meet."

"Your aunt lives in Petersham? But—but that's only a few minutes from Richmond, where I live."

"I know that."

"You mean . . . I've had a blood relative nearby all these years and never knew it."

"Yes, yes. Your great-aunt Hilary. I hope you two will be meeting very soon. Now, when shall we meet?"

"Well, Sir Julian wants me to come to Marsden Court again next weekend."

Helen sighed. She could tell that Emma wanted to go to Marsden Court. No wonder. She'd obviously met with a far warmer reception from her real father than from her mother.

She wondered how Richard felt about all this. Poor Richard. He was probably furious. Although the two men had met only once, she discovered later that Richard had disliked Julian.

"Are you still there?" Emma asked.

"Sorry. I was thinking. Why don't we meet in Richmond, then? Say, on the Friday. That would give me a clear day alone with Aunt Hilary."

"Friday would be fine, but my—Sir Julian is hoping you'll come to Marsden Court for the weekend as well."

Helen almost exploded. "You must be joking."

"I wasn't sure it was such a good idea, either."

"I'm not sure I ever want to see Julian again." Helen was fighting to remain calm.

"Well, I shall be going to Marsden Court on Saturday morning. You see, we—that is, Alan Grenville and I—were down here on a restoration project. As you can imagine, it somehow got shelved after . . . after all this happened."

So that was how it had happened. A sheer fluke. A Dickensian coincidence. Not a result of Emma's digging at all. *I see God's hand in this,* she heard her father say as if he were standing right beside her. "Where is it?" she asked, hurriedly pushing all thought of her father back into the deepest recess of her mind.

"Marsden Court? It's a gorgeous old Jacobean house in Oxfordshire."

So Julian had acquired the beautiful home he had always desired.

"Just a minute." Emma began speaking to someone else.

"Helen, are you there?"

Helen stiffened at the sound of Julian's voice on the line. "Yes."

"Sorry about waking you up. In the excitement of the moment, I completely forgot what time it was over there. Emma tells me you really are flying over. You must come and stay at Marsden. We have a great deal to discuss."

"I have nothing to say to you, Julian. Nothing. It was all said years ago."

"We both owe some sort of explanation to our daughter, at least."

She was about to flare up at him again, then realized that, in a way, he was right. What mattered now was Emma, not the unhappy past. "That's true."

"She's a beautiful girl, Helen. Looks very like you."

Helen blinked back tears. "I'm longing to see her."

"It would make Emma very happy if you were to come here, to Marsden Court." His voice was warm, persuasive.

Helen hesitated. Emma's happiness was now uppermost in her mind. "I'll think about it."

"Good. If you do decide to come, Grenville says he will drive you both down here on the Saturday morning." A moment of hesitation, then he said in a low voice, "Would I recognize you, do you think?"

"I doubt it very much. After all, it's more than thirty years since we last saw each other."

"At least your voice sounds much the same. No hideous American accent to mar its lovely quality. It was your voice I fell in love with first, you know."

"Please put Emma on," she said, anxious to put an end to this maudlin conversation. It reminded her of Katharine Hepburn and Laurence Olivier in *Love Among the Ruins*.

Another short exchange with Emma and it was all arranged. In a matter of a few days she would be making a rendezvous with the past, returning to those places and people she thought she had left behind forever when she had fled to Canada with Ann after Emma was born.

The thought so paralyzed her with fear that for a long time after she had replaced the receiver she was incapable of moving from the chair.

18

By the time Tuesday arrived, Helen was operating mainly on adrenaline. Monday had been a whirlwind of phone calls and packing and stocking up the freezer. It didn't help that her entire family was against this sudden decision to fly to England.

Karen actually came over to tell her that she was out of her mind to be leaving at this time, with Dad under so much stress.

Even David was unsupportive. "I suppose it's your business," he had said with a shrug as if he didn't really care.

"What will you do?" she asked him as she unpacked frozen dinners, piling them up in the basement freezer.

"How long will you be away?"

Helen leaned over the freezer to hide her face from him. "It depends on how my aunt is when I get there."

"So it could be a while?"

She straightened up, rubbing her hands to get the circulation going. "I'm afraid so."

"I'll have to see if I can move back in with Phil."

Any other time she would have pleaded with him to stay, to try to get on with his father, but this time all she said was, "Good idea," and pulled down the freezer door.

They would all have to get on with their lives without her for a while.

The one bright spot in her otherwise frantic Monday had been her brief telephone conversation with Ann.

"Want me to come with you?" had been Ann's half-comic, half-serious reaction.

Helen hesitated for a moment and then said, "No, Annie. This time I must do it by myself."

"Good for you. Go for it, girl. And while you're at it, you can give Julian a punch on the nose from me."

Helen laughed. "He won't have a nose left after I've been there. Seriously, though, Annie, next time I go, you'll be coming with me and we'll have a great time."

"I'll keep you to that. Give Emma a big hug from me. Don't forget to tell her I'm her unofficial godmother."

It was wonderful to speak to someone who knew the real reason for her sudden visit to Britain.

Bruce was her main worry, of course, but her decision to leave almost immediately meant that she had little more than one evening of his sullen mood.

"I've spoken to Magda," she told him, "and she's going to take over all the arrangements for the party for me."

"Magda? Why not Joan?"

"Because Joan's a rotten organizer. Besides, Magda will be in her element."

"I thought you couldn't stand Magda."

"I decided it was safer to have her as a friend than an enemy. Besides, she'll take a load off your shoulders."

Bruce gave her a puzzled look over his copy of the *Globe and Mail*. "I don't know what's happened to you recently. I feel I don't know you anymore."

Helen smiled enigmatically at him across the ironing board. "Maybe you never did know me, Bruce."

By the time the plane landed at Heathrow at seven-thirty Wednesday morning, her body was aching with tiredness, but her mind was still going full tilt. She followed the other passengers to Immigration and then the luggage carousel, glad to stretch her legs. Yet at the same time, she was longing to lie down.

Apart from another call to Emma, she had made no arrangements. As she followed the porter and her bags on his trolley, zigzagging through the crowds, she scanned the sea of faces before her, wondering with a lift of her heart if Emma might be there to meet her.

Then she remembered that she'd told Emma she would be seeing her aunt first, allowing herself time to settle in before the big reunion with her daughter . . . and, if she could find the strength for it, Julian.

But Aunt Hilary knew nothing about her arrival. Should she call her first, to avoid it being too much of a shock for her?

"Want a taxi, love?" the porter asked her.

The strange yet familiar cockney accent, the milling throng, the constant announcements, the hurried pace—all assaulted her, so that she felt light-headed for a moment.

"D'you want a taxi?" the porter repeated impatiently.

"Yes. Yes, I do." Shock or not, she wanted to be able to see Aunt Hilary's expression when she opened the door.

It wasn't until she was bowling along the Great West Road in the high-roofed black taxi—so many cars, and where was the old Firestone Building?—that she suddenly thought, What if Aunt Hilary isn't at home? What if she's sick? Or away visiting someone?

If she isn't there, she answered herself resolutely, I shall go and stay in one of those swanky hotels on Richmond Hill that we could never have afforded in the old days.

Or she could even call Emma.

The thought made her light-headed again.

No, no. Much as she ached to see Emma as soon as possible, she must get her bearings first, recover from jet lag. Most of all, she had to discover what it was like to be set down in her old surroundings thirty years later, like someone in a time warp.

Her excitement at seeing the old familiar places increased as the taxi drove along the Petersham road. Little had changed. There was the Dysart Arms, where Julian had taken her for their first drink together. And there River Lane, where he had first kissed her. A tide of warmth swept over her face as she remembered the response of her innocent yet eager seventeen-year-old self.

When the taxi turned into her road, she leaned forward, anxious to catch her first glimpse of Lansdowne House since she had fled from it.

But as the taxi turned into the driveway, Helen felt a sudden sense of foreboding. This was not the same lovely house she remembered. Weeds had sprung up in the gravel driveway, and the curving flower beds were overgrown. The ivy her grandmother had always ordered the gardener to prune rigorously now covered the front of the house, hiding the rosy brick, its tendrils even trailing across the grimy windows. The once pristine white paint was gray and peeling.

In the dull, sunless light it looked more like a house in a Gothic novel than the home she had loved.

She shrank back into the corner of the taxi, fear swelling in her throat.

What if Aunt Hilary was no longer there and a stranger answered the door, demanding her business? Worse still, what if Aunt Hilary herself met her with a stony face and no welcome, as well she might?

Certainly the beloved house issued no welcome to the returning exile.

"This the right place?" the taxi driver demanded.

She felt like saying, "I'm not sure." Swallowing the lump in her throat, she replied, "Yes, it is." She reached for her carry-on bag and then opened the door.

The driver heaved out her suitcase and set it down on the step. "That'll be twenty-seven pounds," he told her.

Helen paid him. Then, as he went back to the taxi, she called after him, "Would you mind waiting? In case no one's in."

He grunted a reply and went to sit in the taxi, lighting himself a cigarette.

Her heart pounding, Helen mounted the steps. "It's me, Gran," she whispered. "I've come back."

But it was too late for her grandmother. Thirty years too late. She had suffered a fatal stroke three months before Emma had been born. Helen closed her eyes. "I killed you, Gran," she whispered.

"You going to try the bell?" the driver yelled from the taxi. "Can't wait around all day."

He was right. She pressed the bell, a replacement for the old pull bell she had known so well. She could hear its faint pealing beyond the door.

No response.

She pressed it again and waited. Eventually she became aware of a shuffling sound, punctuated by tapping beyond the door. Then the letter-box flap opened from the inside and a voice, unmistakably her aunt's, shouted, "What do you want?"

Helen was so surprised that she didn't answer at first. But after another imperious, "Who is it?" she bent down and said, "It's Helen, Aunt Hilary. I've come to visit."

Fatigue and her awareness of what a strange sight she must appear to the taxi driver made hysterical laughter gather in her throat.

Silence from behind the door.

The wind swirled the fallen leaves about the step. Helen pushed the letter-box flap open and shouted, "Let me in, Aunt Hilary. It's cold out here."

Another pause. Then came the rattle of chains and screech of bolts, as if the door to Sleeping Beauty's castle were being unlocked after a hundred years. The door appeared to be sticking. She could hear her aunt cursing it beneath her breath.

"Stand back and I'll push it," Helen shouted. Behind her, she heard the taxi driver pointedly revving up his engine. "Hold on a minute, Aunt Hilary."

She ran down the steps again. "Thanks so much for waiting," she told the driver. She scrambled in her purse, unused to the new British money, eventually holding out a couple of gold pound coins.

He grinned at her, pocketing the money. "Sure you'll be okay?" he asked with a grimace at the house. "Looks a bit spooky to me."

"I'll be fine," she assured him, and ran back up the steps again.

By this time her aunt had wrestled the door open and stood in the entrance. Pity tightened Helen's throat. The once upright Hilary Barstow was bent over a stout walking stick, her back curved into a dowager's hump. But her eyes, at least, had not changed. They flashed behind tape-bound spectacles, bright with anger or excitement, Helen wasn't sure which.

"So. You've come back." There was no welcome in the harsh voice.

"Yes, dearest Aunt Hilary, I have." Helen hugged the unyielding old body against her, her nose wrinkling at the musty smell of age and neglect that emanated not only from her aunt, but also from the house itself.

"Are you intending to stay?" Aunt Hilary looked past her to the suitcase on the step.

"I am." Helen turned to pick it up and carried it past her aunt into the hall. In the dim light from the bare bulb hanging from the ceiling, she could see patches of damp wallpaper peeling from the walls.

"You should have telephoned first. There's no room ready for you."

Helen slammed the door, leaning her shoulder against it to force it shut. "I can prepare my own room." She gazed at her aunt. "The main thing is, I'm here."

"Thirty years too late." Aunt Hilary turned. "Thirty

years too late," she repeated, shuffling down the hallway.

Helen closed her eyes, squeezing back tears. She was right, of course. Taking a deep breath, she followed her into the drawing room.

The high-ceilinged room was gloomy, the curtains closed, the chairs and sofa swathed in drab dustcovers. Her aunt switched on the light and dragged the cover off the sofa, to reveal the same ivory-and-burgundy-striped sofa, its colors remarkably fresh after so many years.

"It's all the same," Helen said, looking about her with wonder. Her eyes devoured the dear, dear things that had been such an important part of her life.

"Sit down and I'll make a cup of tea."

"I'll make it, Aunt Hilary."

"You'll do no such thing. You're a guest."

An uninvited guest, her tone implied.

"I'll come into the kitchen with you, if I may."

"As you please." Her aunt turned abruptly.

The kitchen was cluttered and grubby. What appeared to be a year's supply of newspapers was piled in the corner.

Helen looked about her, trying to hide her dismay. "Don't you have any help?"

"Cleaning woman once a week." Her aunt busied herself setting the battered aluminum kettle on the gas stove. She took a crumpled lace tray cloth from the drawer and set cups and saucers on a tray.

There was the teapot Helen last remembered seeing on her grandmother's tray, the white china one with pink rosebuds. Only now the spout was chipped and the handle bound with a piece of grubby waterproof tape.

Helen ran her finger over it. "The same teapot."

Her aunt slammed the bread-and-butter plate on the table. "It's all much the same."

Helen smiled. "I'm glad."

Her aunt cast a sharp glance at her and began taking

biscuits from the large, square tin with a picture of Anne Hathaway's cottage on it.

"Barstow's Biscuits," Helen said eagerly. "Are they still in business?"

"Not for much longer. Some big company's trying to buy us out."

Helen reached for an orange crumble. "But that might mean you'd make some money."

"You're like all Americans. Think only of money."

"Canadian, Aunt Hilary, not American. There's a big difference."

"Hm. Can't see it myself. You're dressed like an American. Thank God you don't sound like one, at least." She picked up the heavy tray, but Helen took it from her.

"What's wrong with making money from the biscuit shares?" she asked her aunt, following her down the hall and setting the tray on the oval table in the drawing room.

"It would mean the end of Barstow's, that's what's wrong."

"Oh, you mean they would buy them out completely and—"

"The Barstow factory would manufacture the biscuits for some big company, but the name wouldn't be used. No more Barstow's Biscuits."

"That would be a shame."

"It would be."

Discomfited by the silence and tension that followed, Helen put out her hand to pick up the teapot, to find herself waved away imperiously.

"I am perfectly capable of pouring out tea in my own house, thank you."

Helen flushed. Childish tears welled in the back of her throat. She was aching with tiredness, and more than anything she longed for the familiar comforts of her home in Winnipeg. What she wouldn't give for the warmth of Bruce's arms about her now. But he was probably making love to his mistress at this very moment.

Turning her face away, she took a tissue from her handbag and rubbed at her eyes with it.

"What's the matter with you?"

Helen blew her nose, sat up, and looked straight at her aunt. "I've been traveling for more than fourteen hours. I've missed a whole night's sleep. And I don't feel at all welcome here."

Her aunt set down the teapot with a sharp crack. "What did you expect? Waltzing in here without even a telephone call, as if you had just left here yesterday."

"I thought I'd surprise you."

The old eyes sparked with anger. "Oh, you surprised me all right."

"I found it hard to summon up the courage to come here."

"I can imagine. I'm not sure I'd have the nerve to do it if I were in your shoes."

This conversation was getting them nowhere. If it was this difficult with her aunt, what in God's name would it be like with Emma and Richard . . . and Julian?

Her aunt's eyes were flint hard. "When I saw you there on the step, I thought of that day you moved out to your parents' with your things, all smiles. Little hypocrite!"

A feeling akin to hatred filled Helen. "How cruel you are, Aunt Hilary. When I left Lansdowne House that day, my heart was breaking. I knew I'd never live here again."

"Well, you'd never have guessed it from the way you were acting."

"That's what I was doing, acting. For God's sake, Aunt Hilary. I was only eighteen, and—and I was pregnant." Helen didn't trust herself to say any more. The old memories of that dreadful day flooded over her.

"Drink your tea or it will get cold."

Helen put out a hand to pick up the cup, but it shook so hard that the cup rattled in its china saucer.

"For heaven's sake, you are in a state. Give me that

before you break it." Hilary grabbed the cup from her.

Now the tears started in earnest. Helen couldn't stop them. She felt as if she were drowning in her own sorrow. She was only dimly aware that her aunt had dragged herself up on her feet and was crossing the room, but she knew nothing else until she found a glass pushed into her hand.

"Here, drink this down."

"What is it?"

"Whiskey."

"I hate whiskey."

"Too bad. Drink it."

Helen took a gulp and grimaced. "Thank you. I—"

"Drink it all," came the command.

She did as she was told, loathing the taste but not caring. When she had finished, the glass was taken from her.

"Now, you'd better have some biscuits or you'll be intoxicated."

Like a zombie, she ate three biscuits, drank a cup of tepid, sweetened tea—another grimace, as she never took sugar in her tea nowadays—without one more word passing between them.

Then she felt her aunt's bony hands on her shoulders. "Lie down," she was told.

Helen kicked off her shoes and swung her legs onto the sofa. She heard the hiss of the gas fire and felt its warmth on her face. Then, a little later, the soft weight of an eiderdown quilt upon her. Was it her imagination or could she smell a faint trace of Apple Blossom perfume from it?

This was how it had always been when she was not well: a fire in the drawing room, her grandmother's fragrant quilt wrapped around her. "Thank you," she whispered, not even sure if Aunt Hilary was still in the room with her.

19

Helen awoke to the muffled roar of an ancient Hoover vacuum cleaner rumbling over her head. She swung her legs to the floor and stood up, then abruptly sat down again. Her head was swimming. A combination of tiredness, whiskey, and strain, no doubt.

She looked at the clock on the mantelpiece. Ten past two. Surely not. That would mean she had slept for almost four hours. She looked at her watch. Ten past eight. That would be right, then. She hadn't adjusted her watch to the six-hour time difference.

She had promised to phone home to let Bruce know she had arrived safely. Maybe he wouldn't even be at home. She'd leave it for a while and call him at the office. She didn't want to have her suspicions about Bruce finally confirmed.

For a few minutes she sat gazing at the ornate fireplace and the crimson velvet curtains, which had faded in places to pale cerise, and wondered if she was really in her king-size bed in Winnipeg, dreaming all this.

She got up, crossed the hallway, and went into the dining room. The long table was covered with a dust cloth. She switched on the light and looked up at the ceiling. Yes, the painting was still there: the rampant blues and reds and gilt needed cleaning even more now, but they were still vivid enough to be a shock.

As she gazed at the cherubim in their loincloths and the golden-haired Diana in her blue robes, she recalled Julian's pleasure in the painted ceiling. This had been his favorite room in the house.

She turned abruptly, pushing away the thought that she might be seeing Julian again in a few days.

She could hear voices upstairs. Who on earth was her aunt talking to? For a fleeting moment she thought it might be Edith. But that was nonsense. Edith had died more than twenty years ago, leaving Aunt Hilary alone in the house.

She mounted the stairs, her hand curving around the familiar banister rail. When she paused on the landing, she could hear voices coming from her grandmother's bedroom.

Her feet froze. She stood there, unable to move. Then, steeling herself, she walked to the open door . . . and into the room.

Hilary and another woman—the cleaner, probably— were making up the large, four-poster bed.

"So you're awake," her aunt said. "Mrs. Brown, this is my niece, Mrs. Lawrence."

Mrs. Brown wiped her hand on her faded floral apron and held it out. "How d'you do, Mrs. Lawrence."

"How do you do." Helen smiled and shook her hand. "This room hasn't changed, either," she said softly, not daring to meet Aunt Hilary's eyes.

"If you're expecting change, this is the wrong place for you." Her aunt lifted the sheet, snapping it to emphasize her point.

Helen looked into the tarnished mirror of the dressing table, expecting to see a girl with long auburn hair, and was shocked to see the face of a middle-aged woman, her faded red hair badly in need of a brushing.

"I wanted it to be exactly the same," she said, her fingers

lingering over the crystal bowls on the dressing table, the silver hairbrushes and comb.

"Well, it's certainly not exactly the same."

"No, it's not." Helen turned to look out the front bay window. "Gran's not here."

"Thank you, Mrs. Brown," she heard her aunt say. "I think that will do for now. It was good of you to come in specially."

"Pleasure, Miss Barstow. Bye, Mrs. Lawrence. Nice meeting you."

"Good-bye, Mrs. Brown," Helen said, but she didn't dare turn around. Her eyes were too blurred with tears.

The two women went from the room, leaving her alone. She had been a fool to come. It was all too late. Returning had caused nothing but pain and bitter memories.

Gazing out the window at the windblown trees that lined the driveway, the strands of ivy tapping at the window, she didn't hear her aunt come in until she spoke.

"Every day she used to sit there in her chair, watching the driveway, waiting."

Helen squeezed her eyes shut. "Oh, Aunt Hilary, please don't."

"'I don't understand,' she'd say. 'Why does she never come to see us anymore?'"

Helen kept her back to her aunt. "Did you tell her the truth?"

"The truth? How did we know what the truth was? We'd been told so many lies by your parents . . . and by you."

Helen turned from the window, her arms folded tightly across her breast. "I never lied to you. I left this house to avoid hurting you and Gran, so there wouldn't be any scandal. Imagine how I felt, knowing I might never return."

Her aunt turned abruptly. "I can't stand here debating all that rubbish with you."

Helen darted forward, grabbing her aunt's arm. "It's not rubbish, Aunt Hilary. It's the truth. I left because I loved you both so much. You had been so good to me. I thought it would break Gran's heart if she knew."

"You broke her heart all right. She was so frantic when you disappeared that she'd pace this room, back and forth, back and forth, for hours at a time."

"I sent a note to say I was safe and being well cared for."

Hilary turned, lifting her stick, so that Helen flinched, afraid her aunt would strike her. "And you thought that was enough to set our minds at rest? We should get on with our busy lives and forget you entirely, eh?"

Her aunt's heavy sarcasm bit into Helen's heart like acid. She heard the excuses of a child issuing from her own mouth, but the experienced mind of a middle-aged woman realized, as she spoke them, how ridiculous they were.

"Tell me what you would have done, had I told you I was pregnant," she said, knowing the answer before it came.

Hilary shook her head. "I'm not going to stay here playing games with you. My legs are getting tired from standing." She shuffled away and began to descend the stairs slowly, one at a time.

Helen followed her. This was all so useless. What was she achieving with this postmortem? If she wanted an endorsement of the decisions she had made thirty years ago, she certainly wasn't going to get them from Aunt Hilary.

When they reached the foot of the stairs, they stood awkwardly in the dingy hallway.

"I'll phone for a taxi," Helen said.

"What for?"

"So I can move into a hotel."

"Running away again, eh?" The challenge was there, in her aunt's eyes. "You're just like your father."

Helen winced. "I wasn't running away. I just don't

see the point of us quarreling and you being upset."

"Who said I was upset?"

Helen released a long sigh. "For heaven's sake, Aunt Hilary. It would be easier for us both if I checked into a hotel in Richmond. If you'd like to see me again, then that's up to you."

She walked to the phone table in the corner of the hall and picked up the tattered directory, noticing that it was dated 1981.

She was about to ask her aunt if she had a Yellow Pages directory, but Hilary spoke first.

"We would have cared for you."

"I beg your pardon?"

"You asked me what we would have done if you had told us you were pregnant. I'm telling you now, we would have cared for you."

Helen let the directory slide from her grasp.

"Not only because we loved you," her aunt said, "but also because your grandmother felt responsible."

Helen shook her head vehemently. "Of course she wasn't."

"Yes, she was. And I told her so. Frequently. She encouraged that bloody actor. She liked his flattery. I told her that." Hilary's mouth quivered. "'You're a silly old woman, Mother,' I told her. 'You fell for him as much as Helen did, and I hope you're satisfied now.'" Her face crumpled. "That's what I told her. I said she was responsible for us never seeing you again. I killed her as much as you did."

Helen ran to her, gathering the rigid figure in her arms. "No, no, Aunt Hilary. Of course you didn't. No one person is to blame for any of this. You must understand that. It happened, that's all. It just happened."

Her aunt pulled away from her, searching for something in the pocket of her tweed skirt. She pulled out a grubby handkerchief and blew her nose. "It would never have happened if Geoffrey's wife had been a proper mother to you."

"Oh, Lord, Aunt Hilary, how often have I gone through all those if onlys. If only I'd had different parents. If only I'd never met Julian. And so on and so on. We can't change the past." Helen sighed. "I'm just finding it very tough to face up to the present I've created with all the mistakes I made." She looked at the wrinkled hand gripping the damp handkerchief. "I've hurt so many people."

She became aware that her aunt was shivering. "Let's go and sit down by the fire and start all over again."

Her aunt put up a hand to brush Helen's cheek. "I should like that. I didn't give you a very warm welcome, did I? I was shocked to see you there." The old gray eyes blazed. "You could have given me a heart attack, arriving like that, without any warning. Very thoughtless of you."

Helen hid a smile. "It was. Very thoughtless. I just wanted to see the expression on your face when you first saw me."

"Well, you got what you deserved, then, didn't you?"

"I did. Now, can we please go into the warm, before we both freeze in this drafty hallway?"

She took her aunt's arm and led her into the drawing room. "Have you eaten any lunch?"

"Too busy to eat," Aunt Hilary said.

"Sit down," Helen told her. "I'm going to make us some tea and something to eat."

Aunt Hilary snorted. "Hm, getting very bossy in our old age, aren't we?"

"I'm afraid so. I must take after my aunt." Helen left the room before her aunt could respond.

When she had put on the kettle, Helen stood in the center of the kitchen, surveying it. As soon as she was properly rested, she would give it a good clean. Mrs. Brown was friendly enough, but she obviously didn't believe in thorough cleaning.

She looked at the large breadboard. There was a fresh loaf on it, brown and crusty, but it was standing in a pile of old bread crumbs that had probably been accumulating for days. Helen took up a gray dishcloth, grimacing as her fingers encountered cold grease.

She opened a drawer and pulled out a threadbare but clean dishcloth and wiped the breadboard. Honestly, it would take her a month to get this entire house clean. It needed so much done to it: paintwork, wallpapering . . .

No point in thinking about that now. There were too many other priorities.

A tin of corned beef provided a filling for sandwiches. She found a rusty tin of Colman's mustard powder and made some, spooning it into an eggcup. Unless Aunt Hilary's tastes had changed, she had always liked hot mustard on her corned beef sandwiches.

The tiny memory made Helen feel a warm glow of happiness, quite out of proportion to its importance. Somehow, recalling the mundane fact of Aunt Hilary's preference for hot mustard showed that all those little day-to-day things she thought she had totally forgotten were still there, buried in her subconscious.

"I am right, you do like mustard with corned beef, don't you?" she asked when she carried the tray into the drawing room.

"Not any more. Goes for my stomach."

"Oh."

She must have looked disappointed, because Aunt Hilary said, "I'll take it if you've already put it on. Won't hurt to eat it once, on a special occasion."

"No, it's all right. I put it in an eggcup."

Stupid of her. She should have realized that someone her aunt's age wouldn't eat hot spices. "I can't take onion anymore," she told her aunt.

"What rubbish. You're a young woman. You should be able to eat anything. I had a cast-iron stomach at your age."

Helen smiled. "I'm not a young woman anymore, Aunt Hilary. I have two grown-up children."

It came out without her thinking. For years it had been an automatic response. "I've been saying that for years. But, of course, I actually have three children."

"Well, you don't have to count the first. After all, she—"

Helen set the tray on the table. "Oh, yes, I do. That's my reason for being here. To meet Emma, the baby I gave up for adoption. But let me pour out the tea first."

Once she had poured out tea for them both, it was a tremendous relief to be able to tell Aunt Hilary all that had happened since the first call from Emma. Her aunt made no comment, apart from a few snorts when Julian's name was mentioned, until Helen had finished.

Then she said, "Emma sounds like a nice, properly brought-up girl to me. Full of spunk as well."

Helen beamed. Her aunt couldn't have said anything that would have pleased her more. "That's what I thought." She folded her paper napkin over and over, creasing it with her finger. "I've treated her so badly these past months. Can you imagine what that poor girl has gone through? Rejected twice by her own mother." She looked down at her lap, not wanting her aunt to see her crying again.

"Now just you stop that. It doesn't help one bit. Be honest with her, tell her exactly why it was difficult for you, and she should understand. When are you meeting her?"

"Friday. She wants me to go down with her to Julian's place on Saturday morning. *Sir* Julian," she added with a ghost of a smile.

Another snort from Aunt Hilary. "In my opinion, seeing that wretched man would be a big mistake, but I realize you would do it to please your Emma. Where will you meet her?"

"Heaven knows. I must admit I'm absolutely dreading it. I certainly don't want Richard Turner to be there. Not at first, anyway. Just thinking about it gives me a panic attack."

"Why not ask Emma to come here?"

Helen's eyes widened. "Here?"

"Yes, here. Lansdowne House. Show your daughter the place where you grew up, where you were at your happiest. And—if you must bring the bloody man's name up—show her the dining room ceiling her father loved so much. Probably thought this all might be his, one day."

Helen opened her mouth incredulously. "Julian did? You're not serious."

"Certainly I am. I swear he had his eye on this place."

Helen didn't know whether to laugh or be furious. "Are you trying to tell me he seduced me for Lansdowne House?"

"Oh, I shouldn't think he'd have done so deliberately. But I should imagine part of your attraction for him was that he thought the family was well off or something like that."

Some buried memory of something Julian had said stirred in Helen's mind, but it refused to come to the surface. "I don't care about Julian, damn him. It's Emma I'm worried about. I want to make a good impression on her, after the terrible way I've treated her."

"Then you should get your hair dyed or colored or whatever they do to it nowadays."

"Aunt Hilary! Are you trying to totally demolish my morale?"

"Certainly not. But you're too young to let yourself go. Your hair was always your crowning glory."

"I'm a middle-aged—"

"I know, I know. A middle-aged mother with *three* grown-up children. Doesn't mean you have to look like one, does it?"

"I'll think about it. But I want to be myself with Emma. She must take me as I am."

"Whatever that is," her aunt said enigmatically.

Their eyes met. God, she always could see through me, thought Helen.

She busied herself with sweeping bread crumbs from

the table onto a plate. "I must phone her sometime today to make arrangements for Friday."

"You should phone your husband first to tell him you've arrived safely. I am utterly amazed that you have told him nothing about all this."

"I think it's better that way."

"Better for whom?" Aunt Hilary sighed impatiently. "You would always do anything to avoid a confrontation. I can see that hasn't changed. Just like your father. And while we're on the subject—"

Helen jumped in. "I'll phone Bruce to tell him I've arrived. He should be in the office by now. Then I'll phone Emma."

"Very well. And what about my suggestion for Friday? Why not have her come here? I can keep out of the way, stay in my room while she's here."

"What utter nonsense! She wants to meet you, and I know you'll want to meet her." Helen mulled the idea over for a minute or so and then nodded. "I like it. I'd feel more at home here than anywhere else. And Emma would see the place where, as you said, I spent the happiest days of my life." She leaned over to take her aunt's hand. "I hope you will like Emma," she said shyly as if she were talking of a childhood friend.

Aunt Hilary squeezed her hand. "I love her already for having brought you home before it was too late."

When Helen had helped her aunt to tidy away the lunch things, she phoned Bruce at the office. In answer to his cool inquiry, she told him that her aunt was better than she had expected. Which, in a way, was true. She also told him that she would have to stay for a week or so to help her back on her feet when she got out of hospital. Which wasn't.

"The house is a mess," she told him. "It's too big for her to look after on her own. She needs help with it."

"Then hire a companion or something for her,"

Bruce said impatiently. "I'll be happy to pay for it, so long as you can come home soon."

He sounded absolutely sincere. Helen felt a rush of longing to be back home with him, to return to the old days.

"Don't tell me you're missing me," she said, smiling.

"You're damned right I am. You forgot to pick up my shirts at the laundry. I had to wear yesterday's shirt and change at the office after I'd picked them up."

Hearing humor and warmth, not anger, in his voice, she laughed out loud. "You're kidding me."

"It's true. But that's not the main reason I'm missing you. Our bed is too damned big without you. When I woke up this morning I almost fell out. I'd been working my way across to your side looking for you." Oh, Bruce, she wanted to wail, I need you desperately.

Why not tell him everything now?

No, no, she couldn't. Especially not over the phone. She dreaded hearing the warmth in his voice turn to cold steel. He might even tell her just to stay on that side of the Atlantic and not bother to come home.

"Are you still there?" he asked impatiently.

"Sorry. I'm sort of squiffy from jet lag. I'm missing you, too, darling. I promise I'll be home as soon as I can get my aunt settled."

When she replaced the receiver, she stood looking at herself in the brown-flecked mirror on the wall. He'd slept at home last night. If he hadn't, he wouldn't have mentioned their bed. And he was genuinely missing her.

"Thank you, God," she whispered.

Her reflection sneered at her. This is just the first night, Pollyanna. The question is, will he still be sleeping alone a week from now?

20

Helen decided to phone Emma at the office. If she called her at home this evening, she might have to speak to Richard Turner. She couldn't face any more reunions today. Not even by telephone.

"Forgive me for bothering you at the office," she told Emma after they'd exchanged stilted greetings, "but I'm not sure I can stay awake much longer. I was wondering if we could meet here on Friday, at my aunt's house, rather than your place."

She had stood over the phone for more than ten minutes, putting off calling. Now Emma's cool reception chilled her. Evidently she still believed everything Julian had told her.

"There is a little bit of a problem," Emma said after a moment's pause. "Do you think it would be possible for us to meet tomorrow evening, instead of Friday?"

Helen hesitated. It's far too soon, she wanted to say. I need more time.

"I know we'd talked about meeting on Friday," Emma continued. "Alan and I were hoping you wouldn't mind coming down with us Friday evening instead of Saturday morning."

Everyone seemed to have taken it for granted that

she was going to Marsden Court. "No, of course I don't mind," she said, her desire to please Emma overcoming her misgivings.

"I could come to Petersham tomorrow evening, but Daddy would be disappointed not to see you. He wants to have a little dinner party for the three of us, if you're free."

Again Helen hesitated. The day's grace she thought she'd have was being taken from her. Besides, she wasn't sure she could face Richard Turner that soon.

What the heck! "Why not? But I must see you alone first, Emma," she said firmly. "Is there any chance you could take tomorrow afternoon off and come here? Then I might feel more able to face your father— Richard, I mean—in the evening." She gave a shaky laugh. "This is all very scary for me, you know. I'm not sure I could manage—"

"You're not the only one who's scared." Now it was Emma's turn to laugh. "I thought it might help me to have Daddy there for the first meeting."

"We don't need to be alone tomorrow—if you come here, I mean. Aunt Hilary, your great-aunt, will be here."

"Oh. But then she'll be your supporter, won't she?"

Like hell she will, thought Helen. "Somehow I don't think so. She knows what a mess I've made of all this."

There was a pause. Then Emma said, "Hang on a minute and I'll just see if I can take the afternoon off tomorrow."

Minutes passed, marked by the loud ticking of the grandfather clock in the hall. Helen picked at a piece of peeling wallpaper while she waited.

"Hallo?" Emma said. "I've managed to clear tomorrow afternoon. Actually, Alan said I should take the whole day, but I told him the afternoon will be fine."

"That's great."

"Will you still come and have dinner with us—Daddy and me, I mean?" Emma asked. "I'll have the car, so we can drive there. It's only a few minutes away. But you know that, of course. Or will you be too tired? We could make it nice and early."

Helen couldn't help smiling. Emma seemed to have her habit of gabbling when she was nervous.

She didn't reply immediately. She wasn't sure she wanted to see Richard at all, never mind directly after her first meeting with her daughter. Yet she could tell that it was important to Emma.

"I'd be happy to come and have dinner with you and Richard."

"Good. He'll be pleased, I know."

Helen gave her the directions to Lansdowne House. "I'd really like you to see the house where I spent the happiest times of my life," she told Emma.

But later, when she was roaming the grounds, Helen wondered what Emma would think of Lansdowne House.

It was no longer the beautiful home of her youth. Everywhere she went, she found rampant growth and neglect. The rosebushes were choked by bindweed. The toolshed windows were broken, the door hanging on loose hinges, the tools inside crumbling with rust. When she looked up at the rear of the house, she saw that the curtains were drawn across the windows, repelling her, like dark glasses over blind eyes.

Shivering, she went in by the kitchen door, which scraped across the tiled floor.

"That door needs fixing, Aunt Hilary," she told her aunt, who was making something cheesy for supper, from the smell of it.

"Everything needs fixing," her aunt snapped. "But I don't have the energy to do it myself or the money to have someone else do it."

"Of course you don't. I intend to help you."

"You just look after your own affairs and leave me to deal with mine. And by the way, I think it's time we dropped the 'Aunt Hilary' bit, don't you?"

"What on earth do you mean?"

"At your age I think 'Hilary' would be sufficient."

Helen wasn't sure if it was a concession or a criticism. "It won't be easy to change. After all, I've been thinking of you as 'Aunt' since I was an infant."

"Makes me feel ancient, having a woman your age calling me 'Aunt.'"

"I'll try to remember that . . . Hilary." Helen quickly changed the subject. "What are you making? It smells delicious."

"Welsh rarebit. I've only got cheese in the house. Can't expect me to provide steaks when you don't tell me ahead of time that you're flying in after thirty years."

"I don't expect it. I haven't had Welsh rarebit for years. Can I help?"

"Make the toast. The cheese is almost ready. Talking about food, what am I supposed to serve tomorrow afternoon, when your Emma comes for tea?"

"I thought I'd take the bus into Richmond in the morning and pick up some cakes."

"Bought cakes? I'll not have your daughter come here for her first visit to eat bought cakes!"

Helen had to smile. "Would you let me bake something, then?"

Hilary poured the melted cheese mixture over the toast Helen had laid out on plates. "Why don't we both bake something." She lifted her face. A wash of red streaked her gaunt cheekbones. "It would be like old times again."

Tears welled in Helen's eyes; she seemed to be doing far too much weeping lately. Strange, that. Since she had given up Emma, she had rarely cried. She blinked and then blew her nose. "I'd love that," was all she said.

The next morning, when she checked the refrigerator and larder, Helen found that both were almost empty. She had to spend most of the morning grocery shopping before they could start baking. Perhaps it was a good thing, she thought as she rolled out pastry dough, otherwise she might have gone stark crazy waiting for Emma to come.

"I've a feeling this Alan Grenville is someone special to Emma," she said to her aunt as she spread raspberry jam onto the pastry for the bakewell tart.

Hilary bent down to take a tray of oatmeal flapjacks from the Aga oven. "Really? What makes you think that?"

"I don't know it. I just have a feeling, that's all."

"Mother's intuition?" her aunt said caustically.

Helen was about to snap at her, but then, seeing the devil dancing in her aunt's gray eyes, laughed. "I always wondered who David reminded me of. Now I know. It's his great-aunt."

"David?"

"My son. Your great-nephew," Helen reminded her patiently. Her aunt's short-term memory was not good. She had tried to tell her all about Canada and the family over supper the previous night, but some of it hadn't sunk in.

Hilary looked at the man's watch on her bony wrist. "Quarter to two. Is that tart ready to go in?"

"It is."

"Then you go up and change. I'll just finish the scones. She's coming at three, you said, didn't you?"

"That's right." Helen's heart hammered. "There's plenty of time yet." She preferred not to be alone with the dread that was creeping over her.

"You go on up. You want to look your best for the first meeting with your daughter, don't you? I still think you should have had your hair tinted, but it's too late for that now. Off you go."

Reluctantly, Helen did as she was told. It was a strange feeling for her to be bossed around after all the years of being the matriarch of her family. She felt as if she were seventeen again and fast losing control.

As she paused outside the bedroom door, she half expected to hear her grandmother's voice ordering her to "Come in, child, and don't hover out there."

She went in and stood in the doorway, surveying the frilly room that had been her grandmother's, seeing it with fresh eyes now that she was not exhausted from lack of sleep.

The muslin curtains at the windows were gray and ripped from countless washings. The glazed-chintz quilt was stained and worn almost bare in places. Had it always been this shabby? Had her memories gilded everything?

"God, how I wish I could make it as perfect as I remembered it to be."

"You always were a dreamer."

Helen started and swung around. "Oh, you gave me a fright."

Her aunt snorted. "Did you think it was your grandmother's ghost come to haunt you? I was just up to the linen cupboard for a cloth for the tea trolley and heard you muttering to yourself. What are you going to wear?"

"I have no idea. Come and help me choose. I spent half an hour this morning trying to decide and got nowhere."

Helen's hands were shaking as she opened the wardrobe door. The interior smelled of cedar and mothballs. She gave a little exclamation as her hand brushed against her grandmother's old fox cape.

Her aunt pushed her aside. "Get away from there. You're a bundle of nerves. At this rate she'll be here and you'll still be in trousers."

"Perhaps that would be better. No formality."

"Nonsense. How would you like to be meeting your mother for the first time, only to find she couldn't be bothered to dress up for the occasion?"

The very possibility of meeting her mother for the

first or any time made Helen's blood run cold. Thank God that's one person I don't ever have to see again, she thought, and then was swamped with guilt for thinking it.

"Oh, Aunt Hilary, I'm sick with nerves." Helen plugged in her curling iron and then sank onto the bed. "I know I'm going to make a mess of this, I just know it."

"I hope you aren't like this with your family in Canada."

"Of course I'm not. If you were to ask any of them, they'd say I was famous for being totally unflappable. Cool, calm, and collected, that's me."

Her aunt grunted disbelievingly and went back to looking over her clothes. "This is attractive." She held up the heather light wool suit Bruce had persuaded Helen to buy several Christmases ago. It seemed like ten years ago. Another world.

"Not too dressy?"

"You're going for dinner afterwards, aren't you?"

"Unfortunately, yes. I'm not sure I'm going to survive all this. I am absolutely terrified."

Aunt Hilary put the suit on the back of a chair and shuffled over to Helen, her stick banging on the floor. "You're going to be just fine," she said firmly, running her bony hand up and down Helen's back. "Now, let's get this show on the road, as they say, or Emma will be here and you'll still be shilly-shallying about what to wear."

Helen took in a deep breath. "I agree. The suit will be fine," she said, pulling off her sweater.

"Excuse me, I have to change, too. Anyone would think you were the only one who wants to look her best."

By five to three both of them were ready—Helen in her heather suit, her aunt in a blue silk dress—sitting on the edge of their seats in the drawing room. Beside Hilary's chair stood the tea trolley laden with what was left of the best blue-and-gold tea service with the newly polished silver teaspoons. The two silver cake stands bore enough cakes and biscuits to feed ten people, not three.

"Should I kiss her, do you think?" Helen asked.

"You should do what comes naturally."

"Perhaps not. She's not very pleased with me." She looked bleakly at her aunt. "Who can blame her? I rejected her a second time, and Julian's been filling her head with lies about me."

"Too late to be thinking of that now." Hilary tapped Helen on her knee. "You'll manage, just you wait and see."

It was too late for anything. She could hear the crunch of wheels on the gravel driveway. The terror she felt was far worse than the bowel-churning stage fright she used to have while waiting in the wings for her first entrance.

The car engine was turned off. Then silence.

"Go and meet her," Hilary said.

"I'll wait till she rings the bell."

"She's sitting in the car, as terrified as you are, you silly ass. Go on."

Helen stood up. "Won't you come with me?"

"No, I won't. This is your show."

Helen gave her aunt a wan smile and went out into the hall. She had been dreaming of this moment for years. Now it was like her worst nightmare.

She opened the front door. Emma wasn't sitting in the car. She was standing by its open door, gazing up at the house. That was Helen's first impression.

Her second impression was that her firstborn daughter was beautiful beyond belief. Small-boned, slim, her red-gold hair swinging about her face. She was dressed in a green wool suit, with a long jacket and short, pleated skirt that showed off her shapely legs.

"Hallo, Emma."

Emma started. "Oh. I am sorry. I didn't hear the door open. I was too busy admiring the house." She leaned into the car and brought out a huge bunch of flowers and her leather briefcase.

Helen came down the steps, watching her daughter

as she juggled the flowers and case, trying to shut the car door. "Let me help."

"Thank you. Would you mind taking the flowers? They're for you, anyway." Emma turned away to close the car door. "I'm not usually this useless. I seem to be all fingers and thumbs today."

Helen smiled, feeling instant empathy. "I know what you mean." She shifted the flowers to her left arm and held out her right hand. "Hallo, Emma. I'm Helen Lawrence."

It sounded terribly formal, but she didn't want to frighten her off by saying "I'm your mother."

Emma took her hand and then quickly released it. "Hallo. I would have known who you were even if you hadn't said so."

"Would you?" Helen gave a nervous little laugh. "I don't know how."

Emma waved her hand. "Your voice. The red hair."

"Not very red anymore, I'm afraid. My aunt said I should have tinted it, to look my best for you, but I thought—" She halted midsentence, aware that she would gabble on forever once she got going. She gazed at her daughter. "You are very beautiful." The words came out before she could stop them.

Emma flushed, the tide of pink coloring her pale gold skin. "Thank you," she said formally.

Helen could have kicked herself. "I'm sorry. I didn't mean to embarrass you. Shall we go inside?"

"Of course." Emma followed her up the steps and then turned to look out at the semicircular driveway, like a prisoner taking a last look at freedom. "Will there be time to see the garden later?"

"Definitely. But I'm afraid it's in pretty poor shape." Helen lowered her voice, in case her aunt should hear. "I was shocked to see how much the house and grounds had deteriorated when I arrived yesterday."

"Oh? Is it a while since you were here, then?"

"Thirty years. I hadn't seen it for thirty years."

Emma gave a tentative little smile, not knowing what to say. "I hadn't realized," she murmured. "When you said you had an aunt in Petersham, I thought—"

"I hadn't seen her for thirty years, either." Helen looked down at the tawny and yellow chrysanthemums.

This time Emma said nothing.

Helen pushed open the front door and led the way. "Here we are," she announced in an artificially hearty voice. "This is the drawing room. Aunt Hilary, this is Emma."

Emma went forward. "Please don't get up, Mrs.—"

"Miss. Miss Barstow. But you shall call me Aunt Hilary. Not Great-Aunt, if you please. I've told Helen she's too old to be calling me 'Aunt,' but you may do so."

Emma looked overwhelmed for a moment. Then she smiled. "Hallo, Aunt Hilary."

"Hallo, Emma. Do I get a kiss?"

Helen squirmed. This was too much. "Perhaps Emma—"

But Emma was already making her way to the wing chair and bending to kiss Hilary's powdered cheek.

Hilary grasped her hand and held it. "You realize that you are the first of Helen's children to kiss their old great-aunt, don't you?"

"I—I don't understand," Emma said.

"She has never brought her children or husband here to meet me."

Helen closed her eyes for a moment.

"But," continued her aunt, still grasping Emma's hand, "it's right you should be the first to kiss me, because you are her firstborn child. In fact, when you think about it, you've been here before, Emma, but we didn't know anything about you then. You weren't even born."

Helen had to escape. "I'll put these flowers in water and put the kettle on for some tea."

"And take the scones out of the warming drawer," her aunt shouted after Helen, who almost ran from the room.

As she hacked off the ends of the stalks and arranged the flowers in a cut-glass vase, Helen was seething. She had tried hard to start the meeting off on a quiet, unemotional note, and Aunt Hilary had torpedoed it, damn her. She should have met Emma on some neutral ground, where she could have been in control of the situation.

But when she went back into the room, it was to find Emma bent over the fireplace examining the carved surround and her aunt in the middle of telling her about it.

". . . so we're not sure exactly who did it."

Emma's face was alive with enthusiasm as she turned to reply. "I'm sure it's an Adam. It has all his hallmarks. This is such a wonderful room." She extended her arms exuberantly and turned to take it all in. "I do hope I'll be able to see the rest of the house."

"I'll be happy to show you around," Helen said, setting the teapot on its stand. "I haven't seen it properly myself. I was too tired last night."

The best part of half an hour was taken up with tea and an interchange of general questions about the Barstow family on Emma's part and replies from Aunt Hilary, mainly. She and Emma seemed to be getting along very well.

But Helen was aware that all the chitchat in the world couldn't permanently postpone what might prove to be a nasty confrontation between her and Emma.

"So your mother died several years after you went to Canada," Emma was saying to Helen. "She would have been my grandmother, of course."

"That's right," Helen said abruptly.

"I'm sorry I never knew her."

Helen bit her bottom lip hard to stop herself from saying it was no loss, but Hilary was not so tactful.

"You wouldn't be if you'd known her."

Emma looked startled.

"She was a prize bitch," Hilary said succinctly.

Emma wasn't sure what to say. Helen could see her bottom lip quivering and knew that she was trying hard not to laugh at Aunt Hilary's bluntness.

"And what about—"

Helen got up, cutting Emma short. "If you don't mind, Aunt Hilary, I think Emma and I should spend a little time alone together."

Hilary frowned at her. She looked as if she were about to say something to Emma and then decided against it, to Helen's relief. "Very well. I'll go and wash up."

"No, leave the dishes. I'll do them later. Please don't move. We can go into the breakfast room or Gran's bedroom to talk."

"You'll stay here." Her aunt stood up, leaning heavily on her stick to lever herself out of her chair. "Push the trolley out into the hall for me," she ordered Helen. "I'll see you later, Emma."

Emma smiled at her. "Thank you for the lovely tea, Miss Bar—"

"Aunt Hilary."

Emma's smile widened. "Aunt Hilary."

Helen pushed the tea trolley into the hall. Her aunt followed her, closing the door behind her.

"I'll roll it into the kitchen."

"Leave it there and stop treating me like an invalid. I've managed very well by myself these past years." Hilary's hand gripped her arm. "Mind you tell that girl everything. No holding back. You owe that to her."

"Of course I will." Helen shifted from one foot to the other. She wished she hadn't put on her high heels. The corn on her left foot was killing her.

Her aunt's grip tightened. "Everything, mind. And I'm not just talking about Emma and the famous Sir Julian, either. It's time you faced up to reality. You've been hiding from it for too long. No more family secrets."

Helen met her aunt's fierce expression. "No more secrets," she whispered.

"Because if you don't tell Emma the entire truth, then I will."

21

When Helen went back into the drawing room, Emma was on her knees before the fireplace, closely examining the molding. "Sorry." She scrambled to her feet, her face flushed. "This house must be an absolute treasure trove."

"Wait until you see the dining room." Helen sat down. "But I think we should talk first, don't you?"

Emma chose the far end of the sofa, setting as much space as possible between them. "It's strange to think," she said, looking everywhere but at Helen, "that I've walked around Ham Common, right past this house, and never realized that it belonged to a member of my—my . . ."

"Your mother's family," Helen prompted gently.

"Yes." Emma straightened her short skirt, pulling it down almost to the top of her knees. Then she looked at Helen, her lips tight. "I'm sorry. I'd always imagined that you must have been too poor to keep me. But since I've met Sir Julian, and now that I've seen this house and met your aunt, I find it even more difficult to understand."

Emma's bewilderment made her appear much younger. Helen wanted to hold her and comfort her, like a real mother.

She folded her arms stiffly across her chest. "It's hard

for you to understand, Emma, because we live in such a different world nowadays. People live together openly before they're married. No one talks about the stigma of illegitimacy or the horrors of an unwed pregnancy."

"I know it's different now, but you had your family to help. After all, your aunt seems to be accepting me without being at all shocked."

"My aunt was always a law unto herself. You seem to have forgotten my parents. They—they weren't like Aunt Hilary at all, I'm afraid."

"Julian—he said to call him that—Julian told me your father was a vicar." Emma looked directly at Helen. "It felt very odd hearing all about your background from him."

Helen closed her eyes for a fleeting moment. "Before we go any further, Emma, let me say that I was utterly wrong to reject you when you phoned me. I've regretted it ever since. I was selfishly thinking of myself and my family."

"But you haven't regretted it enough to tell them."

"No, I'm still hoping I won't have to."

Emma jumped up and went to the window. She looked out for a moment and then turned, her hair gleaming like polished copper in a shaft of sunlight. "We're not very alike, are we, you and I?"

"What do you mean?"

"I would have fought to keep my baby, whatever era I lived in. You told me that Julian was the love of your life. If you really loved him, how could you give up his baby?"

This was even worse than Helen had expected.

"You don't know how hard I fought to keep you," she protested. "My parents were going to send me away and have you adopted by strangers. They made me feel like a—a slut. That's what my mother kept calling me. Then they talked about having Julian charged with rape, but I told them that it hadn't been rape, of course. That I had wanted to—to sleep with Julian." Her face felt as if it were on fire.

"My father said you ran away from your parents' home."

"Yes, I did. I was determined to keep you myself. But I was only eighteen, legally a minor, with hardly any money. There weren't the social services to help unwed mothers there are today. Mr. Turner, I mean Richard, whose firm I'd been working for, helped me." She smiled rather sheepishly. "It's hard to think of him as Richard, even after all these years."

"He told me something about your friend. The one I phoned in Toronto."

"You mean Ann. Ann Sturgis. The best friend anyone could have. She still is."

Once this was over, she must call Ann and tell her what was happening.

"Ann stayed with me the entire time, and then, when Mary and Richard Turner adopted you, we decided to go to Canada to work for a while. Did Richard tell you that it was I who named you Emma?"

"Yes. He said it was your last wish before you handed over the baby—me—to them."

Helen swallowed and turned away. "I'm not sure I would have survived that time, that entire year, without Ann's help."

"You didn't ever consider having an abortion?"

"No. I was determined to keep you, Emma. I loved Julian. Besides, abortions were still illegal then. Oh, there were doctors who'd do them for a price, of course, but I knew nothing about such things." No need to tell Emma that Julian had wanted her to have an abortion, had given her a list of doctors and tried to pay her off with a check for a hundred pounds.

"We were very naive in those days, I'm afraid. At least, I was. I knew practically nothing about birth control. I left all that to Julian."

"Why didn't you tell Julian?"

Helen went cold. "That I was pregnant, do you mean?"

"Yes."

God in heaven, anything she said would put Julian in a bad light. But she could not, would not, let him get away with everything, including Emma's total love and respect.

"I did tell him."

"He said he knew nothing about it."

Helen gave her a wry smile. "Yes, I gathered that's what he told you, but it's not true."

"You say you told him you were pregnant. Were you sure he was the father?"

Helen winced. "I expect it's hard for you to believe, in these days of the pill, but I've slept with only two men in my entire life—Julian and Bruce, my husband."

Emma bristled visibly. "No, it's not that hard for me to believe. As a matter of fact, I haven't slept with *anyone* yet. I'm still trying to sort myself out before I make any commitments. And that includes making love with someone."

"I'm so sorry, Emma." Helen stood up, arms clutching her stomach. "I've ruined your life, haven't I?"

"Nonsense." Emma lifted her chin. "I've got a very full and rich life. It's just that I need to know the truth. I don't want any more lies, *please*. You owe me the truth."

"That's why I'm here. Just ask me what you want to know."

"You say you told Julian you were pregnant. He says you didn't. How do I know which one of you is telling the truth?"

"I am. Ask Richard. He knows what happened. Naive little fool that I was, I thought Julian would marry me. But he was going to Hollywood to be a big star."

"And that's all?"

"He gave me a check for—for my expenses."

"That's not what he told me at all."

"No, I don't suppose it is."

"He said he didn't know you'd had a baby. You never told him."

"That was true. I didn't."

"Why on earth not, when it was his child?"

"Because—" Because he didn't want you. That was what she was about to say. Oh, God, how could she tell Emma the truth and yet not tell her about Julian's cruelty? "Because we'd lost touch with each other, and Mary and Richard were wanting to adopt you. I didn't want to give you up, but I had no home and no money. I was thinking solely of you. I knew they'd give you a stable home and a good education."

Emma shook her head vehemently, her bright hair brushing her face. "That's all very nice, but I still don't understand why you had to give me up. What about this house? Your aunt and grandmother? You said you'd spent your happiest times here. Couldn't you have brought me here?"

Helen gazed at the china cupboard, suddenly realizing that the collection of Sevres was no longer there. "My grandmother was very frail," she said, staring at the bare shelves behind the glass doors. "She and Aunt Hilary had been so good to me. I didn't want to bring shame on the family. I was afraid it would kill Gran."

"They didn't know you were expecting a baby?"

"No. I left here and went back to live with my parents. Gran never knew. All she knew was that I had disappeared without a word. I wrote her a note, saying I was well, not to worry. She died a few months later, before you were born."

The china cupboard blurred before her eyes.

"So I killed her anyway." Helen turned away.

She heard movement, smelled Emma's fragrance. "This must be an awful strain for you," Emma said slowly. She stood, rubbing her palms together.

"It's just as much a strain for you." She lifted her hand and gently brushed the hair from Emma's cheek.

The brief contact was like an electrical jolt between them. Helen stepped back. "Why don't we go and look at the house and you can ask me more questions as they come to you?"

Emma looked relieved. "I'd like that." She grinned. "I find it hard to keep still, especially under stress."

"Just like your father."

Their eyes met and held.

"Perhaps he's slowed down now, but he had tremendous energy when I knew him." It was hard for Helen to talk about Julian, but she knew that she must, for Emma's sake.

"Was it strange to see him in movies and the theater? Afterwards, I mean."

"I tried to avoid it as much as possible. It hurt too much."

"You really did love him, didn't you?"

"I adored him." Helen smiled wryly. "That was the trouble. It wasn't a very balanced relationship."

"I'm sure he loved you, too. His eyes light up when he talks about you."

Helen's smile faded. "Before we go any further, Emma, you must understand one thing. All this happened a long, long time ago. I'm a happily married woman with a grown-up family. This isn't one of those forties movies, where they've loved each other all the time they've been apart. Since we parted, Julian's been married and divorced twice. If his eyes light up when he talks about me, it's because he's nostalgic for his youth, not me."

"But he did love you . . . before I was born, I mean."

For Emma's sake, Helen replied, "Yes, of course he did. I certainly wasn't a one-night stand. Julian taught me a great deal."

To her surprise, Helen realized that what she said was true. Before Julian, she had known precious little about theater and art and life in general. In her bitterness against him, she had forgotten all the positive things.

She smiled to herself. "He called me a little Philistine and said something about having to be my instructor in all matters cultural."

Emma threw back her head in a peal of laughter. "Oh, I can just hear him saying it. He has an incredible ego, doesn't he?"

"I don't know, Emma. I haven't seen him for thirty years, remember?"

"I think he has. But you can't have been a complete Philistine. You were an actress. A very good one, he told me."

"An amateur in every way. I never stood on a stage again after playing the princess in *Henry V*." She made an abrupt move to the door. "Enough about me. I want to hear all about you and the firm you work for."

Emma seemed reluctant to move from the window. "I haven't even asked you about—about . . ." She paused, waving her hand in the air, her face pink. "Rats! I don't know what to call them. Your children."

"Karen's a lawyer. She's twenty-seven. David's just twenty-one. He's still at university, taking his BA, but what he really wants to do is go into drama."

"How strange. Does he know you were an actress?"

"No. No one in Canada knows anything about my life in England before I emigrated."

Helen was deliberately abrupt. She felt reluctant to merge the two sides of her family. Those in Canada knew nothing about Emma. She would have preferred to have kept it the same way in England, but that wasn't possible.

She opened the door. "Excuse me, but I think we should have a quick tour of the house, if you still want to see it."

"Of course I do." She joined Helen at the door. "I am sorry. I've been asking too many questions."

"Not at all. It's just that as it's only my second day with my aunt, I don't want to leave her alone too long, especially as we're going out this evening. That is still on, is it?"

"Daddy said it was up to you. If you felt it was too much all at once, we could do it another time."

Helen felt a rush of warmth at Richard Turner's sensitivity. He obviously hadn't changed. "He was always so kind," she murmured half to herself.

"Daddy? Yes, I suppose he is kind. I'm afraid I take him for granted. I shouldn't, really. Not all fathers are like him."

Helen turned away to switch on the light in the dim hall. "No, they're not." She suddenly felt extremely tired.

"Are you all right?" Emma asked anxiously.

"Yes, thank you. I'm still a bit worn out from the long journey." Helen crossed to the opposite door. "Come and see the dining room. Then we'll go upstairs."

She opened the door, gesturing to Emma to go ahead of her.

A gasp followed by silence was Emma's initial response to her first sight of the painted ceiling. Then, "Oh, my God! It's wonderful." She gripped her bottom lip with her teeth, sucking in a breath. "I wish I had a stepladder to get a closer look."

Helen smiled at her enthusiasm. "I thought you'd find it interesting."

"Interesting? It's incredible. Have you had it examined? I mean, an assessment done by a professional?"

"You forget," Helen said gently. "I only just arrived."

"Sorry. I did forget. What about when you visited here as a child? Did your grandmother say anything about having it examined to determine the artist?"

The professional had taken over from the personal. Helen was quite relieved. It helped to take some of the strain away for a little while.

She looked up at the cherubim floating under their fluffy clouds. "I'm afraid Gran was terribly casual about the whole place. We all took it very much for granted. All this restoration wasn't being done then. You, especially, must know all about that, Emma. Some beautiful houses were just left to rot until they had to be torn down."

"Ah, but some of the restoration was worse than letting it rot, I'm afraid. From what I can see, Lansdowne House is one of those gems that hasn't been ruined by improvement."

"You can say that again," Helen said, smiling.

"I wish Alan could see this." Emma's eyes were bright with excitement.

"He can, if you want him to. After all, you said he would be driving us down to Marsden Court on Friday, didn't you?"

Emma went pink. "Well, I haven't actually asked him about—"

"You wanted to make sure I was presentable first."

"Not at all. I wanted to make sure you were coming to Marsden Court."

"Be honest with me. Weren't you dreading what you might find?"

Emma gave her an attractive grin. "Well—"

"I can't say I blame you. I hadn't given you much cause to trust me or to like me enough to have me meet your friends. That's my fault, not yours."

Emma rubbed her palms together again. "I'm trying very hard to understand what happened, I really am. I know there's the generation gap and things like the Pill and the new morality, but . . ." She shook her head.

"If I told Karen, she'd probably say the same thing. She thinks I belong with the dinosaurs, even now."

"Oh, I wouldn't say that."

"You don't have to be polite with me, Emma."

"I'm not. I don't want to make comparisons, but I am sure I couldn't have talked like this with my mother." She grimaced. "If you know what I mean. Oh, dear, I really am putting my foot in it, aren't I?"

Helen laughed. She wanted very much to put her arm around Emma's waist and hug her. It was ironic that if Emma had been anyone other than her daughter, she was sure they would have hit it off immediately.

As they went out into the hall again, the breakfast room door opened and Hilary peered out. "Is it safe to come out yet?"

"Of course it is," Helen said. "I am sorry we've kept you from the drawing room."

"You haven't. I never sit in there. Too damned cold." Hilary turned to Emma. "Have you seen Helen's room?"

Helen replied for her. "We were just going up. I haven't seen it myself yet."

"Did you have your own room here?" Emma asked.

"She still does," Hilary replied. "But she's in her grandmother's room now."

"What have you done with my room, Aunt Hilary?"

"Nothing," said her aunt, and went back into the breakfast room, shutting the door.

Helen led the way up the main flight of stairs, pausing before the open door of her grandmother's bedroom. Her heart was knocking against her ribs. She didn't want to turn and take the six stairs up to her room. It held too many painful memories.

"What a beautiful room!" Emma peered over her shoulder.

"This was Gran's room. Would you like to see it?"

"I'd rather see yours first, if you don't mind."

"Not at all." Helen led the way up the short flight of stairs. "Of course," she said, the door creaking open, "it won't be the same as it was when—"

Dear God in heaven.

She wasn't sure if she actually spoke the words aloud. Her head spun, so that she felt she was going to fall. She clutched at the doorjamb to steady herself.

Her panda and teddy bear lay on the pink-rose chintz bedcover. Her books stood on the shelves of the little wooden bookcase.

Not a thing had been changed. The room was exactly the way she had left it.

22

Helen became aware of Emma behind her. "I'm sorry. I didn't expect this. Nothing's been changed since I left it."

Emma touched her arm. "You look awfully white. Are you feeling okay?"

"I'm fine. It's just a bit of a shock, that's all. She felt dazed, disoriented.

The curtains were drawn almost shut. She crossed the room and opened them, dust filling her nostrils. "Take a look, Emma," she said, sitting on the window seat. "It's a sort of 'This is your life, Helen Barstow.'"

But Emma remained in the doorway, looking extremely uncomfortable. "I feel I'm intruding."

"You're not." Helen took a deep breath and let it out in an audible sigh. "As I said, it came as a shock to see it the same after all these years." She went to the dressing table and took up a silver-framed photograph. "Come on in and meet your mother when she was eighteen."

Emma moved hesitantly across the room to take the photograph from Helen. "Oh. We are alike, or . . . we were."

"Were is right." Helen looked down at the photograph

again. "Shame it's black and white. I think your hair's a more golden red than mine was."

There was another photograph on the bedside table. Helen gazed at it for a moment, with the familiar lurching of her heart she felt whenever she saw a picture of him. "And here he is, your father."

Emma took it from her. "Wow. He was quite something, wasn't he?"

"He certainly was. Here's another one. This was taken in the garden. That's my grandmother in her favorite straw hat." Helen swallowed, trying to dislodge the tears that tightened her throat. Oh, Gran, I wish you were here.

The damned tears wouldn't budge. She turned away.

Emma tactfully moved to the bookcase. "We obviously liked the same books. *Jane Eyre. Pride and Prejudice* . . . What's this?" She held up a tattered red-covered book that was lying on top of the bookcase.

"Shakespeare. I was Titania in *A Midsummer Night's Dream.* I met Julian after the opening night."

Emma opened the book and skimmed through the pages. Helen saw them in her memory, the tissue-thin pages scored with red pencil marks, where she had underlined her part.

She got up and crossed the room to unlock the wardrobe. The door opened with a squeak of unoiled hinges.

The few clothes she had left behind to emphasize the pretext that she was returning were still there.

She took out the tartan wool dress with the white collar. "I wore this on my first date with Julian."

Emma smiled uncertainly but made no comment.

"I don't think I'd fit into it now," Helen said wryly. She put the dress back, and her fingers encountered the stiff skirt of her taffeta-silk evening dress. She hesitated and then lifted it out. The iridescent green still shimmered.

Emma walked around the bed. "That's lovely." Her fingers ran over the fabric.

"Yes, it is. It would look good on you. Short skirts and bare shoulders are in again." She paused, looking at Emma. With her high-heeled shoes on, she was a little taller than her daughter. "You were conceived on the night I wore this."

Emma's eyes widened. "Oh."

"We had a wonderful, romantic evening. He took me back to his flat for the first time." She smiled. "That was it."

"He seduced you?"

"I didn't need much seducing. I was head over heels in love with him. We'd been going out together on and off for a year. I was ready."

She threw the dress on the bed and went to stare out the window, her arms locked together across her chest. "What I wasn't ready for was a baby and being abandoned by Julian when I told him about it."

The silence stretched between them. She doesn't believe me, Helen thought. She's probably thinking what a good actress I still am.

Emma spoke to her from across the room. "Seeing this room has made it all so real for me. I can tell from it how young you were. How much you loved my father."

Helen turned slowly. "I did. I truly did."

"It means so much to me, to know that. I just wish my coming hadn't made you so unhappy."

"Unhappy? I was then, of course. It changed my entire life. But all the time I was carrying you, I loved you very much. Giving you up almost drove me insane."

"And now?"

"Now? I've never stopped loving you, Emma. My negative reaction was not because I didn't love you, but because I was afraid."

"Are you still angry with me for contacting you?"

"I was never angry. Terrified that I'd been found out. Afraid that my carefully built facade would crumble. But since the day I watched the Turners walk out of the nursing home carrying you, I have never been truly happy. All these years there's been an emptiness in my life where you should have been."

Emma's eyes filled with tears. "Thank you," she whispered.

They stood, the bed dividing them.

"Would it be all right if I hugged you, do you think?" Emma asked. "I mean, even relative strangers hug each other nowadays, don't they?"

Helen opened her arms. For a moment she felt extremely vulnerable, her armor stripped away. Then Emma was close and she felt her firm young body against hers.

She had a fleeting thought that Karen had never hugged her so tightly and felt a spasm of guilt.

They moved from each other after a moment, exchanging embarrassed smiles.

"I thought you were so cold," Emma said, "but you're not at all."

Helen smiled. "Freezing helps kill the pain." She put out her hand to touch her daughter's lovely face. "It will take us some time to get to know each other. I'm prepared to stay in England for as long as it takes."

"You have your family to think of."

"They've had all my time. You're my family, too. Now it's your turn. That is, if you want me."

"Of course I want you. You seem to forget I've been wishing I could find you for ages."

"Ah, but that's not the same as wanting me once you've found me, is it?"

Emma sat on the bed. "There's so much more I'm dying to ask you. How you did at school. Your life in Canada. Our family history. I gather your mother wasn't . . ." Emma raised her eyebrows. "I don't know how to put it."

Helen felt the usual shriveling in her stomach when her mother was mentioned. "I'm afraid Aunt Hilary was a little blunt. My mother was hardworking, thrifty, and ever aware of her duty."

"She sounds cold and hard."

"If she was, life had made her that way. She'd had a very tough childhood. Her mother died when she was only twelve, and she had to take over as mother to the younger children, as well as trying to keep up with her schoolwork."

"Have you forgiven her?"

Had she? Helen closed her eyes for a moment. "Forgiven, yes. Forgotten, no. I think I understand her more now that I've had a family." Her eyes met Emma's, then slid away. "Maybe I'm more like her than I'd like to think. After all, I rejected you when you called me. The way she rejected me when I needed her most."

"Of course you're not like her," Emma said indignantly. "And what about your father? Where was he when you needed him?"

Helen put the green evening dress back in the wardrobe and closed the door. "We'll have plenty of time to talk about my family later. Now we really must go down. It's not fair to leave Aunt Hilary alone any longer."

"I'm sorry. There's so much I want to know." Emma gave her that shy smile that made her look so much younger. "I think we've done quite well for our first day, don't you?"

"Extremely well." Helen squeezed Emma's upper arm. "Thank you for being so understanding—and forgiving. The only thing is," she said briskly, "we've talked all about me and very little about you."

"I expect Daddy will make up for that this evening. I warn you, he's very much the proud parent."

"Good for him. He has every reason to be so."

"Will we have time to see the rest of the house?"

"Oh, I'm sure we will. We can take another quick tour before we leave and see the garden then, too."

"Did you tell her everything?" Hilary asked when Helen was helping her make more tea in the kitchen.

"We haven't finished asking each other questions. I can't pile all the information on her at once, you know."

"No need to snap at me. I just know you. Anything to wriggle out of the unpleasant truth."

"I do wish you'd stop thinking of me as a naive schoolgirl, Aunt Hilary. You haven't known me since I was eighteen. People change, you know."

"You haven't changed that much," Hilary said tartly. "After all, you haven't told your husband anything about Emma. If that isn't hiding from the unpleasant truth, what is? But, however long it takes, truth will out eventually, mark my words."

Helen put Aunt Hilary's warning out of her mind and enjoyed the rest of the afternoon with her and Emma. But, later, as they got into Emma's small red car and drove away from Lansdowne House, she again experienced the strange feeling that she was in a dream and about to wake up in her bed in Canada.

If she did, she asked herself, would she tell Bruce now, at this very moment, about Emma?

"I'm sorry Aunt Hilary wouldn't come with us," Emma said, bringing her back to reality. "I'm sure Daddy wouldn't have minded. In fact, I think he would have enjoyed her. Did they ever meet?"

Helen frowned, trying to remember. "I think so. I'm sure she came into the office occasionally." She shivered.

"Are you cold? Sorry, this car takes a little time to heat up."

"No, it's fine. I was just remembering something. The first day Julian came into the office, actually. I think it was the only time he and Mr. Turner—Richard—met. Richard didn't like him."

"I'm afraid he still doesn't. He pretends to be noncommittal, but I can tell."

"He's probably worried. It must have been a shock to him, your finding out that Julian was your real father. Perhaps Richard's afraid he'll lose you to him."

"Of course Daddy won't lose me," Emma said indignantly. "I've got love enough for both of them. Besides, it's a different feeling."

"*You* know that, but Richard may still worry."

"No, it's more than that. I get the idea he's always hated Julian."

Helen gave her a faint smile. "He barely knew him." The car made the turn around the dangerous bend on Petersham Road. "Oh, look," she cried, glad to have an opportunity to change the subject. "The Dysart Arms. That's where your father and I had our first drink out together."

"You and Richard?"

Helen laughed. "Heavens, this is going to be difficult, isn't it? No, me and Julian. Richard and I never went out together." She felt a flush rising into her face. "Richard was married to your mother when I worked for him. I was just a humble little office clerk. He must have been almost ten years older than I was."

"He's fifty-nine now."

"Right. A little older than Julian. Heavens, it's hard to think of them as that age. We all must seem positively ancient to you."

"Daddy does, but somehow Julian seems much younger."

"See what I mean? Watch out. It's dangerous to compare them. Anyway, what was I saying? Oh, yes. From now on I shall call Richard your father, and Julian shall be just Julian."

"That's what he wants, anyway."

"It will make him feel younger," Helen said—and immediately realized how spiteful she sounded. "By the way, don't be surprised if I call your father 'Mr. Turner.' It wasn't until much later—when he and your mother were organizing the move to Devon—that he insisted I call him 'Richard.' I'm not even sure I'll recognize him after all these years."

But when Richard opened the door the instant Emma put the key in the lock, Helen would have known him anywhere.

He stood in the doorway, gazing at her, his eyes warm behind his glasses. "Helen," he said, smiling that slow smile of his. "I would have known you anywhere."

She laughed nervously. "That's funny. I was just thinking the same about you."

"Is it permissible to kiss you? After all, you are the mother of my daughter."

They all laughed. "Of course." Helen felt his mouth brush her cheek and caught the faint hint of his fresh-smelling after-shave.

"Let me look at you properly." He took her hands in his. "No," he said after a moment. "You haven't really changed at all." He released her hands, but Helen still felt their impression on hers.

"I wish that were true," she said ruefully. "I'm afraid I've put on a few pounds since you knew me."

"Ah, but you were always too thin, you know," Richard said, tactful as ever. "You remember I used to try and fatten you up with cream cakes?"

"So you're the one responsible for my passion for rich cakes," she said.

Laughing, they all went into the living room. Helen had forgotten how much more cluttered homes in England were than in North America. Books on every surface, stacks of magazines by the fireplace, photographs on the mantelshelf—the Turners' flat looked comfortably lived in. Not at all like the home of an interior designer.

But then, it was also Mary and Richard Turner's home, and Mary had been dead less than a year.

As she sat, waiting for the dry sherry she'd asked for, Helen wondered when the small talk and banter would fade into awkward silence, leaving only the memories she and Richard Turner shared.

Richard's light brown hair was thin now and graying, but the kindness hadn't changed, or the humor.

He set her glass of sherry on the low table. "Emma's just laying the table. She said this would give us a few minutes to talk about old times together."

Helen smiled and then looked away from his watchful eyes to pick up her glass. "It's so difficult for her to understand. I tried to explain to her that I was the junior office clerk and you a partner of the firm." She took a sip of her sherry and then licked her lips to relieve their dryness. "She likes to think we were . . . friends."

"I like to think that, too," he said softly. "I think we became so later, don't you?"

She nodded, unable to speak for a moment. Then she said, "You were the best friend anyone could ever have." Her lips quivered. "I've never been able to thank you enough for all you did for me."

He took her hand in his. "I have my thanks a thousandfold every time I see our Emma's sweet face."

Our Emma.

She dared not meet his eyes. Gently she drew her hand away. "I was so sorry to hear about your wife." She hoped that mention of Mary Turner would break the spell that held them.

Richard moved away to pick up a briar pipe from the mantelshelf. "Thank you. It was a difficult time for us all." He put the pipe in his mouth but didn't light it. "Poor Mary. She suffered for a long time. Emma was wonderful."

"How was Emma wonderful?" Emma herself said, coming into the room.

"Looking after your mother."

"Oh, yes, poor Mummy. You were the wonderful one, Daddy. He took over all the cooking and grocery shopping," she told Helen.

"Emma tells me the dinner tonight is all your doing." Helen smiled at him.

"I find working in the kitchen a marvelous antidote to the boredom of wills and house purchases."

"You've been successful, though." She glanced around the large room, with its expensive, comfortable furniture and curving, art deco windows. Although the block of flats they lived in had been built before the Second World War, it was still one of the most prestigious addresses in Richmond.

"I suppose I have. I'm the senior partner now. Richmond has become one of the most fashionable and expensive places to live, which means we can charge nice fat fees. We've even got computers." He grinned at her. "Miss Price would turn in her grave."

"Oh, my goodness. I'd forgotten Miss Price. How she disapproved of me, didn't she? Especially when I began to wear my hair loose."

"It looked glorious that way."

Please don't, Richard, Helen thought. Especially not with Emma here.

Emma glanced from one to the other of them, sensing the sudden tension between them. "Sorry to butt in. I just came in to say that you're needed in the kitchen, Daddy. The duck is getting all black on top."

"It's supposed to get black on top, my pet." He set down his cold pipe. "Excuse me, Helen, I must don my chef's hat. This is a very important evening, necessitating a very important meal to celebrate our reunion."

It was a wonderful meal. Prawns and avocado in a vinaigrette, roast duck with blackcurrant sauce, a gooseberry fool with thick Devonshire cream. Helen suspected that Richard had stayed home all day to prepare it.

"I thought you'd like a truly English meal," he said.

"It was absolutely marvelous. Until today I thought I was a passably good cook, but I'm a novice compared to you, Richard."

He beamed at her praise. "I am glad you enjoyed it. Some more Stilton?"

"I couldn't eat another bite."

"Then we'll adjourn to the lounge and have coffee. You and Emma can have liqueurs. I won't, as I shall be your chauffeur for your return journey."

"That's okay, Daddy," Emma said. "I don't need another drink. I can drive."

"You are both my guests of honor tonight. You can come with us, of course, Emma, but I shall drive Helen home."

Helen sat back and relaxed, glad that she wouldn't have to be on her own with Richard in his car. She knew there was something unspoken hovering between them. Something more than their shared interest in Emma. She preferred that it remain unspoken.

For a while, the conversation was general. The cost of houses in the London area. The changes in Richmond, which Helen had yet to see for herself. Then it returned to the personal when Emma began telling Richard about Lansdowne House.

"You should see it, Daddy," she said after describing it to him. "It's an absolute gem. Alan would love it."

"And if Alan Grenville loves it, then it must be truly wonderful," Richard said, teasing her.

Emma laughed, her cheeks pink. "You know what I mean. I'm speaking professionally now."

"Of course." Richard's face became extremely serious. "What else would I mean?"

"Oh, Daddy." Emma slapped him playfully on the arm.

The rapport between father and daughter warmed Helen. They were completely at ease with each other. Even Bruce and Karen were not this close. On the other hand, she wondered how Richard was going to feel when Emma left home, as she must do soon, to achieve her independence of him.

"So your aunt Hilary is the only member of your immediate family left here?"

The question came at her out of the blue, taking her by complete surprise. "Sorry, Richard. I was dreaming for a moment."

"I was asking about your remaining family."

Her remaining family. The warmth Helen had felt only a moment ago seeped away, leaving her cold and shivery. "I never knew my mother's sisters and brother. They lived up north somewhere, I believe."

Her mother had rarely spoken of them. Helen suspected that she had been ashamed of her family and that the very proper accent her mother used had been acquired.

"When did your mother die?"

She was beginning to feel sick now. Too much rich food, she told herself. "In 1973, I think it was. Karen was eight."

"And your father?" Emma asked.

Here it was at last. The seemingly innocuous question. The question she dreaded but had to answer. Tell her everything, Aunt Hilary had said, or I shall.

"My father?" she repeated.

"Yes, when did your father die?"

Helen's brain was numb.

"I'm sorry," Emma said when she didn't answer, "I don't want to upset you. I'm just interested. He was my grandfather, after all."

"Yes, of course he was." Helen shut her eyes for a moment, swallowing the tight lump that closed her throat. "My father isn't dead. He's living in a home for retired clergymen in Hampshire."

23

Emma looked utterly bewildered. "I don't understand. I thought both your parents had died a long time ago."

"To me they had."

"You mean you've never visited your father, written to him?"

"Not since I went to Canada, no."

Emma's eyes blazed. "I think that's awful."

"Yes, I suppose it is."

"Hold on now, Emma," Richard said. "Don't jump to conclusions before you know all the facts."

Helen had to smile. "You sound like Bruce. No, Richard, she's right. It is awful, but I can't help it."

"Of course you can help it," Emma protested hotly. "He's your father. Even if you don't love him, how can you abandon your own father?"

Richard rubbed his hand over his mouth. "I don't think we should delve into other people's personal lives, Emma."

"She's not just 'people,' Daddy. She's my mother. And this is my grandfather we're talking about. If I hadn't asked point-blank about him, she wouldn't even have told me that I had a grandfather." She turned aggressively on Helen. "Isn't that right?"

"I'm afraid it is. Except that your great-aunt warned me that if I didn't tell you, she would."

"Why?" Emma asked. "Why have you abandoned your father all these years?"

Helen's long pent-up annoyance at being the bad guy spewed out. "I abandoned him because he abandoned me at a time I most needed him. Not only was he the father I adored, he was also a clergyman, someone who was supposed to help people. But it was always others he helped, not his own."

She turned on Richard. "You won't remember. It's all so long ago. But the day you drove me home from the office because I had so-called stomach flu—"

"I remember," Richard said quietly. "I remember thinking that your home looked cold and forbidding."

"My father was home, working on his sermon. I knew I had to tell him. I was terrified of telling my mother." Helen was aware that she was shaking, but she couldn't stop. "He didn't want to hear. All he could think of was what my mother was going to say, what his bloody parishioners would think of their vicar having a pregnant, unmarried daughter."

She turned to Emma, who sat, white-faced, dismayed at the floodgates she had inadvertently opened.

"You asked me if I'd forgiven my mother, Emma. I told you I had. That was true. I forgave her because I didn't expect anything more than I got from her. But I can never forgive my father. I thought he loved me, cared about me. He was my one hope when I felt so desperate. But all he cared about was my mother and his parishioners."

To her horror, she began to cry. She lowered her head and sobbed quietly, her hands dangling at her knees. "I'm so sorry," she whispered eventually. "I'm so ashamed of myself for this, for spoiling the evening."

Emma sat beside her and put her arm about her.

"I'm the one who should be sorry. I could kick myself for prying."

"No," Helen said vehemently. "You had to know everything. I promised. It's just that—that for a long time I've never allowed myself even to think about my father. Aunt Hilary would send me news of him and beg me to send him a Christmas card, at least, but I just couldn't do it."

Richard stood in front of them. "Drink this."

Helen looked up at him. "Oh, Mr. Turner, I'm so sorry." Immediately she clapped her hand to her mouth and laughed, even though she was still crying. "Damn, I told Emma I'd call you that. Must be all this bloody reminiscing."

She accepted the glass of brandy from him and took a large sip, the golden liquid tracing a path of warmth down her throat. "Oh, that's good."

He sat on the coffee table in front of her, his knees brushing hers. "This is all far too much for you in one day."

"It probably is. I must admit I do feel that I've been through an emotional wringer. I think I've cried more in these past few months than I have in my entire life."

Emma slid her arm away. "That's my fault."

"No, darling, it's not," Helen said. "It's good. I've been bottling all this up for years. It can't have been good for me—or my poor family in Canada."

"Did you know about this, Daddy?" Emma asked Richard. "I mean, my mother's—"

"Helen."

Emma smiled. "Helen's parents."

"Yes, I knew about it," he said quietly. "They were going to send her to some appalling church home for unwed mothers and have her baby adopted."

"But that's what happened anyway, wasn't it? I mean . . . I was adopted."

"Yes, but you went to someone Helen knew, and—"

Helen intervened. "I've told you, Emma, I wanted to keep you. I had no idea how I'd manage, but I still hoped that Julian would come back into my life and marry me. I was very young, remember, and remarkably naive. It was Richard who persuaded me to give you to him and Mary."

"Was I wrong?" He looked at Helen and then Emma, as if he expected both of them to give him an answer.

"Are you asking me?" Emma asked.

Richard shrugged his shoulders under the gray tweed jacket. "Both of you, really."

"You and Mummy were the best parents in the world." Emma reached out and hugged him and then, shoving aside the pile of books, went to sit beside him on the coffee table.

They sat there, side by side, waiting for Helen's response.

"If Emma hadn't called me, I might have answered that question differently," she said slowly, thinking as she went along. "Now that I am here, reunited with my lovely daughter, able to see how happy she has been, I can say unequivocally that you were right to persuade me to give her up."

Emma leaned forward to squeeze her hand. Then she stood up. "I'm going to clean up the kitchen."

"I'll help," Helen said.

"No, you two sit and enjoy your coffee and brandies and talk. Don't forget we're going to have the entire weekend together."

Before Helen could say any more, Emma bounced from the room.

Richard retreated to his chair, setting a distance between them.

"I'm dreading it, you know," Helen said.

"The weekend at Marsden Court?"

She nodded.

"Then don't go."

"I have to."

"This must all be a tremendous strain for you, Helen."

"It is." She swirled the brandy around in her glass.

"If you were to consult me, my advice would be to postpone seeing Julian for a while longer."

"I can't. It's terribly important to Emma."

"What in God's name does she expect? A Hollywood finish, the two of you coming together in the end?"

"Something of the sort, I suspect. Although, actually, she's pretty realistic about the whole thing. I've told her I'm a happily married woman."

"And are you?"

"Am I what?"

"Happily married?"

"Of course I am. My goodness, this really is an evening for personal questions, isn't it?"

She had hoped this would put Richard off, but it didn't.

"Are you really happy, Helen? I keep asking myself what sort of a person your husband must be, that you're afraid to tell him you had a child before you were married."

Helen was tempted to tell him it was none of his business, but how could she? This man had been her child's father. He had also been a supportive friend, both emotionally and financially.

"It's not my husband's fault," she said in Bruce's defense. "It's mine. When I first met Bruce, he was like the answer to all my prayers. He was dependable, and miracle of miracles, he loved me."

"He was, in fact, all those things the other men in your life had not been."

"I believe you've been reading too many psychology magazines," she told him.

"I doubt I needed to have done so to come to that conclusion." He tapped his tobaccoless pipe against the tiled fireplace. "I note you don't say you loved him."

"That came later. At the time, I was too numb to love anyone. I couldn't believe my luck in finding someone who truly cared about me."

Remembering Bruce's wooing, she smiled. Then the smile faded. "I think he thought of me as an untouched ice maiden, waiting to be thawed by the right man. If I had told him the truth, his fantasy would have been shattered. Having found him, I just couldn't risk it." She raised her eyes to meet Richard's. "He represented all that I needed at the time—devotion, shelter, security. When you say it out loud," she added bitterly, "it makes me sound like nothing more than a kept woman, doesn't it?"

He offered her no platitudes. "What about later, when you were expecting your next child?"

"Karen. Of course I had to tell the gynecologist. He promised to keep the fact that I'd had a child secret. Once that hurdle was over, there was no reason to tell Bruce."

"You put it all aside, forgot about Emma, and got on with your life." The cynicism in his tone was inescapable.

How dare he, a virtual stranger, read her so well! "You know damn well I didn't." Her fingers tore at the maroon cocktail napkin. "Not a day went by that I didn't think of Emma." She smiled and knew it was not a warm smile. "But I learned to distance myself from it all. I became a cool, calm person. The perfect wife and mother. Gourmet cook. Beautifully kept house. Hostess supreme. I was often tempted to tell Bruce the truth, but the more I put it off, the more impossible it became."

"And now?"

She laid the shredded napkin on the table. "Now it could mean the end of my marriage. Bruce hates lies. To shatter the illusion that he was the first man in my life, to tell him that I have an entire past life he knows nothing about, would be the last straw."

"The last straw? You make it sound as if all isn't well between you."

"All was very well with us until Emma called."

What a bare-faced liar she was!

"But you still haven't told him about her?"

"No. I've been a bundle of nerves trying to hide it from him. The guilt I felt at rejecting Emma when she called me has been tearing me apart."

"And you intend to return home and still not tell him one word about all that has transpired today?"

"You should have been a barrister, not a solicitor, Richard. I have the feeling I'm on the witness stand."

"I'm sorry. It's just that I'm worried about you."

"You have no need to be. I'm perfectly capable of taking care of myself nowadays. I am no longer eighteen and pregnant."

He accepted her rebuke with a wry smile.

"I will answer your last question and then I hope we can change the subject," Helen said. "I have every intention of staying here for a while to get to know Emma and to see that Aunt Hilary is all right. After that, I shall return home to Canada, my mind at ease, and resume my former life." She held up her hands to intercept his next question. "Without having to tell Bruce anything."

"And you will never see Emma again?"

She glared at him. "Of course I shall see Emma again. I'm not a monster, you know. I shall come over for regular visits to Aunt Hilary."

"And when she dies? She must be in her mid- to late seventies by now, surely."

"I shall deal with that when it happens. Now . . . enough, Richard. No more on the subject of my husband, please."

She sat back, gazing around the comfortable room, all the time aware that Richard was watching her.

"You're very pensive," he said. "Forgive me if I've upset you. That was not my intention, I assure you."

She was about to make some light remark, to avoid any embarrassment, but then remembered that this was a time for honesty. "I was just thinking about the past, remembering why I felt it was right to entrust my daughter to you." She leaned forward. "But you never suggested that I should keep my baby, did you, although I desperately wanted to?"

"No. I knew you were alone and would have found it very difficult to manage." He met her eyes, but this time his were the first to look away. "I was not well off. Besides, Mary would never have countenanced supporting you and the baby. The one way I could help you was to take Emma."

"I notice you haven't mentioned the fact that Mary couldn't have children. I thought that was the main reason for your adopting Emma." Why was she sounding so accusatory? Helen wondered. After all, hadn't they done a wonderful job with Emma? And why in God's name was she asking these questions, knowing where they might lead?

"It was Mary's main reason, not mine. When I suggested adopting the baby, I was thinking solely of your needs, not ours."

He got up to stare out the window at the view of the almost bare trees and the Thames beyond the terrace gardens. "And, after all, she was the only part of you that I could make my own."

There was nothing she could say. A devil in her mind marveled at how one innocent girl could unwittingly have created so much havoc in other people's lives, including those as yet unborn.

The thought came out involuntarily. "I sometimes wish I had never been born."

He turned, his sagging shoulders suddenly straight again. "Don't ever say such a thing. Don't even think it."

"How can I not, when you see all that's happened because of me?"

"I hate to hear a patently sensible woman speaking that way. You have brought beauty into people's lives. Not only mine, but also your aunt's and grandmother's."

"I killed my grandmother," she said flatly.

"What utter rubbish! I am surprised to hear such defeatist nonsense from you. It's time you stopped blaming yourself for every little thing that happens in this world."

She smiled. "It's remarkable how well you know me, considering we hardly knew each other."

"Each time I looked at Emma, I saw you."

"Emma's nothing like me. She's sunny and confident and well able to stand up for herself."

He beamed at her, suddenly the proud parent, as Emma had called him. "She is something special, isn't she?"

"You'll miss her when she goes," Helen said lightly.

He frowned. "Goes?"

"Yes, leaves home. She's thirty, Richard. It won't be long before she moves out, will it? Either to marry or live with someone."

A spasm crossed his face. "You seem to be very up-to-date with modern mores."

"Of course I am," she snapped. "I'm not a long-haired princess in an ivory tower, you know. My daughter, Karen, is having an affair with someone at present."

"I see."

"You don't see at all. The bloody man's married and is just using her. And if he's using her, he might be using others. I worry about all sorts of things—a nasty divorce, AIDS, but what can I do, other than warn her? She's an adult and must make her own life and her own mistakes."

"I sense a message in there somewhere."

"Oh, God. Who am I to be giving anyone advice?"

"Emma's mother, that's who."

"What about this Alan Grenville?" she asked quietly. "Is he someone special in her life? Have you met him?"

"He is and I have."

"What do you think of him? Besides the suspicious jealousy natural to a father," she added with a smile.

He looked at her over his glasses but chose to ignore the remark. "When I first met him, I liked him very much. But there's something about him that doesn't quite ring true. I'm damned if I can put my finger on it. When I ask Emma about him, she says there's nothing between them, bar their professional relationship, but I know she would like it to move on to something else. Apparently he doesn't like long-term relationships."

"Oh, dear. One of those."

"Yet when you meet him, he seems a sincere enough chap."

"He sounds like a man of the eighties, not the nineties. This is supposed to be the decade for commitment."

"You'll be meeting Alan Grenville tomorrow. I'll be interested to see what you think of him."

Her eyes gleamed. "Conspirators?"

"Exactly." He picked up his pipe to chew on the end. "I'm almost tempted to come with you."

"To Marsden Court? I wish you could. I'm dreading it."

"Would you like me to come?"

"How could you?"

He grinned, forcibly reminding her of the young solicitor in his twenties who used to tease her in the office. "Believe it or not, the mighty Sir Julian has issued an invitation to Emma's other dad."

"Never."

"Indeed he has. Just imagine it. Your first meeting with him in thirty years. His son by his first marriage. Emma and her two fathers—"

Helen began to laugh. "Stop, stop. I can't bear it."

"And Alan Grenville, Emma's potential suitor. Oh, I almost forgot the housekeeper and kitchen maid."

By now Helen was laughing so much that it hurt.

"You know what it's like?" she gasped. "A soap opera. 'All My Children.'" At this she went into another peal of almost hysterical laughter.

Emma stood in the doorway, staring at them. "What on earth's so funny?"

They were both laughing so hard that neither of them could answer her. Then Helen gasped to Richard, "We could create our own soap opera and call it 'The Grand Reunion.'"

"Beats 'EastEnders.'"

Drying her eyes, Helen turned to Emma. "Sorry about that. We were just discussing the weekend." She took a long breath. "I think hysteria set in—at least where I'm concerned. I'm feeling slightly punchy."

"You must be very tired. It's been a long day for you."

"You're right. I think I'd like to go home now."

Home to Lansdowne House.

"I was just asking Helen if she'd like me to come down to Marsden Court," Richard told Emma.

"I thought we'd already discussed that, Daddy."

"Perhaps Helen would like me to come."

Helen looked from one to the other, sensing tension. "To be honest, Emma, I'm scared stiff, but I know you'll be there, so—"

"I just don't think it would be a good idea for Daddy to come with us this weekend."

"Afraid I'll challenge the notorious Sir Julian to a duel, darling?" His tone was light, but Helen could hear the acid beneath.

"I think Emma is right, Richard. It might be easier for me to clear the air with Julian first."

Richard took his defeat well. "Then the nays have it. I shall spend this weekend at home alone, staring at the empty hearth."

"Poor Cinderella," Emma teased him, kissing him on the cheek. "He'll spend the entire weekend on the golf course, Helen, so don't feel one bit sorry for him."

But as she sat beside Richard in his Rover, driving at a sedate pace down the hill, Helen did feel sorry for him. He was patently concerned about Emma's relationship with Julian. She wished she could tell him that he couldn't keep his daughter tied to him. That letting go would be better than binding her close.

There were many things she would like to share with Richard about relationships with adult children, but she could not allow herself to get into any more intimate family discussions with him.

Thank God Emma hadn't wanted Richard to come with them to Marsden Court. The thought of that added dimension to what promised to be a stress-filled weekend made her head whirl.

24

Emma worked for most of Friday morning and through her lunch hour, putting the final touches to the preliminary sketches for Marsden Court. She was just rolling up the house plans when the telephone rang.

"Emma? Alan here. I've been held up at the other end of town. Sorry, but I'm going to be late. Why don't you go home and I'll pick you up there?"

"I've got my suitcase with me. Thought it would save having to stop off at my place before we go to Petersham."

"Damn."

"I'm sorry, but I really don't feel like lugging it back on the tube." Emma was annoyed. Couldn't he put himself out and be on time for her just this once? After all, this was rather a special day for her.

"You didn't bring your car, then?"

"No, of course I didn't. What was the point of bringing it when I was supposed to be driving down to Oxfordshire with you?"

She suddenly realized how bitchy she was sounding. Unnecessarily so, considering anyone could get caught in a London traffic snarl. "Sorry," she said briskly. "I don't mean to whine. I'm just a bit tense about today."

"I know. This delay's a bloody nuisance. I'll get there

as soon as possible, I promise. Let your mother know we'll be late picking her up, would you? No, I've got it wrong. Not your mother. It's Helen, Helen Lawrence, right? You can kick me if I screw it up."

Emma laughed. "I don't think anyone expects you to remember it all. I get muddled myself."

"Okay. I'll be there as soon as I can."

She was glad she'd apologized. Stupid to start off annoyed with each other. Something was worrying Alan, she was sure. Something beside the holdup. He'd been short-tempered all morning, and she'd heard him ask the receptionist to put any calls directly through to him, without vetting them first.

At eleven o'clock he had dashed off, muttering something about an important meeting, he'd be back by one at the latest.

She gathered up her sketches and shoved them into the Marsden Court portfolio. "You really are a bit thick in the head, Emma Turner," she told herself out loud. "Give it up. It's not like you to go moping around about a man."

Maybe she should do what the women's magazines kept telling women they could now do. Ask him outright. She imagined herself saying to Alan Grenville, "Are you one bit interested in me as a woman?"

She imagined him running his hand through his hair, a look of pity or perplexity on his face. "Emma, I am sorry," or "What in hell could make you think I was?" And then where would they be, professionally speaking?

To hell with the magazines! It was all very fine to give advice. Not so easy to carry it out without repercussions, however emancipated women might be.

She picked up the phone and punched out the number at Lansdowne House.

Helen wasn't sure whether to be glad or sorry that Emma and Alan would be late. She had been ready since lunchtime, dressed in the new sapphire-blue silk suit she'd bought at Holt Renfrew for the merger party.

When at last she heard the car pull up in the driveway, it was almost three o'clock.

"Are they coming in?" Hilary asked, peering through the net curtain in the drawing room.

"I doubt it," Helen said, already going to the door. "We're very late. They were supposed to be picking me up just after lunch."

When she opened the front door, Emma was on the doorstep, all apologies. "I am so sorry about this," she said in a low voice.

Behind her, Alan Grenville was staring up at the house. No wonder Emma was smitten, Helen thought. He was an extremely attractive man.

"Alan, come and meet Helen."

Smiling, he came forward, hand outstretched. "How do you do, Mrs. Lawrence." His voice was pleasant, too.

"Helen, please."

Aunt Hilary limped out onto the step and had Alan presented to her. "You have a beautiful house, Miss Barstow," he told her. "Perhaps you would kindly give me a guided tour on Sunday, when we bring Helen back." He looked at his watch. "We're running rather late, I'm afraid. My fault entirely."

As they were driving along the M40, Helen sensed the tension between Emma and Alan. They'd obviously had words on the way from Chelsea. She felt sick, her usual reaction when others quarreled.

"You realize that all this is entirely new to me." She waved her hand at the motorway, the cars hurtling in both directions. "I feel like Sam Beckett in 'Quantum Leap,' only I've leaped forward thirty years instead of back. When I left England, not that many people owned cars."

She rattled on, filling up the silent void, until she had drawn them both into the conversation. Gradually the atmosphere warmed and she was at last able to sit back and relax. "I'm sorry, I'm talking far too much. I tend to do that when I'm nervous," she confessed.

"So do I," Emma said from the back seat.

"Genetics," Alan said, and they all laughed.

Once they turned off the motorway, despite her anxiety about the coming ordeal, Helen delighted in seeing the English countryside again. Although the leaves had begun to fall, it was a crisp, bright day and the reds and golds of autumn lifted her spirits, despite her apprehension.

"We're almost there," Emma said. "Are you nervous?"

"Terrified." Helen turned to give her a faint smile. "I hope Alan realizes what he's letting himself in for."

"Oh, I've promised to keep my head down and not get involved," Alan said, his eyes on the road as he negotiated a tight bend in the narrow country lane. "If it gets really nasty, I shall disappear into the tithe barn with my trusty slide rule and leave you all to it."

Emma leaned forward. "Could you pull up here for a moment, Alan? This is the best place to see the house properly," she told Helen. "Once we go down into the valley, the trees tend to hide it."

Alan checked in his mirror and then pulled over onto a stretch of grass at the side of the road. Just beyond it was a break in the hawthorn hedge, where a wooden gate and a dirt track led to a farm.

They got out and climbed onto a grassy knoll just inside the gate. "There it is, Marsden Court," Emma said, pointing to the gabled limestone house that stood in the shelter of trees in the valley below them. Helen could tell from her voice how much she loved the place.

A shaft of late afternoon sunlight bathed the western wing of the house, turning the stone walls to gold. The remainder—with its many chimneys and mullioned windows—was warm creamy gray.

"It's beautiful," Helen breathed.

How inadequate a word to describe a house that

looked so utterly right in its surroundings. It was as if it had grown out of the ground, its roots mingling with those of the trees that both protected and enhanced it.

My ambition is to be so rich that I can surround myself with beautiful things. Julian's words came back to her, as clearly as if he had just said them.

It seemed he had achieved that ambition. "It must be spectacular in the summertime, when everything's green," she said hurriedly.

Emma and Alan grunted in assent. Helen knew, without turning to look, that they had moved closer together as they both looked down on the house.

"I wish I could stay here and not have to go down."

"Might I suggest," said Alan, "that the quicker you get there, the easier it will be."

"Julian's really very charming," Emma assured her.

"I am well aware of Julian's charm."

"Oops." Emma grimaced. But then she saw that Helen was smiling and she began to laugh. "Yes, you would be."

They drove down into the valley, but Helen was so nervous that she saw very little. Everything looked blurred, distorted, the only reality the sick galloping of her pulses. She should never have come. There had been no need to put herself through this agony.

Past the gatehouse, with its guard dogs; then a long driveway lined by horse chestnuts, and they were there, pulling up before the house.

There were two men on the steps. The younger— "That's Martin Holbrooke," Emma said—raised his hand and came down to greet them.

Julian stood, a lone figure, on the top step. Coriolanus on the steps of the forum, Helen thought with a stab of annoyance. Then, lithe as a thirty-year-old, he ran down to greet Emma, his arms around her, kissing her.

Helen felt a strange sense of déjà-vu.

Alan's hand was on the door handle. Julian came

toward her. The car door opened and she got out, feeling rather like a film star arriving at the Academy Awards. Unfortunately, her silk suit was creased around the middle and she forgot her handbag and had to bend back into the car to pick it up.

Feeling extremely flushed and inept, she turned to Julian just in time to catch the look of dismay on his face.

He immediately rearranged his expression and took her elbow. "Helen. My God, it's hard to believe, isn't it? Together again after all these years." He looked at her with smoldering eyes. "You've hardly changed at all."

Helen stifled a hysterical giggle. It was exactly like a scene from an old movie. She smiled at him, wishing he wasn't so close, too close to shake hands.

He bent his head and kissed her on both cheeks. "I hope you don't mind," he said softly. "But, after all, we were much more than mere friends, weren't we?"

Anger tightened her chest and rose, like bile, into her throat, threatening to undo her right then and there.

Damn him. Damn him to hell.

Aware that everyone was watching them, she drew away from him. "Your house is very beautiful."

"I am glad you like it, darling." There was a strong emphasis on the "you."

He introduced Helen to his son, Martin, and then extended his hand to Alan. "Welcome, again. Perhaps *this* weekend we may get a start on discussing our plans." He turned to Helen. "Last weekend was a trifle disrupted by the discovery that my interior designer just happened also to be my daughter."

They all laughed, but Helen caught the hint of accusation in Julian's voice.

Her determination not to upset Emma was fast being replaced by a strong desire to denounce Julian before them all as a lying hypocrite.

Shivering, she pulled the black wool serape more

tightly about her. She should have brought her sensible wool coat instead of catering to her vanity.

"You're cold," Julian exclaimed. "What am I thinking of, keeping you out here? Come on inside, everyone. Don't worry about the cases now. I'll send someone to get them."

Once inside, Helen took refuge in admiring the great hall, with its oak beams and narrow, leaded windows. A giant bowl of cream and gold crysanthemums stood on the long, polished oak table in the center.

Martin took Emma and Alan into a room to the left, leaving her and Julian alone in the hall. She felt like a tongue-tied schoolgirl again.

The man before her was a stranger, yet she had known his body intimately. It was still a good body, she noted. No sign of a paunch or sagging neck muscles. How on earth did he do it?

She glanced around the hall, to avoid the still brilliant eyes that were assessing her openly. "This is lovely, Julian."

"Would you like to see the rest of it?"

"Not yet, if you don't mind." She was dying to go to the bathroom. "Perhaps I could go to my room?"

"Of course, darling. My housekeeper, Mrs. Pennington, will take you up."

As he strode off down the hall, Helen sighed. For heaven's sake, couldn't he just tell her where her room was?

She stifled a giggle when she saw Mrs. Pennington. The perfect stage housekeeper, complete with west country accent and black silk dress. She was led up the wide staircase with its carved banisters.

The elegant bedroom was like something out of *Architectural Digest.* Ivory carpet and turquoise-and-ivory chintz covers. A creamy gardenia plant on the table filled the room with its heady fragrance.

Having told her where everything was, the housekeeper

said, "When you're ready, Mrs. Lawrence, Sir Julian has asked that you join him in the library for tea. The library's the second door on the right when you go down."

To Helen's relief, the excellent Mrs. Pennington slipped away, leaving her to find the bathroom and then to look about with great misgivings.

The house was undeniably beautiful. Julian had always had good taste. But she felt as if she were an alien in it. She didn't belong. Everyone else was attached to Julian Holbrooke in some way.

She was most definitely alone. If she confronted Julian, the weekend would be spoiled, and everyone—especially Emma—would blame her for it.

Her eye caught sight of the ivory telephone on the curtained bedside table. She picked it up. Automatically her fingers pressed 0101 before she realized it.

She put the receiver down again. She couldn't phone Canada without asking first, could she?

She caught her worried reflection in the long, gilt-edged mirror. What a fool! Here was Julian rolling in money, and she was concerned about making a little long-distance call.

What time was it? Five-thirty. Twelve-thirty in the afternoon in Toronto. That was okay.

As she heard the familiar Canadian ring, she crossed her fingers. "Please be in, Annie," she said out loud.

"Hallo."

Thank God. "Ann. It's me, Helen."

"Crikey, what a coincidence. I was just thinking of you. How's it going?"

"If I started to tell you, it would take two hours. I can't stay long. This is just a quick call."

"How's Emma?"

"Oh, Annie, she's absolutely wonderful. I'll give you all the details when I get back to Richmond." She quickly gave her an outline of their meeting.

"Where are you now?"

"Julian's place. You should see it! Like a film star's house."

She heard Ann's burst of laughter and joined in with her, realizing what she'd said. "Oh, Annie. You're making me feel better already. I want advice—and quickly. Julian's waiting for me. He's got some wonderful fairy tale made up about what happened between us. Emma adores him. Should I play along for her sake and not make a scene?"

"Not bloody likely," Ann screeched across two thousand miles. "Emma wants the truth, you told me. So give it to her. She can take it. If you let Julian get away with it, you're the scapegoat. Kick him off his bloody pedestal."

"They'll all hate me."

"Who the hell cares? Stand up to him. Do it for yourself, not Emma. Then, if you feel you have to get away from the place, walk to the nearest station."

"But—but I'm wearing my high-heeled shoes." Hysteria bubbled in Helen's throat. She began to laugh and couldn't stop.

"Then take 'em off."

The laughter subsided. "God, Annie, you're good for me. What would I do without you?"

"I'm in your corner, remember. Go get 'im, baby."

"I will. Thanks. Love you. Wish you were here."

"I'd love a ringside seat. Do it *now!* Love you. Bye."

"Bye." Helen put down the phone. She paused only to check her hair and makeup, dragged ineffectively at her creased skirt, and opened the door.

25

As *Helen walked down* the stairs, she could hear voices and laughter from below. When she reached the bottom step, Martin Holbrooke came out of a room on the left of the hall, carrying three empty beer bottles.

"Oh, hallo, Mrs. Lawrence. Were you looking for my father? He's in the library, waiting for you." He grinned. "I believe you've received the royal summons."

She liked him at once. "Yes, so I understand. By the way, would you mind calling me Helen? Don't forget I'm Canadian. We tend to go in for first names across the pond."

"Helen it shall be."

They stood looking at each other, Julian's son and the mother of his only other child, and Helen felt instinctively that perhaps she did have an ally after all.

"Emma's very like you," Martin said softly. "If it's any help to you at all, I'm extraordinarily grateful to you for having given me such a terrific sister."

It was such an unexpected and obviously sincere compliment that she felt like hugging him. "Thank you, Martin." She smiled. "I'm scared stiff, you know."

"Of my father?"

"No, not of *him*. Of his . . ." She hesitated, not

knowing how to explain it to Julian's son. "Of his ability to distort the truth."

He smiled, raising dark eyebrows at her. "Ah, yes. He does have a tendency to rearrange the facts, doesn't he? You aren't the only one to have realized that, you know."

Helen heard the touch of bitterness in Martin's voice. For a fleeting moment his hand was at her elbow. Then it was gone. "But I believe he must have hurt you more than he did anyone else in his life."

More even than Martin's own mother? Helen wondered about that, but she knew nothing about Julian's marriages, and this was definitely not the time for personal questions.

"Are you ready for your grand audience?" he asked.

She nodded, grateful for his attempt to lighten the tension.

"Then here we go." He strode to the second door on the right and opened it. "Helen's here," he shouted unceremoniously, and backed out again, leaving Helen to enter the room by herself.

She had an impression of bookcases crammed with books, lovely antique furniture, color and warmth everywhere. An old spaniel, his golden fur turning white in places, stretched out before the crackling fire.

Julian had jumped to his feet as soon as she entered. "You must forgive Martin," he said, glaring at the empty doorway. "For all his expensive education, he lacks the social graces, I fear."

"I like him very much. He's warm and sincere."

There, she had fired the first salvo by disagreeing with him about his son.

Julian took both her hands in his. "Let me look at you again. You really haven't changed as—"

"As much as you thought I had?" Helen finished for him. "Oh, come off it, Julian. Admit it, you were absolutely shocked when I got out of the car. You were expecting to see a willowy eighteen-year-old and got a middle-aged mother of three adult children instead."

The smile faded. "Well, all right, then. It was a bloody shock to see your hair going gray. Why the hell haven't you colored it or something? It was your most beautiful attribute."

This was better. This was more like the old Julian, the one she had come to confront with the truth.

"May I sit down?" Without waiting for his permission, she sat at the end of the green-and-ivory-striped sofa.

"Of course. Sorry. Would you like tea or a drink?"

"I think I'll take the drink. Not sherry or Babycham, thank you," she added sweetly. "I'll have a gin and tonic."

The old spaniel came to sniff at her. "Who's this?"

"That's Jasper."

"Jasper?" She couldn't help smiling.

"What's so funny?" He sounded annoyed.

"Jasper was the dog in *Rebecca*, remember?"

He didn't reply. He was pouring the drinks at the cabinet that was built in below the bookshelves and set the bottles down just a little hard on the glass shelf.

Good, she had riled him. She remembered, with sudden clarity, that Julian always came closer to the truth when he was angry.

He put the drink in front of her and then sat on the leather chair opposite. "Do you have to wear glasses?"

"Not if you don't mind my spilling gin all over your lovely sofa, no."

"If you have to wear them, why tinted ones? Forgive me, but I hate to see your lovely eyes hidden."

Bruce had often said the same thing. Slowly she took off the glasses and laid them on the table. "There, is that better?" She felt uneasy without them, the light too bright.

"Infinitely. You must think it's bloody rude of me to make comments about your appearance. It's just that the Helen I remember—"

"No longer exists," she said firmly. "You cannot turn back the clock, Julian."

"Have I changed that much?"

She was forced to look at him. What should she say? For a man of fifty-seven, you look marvelous? The truth was, he looked as attractive as ever. In him, the graying of his hair merely enhanced the aquiline features. His body seemed as graceful and agile as it had been thirty years ago.

"Well?" he asked impatiently.

"I think you've changed remarkably little in looks," she told him coldly. "As for you yourself, I have no idea what you are like. We are strangers." She looked down at the glass. "In fact, we always were strangers. I never really knew the real you."

"What utter rot! We were lovers, for Christ's sake."

"Hardly. We slept together twice, that's all."

"Do you need to be quite so crude about it? God, Helen, you really have changed. And as for us sleeping together twice, that wasn't my fault, was it? Considering you were Miss Prude of the sixties."

She pressed the backs of her knees against the sofa's base to stop her legs from shaking. "I was a girl of seventeen who'd never had a boyfriend before you came along. It was a more innocent age, Julian, in case you've forgotten. The swinging sixties hadn't got into their stride. At least, not for me, they hadn't."

"And I was a randy goat, I suppose. Did I force myself upon you, is that what you're saying I did?"

"Not at all. But I object to you suggesting that ours was the grand love affair. I'm sure you were going out with other women at the time."

He ignored that. "I still find it amazing that you would talk of us as strangers. We went out together for almost two years."

"One year. We met in July 1960, and parted forever in October the following year."

"Not forever. You are here now, in my home." He

gave her the dazzling, intimate smile that still made her heart turn over. Damn him, damn him, damn him, that he should still have the power to do that to her!

She glared at him. "Did you ever let me meet your friends, your family? No. Did you ever even talk about them to me? No. You knew absolutely everything about me. I knew nothing about you."

"Except that I loved you."

"Did you, Julian, did you really?"

"I have never forgotten you, darling. When I saw Emma for the first time, I was bowled over. For a moment, I thought it was you come from the past to haunt me."

"Yes, me as you remembered me. A fantasy me. Not a fifty-year-old woman with gray hair and a thickening middle."

"You're not fifty."

"Almost. Who cares?" she said, exasperated. "I'm not the Helen who adored you and would have done anything for you, the Helen you saw as a clean slate to be written upon."

"The Helen who ran away from me."

It was like a fist in her stomach, taking away her breath. Her instinct was to leap on him and scratch his eyes out. She took a deep breath. "*I* ran away from *you?*"

"You disappeared completely, remember? Even your family didn't know where you were."

"How would you know what my family knew? You were in Hollywood."

"I couldn't get you out of my mind. I hated parting from you the way we did. I phoned Lansdowne House and spoke to your aunt Hilary. She told me you'd disappeared and no one knew where you were."

Helen was bewildered. In all the years they'd written notes to each other at Christmas, Aunt Hilary had never mentioned that Julian had phoned. "I don't believe you."

"I wrote you a letter, begging you to tell me what had happened to you. I was desperately worried about you."

She shook her head at him and licked dry lips. "I don't believe one word of it. You're making it all up to appear the hero in Emma's eyes."

"No, I'm not. And if I'm not a hero, you're certainly no heroine. You gave up your baby to strangers to bring up and never told me I had a daughter. How could you have kept that from me?"

This was all a nightmare. She was light-headed with tension. "Because the last time I saw you, Julian, you were telling me it was over, that you were going to Hollywood. You were cooking spaghetti, I remember. I've loathed spaghetti ever since. You gave me money, as if"—she choked, unable to say it—"as if I were a whore. Money for an abortion, you said."

He put his hand over his eyes, hiding his face.

"I threw it back at you," she continued. "Then you sent me a check and a list of doctors who performed secret abortions. Or have you forgotten that as well?"

He rubbed his fingers across his forehead. "I thought . . ." He seemed bewildered for a moment. "I had, but now it's beginning to come back to me," he murmured.

He suddenly looked his age, and she felt sorry for him. But she mustn't allow him to manipulate her. She could hear Ann in her corner, urging her on.

"What would Emma think of it all?" she demanded. "The money you gave me, the list of doctors?"

He paled. "You haven't told her, have you?"

"No, not yet. But she should know. I'm growing a little tired of appearing the bad one in this story."

"It's not true that I demanded you have an abortion. I merely suggested it as one option that we might consider." His voice had a querulous tone, as if he were begging her to confirm his memory.

"*We* weren't considering any options. You had opted out." She gave him a bitter smile. "I wouldn't kill your baby. Despite the fact that you'd abandoned me, I still loved you desperately. When I told my parents, they wanted to put me in some dreadful religious home for unwed mothers. They even threatened to charge you with rape. So I ran away."

"Oh, God. I hadn't realized . . ." He leaned forward, his hand outstretched to her. How gracefully he moved. "But what about your grandmother, your aunt? Surely they would have looked after you."

"I was ashamed. They had done so much for me. I couldn't bear to ask them to do more. They would have been so disappointed in me. I left without telling them. I never saw Gran again. She died a few months later."

"Christ!" He put his head in his hands and stared down at his feet. She could hear him breathing. "I am so sorry, Helen. I was a bloody swine to abandon you like that."

She had meant to keep so calm, to remain so cool, but the suddenness of his admission, the words she had wanted to hear for so long, undid her. She began to cry, the tears trickling down her face.

He came swiftly to kneel before her. "Don't cry, darling. I can't bear to see you so unhappy." His arms were around her and she was sobbing against him, her face pressed to his chest.

After a minute or so she pulled away, embarrassed and annoyed at herself. This dissolving into tears was getting to be a bit too much. She put on her glasses again.

He stood up, wincing a little as he did so. She was glad to see that he hadn't entirely escaped the ravages of time. "How about another gin?"

She shook her head. "I'm light-headed enough as it is." She looked up at him. "I've been dreading this."

He sat beside her, turning so that he could see her face. "I can see why. All that anger bottled up all these years. God, what a bastard I was. My mind was full of the Hollywood offer. I couldn't think of anything else."

"I know that. Particularly not marriage and a baby. But, at the time, I would have taken anything. I even had dreams of keeping a little cottage in the country where your baby and I would wait for you to visit us at weekends." She gave him a rueful smile. "Pathetic, wasn't I?"

He took her hand. "If you had been at Lansdowne House when I called and I had known you'd kept the baby, I might have offered you that."

"On the other hand, you might not."

"I doubt it would have lasted, anyway. Not at the time. I was too bloody selfish then. You needed someone like Turner, someone safe and reliable."

She smiled. "You make me sound extremely boring."

His hand tightened on hers. "I don't find you boring at all. In fact, my Titania has matured into a very attractive and sexy woman."

She laughed outright at this—and then the laughter died when she saw his expression. God in heaven, he really did find her attractive.

Once again it was time to bring Julian back to reality. "My husband's a safe and reliable lawyer, but he's not at all like Richard in other ways."

"What I would like to know is why you haven't told him about Emma. Is there some problem with your marriage?"

"That's really none of your business."

"Emma's happiness is my business. And she thinks you're ashamed of her."

"Of course I'm not ashamed of her."

"It also saddens her to think that she will never meet her half sister and brother. She and Martin get along remarkably well, you know."

"I'm not surprised. He's a very nice person." They were back where they had started.

Julian grunted. "He runs the estate well, I'll admit."

Her hand was still in his. She tried to take it away, only to find it gripped more tightly.

"I was a fool to let you go, my sweet Helena. A damned fool. It's only now that I realize what I lost." He bent his head and kissed her.

She closed her eyes, for a moment responding to him instinctively, then pushed him away.

"That's enough, Julian." She sat upright, trying to smooth down the skirt that had ridden up to the tops of her thighs.

His eyes gleamed. "It's still there, isn't it, that old feeling between us?"

"For God's sake, stop talking such melodramatic garbage."

"Methinks she doth protest too much."

He looked down at her, but she avoided those brilliant blue eyes. She stood up and found her legs were unsteady.

He took her elbows and drew her closer, so that their bodies touched. Helen was finding it difficult to breathe. "Excuse me, I'd like to go upstairs to my room."

He released her. "One thing before you go," he said urgently. "What will you tell Emma?"

"About what?" she asked. Although she knew exactly what he meant, she wanted to hear him say it.

"About my . . ." He shrugged. "My response to your pregnancy. Will you tell her I suggested an abortion?"

"Not suggested, Julian. You *expected* me to have an abortion, remember?"

"Whatever," he said with an impatient wave of the hand. "Will you tell her?"

"I'm not sure yet what I shall tell her." Seeing his anxiety, she added, "I will tell her that you tried to contact me when you got back to England, if that's the truth. Don't forget that I can verify it with Aunt Hilary."

"Your aunt may deny it. After all, she hasn't mentioned it to you before. She never liked me, did she?"

"No, she didn't fall for your charm like Gran and I did. But if what you say is true, however much she disliked you, she still should have told me you had called."

"I called twice."

Helen frowned. "Of course, she didn't know where I was until much later. When did you call, by the way?"

"The first time? November sometime, from the States. Then I phoned again, as soon as I got back from Hollywood. Must have been April, I suppose."

"April? *April?* But . . . that was only a month before Emma was born. I don't understand. Aunt Hilary knew how to get in touch with me by then. Richard had contacted her and told her . . ."

Their eyes met.

"Your aunt Hilary definitely didn't like me, did she?" Julian smiled sadly.

Helen drew in a long breath and released it in a sigh. "You said yourself it wouldn't have lasted."

"True. Not then, at least. Still, one never knows."

The silence between them was broken only by the crackling of the fire and Jasper's snoring.

Helen spoke at last. "We shall always have Emma."

"True. She's lovely, isn't she? Not only lovely to look at, but bright, intelligent . . ."

"I think so."

"That's one thing that can never be taken away from us. Our love created a beautiful person." Julian smiled his siren smile at her.

"Yes."

His bronzed face glowed with sudden excitement. "It might not have worked then, but it could be very different now, my darling."

Helen's eyes widened. As he came toward her, she took an instinctive step backward.

"You look so wonderful in this room, Helena," he said. "You suit this house perfectly."

She stared at him in silent amazement. Before he could say any more, she opened the door and went out.

26

"*Why don't we all* go to church?" Julian suggested after breakfast on Sunday morning. "Mind you, I'm not sure the vicar could withstand the shock of seeing some live bodies in his pews."

"I'd like that," Helen said. "How about you, Emma?"

Emma nodded. "I think we've got something to celebrate, don't you?" She turned to Alan. "Would you prefer to stay here and work?"

He gave her a strained smile. "No, I'll come along."

"Count me out," Martin said, scraping back his chair. "I've heard too many of Jeremy's pseudomod sermons, I'm afraid. I don't know why he bothers, considering not one member of his tiny congregation is under sixty."

Julian gave him a baleful look as he went out and then turned to Alan. "You'll like the church, Alan. It has some particularly fine carvings in the choir stalls."

"Then I'll definitely come. If you'll excuse me, I must make a phone call first. I'm keeping a note of my calls, by the way."

Julian looked astonished. "For God's sake, man, whatever for?"

Color flared on Alan's cheekbones. Emma looked down at her piece of toast, feeling embarrassed for him.

It *must* be a new woman. Nothing else, surely, would cause him to act so strangely about making a few phone calls. Come to think of it, he hadn't really relaxed since they'd arrived.

To Emma's relief, Helen jumped in. "As a matter of fact, I've made some calls to Canada, Julian. I'll settle—"

"For Christ's sake," Julian exploded. "What's the matter with you all? Does it look as if I can't afford a few phone calls for my guests?"

Alan murmured his thanks and slipped away.

"Whom were you calling in Canada?" Julian asked.

Helen looked as if she were about to tell him it was none of his business. "Bruce, of course," she said.

Emma could tell that it still upset her mother to talk about her family in Canada.

"And I also called my friend Ann. You remember Ann Sturgis, Julian?"

"Vaguely. Emma said she'd spoken to her, I believe, when she was looking for her father." He gave Emma a loving smile. "I must admit I'm surprised you're still friendly with her, Helen. Rather a common girl, if I remember."

"What a snob you are. Ann was and still is my dearest and best friend. She stayed with me all the time I was expecting Emma. Then we went to Canada together."

"I'd love to meet her," Emma said.

"Maybe you will one day. She's divorcing her husband and would like to come back to England permanently, if she could afford it." Helen smiled at Emma. "When I was staying with her in Toronto she said she was dying to meet you, considering you had made such a change in her life."

Emma grimaced. "Oh, dear, I seem to have changed a great many people's lives."

Julian jumped up to kiss her cheek. "For the better, I'd say. To know you is to love you."

Emma saw Helen thank him with her eyes. She

drank down her tea and pushed back her chair. "Well, if we're going to church, I'd better change. I put on jeans, as I thought we'd be working this morning and that barn is filthy." She shuddered, thinking of the rat she'd seen there yesterday.

"Don't dress up," Julian said. "The Reverend Jeremy Ravelstone will be so delighted to see some people in his pews, you could be naked for all he cared."

Emma thought Julian was exaggerating, but in fact there were only seven other people in the congregation, apart from the choir of elderly, quavering voices and a decidedly off-pitch organ hidden away somewhere above them.

As she sat in the ancient church, breathing in the dank, musty smells of the old stones and timbered roof, she thought about all that had happened this weekend.

Her birth parents sat side by side at the end of the special pew for Marsden Court. They looked good together. A beautiful couple, she thought wryly. At least they seemed to have resolved a great deal of their conflict.

Whereas she and Alan seemed to be farther apart than ever. They had worked most of Saturday, measuring and examining the tithe barn and discussing their ideas with Julian, but whenever she had spoken to Alan he had answered her only in monosyllables.

Now he sat beside her, his shoulder pressed against hers because of the constricted room in the pew. She could feel the tension in him. What on earth was wrong with him?

She touched his hand. He turned, startled, as if he had been miles away. "It's a lovely old church, isn't it?" she whispered.

"Full of dry rot," he whispered back.

She was tempted to kick him hard on the ankle.

After the service—having escaped from Reverend Ravelstone's effusive thanks for having deigned to attend his humble little church—they piled back into Julian's dark green Jaguar, license-plate JH1.

"Let's go for a pint before lunch, shall we?" Julian suggested.

"What a great idea," Helen said. "I haven't been into a country pub for—"

"Thirty years?" Julian smiled at her. "Remember the Dysart Arms?"

They pulled away from the church and drove off down the sunlit lane, beside a winding stream. There were still leaves on the trees here in this sheltered lane. The branches formed a canopy of gold and bronze overhead.

"This is all so lovely," Helen said with a sigh.

A car hurtled past them, going far too fast for the lane. "Strange, that," Alan said. "That's the second car I've seen speeding down here. Wonder what's up."

With a screech of brakes, the car came to a halt just beyond them, blocking the lane. Julian was forced to stop. Two men jumped out and came running toward them.

"I don't like the look of this," Julian said, visibly nervous.

"Lock the doors," Alan said from the rear seat.

Julian did so, but the windows were still halfway open. "What the bloody hell do you think you're doing?" he demanded as the two men reached them.

One, a thin-faced man in jeans and a windbreaker said, "'Scuse us, Sir Julian. This'll just take a minute." Bending to the open window, he addressed Emma. "Miss Emma Turner?" he asked.

"Yes, that's right. Has something happened?"

The man straightened up. "We've got 'em," he yelled to his companion, and before anyone had time to do anything, the other man bent down and began taking pictures of the two women, the camera whirring and clicking at tremendous speed.

Instinctively both Emma and Helen put up their hands to shield their faces from the cameras.

"All done. Thanks, love," Emma heard the man say.

"Open this bloody door, Holbrooke," Alan yelled, "so I can get their camera." He leaped from the car and ran after the two men, catching up with them just before they reached their car.

Yet another car screeched to a halt behind the Jaguar. Two men jumped out. The woman driver kept the engine going.

Julian seemed frozen at the wheel. "I'm so sorry about this," he said, shaking his head. "I'm so very sorry."

Emma looked at Helen. She was deathly white. "Don't worry." She leaned forward to squeeze her mother's shoulder. "They won't hurt us."

"Not physically," Helen whispered.

Alan came running back. "Get the hell away from that car," he yelled, moving menacingly toward the two men.

"It's all right, sir," said the man, his tape recorder in his hand. "Nothing to get excited about."

"I'll get excited all right, if you don't get back into your car."

The reporter ignored him, thrusting first his elbow and then the recorder into the few inches of space at the top of Helen's window. "Care to make a statement about your love affair with Sir Julian, Mrs. Lawrence?"

Alan dragged him away from the window and shoved him and his recorder into a bramble hedge. Hearing his friend's yelps and curses as he encountered the sharp thorns, the photographer lowered his camera and retreated hastily. Both men hightailed it back to their car.

The woman driver reversed at top speed down the lane, leaving ruts in the soft ground of the hedgerow. Then the car in front of them roared off, leaving the lane free ahead of them.

"Thank God they've gone," Emma said. She was shaking all over and felt as if she had been violated. "Now I know how Princess Di must feel," she said with a shaky laugh, trying to ease the tension. Helen looked utterly stunned with shock. Emma leaned forward to rub her hand up and down her mother's arm.

Alan got in the back. "Bloody bastards," he said, breathing heavily.

Emma grabbed his arm. "Are you all right?"

"I'm fine." He was rubbing his hand. She could see that the knuckles were scraped and bleeding.

"Oh, Alan." She had a sudden mad impulse to throw her arms around him and kiss him. Instead she said, "You were absolutely wonderful."

He was furious. "We were all bloody useless against them. The other two threatened to charge me with assault. Can you believe it?"

"Trouble is, they'd probably say you used undue force," Julian said dryly, "that the media was just doing its job, getting the news to its public."

"But we're not news," Emma said hotly.

"Oh, but we are." It was the first time Helen had spoken in ages. "We are all connected with the great Sir Julian Holbrooke in a big, juicy story."

They huddled together in the car, silent for a moment as the reality of this sank in.

"Sorry to be a party pooper, but I'd like to go back to the house," Helen said wearily.

Julian made no move to start the car.

Helen's voice rose. "Julian. Please take us back."

"I'm sorry, darling. I hate to say this, but I've a feeling they'll all be waiting for us at the gates."

"Damn," Alan said. "You're probably right. There were two other cars, weren't there?"

"Probably a great many more than that by now. I know how the press works." Julian took Helen's hand. "The only way to get rid of them is to give them a story."

"I won't. I refuse to." She snatched her hand away so furiously that Emma thought she was going to strike Julian.

"Darling, be reasonable," he pleaded. "They've got our pictures anyway. They've obviously got the story as well. Surely it's better to give them the truth, rather than let them print their filthy inventions?"

"We can't," Helen whispered. "Don't you see we can't?"

Emma felt a stab of anger. All her mother could think of was her precious family in Canada. It was obvious that that was what was uppermost in her mind.

"I think Julian's right," she said. "Much better to make a statement and then we can get on with a normal life."

"That's true, Mrs. Lawrence," Alan said. "There's not much else we can do."

Emma could see only Helen's white-faced profile. She felt immensely sorry for her, but she was also glad that this miserable episode might put an end to all the secrets.

There were several cars and vans at the gates, the reporters and cameramen lined up, waiting for them. Two local policemen ordered them to clear a way for Julian's car.

Julian stopped the car and got out, all smiles and bravado. He looked, Emma thought, as if he should have a sword in his hand and be making little circles in the air.

"You've caught me out, damn you all," he said good-naturedly as the cameras whirred and clicked. "If I promise to give you a statement within the next half hour, will you go away, like good chaps, and leave us all alone?"

"How about a photo of you all together?" a woman's voice shouted.

"And who's the guy in the back who assaulted us?" demanded another.

"We'll see about the photo later. The statement will tell you about everything and everyone, I promise you." Julian gave them a smile of camaraderie. "Trust me. Have I ever let you down before?"

Some of them laughed. The mood became less frenzied. The cameras kept going, but a path was cleared and Julian allowed to get back into the car.

The gates opened slowly. Emma held her breath for a moment, fearing the reporters would all pour in behind them. Looking back, she saw the gates close. As Julian drove off, the driveway was empty behind them.

Thank God. She saw now the reason for the gates and security. It was more than just a symbol of Julian's fame and wealth. She wondered if it was all worthwhile. For Julian, perhaps, but it was not her sort of life. Nor, she imagined, would it be Helen's.

27

"It was all going so well," Emma said to Alan as they were working in the barn later that afternoon. She had changed back into her jeans and wore long leather boots, necessary protection against the spiders and rats and mice, all of which she loathed.

"I know. Your mother's really upset, isn't she?"

"It's understandable. If her family in Canada reads anything about this, her cover's blown."

"You don't sound too sorry about that part of it."

"I'm not. I hate secrets. Why can't people just be open with each other? Secrets make people sick, literally."

He turned away abruptly. "I'm hoping we can keep the main cruck beams, but we may need something stronger to hold the dividing wall."

Whenever we start talking about emotions, it's back to work, Emma thought. Why on earth should she be interested in someone who was totally incapable of commitment or even of just discussing feelings?

"Hallo there." Julian appeared in the dusty sunlight streaming in the open door.

"Hi." Emma came to him, leaving Alan to climb up the long ladder to examine the crumbling beams. "How's Helen?"

"She won't talk to me," Julian said gloomily. "She's locked herself away in her room. That's what I came for. Would you be a sweetheart and see if she'll talk to you?"

"Of course. Alan's got some questions for you, anyway." She was about to start off for the house but turned back. "Have you been able to find out who it was who spilled the beans to the press?"

"Must have been one of the gardeners," he said. "Whoever it was will receive his marching orders."

Suddenly she knew. "It was you, wasn't it?" His face told him she was right. She shook her head in amazement. "You told the press about Helen and me. How could you?"

He opened his mouth to deny it. Then closed it again.

"What's wrong?" she asked. "The autobiography not selling well enough?"

"That's rather bitchy."

"Is it? I see you don't deny it, though. I think what you did was absolutely awful. How could you, especially when everything was working out so well?"

"Oh, come off it, darling. They'd have found out soon enough, anyway. I did it because I wanted to share my happiness with everyone. I never dreamed they'd go that far."

"You may be used to sharing your most intimate life with the press, but we're not. What about our right to privacy? Helen's terribly upset, and Daddy's going to be furious when he hears what's happened."

He cast his eyes up to the rafters. "Who gives a tinker's curse about Daddy?"

"I do, and don't you ever forget it, Sir Julian." Emma jabbed her finger in the air at him. "He was—and still is—a wonderful father to me. If you want me to keep in contact with you, you'll do well to remember that."

He ran his hand distractedly through his hair. "Sorry, darling. This has all been very upsetting today."

"Damned right it has been. Let's not forget whose fault it is, shall we? I bet Helen knows it, too. That's why she won't speak to you."

"What's going on down there?" Alan shouted from above them, his voice deadened by the musty bales of straw.

"Julian's here to talk to you," Emma yelled back. "I'm just going to the house for a while."

She marched out before either man had time to respond. "Men! Effing, bloody men," she muttered, striding across the lawn and up the terrace steps.

She dragged off her muddy boots and was crossing the hall when Mrs. Pennington came out of the library.

"Oh, Miss Turner. I wonder if you could tell me where Mr. Grenville is? There's a telephone call for him."

"He's out in the barn with Sir Julian. I'll take the call for him."

"The person on the phone said she must speak to Mr. Grenville only."

Emma raised her eyebrows. To hell with the caller, whoever she was. She'd have to put up with Mr. Grenville's lowly assistant. "Don't worry. I'll take a message for Alan." She marched to the door.

"It's the phone on the desk." Mrs. Pennington hovered in the library doorway. "She said—"

"Don't worry about it, Mrs. Pennington," Emma said, brushing past her.

She picked up the phone. "Hallo?"

She could hear someone breathing on the other end of the line. Then a woman's voice said, "Oh, dear. I was wantin' Mr. Grenville. I—I can try later."

This surely couldn't be one of Alan's women friends, Emma thought. The voice was that of an older woman, with a strong cockney twang. "Why not leave a message with me for him? This is his associate, Emma Turner."

"Oh, so you're Emma, eh?"

"That's right. I'm Emma."

Silence, during which Emma puzzled over who this could be. It sounded like one of the women who cleaned the office.

"I'm sorry, dear," the woman said hesitantly, "but he said as I must speak only to him, see. It's about his dad."

"His father? Is he ill?" Could this be a nurse, perhaps?

"Yes, but he's ever so much better now. I expect Alan didn't want to tell you, seeing as you had important plans for the weekend. I promised I wouldn't bother him, but—"

Silence again. Slowly it began to dawn on Emma who this was. It was the use of Alan's first name that did it.

"Is this Mrs. Grenville, Alan's mother?" she asked.

"Yes, that's right," the woman said eagerly, as if relieved to be recognized. "Alan was so worried about leaving and he may've tried to get me, but I've been at the 'ospital all day. He doesn't like me to call him at work, but I thought this was different."

"Bloody right it's different," Emma murmured, anger building.

"Beg your pardon, Miss Turner?"

"I said you were quite right to call. And it's Emma, by the way, not 'Miss Turner.'"

"It's nice to talk to you, Emma. We don't often see Alan, but when we do he seems to mention you a lot."

More than he mentions his parents to me! Emma thought. "I'll go get him right away. Where can he reach you?"

"Trouble is, I'm at the 'ospital, dear. It's one of them pay phones."

"Oh, I see. Which hospital?"

"St. Mary's. Alan knows. He visited his dad there on Friday, after he'd had the operation."

Friday lunchtime, when he was late. Emma drew in a breath between clenched teeth. "Can you put in another pound, Mrs. Grenville? That should be enough, as it's Sunday. I'll hare off and fetch Alan as fast as I can."

"Oh, would you, dear? That is nice of you. There, I've put in another pound."

"Okay. Here I go."

Emma put the receiver down on the desk and ran from the room. Cursing, she dragged on her boots and then went out, crashing the door shut behind her.

Martin came round from the front of the house. "What's up?"

She glared at him and then remembered that he wasn't to blame. "Tell you later," she threw over her shoulder at him as she ran across the lawn.

When she burst into the barn, Alan and Julian were poring over the plans by the light of Alan's powerful worklight, which hung from a hook in the wall.

"Urgent phone call, Alan. Your mother."

"My mother?" he repeated incredulously.

"Yes, your mother. It's nice to find you have one, like us lesser mortals."

She stalked away from him, back across the lawn.

"What the hell's that supposed to mean?" he shouted, grabbing at her elbow from behind.

"What it says. And there's no need to shout."

"Damn. I told her not—" He stopped short, seeing the expression on Emma's face.

"Not to call here? I can't think why she didn't obey you, can you? After all, she's only calling because your father's in hospital."

"That's not what I meant."

She stopped short of the terrace and faced him. "Go and speak to your mother or her money will run out."

"Aren't you coming in?"

"No, I'm going for a walk." She turned and walked away in the direction of the beech coppice.

For more than half an hour she scuffed through the dead leaves, watching the sunlight come and go through the lattice of branches above her. When Alan came to find her, she was picking hazelnuts and eating the ripe brown kernels.

She heard him approach from behind her. "I'll probably be damned for this," she said, not turning around.

"For what?"

"Eating hazelnuts on a Sunday. When I was a girl, my father told me that in some parts of the country, picking nuts on the Sabbath is supposed to bring bad luck."

"Well, it certainly looks as if something's brought bad luck on us all this Sunday."

Emma turned quickly. "Is your father worse?"

"No, as a matter of fact it was good news. The growth they removed was benign."

"That's wonderful. So, where's the bad luck—for you, at least?" she asked belligerently.

He shrugged and kicked at a tree stump.

"Look at me, Alan."

He did so, reluctantly. His face was shuttered, no emotion filtering through.

"Just for once, could we forget you're a partner and I'm an employee?"

"Go on. Say what you have to."

Emma came one step nearer him. "Will you listen to me, though? The way I listened to you that awful night after the phone call with Helen, the night you were so kind to me?"

He glanced up at the tree branches above him. "Could we go somewhere more comfortable, do you think?"

She was about to snap at him and then saw that he was serious. "You don't like the countryside, do you?" she said.

"Not much." He gave her a faint grin. "I like to feel cement beneath my feet."

"Is that why you can't relax when you're here?"

His spine stiffened. "I hadn't been aware that—"

"Oh, for heaven's sake, I'm not criticizing you. I know you haven't been relaxed here. Yet you love the work itself. So it had to be the place."

He drew in a deep breath and, as he let it out, relaxed his shoulders. "Something like that."

"I remember now. You said last weekend that you thought the country house atmosphere was a bit too precious for your liking."

"So it is."

"Now I know that you don't like the countryside very much. What else can I find out about you?"

She waited for him to say something, but he stood in the clearing, tall and tense, the sunlight gilding his hair, glowering at her as if he would like to strangle her.

"Come on, Alan," she said in a coaxing voice. "I've told you all about myself. I don't think there's anything you don't know about me. Now it's your turn." She held out her fist as if it were gripping a microphone. "Alan Grenville. This is your life!"

She waited as he rubbed his hand over his mouth, his brown eyes wary.

"I don't gossip. It won't go any farther than"—she looked up—"than these trees."

Still she waited. "You'd probably like to tell me that it's none of my business, but I think it is. It makes me feel awfully vulnerable when I've poured out my life story to you and I don't know one thing about your life."

"My work is my life," he said through gritted teeth.

"No, that's not so, not for any one of us," she said fiercely, "however much we might feel it is. I've learned through this whole crazy experience of mine that family means a great deal. We can't do our work properly until we get our private lives worked out."

"I hadn't realized you were a part-time psychoanalyst."

She ignored the gibe and came another step closer. "I speak from experience. I can't even go to bed with a man until I get myself sorted out."

He looked startled at that. "I didn't know."

She laughed. "How could you? I don't have it carved into my forehead. There, I've told you my last awful secret. Let's sit down and you can tell me yours. Although I'm sure I know it already."

She sat herself down on a cushion of dry leaves with her back against the trunk of an ancient beech tree.

He looked down at the ground with obvious misgivings. "Are you sure it's not wet? Couldn't there be voles or moles or something?"

For the first time in ages, it seemed, Emma let herself go in a peal of laughter. "For heaven's sake, let your hair down." She took his hand and dragged him down beside her. "What's a squashed vole between friends?" She went off into another shout of laughter and was glad to see him grin, at least, in response.

"Okay, I'm going to make this easy for you. I'll ask the questions. Where were you born?"

He hesitated.

"Come on, don't even think about it. Just give me straight answers, as if we were in court and I was a lawyer."

"I was born in Bermondsey."

"My God, you really are a true Londoner, aren't you? Wasn't Michael Caine born there? Somewhere nearby, I think. Tommy Steele certainly was. Did you know him? No, he'd have left Bermondsey by then. He was living in that gorgeous house in Petersham when you were still a kid."

Emma was painfully aware that she was rattling on, as usual. She paused and then said, "Okay, so you're a real Londoner. That's a rare breed nowadays. How many siblings?"

"Three. Three sisters."

"Oh, poor you. Younger than you?"

"No. All older. I was hopelessly spoiled."

She held her breath for a moment, realizing that it was the first fact he'd volunteered.

"What did your father do?"

She could sense him steeling himself. "He was a plumber."

"A good, lucrative business, plumbing. Schools?"

"I won a scholarship to a private school, at first. Then my eldest sister married a clothing manufacturer and she paid for me to go to a minor public school, a boarding school." He looked down at his hands, the well-manicured nails grimy from the barn. "I loathed every minute of it."

"I bet you did. Is that where you got rid of your cockney accent?"

"My mother and sisters worked on me before that. 'You can't get on in this life if you speak common,' they'd say."

"Doesn't apply so much nowadays," Emma said lightly, "but I expect it did when you were growing up."

"Don't kid yourself. Even now I don't think you'll find too many architects with cockney accents. Actors, musicians like Nigel Kennedy, maybe, but not architects." He raised golden-brown eyebrows at her. "What would your Sir Julian think of me if I dropped my aitches?"

She didn't answer. "And then you went to Cambridge?"

"You know the rest, professionally speaking."

"And all that time you were growing away from your family?"

He picked up a large twig and, one by one, stripped it of its leaves. "It wasn't just me," he said in a low voice. "They encouraged me to break away from them. 'You don't want your posh friends meeting us,' Mum would say."

Tears stung Emma's eyes. "It must have made you feel very lonely. Especially if you'd been a close family."

"We had been."

Emma watched his profile, wishing she could hold him in her arms and comfort him, as he had held her that night. But she knew better than to invade his space until he invited her in. If he ever did.

"I felt rather like an orphan for a while. Abandoned. They kept pushing me away and I wanted to cling on. Then, as I got older, I adjusted. I learned to keep my friends and my family apart."

You didn't have to be a psychologist to see why he'd never married, Emma thought. Marriage usually involved one's family, whether one wanted it to or not.

"No wonder you were so kind to me when I told you about my mother rejecting me." Emma shifted a little, as if she were making herself more comfortable, but now her shoulder and thigh were pressed against his.

"That was different."

"Yes, I suppose it was. I was given up by my mother, and it seems my real father conveniently chose Hollywood over me," she said in an acid tone. "Whereas you, Alan, had a loving family. In fact, they loved you so much that they pushed you out of the nest so you could better yourself. Now that was true sacrifice."

He turned his head to give her a wry smile. "Are you trying to make me feel guilty?"

"Not really. It's understandable that you'd feel awkward with them now. Socially, you're poles apart."

"But I'm still a cockney at 'eart, right?" he said, affecting a cockney accent.

"Maybe you are, without knowing it. Have you ever wondered why you still hang on to the Docklands flat, when you say it doesn't suit your image anymore?"

"Because I'd take a gigantic loss if I tried to sell it, perhaps?" He was beginning to look and sound his old self again. Only now it was different. Now she knew who he was.

"No, silly. Because you can just about see Bermondsey

across the Thames from your place. Hadn't you realized that?"

"Actually, I hadn't. My God, Emma, you really have missed your true vocation," he said, mocking her. "You definitely should be a psychoanalyst."

"Oh, stop that." She punched his arm playfully and then settled back, only this time even closer to him than before. "Do your parents still live in Bermondsey?"

"No. I moved them into a nice house in Fulham. That was as far as they'd go from the center of London."

She slipped her hand into the crook of his arm. He didn't pull away. "I remember reading a magazine interview with Kenneth Branagh. He said he took his parents to one of his plays and when he asked them afterwards whether they'd liked it, they wouldn't give an opinion, because they were so afraid of saying the wrong thing and embarrassing him."

Alan turned to her, his face animated. "That's it. That's it exactly. If only they'd be themselves, but they worry themselves sick about saying the wrong thing."

"See? They're thinking about your feelings, all the time. But although you've been phenomenally successful, the feeling that you were rejected still hurts, doesn't it?"

"Yes, you're right. It still hurts like hell."

"But you're a wonderful architect. And you love your work. Never forget that's their gift to you. You can repay them by excelling in the work you love."

For a while they sat, her hand tucked in his arm, pressed against his heart. Then he turned his head and looked down at her, his eyes glowing with a golden light. "You surely are something special, Emma Turner," he said slowly.

He pulled his left arm away to put it around her shoulders, and she lifted her face. It was as easy as that. No fireworks, no trumpet blasts. Just the warmth of his mouth on hers and a feeling of rightness about his kissing her.

"Emma, my darling, darling Emma," he whispered,

coming up for air. "Where have you been all my life?"

"Working right beside you, Mr. Grenville. Waiting a hell of a long time for you to find me."

He ran his fingers down her cheek. "I thought it was you who'd found me." He kissed her again, this time pulling her closer to him so that they were half sitting, half lying against the tree trunk.

His hand slipped inside her heavy Aran sweater. Her entire body seemed one great pulse beating against his, but she was also growing increasingly aware of a knotty root under her right side and a large stone digging into her hip.

"This isn't very comfortable, is it?" she said when the discomfort began to outweigh the pleasure.

"I thought you loved the countryside."

"I do, but I can think of more comfortable places to make love."

His eyes darkened. "Is that what we're doing, making love?"

A tide of warmth flooded into her face. "That's what it felt like to me. At least, the preliminaries. But then, what would I know?"

He took her face between his hands and looked into her eyes. "You're a boundless fount of knowledge, Emma Turner."

He looked away to glance down at his watch. Normally she might have felt the gesture was a brush-off, but this time was different.

"You'll be wanting to leave right away."

"Would you mind? I'd like to be able to get to the hospital this evening."

Emma stood up, brushing leaves and twigs from her clothes. "May I come with you?"

"Of course. I intended to drop you and Helen off at Richmond first."

"No, I meant I'd like to come to the hospital. If that's all right with you."

His face was like sunlight in the darkening wood. "It

certainly is. I must warn you, though, my mother will think you're someone very special to me. Nadia only met my parents once. It was a disaster," he added. "I vowed I'd never bring another woman home until—"

"Until?"

He quickly changed the subject. "Will Helen mind leaving early?"

"I doubt it. Actually, I think she'll be delighted. Apparently she's refusing to talk to Julian."

"Good God, I'd completely forgotten all about the reporters. Can you believe that?"

"Yes, I can believe it." She laughed up at him. "But I'm sure we'll be forcibly reminded tomorrow, when we see our photographs plastered all over the newspapers."

28

Karen was watching the Wednesday "Tonight" show, eating a low-cal meal, and reading the *Winnipeg Free Press.* The news item was tucked away in the People section of the paper.

FAMOUS ACTOR FINDS LONG-LOST DAUGHTER, screamed the headline.

She idly scanned the story of Sir Julian Holbrooke's recent discovery that the interior designer he'd engaged to renovate his house just happened to be a daughter he didn't know existed. Ridiculous! Did they really expect people to believe such garbage? Trash like that was suitable for the *National Enquirer,* not the *Free Press.*

She came to an abrupt halt at the name that jumped out at her.

The mother of Sir Julian's daughter is Helen Lawrence, a Canadian, who was Sir Julian's first love thirty years ago.

Karen almost dropped the foil container on the floor. "Shit!"

It couldn't be the same Helen Lawrence. Karen read on, her heart beating faster.

Sir Julian's beautiful Elizabethan mansion in Oxfordshire was the setting last week for the grand reunion of the two lovers and their daughter. "I am an extremely fortunate man to find such a lovely daughter," Sir Julian said to reporters. "Had it not been for an absolutely freakish coincidence, I might never have found her."

Karen was beginning to feel sick.

She picked up the telephone and started to punch out her father's number. Then she put the receiver down again. "Don't be such an idiot," she said out loud to herself.

Helen Lawrence wasn't an unusual name. There must be a dozen of them in Winnipeg alone.

But how many of them had migrated to Canada from England around thirty years ago?

She picked up the paper again, this time reading it more slowly. It didn't give her a clue as to which Helen Lawrence it might be. It wasn't a local news item. Just a news bureau pickup from London.

The only photograph was one of Julian Holbrooke as he had appeared in his youth. Very good-looking.

Setting aside the paper, she pressed her father's number, this time completing it.

David answered.

"Hi, Dave. I thought you'd be at Phil's."

"I was watching the game with Dad. Don't tell me you didn't know Toronto won the pennant tonight," he said in a derisive tone.

"Sure I knew. I heard about it on the radio when I was driving home from the office. Shame I had to work tonight or I could have watched it with you."

"Is that why you're calling?"

"Not really. Can I speak to Dad?"

"He's upstairs in the bathroom. I'll get him to call you back. Are you okay? You sound sort of strange."

"Has Dad mentioned reading something in the paper?"

"Nothing other than the score of the last Blue Jays game. We didn't talk much tonight, if you know what I mean."

"Have you two been fighting again?"

"More icy silence than actual fighting. What's this about something in the paper? No doubt it's something legal."

"As a matter of fact, you're wrong. Go get today's *Free Press.*"

"Yes, ma'am." David clunked the receiver down in her ear. "What page?" he asked when he came back.

"Twenty-three. A column on the left-hand side. See the heading? 'Famous Actor Finds Long-Lost Daughter.'"

"Yes."

"Read it."

Karen could hear the rustle of paper. Then David said, "Yo! That's weird. Same name and everything."

"It couldn't be Mom, could it?" Karen knew she sounded scared. The fact that David didn't reply straight away bothered her. "Tell me I'm crazy even thinking it."

"I don't know. Mom's been acting pretty strange lately," he said slowly.

"Oh, shit, Dave. If it is her, it would kill Dad."

"I think you'd better speak to him. I'm not sure I want to be around when he hears, even though he'll know it's not her, of course." His voice sounded hollow, as if he were trying to persuade himself as well as Karen. "Here he is."

"Hi, sweetie," her father's voice boomed over down the line. "Can't you sleep?"

"At eleven-thirty? You must be joking. I'm just getting my second wind." She laughed nervously. "I was just telling Dave about a weird coincidence and wondered if you'd seen it, too. Dave will show you."

The rustle of newspaper. Then an ominous silence.

"What do you think of it, Dad?" Karen asked.

"I think you've got an overactive imagination. Your

mother's staying with her aunt near London, not on some actor's estate in Oxfordshire."

"You're absolutely sure of that?"

"Damned right I'm sure. She phoned me from there just yesterday to ask how the merger party had gone. Said her aunt Hilary was still not too well, so she was staying on another week to get her sorted out and clean the house up."

"I didn't think it was Mother, but I just thought I should call."

"Of course it's not your mother. Did you ever know her to tell us lies about anything?"

"That's true. Sorry to bother you. Go back to bed."

"I wasn't in bed."

"Okay, go back to wherever you were. And enjoy your visit with Dave. See you Sunday, for lunch. Tell you what, let's go to Rae and Jerry's for a good steak. Dave, too."

"Okay. That's a date. Bye, sweetie."

Bruce put down the phone and then reread the piece in the newspaper. It was utterly preposterous to think it might be his Helen Lawrence.

Except for that damned "thirty years."

"What do you think, Dad?" David asked.

"I think Karen's working too hard, that's what I think."

"Mom hasn't really been herself recently, has she?"

"So that means she's telling us a bunch of lies about her aunt being ill and she's really moved in with some film star and their love child?"

David smiled sheepishly. "Sounds crazy, I agree." He began to move to the door.

"Are you leaving?"

"Yeah. Got some work at the computer to do. Why?"

"Oh, nothing." Bruce opened the refrigerator and then closed it again without taking anything out. "Just gets a bit quiet around here at night, that's all."

"Want me to stay a bit longer?"

"Not if you've got work to do. The Heberts aren't tired of you yet?"

"They haven't said so." David hesitated. "Would you like me to move back in here for company?"

"Some company. We drive each other crazy."

"We don't necessarily have to, do we?"

"I guess not. Come on home, if that's what you want."

David stifled a smile. Strange how his father had twisted it around to *his* wanting to come home.

"I'll move back tomorrow, okay?"

"Fine. Karen and I are going to the ballet next week. Want to come? I can get another ticket easily."

"Sure. That'd be great."

Ballet wasn't really David's bag, but he could recognize an olive branch when he saw one.

After David had left, Bruce watched part of a Jets hockey game he'd taped. But the piece in the newspaper stuck with him.

After a while he switched off the VCR and picked up the current *Maclean's* magazine and leafed through it. Nothing in there about any Helen Lawrence.

It was all garbage, of course. Ludicrous garbage. Yet he couldn't get the damned thing out of his mind. He began working out dates, going back and forth, searching through his memory for anything that might tie this sensational story to his quiet, self-contained wife.

"I suppose I could phone her." He looked at his watch. Damn, it was just before six-thirty in the morning in England. But he could call at seven. Tell her he couldn't find the keys to the toolshed or something stupid like that.

He was missing Helen damnably, anyway. All these years he'd taken her quiet presence for granted. Just one week without her had reminded him how much he needed her.

He missed the discussions over dinner, the laughter. The problem was, though, there hadn't been much of either in the recent months. It was as if Helen had disappeared into a world of her own, behind an impenetrable glass wall.

Most of all, he missed her in his bed. Not just for making love, but for warmth and comfort and the awareness that she was there, beside him, helping him through the night. But that, too, had changed. Even in bed, as they lay beside each other, he had felt that icy wall between them.

"Helen, I miss you," he muttered. "Come home."

What a fool he'd been to think Carla could give him what he was missing in Helen: the old companionship, the fun, the love. . . .

That first night, he was so furious that Helen had flown off to England and left him alone, he'd gone directly to Carla's after work. They'd ordered in a pizza and polished off a bottle of Nuits-Saint-Georges between them.

An excellent cognac and he'd felt primed for his first time with Carla. It was Helen's fault this was happening. She had only herself to blame.

He'd reached the bedroom door. One look at the bed with its black satin sheets and he'd shriveled up like a prune. His face flamed at the memory.

"This isn't going to work," he had murmured, turning to escape and finding Carla there.

She'd tried to coax him at first, twining her arms and legs about him, touching him. He felt nauseated when she did that and pulled away.

"I'm sorry," he muttered. "This was a big mistake. I have to go."

She'd screamed at him then. Called him all kinds of names. He deserved them, he knew. He *was* a bastard for jerking her around. Then she'd attacked his masculinity, telling him he was good for no one. No wonder his wife was frigid if that was all he could do.

He felt the bitter frustration and anger welling up inside him again as he remembered. What in God's name had induced him to get involved with the woman?

As he sat in the den, his head in his hands, he knew he'd deserved everything he'd got. He'd used Carla Remillard to fill that awful void in his life, that feeling of "Is that all there is?" As he remembered his humiliation, the Peggy Lee tune ran through his mind.

Not even the plans for the new offices could excite him now. Nothing mattered without Helen.

For a long time he sat, staring into space. Then he glanced at the clock on the VCR. One-fifteen. Good. Early, but not too early.

He pressed out the number and waited. The phone was picked up on the third ring. "Hallo?" It was Helen's voice.

Bruce suddenly felt a fool for calling her. "Hi, darling."

There was a long pause. Then she said, "Hallo, Bruce," in a stiff, formal manner that chilled him.

"Sorry to call you so early, but I wanted to get you before I went to bed."

Another pause. "Is everything all right?"

"Absolutely fine. Just one strange thing. There's a bit in the paper about the actor Julian—"

He heard a little gasp, nothing more, but the small sound crossing thousands of miles to him was enough to make his heart drop.

"I had meant to call you, Bruce. I really had, but I just couldn't get up the courage. It was foolish of me to think it wouldn't get to Canada eventually."

"Christ! It is you, then?"

"Yes, I'm afraid so. There's so much to explain. I wish I'd done it years ago, but—"

Bruce was swamped with fury and frustration all at the same time. How could this be happening to him? "What the hell is this all about? How can you have kept a secret like that from me all these years?"

"I'll be coming home very soon. I'll tell you everything then." Her voice sounded wobbly.

"Like hell you will. Where are you now? With your

lover, Sir fucking Julian?"

"I'm with Aunt Hilary. She hasn't been well."

"Oh, really," he sneered. "I begin to wonder if you have an aunt at all."

"I don't blame you at all for thinking that. I promise to tell you the truth as soon as I get home."

"You'll tell me before that. I'm catching a plane over tomorrow."

"No, please don't." He caught the edge of hysteria in her voice. "It's all been such a great strain. I'm not sure I could take any more at the moment."

"You mean your husband would just get in the way."

"No. I don't mean that. We—we'd planned a sort of family get-together on the weekend. Emma just got engaged."

"Emma? Who the hell's Emma?"

"Emma's my daughter, Bruce."

Again, rage filled him. "I'm coming over. Tell me where'll you be on Saturday."

Another long pause. "At Marsden Court. We're all going down there. You'd never find it by yourself."

"I'll give it a damned good try."

"No. If you insist on flying over, I'll meet you at Heathrow on Saturday morning."

"So you'll stay in London?"

"No, Bruce, I won't. I can't miss—"

"Your daughter's engagement party," he said with heavy sarcasm.

"Not exactly. Richard's throwing her an official party in a few weeks' time. This is just a family get-together to celebrate."

"Then get someone who can give me the directions to this Marsden Court to phone me. You go on to your family party. I'll join you there on Saturday."

"Oh, Bruce, you can't."

"Like hell I can't. May I remind you that I just

happen to have been your husband for twenty-nine years and that you have two children here in Canada?"

"You don't have to remind me of that," she said, a mixture of tears and anger in her voice.

"I guess you've forgotten us."

"Don't be so ridiculous."

"Get someone to call me as soon as possible. Then I'm going to bed. I've got a hell of a lot to do tomorrow. Cases and appointments to reschedule, meetings—"

"This is all totally unnecessary. I'm sure I'll be able to come home by the end of next week."

"I'm coming. Discussion over."

"Please, Bruce, please wait until Monday. Then we can talk about this in private with no one around."

"I'll be there on Saturday."

"Very well."

The icy wall was up again. Tangible, even across the great distance that divided them.

"How the hell could I wait a week to find out what's going on, Helen? Even three days is bad enough. You've turned our marriage into a sham, a bloody sham. I feel I know absolutely nothing about the woman I've been married to all these years. How could you do this to me?"

"Oh, Bruce," she whispered. "I am so sorry. I wish to God I'd told you."

"But you didn't. I had to find it out from reading the bloody *Free Press*. I was the last to know. Anyway, there's no point in going on about it. Have someone call me. I'll see you on Saturday."

He slammed down the receiver and then stared at the telephone. He must call Karen and David. He didn't want anyone else telling them before he did. He had to give them the facts.

The facts. What were the facts? The woman he'd lived with all these years, his children's mother, was an utter stranger about whom he knew nothing.

"What's wrong?" Karen said when he called her.

"The Helen Lawrence in the paper. It's your mother."

"It can't be," she gasped.

"I called her. She said she'd explain when she got home, but I told her I'm flying over."

"When?"

"Friday."

"How can you, Dad? You've got—"

"Who the hell gives a damn what I've got? This is more important. After all, if I died, someone would have to take over, wouldn't they?"

"I'm coming with you."

"Don't be stupid. You can't just take off."

"If you can, then I sure can. I don't have anything major on at the moment anyway, and I haven't taken a holiday at all this year. Besides, I could do with a break."

"I know that," he said softly. That swine Michael Pascal. Karen had told him he'd dropped her without even a telephone call to explain.

"Would you like me to come? I mean, I know it will cost a bomb, but—"

"To hell with the expense." He thought for a moment. "Yes, I would like you to come. Help to pass the time."

She laughed. "Thanks a heap, Dad."

"No, I mean it, sweetie. Come, if you really want to. After all, she is your mother. That, at least, we know for a fact," he said bitterly. "Sorry, my mind's spinning."

"Want me to call David?"

"No, I should do it. I suppose he'll want to come with us."

"Will you take him?"

"If he wants to."

But, to Bruce's surprise, David didn't want to come with them. At first he had been stunned into silence at Bruce's news. Then he said, "You do whatever you want, Dad, but I think we should wait until Mom comes home so she can tell us everything in her own time."

"Frankly, I don't trust her to tell us the truth once

she's back here. I can't wait, Dave. I have to know what's going on, right now."

"I know how you feel. It's like we—we don't even know her. Shit, Dad, why didn't she tell us? We're her family, for God's sake."

Bruce could tell that David was really upset. It would hurt him especially. He and Helen had always been particularly close. "Come on home, son."

David sniffed. "I'm okay."

"You may be okay, but I'm not. I need you, Dave. It's going to be a long night."

"Okay, Dad. I'll be right over."

Bruce was about to get himself a Scotch when the phone rang. An English voice introduced himself as Richard Turner. "I'm Emma's father," he explained.

Bruce was beginning to think he'd fallen asleep and was in some sort of crazy nightmare. "I thought Sir bloody Julian was her father."

"I'm her adoptive father."

"And I'm Helen's husband," Bruce said belligerently. "Perhaps you didn't know she was married."

"Of course we knew." There was a tinge of dry amusement in the man's voice that made Bruce's blood boil. "I can imagine this has come as a great shock to you, Mr. Lawrence. Helen is very upset that you had to hear this way."

"Not half as upset as we are."

"No. I can imagine. She said you were flying over. I gather she told you we were all going to Marsden Court."

"You gather right."

"I shall be driving down to Marsden Court on Saturday morning. Why don't I pick you up at the airport and we can go on from there?"

"Thank you," Bruce said reluctantly. He was annoyed at having to take help from strangers. "Will you have enough room in your car? My daughter's coming with me."

"That would be Karen."

Bruce swore silently. "You seem to know a lot more about us than we do about you."

"I'm afraid that is so. Yes, I shall have ample room. Emma will be driving down on Friday with her fiancé, Alan Grenville, and Helen and her aunt. By the way, Mr. Lawrence, I am a solicitor, so we do have something in common. If you would care to call me once you have all the details of your flight, I shall be happy to meet you at the airport."

"How will we recognize each other?"

"I'll find you. Helen has shown me a picture of you. I believe she said you are rather tall. That will make it easier to spot you."

Bruce promised to call Richard Turner, took down his number, and thanked him. Then he sat, staring at the blank television screen, wondering where this man, also, fitted into Helen's life. The brief conversation had been enough to tell him that Turner had known Helen a good deal longer than just one week.

29

As they drove down to Marsden Court on Friday, Helen and Aunt Hilary sat in the back of the car, so that Emma and Alan could sit together. Their happiness was tangible.

"I did it!" Emma had told Helen triumphantly on Monday evening when she'd driven over to Lansdowne House to share her news. "After we'd been to the hospital and met Alan's parents—they're darlings, by the way— we went back to Alan's flat and he asked me to marry him. I told him I wouldn't give him an answer until we'd made love, just in case that part of me had rusted from disuse."

Helen had to smile as she recalled Emma's laughter as she told the story. In a thousand years she just couldn't imagine herself telling her own mother about her first time with a man, but to Emma it seemed perfectly natural.

"Anyway," Emma had continued, "at first Alan didn't want to. Can you believe that? He said he could wait. I told him he might be able to wait, but I couldn't."

"I hope you were . . ." Helen had hesitated, not quite knowing how to put it.

"Careful? Of course we were. After all, one never

knows where the likes of Nadia Perrin have been, does one?" Another peal of laughter. "So . . . we did it. And it was all right. Then I told Alan yes, I would marry him. Later we did it again and it was much better than all right.

"I know you think we're crazy talking of marriage so early," Emma had said in response to Helen's tentative suggestion that perhaps it might be a good idea to get to know each other a little better, "but we're both absolutely sure. At least we'll wait a couple of months for the official engagement party, just to please Daddy."

Despite her delight in Emma's happiness, Helen felt ice cold with misery inside. Tomorrow she would see Bruce—and her life in Canada would be over. The life she had striven to preserve by lies had been ended by the truth.

Aunt Hilary's hand came out to squeeze hers. Helen turned to give her a wan smile. Her aunt was not looking at all well. Her face was gray and her breathing very shallow. This had all been far too great a strain for her.

"Are you sure you're feeling okay?" Helen asked her.

"I am feeling marvelous, so please don't ask me again. This is a great treat for me. It must be all of twenty years since I last went away to the country."

"How about you, Helen?" Emma turned to look back at her. "How are you bearing up?"

"I'm fine," she lied.

"I'm so excited about us all being together this weekend. The only thing missing is Alan's family. I wish they'd been able to come down, but with Mr. Grenville just out of hospital, it was impossible. Never mind, he and the whole family will be at the official engagement party."

Lucky them to escape this weekend, Helen thought.

Emma turned again to smile at her. "I'm so excited to be meeting my sister. And my stepfather, of course."

Stepfather! Surely Emma had enough fathers without enrolling Bruce as another one.

Alan spoke Helen's thoughts out loud. "Haven't you got enough fathers, greedy?"

"The more the better."

"I hate to be a Jonah," Helen said, "but I don't think Bruce will be in the mood for embracing a new family, just yet." If ever.

"I understand." Emma smiled at her. "Don't worry. I promise I won't be pushy with him."

"Or Karen. She's not like you, Emma. She's a little more . . ." How to explain Karen to Emma, who had love enough for umpteen relatives? "A little more reticent about emotions than you are."

God, how she was dreading tomorrow! Why, oh, why had Julian spilled the story to the press? It would have been so much better if she'd been able to tell Bruce in her own time.

"But David's like you. You and he would get along well, I think."

"What a shame he's not coming, too," Emma said. "That would have made it just perfect. My entire family here for our engagement celebration."

Helen and Hilary exchanged speaking glances.

"What Helen is trying to say, my darling optimist," Alan said, "is that this could be rather awkward for all concerned."

Helen gave him a grateful smile.

"Of course it will be, at first," Emma said. "But it will all work out, you wait and see."

"We'll never find anyone in this mass of people," Bruce said to Karen as they emerged from the customs area into the main airport. In the waiting crowd, people held up cards with individual names printed on them.

"See any with 'Lawrence' on them?" Karen asked wearily.

Bruce shook his head. He felt grubby, bad-tempered, and badly in need of a shower and a shave.

A man was coming toward them, dressed in a tweed jacket and wearing horn-rimmed glasses. "Mr. Lawrence, Miss Lawrence?" he asked with a bend of the head in Karen's direction that was, for all the world, like a little bow.

"That's right," Bruce said. "You must be Richard Turner."

"I am indeed. How do you do." He shook hands with Karen and then Bruce. "I trust you had a good flight."

"As good as any." Bruce knew he sounded surly, but he was dead tired and found the man's very Englishness extremely annoying. All he needed was a pipe in his mouth and leather patches on his elbows and he'd be the epitome of every North American's idea of a country English solicitor.

"You must be very tired," Turner said to Karen as they made their way through the crowd.

"We are. It's a long journey."

"It certainly is. I was over in New York two months ago and that's not nearly as far as you've come today."

"What were you doing in New York?" Karen asked.

"Ah, well you might ask. Richmond—which is where I both live and retain my offices—is a place where many extremely wealthy people live. Actors, rock stars." He cast a smile back at Bruce. "Occasionally, if they are valuable clients, one has to go to them, wherever they are."

Bruce was surprised. He had taken Turner to be an old-fashioned pen pusher, used only to wills and estates.

When they stepped outside, they found it to be a crisp, sunny day with quite a strong breeze blowing through the concrete tunnel.

"Bit nippy," Turner said, "but you're well prepared for it, I see." He indicated Bruce's dark gray wool overcoat and Karen's brightly colored parka.

"Too well," Karen said. "I thought it would be much colder—and raining—here."

His eyes twinkled at her. "It doesn't *always* rain in England, you know. We've had some lovely weather recently."

"It was pretty cold in Winnipeg when we left."

Bruce shifted impatiently and glanced at his watch.

"Quite right, Mr. Lawrence," Turner said briskly. "We should be getting along. Wait here. I'll go and fetch the car. It's a light gray Rover, so you can watch out for me."

"How the hell would I know what a Rover looks like?" Bruce muttered as Richard Turner hurried away.

"I like him, Dad," Karen said. "Stop being a pain in the ass. None of this is his fault."

Bruce sighed. "You're right. Sorry. I'm dead tired. I don't suppose we'll be able to get any sleep until tonight. Can't exactly ask for our beds as soon as we arrive, can we?"

"You might not be able to. I'm certainly going to."

"Don't bother. We probably won't be staying."

"Oh, Dad. We've talked all night about this. You can't walk in and drag Mother out caveman style, can you?"

His face seemed to shiver before her eyes, as if it were about to disintegrate. "I doubt she'd come. Lovers reunited, it said in the paper, remember?"

"Who cares what the papers say?"

"What I'd like to know is where Turner fits into all this."

"He's her—what's her name?"

"Emma."

"Yes, Emma. Her adoptive father."

"I know all that. But there's more to it than that. I'll see what I can find out on the journey to Holbrooke's place."

"Be nice." She squeezed his arm.

He gave her a faint smile. "I promise to be nice until I get to Marsden Court."

"Strange name for a house. Sounds like an apartment block."

"Somehow I don't think it is."

Several times during the drive, Bruce found himself nodding off, and after a few weary attempts at conversation, Karen actually went to sleep in the back, her head pillowed on her discarded parka.

The traffic on the motorway was much heavier than Bruce was used to in Winnipeg. Richard Turner drove skillfully, but not aggressively. He was a middle-lane driver. Not too fast, not too slow. At times Bruce wished Turner would get a move on. He knew that once he'd got the hang of driving on the left side, he would be one of those belting past them in the outer lane.

Eventually they turned off the motorway. When they reached the country roads, not much wider than lanes, Karen woke up, excited by her first view of the mellow English countryside.

"I thought our fall was beautiful, but this is lovely in a different way. Softer, somehow, and greener."

"Regrettably, it won't last that much longer," Richard said. "Soon the leaves will be gone and we'll have November squalls."

"Beats snow."

"Here we are. The entrance to the mighty mansion." Richard drew up before a set of iron security gates.

Despite his lack of sleep, Bruce was able to catch a bite of sarcasm in Turner's tone. He had noticed it before, the few times Turner had mentioned Holbrooke. Jealousy of his daughter's real father, perhaps? Or just plain dislike of the famous Sir Julian?

Three cars were parked in the lane.

"Damned reporters," Richard remarked. "But the Dobermans seem to be keeping them at bay."

Once they were through the security gates, they drove down the long tree-lined driveway to Marsden Court.

"Jesus," Bruce said as the house became visible.

"It is rather impressive, isn't it?" Richard said.

"It's stunning," Karen said. "I've never seen anything so beautiful, except in magazines."

Bruce silently agreed. His heart sank. Helen loved beautiful things. How could a lawyer living in a flat prairie city—however successful he might be—give her anything that befitted her as much as did this lovely old house in its verdant setting?

Anger filled him at the unfairness of it all. All these years he had loved her. Provided for her. Given her the children she loved. And for most of the time they'd been happy. At least, so he'd thought.

Now it was all to be taken away by some film star with enough money to give her all she could possibly want, and more. The man who had been her first lover.

Or maybe he hadn't been the first. Maybe there had been more men in her life. Who knew what kinds of secrets she had harbored all these years? A woman who'd hidden all this away beneath that calm exterior could hide even more, surely.

As he got out of the car, Bruce slammed the door hard.

Waiting in the library, Helen heard the noise of a car door being slammed shut. "I don't want to go out to meet him," she told Julian, panic welling up inside her.

"I hope you're not afraid of him," he said. "If you are, I shall be happy to meet with him."

He made it sound like an assignation for a duel.

"For heaven's sake, Julian, let me deal with this by myself," Helen said. "I'm not at all afraid of Bruce himself. He has never given me cause to fear him. But I *am* afraid of talking to him about all this."

"Then let me do so. After all, I am the one who was at fault."

"It is none of your business," she snapped. "What you did has nothing at all to do with what is between Bruce and me. It all boils down to one thing. I should have told him about Emma before we got married, and I didn't."

"You wouldn't be the first one not to tell." He put his arm around her. "I hate to see you so upset, darling. What sort of man is this husband of yours to—"

The door opened. Helen pushed Julian away, but not before Bruce had seen them. He appeared in the open doorway, quite dwarfing Richard, who was behind him. She had forgotten how tall and solidly built Bruce was compared with other men.

She stifled the impulse to go to him and kiss him.

Julian came forward to greet him. "Welcome to Marsden Court. Helen has been eagerly awaiting your arrival."

Bruce ignored Julian's outstretched hand. "Has she really?" he said with heavy sarcasm.

Had it been any other time but this, Helen would have burst out laughing. Julian's greeting had been so singularly inappropriate for this particular occasion that it was laughable. But, looking at Bruce's rigid features, she felt more like crying. His face looked as if it were carved out of stone, like the faces on Mount Rushmore.

"Where's Karen?" she asked him.

"Someone called Martin has taken her up to her room. I said you'd go up to see her later. After we've spoken." He looked directly at Julian. "Alone, if you don't mind."

Julian glanced from Bruce to Helen. "Will you be all right, darling?" he asked her. "You have only to call if you need anything," he added pointedly.

"I'll be absolutely fine," Helen told him. She turned to Richard, who was quietly observing them with thoughtful eyes. "Thanks so much for driving Bruce and Karen down, Richard," she said with a warm smile.

"My pleasure," he said. "We should leave you alone now." His gaze went from her to Bruce and back again.

"I'll be perfectly all right," she told him softly.

The two men went out, leaving her and Bruce alone.

"Take off your coat, Bruce. It's warm in here with the fire."

He took off his coat and threw it over the sofa. He looked distinctly out of place amid the delicate Regency furniture and chintz covers. It occurred to Helen that he would look more at home in some ancient, craggy castle in Wales or the Scottish Highlands, clad in black armor, his broadsword at the ready to challenge all comers.

She had a sudden annoying urge to rest her head on his chest, to feel the warmth of his arms around her. But she had hidden behind Bruce's strength for far too long.

Now she was on her own.

"Sit down." She indicated the large green leather armchair by the hearth.

"In His Lordship's chair?"

"We might as well be comfortable while we talk," she said, ignoring his sarcasm. She bent to pat the old spaniel. "This is Jasper."

"I don't give a damn who it is." The leather creaked as Bruce sat down. "No more small talk, Helen. I've had enough of that with your friend Richard. I want you to tell me everything. The truth—"

"The whole truth, and nothing but the truth, so help me God."

His face went white with anger. "Christ, Helen, this isn't a joke."

"I wasn't treating it like one." She swallowed the lump of tears that was gathering at the back of her throat. "I meant it. I will give you the whole truth, so help me God."

"That will make a change."

"Remarks like that don't help."

"They help me." The muscles of his square jaw tightened. "I'm so angry I feel like punching someone. Preferably that pansy Julian."

"Julian's no pansy."

"Well, you'd know all about that, wouldn't you?"

She turned away to look blindly into the fire. "Shall we make a pact, Bruce? I'll tell you the entire story as succinctly as possible, and you won't interrupt me."

"So I'm to ask no questions, is that it?"

"Of course you can ask questions. Who could stop a lawyer asking questions? But please would you keep them until I've finished." She leaned forward. "What did Richard tell you?"

"Very little. He said I'd probably prefer to hear the story from you, that he and his wife had adopted your child a few days after it was born, and that she—your child—had called you in Canada."

"Her name is Emma."

"Who cares what her name is?"

"I do. She's my daughter, and I care very much."

This was never going to work, Helen thought with despair. She hadn't even started her story, and they were fighting already.

"I'm sorry," Bruce muttered.

"May I continue?"

"Sure. Go ahead," he said with a shrug as if none of it mattered, really.

"I was seventeen when I met—"

A knock on the door interrupted her. "Damn. Come in," she called out.

Mrs. Pennington entered with a rustle of silk. "Forgive me for disturbing you, Mrs. Lawrence, but we were wondering if you and your husband might like some coffee?"

"Would you like some, Bruce?" He shook his head. "Not just yet, thank you, Mrs. Pennington. Perhaps a little later, though."

"Very well." Mrs. Pennington glanced at Bruce's coat. "May I take Mr. Lawrence's coat and hang it up?"

"Thank you," Bruce said.

"You are most welcome, Mr. Lawrence." She backed out as if they were royalty.

"Is she for real?" Bruce asked as the door closed.

"Priceless, isn't she? I suspect that Julian sent her in to make sure you weren't murdering me."

"I must admit, I feel like it."

She hated to see his pain and anger. "I don't blame you. Let me tell you everything before we get any more interruptions. You can see now why I wanted you to wait until Monday."

"I couldn't wait another day."

Helen met his eyes and turned away to look into the fire. "When I was seventeen, I lived with my aunt and grandmother, in Lansdowne House, which had been the family home of the Barstows, on and off, for over a century."

"What about your parents?"

"You promised not to interrupt."

"No. I did not. You suggested I shouldn't ask questions until the end. I never gave any such undertaking."

She sighed. "All right. But try not to interrupt me too much. I hate being on the witness stand. Where was I?"

"Your parents. Why didn't you live with them?"

"Because my mother and I didn't get along. She objected to everything about me, especially my acting."

"Acting?"

"Yes, I wanted to be a professional actress."

"Ah. So *that's* where David gets it from."

"Yes, I suppose so. Bruce, if you don't stop interrupting me every few words, I shall never get this done."

"You've waited all these years to tell me. Now you don't have the time?"

"This is the wrong place to be doing it."

He came alive then. "Damned right. The right place would have been the restaurant in Toronto, the night I proposed to you."

"I was afraid you wouldn't want me," she whispered. "Once you knew I'd had a baby."

"You should have given me the option to decide that for myself."

"I'd had so much unhappiness, finding you was like a miracle. I was terrified of losing you."

He shook his head, a noncommittal gesture that told her nothing of his feelings.

She swallowed and began again. "I was in an amateur Shakespeare play, and Julian came up to me after it and said he would make me a star."

"Oh, great. Don't tell me you fell for that old line."

"For God's sake, let me tell the story," she said wearily. "To cut it short, I fell in love with him. He was quite a well-known actor, even then. I suppose I was terribly flattered that he'd be even the slightest bit interested in me. For one thing, he was eight years older than me. We dated, on and off, for several months. It was a whole year before we slept together."

"Very considerate of him."

Helen smiled wryly. "I'm sure he was seeing other women as well. But he was my first lover. We slept together only twice. I got pregnant."

"What bad luck. Didn't the famous actor know anything about rubbers, or don't they teach that in English acting schools?"

"I certainly knew nothing about it. He said he'd look after everything."

"A real Romeo, eh? I shall have a few choice words with Sir Galahad before I leave his castle."

"Bruce, stop talking nonsense. This all happened more than thirty years ago. I got pregnant, Julian went to Hollywood, my parents threatened to send me to some ghastly religious home for unwed mothers. I wanted to keep my baby, so I ran away."

"But you didn't keep her in the end."

"No, Richard persuaded me that it would be better for the baby to have two parents and a stable home."

"Ah, so I was right. You knew Turner before he adopted the baby."

"Yes, I worked as a clerk in his office."

"And did he lust after you, too?"

Helen felt her face flare up. "Of course not. He was just extremely kind. It was he who paid for all my expenses and for our flights to Canada."

"Our?"

"Ann's and mine."

"Okay, now I get it. The bond between you and Ann."

"Yes, Ann was the one person who stood by me through it all. She gave up her family and her country for me. Without Ann Sturgis, I'm quite sure I would have gone crazy. I'd lost everything—the man I loved, our baby, my beloved grandmother and aunt, my home—"

"What made you come to Canada?"

"I don't really know. Ann and I had often talked about working our way round the world. Just teenage dreams, really. Canada seemed nearer home than, say, Australia."

"So you left England and never saw any of your family again—until now."

"That's right."

"I take it your parents died."

She twisted her engagement ring round and round her finger. "My mother died . . . and my grandmother."

"What about your father?"

She looked at Bruce, and away again. "Aunt Hilary told me he's in a retirement home for clergymen."

"You mean to tell me your father's still alive?" he said incredulously.

She nodded.

"And all these years you've never even spoken to him or written to him?"

She shook her head.

"Christ! I really don't know you at all, do I? The Helen I know could never abandon her father like that."

She felt tears welling up. "He abandoned me."

He shook his head in bewilderment. "It's as if I've been married to a total stranger all these years. Why the hell didn't you tell me, Helen? Why?"

"I've told you why. I was afraid of losing you."

"So you married me for security, for shelter. Nothing more than that."

She knew that nothing she said would persuade him otherwise. She wasn't even sure herself, after all these years, what her exact motive for marrying him had been.

She answered him with a question. "If I had told you about Emma and Julian, what would you have said?"

"How the hell would I know after all this time?"

"But you're not certain you wouldn't have changed your mind about marrying me, are you?"

"No, I'm not certain. I fell in love with a beautiful young woman. Someone pure and good. I knew you were desperately lonely and missing your home. That's all."

"You make me sound like some innocent waif you wanted to protect." She was suddenly furious with him.

"What's so bad about that?"

"Why is it men project an image onto women and expect them to conform to it? All three of you have done that with me."

"All *three* of us. Who's the other guy?"

Too late, she realized how stupid she had been. "Oh, there was another man who thought he loved me, years ago, in England," she said, trying to get out of it.

"Turner," he said. "I knew there was something about him that bothered me. Is he still in love with you?"

"Of course not. This is all so ridiculous, Bruce. We're middle-aged, ordinary people, for heaven's sake. You make it all sound like some soap opera."

"I think he still loves you. And what about the dashing Sir Julian?"

"What about him?"

"Are you sleeping with him here?"

"No, of course I'm not."

"Don't sound so outraged. After all, the newspapers spoke of reunited lovers."

"I was eighteen the last time I slept with Julian. You haven't much faith in me, have you?"

"No," he said flatly. "Not any more, I don't. Can you blame me?"

"Not really, I suppose. I know how much this must have hurt you."

"Damned right it has. You've made me look a fool."

"Is that all you care about? What other people think?"

"With you at my side I wouldn't give a damn what other people thought. But now it's different. Never mind me, do you realize how much you've hurt Karen and David?"

"They must be ashamed of me."

"Ashamed? You still don't get it, do you? I don't think any of us gives a damn that you had a baby thirty years ago. It's keeping it from us all these years that we can't understand. And didn't you ever consider that they should know they had a grandfather still alive in England?"

"You're right, of course."

He put his head in his hands. "I'm dead tired. I haven't slept for two nights."

"I'll get Mrs. Pennington to show you to your room so you can rest. I didn't think you'd want to—"

"Sleep with you? Don't worry, I shan't interfere with your sleeping arrangements."

Sighing, she shook her head. "Oh, Bruce, I keep telling you, I am not sleeping with anyone."

"I really don't give a damn if you are." He stood up.

She felt like flailing at him with her fists, screaming at him, but what was the use? It was, after all, what she had expected. "I'll get Mrs. Pennington to show you to your room," she said, and walked to the door.

30

"*Sorry yours isn't exactly* the best room in the house," Martin Holbrooke said as he led Karen downstairs, "but we're rather full at present. We really need that new guest house."

"My room's just fine."

He showed her into a sunlit room. "If you insist on staying awake for a while, come and have some coffee to help you out. Hallo, you two. At it again?"

He addressed the tall, fair-haired man and a strikingly attractive redhead who were in a close embrace in front of one of the three windows.

They broke apart immediately.

"Let me introduce you. Karen, this—"

The red-haired girl didn't let him finish but rushed over to hug Karen. "I'm your sister, Emma, and it is truly wonderful to meet you."

Karen stiffened. Immediately Emma retreated. "Oops. Sorry. Helen warned me not to rush you. I am sorry."

Karen didn't know what to say. The only thing that came into her mind was, "You look like my mother," so that's what she said. It was true. Neither she nor David were so obviously her mother's child as Emma was.

"Yes, everyone says that," Emma said. "I saw it myself when we met for the first time last week."

Karen tried to pull herself together. "I'm not very with it at the moment. Jet lag. I'm sorry, but I really don't know the story about you at all." It hurt like hell to admit that to a roomful of strangers. "Only the few things Mr. Turner told us on the drive down."

"Oh, good. I'm glad Daddy filled you in a bit."

"Not much, really. He said he thought my mother would prefer to be the one—" She broke off abruptly. "Could I have that coffee you mentioned?" she asked Martin. "I think it might clear my mind a bit."

"Coming right up. Good and strong. How do you take it?"

"Just cream."

"Will hot milk do? Mrs. P. forgot the cream."

"That's fine," Karen said, although the thought of hot milk in her coffee was repulsive.

"You must meet my brand-new fiancé," Emma said. She took his hand. "This is Alan Grenville, my boss and future husband."

"How do you do, Karen," he said, holding out his hand. "You must forgive Emma. She's been bubbling with excitement ever since she heard you and your father were coming."

"Oh, really?" Karen was well aware that she sounded cold, but she couldn't understand why anyone would be excited about meeting people who were absolute strangers, however close the blood relationship might be.

Her coldness didn't seem to affect Emma one scrap. "I can't explain what it means to me to have found all this new family. You realize Martin is my half brother as well." She hugged him. "Aren't I lucky?"

Laughing, Martin rumpled her hair. "For God's sake, Emma, calm down or you'll explode. Poor Karen's had no sleep. Don't try explaining our intricate family tree to her until she's had her coffee, at least."

I'm not interested in any of it, Karen felt like saying. She was surprised to see the obvious and easy affection between Martin and Emma. According to Mr. Turner, they had met for the first time only two weeks ago.

She had liked Martin Holbrooke from the start. Alan Grenville was far better looking, of course, if you liked that type of blond, upper-class Englishman, but she preferred Martin Holbrooke's easy manner and casual dress. At present he was wearing grubby jeans and a Rolling Stones T-shirt.

Her mother came into the room. Her gaze immediately fixed upon Karen. "Mrs. Pennington told me you were in here." She came forward. "Did you have a good flight?"

"Very good, thank you." Karen knew she sounded horribly formal, but that was how she felt.

"Let's go for a walk," Emma suggested to the men. "We'll leave you two alone together." She went to Helen and kissed her.

Helen's fingers brushed Emma's cheek. "Thanks, darling." They looked so natural together, so *right,* that Karen felt a stab of pain around her heart.

"Sit down and drink your coffee," her mother said when they had gone. "There's cold milk here. You'll prefer that to hot."

Karen sat down and sipped at the strong coffee.

"Your father's very upset."

"Are you surprised?" Karen asked.

"No, not really. I expect you feel the same way."

"I don't really care," Karen said with a shrug.

"Then why did you come?"

"I came so Dad wouldn't be on his own."

"How's David?"

Karen took a piece of shortbread from the plate and bit into it. "Not that hot."

"He hates me, too, I suppose."

"Hate is a heavy word, Mother. Let's say he probably

feels worse than I do, because the two of you were closer."

Her mother didn't even try to deny this, which was a first for her. "Do you want me to tell you all about it?"

"Not really. I'm too tired. Besides, I'm sure Dad will tell me later. Where is he, by the way?"

"He's gone to his room for a rest."

"To *his* room? So you two aren't sleeping together now." Karen struck her forehead with her hand. "Oh, but what a fool I am. You'll be sleeping with your long-lost lover, won't you, Mother?"

"Don't you start on that as well. I'm sleeping by myself. In fact, the way I feel at the moment, that's what I'll be doing for the rest of my life, from choice."

"Oh, poor Mother. Jaded with all your men?"

"That's grossly unfair, Karen. Especially when you won't listen to the truth."

"Your sort of truth isn't much worth listening to. I'd rather hear it from Dad, thank you." Karen got up from the table. "I think I'll go to bed. I'll leave you to your *darling* Emma."

Helen grabbed her arm. "Don't be like that. I love you. I've always loved you."

"Yes, but there was always a part of you that was far away, wasn't there? I was never able to put my finger on it. Now I understand. Every time I did anything, you were probably thinking, I wonder if Emma did that. I wonder how Emma is doing at school."

"You're talking nonsense," Helen said, but Karen could see from her mother's expression that she wasn't far from the truth. "It's true I thought of Emma a lot, but you were always my lovely daughter."

"Oh, please, Mother. Spare me the garbage. I was never lovely. If it was a lovely daughter you wanted, it appears you've got your wish."

Helen put her arms around her. Karen stiffened, trying not to move a muscle. "I'll never forgive myself for hurting you all so much," her mother whispered.

Karen pulled away. "Excuse me. I must get some sleep. We can talk later. Please don't come with me, Mother. I can find my own way up."

When she had gone, Helen remained standing, her eyes closed. She opened them when she felt a hand on her shoulders and saw Richard standing before her.

"Oh, Richard, I've hurt so many people," she moaned.

Then his arms were around her and he was stroking her hair and speaking soothing words to her, though what they were she had no idea. She did know she felt very comfortable here, her face against his tweed jacket.

Now she could make out his words above the pain that pounded in her head. "Let me take you away from all this worry. You're not strong enough to stand it, darling. I've loved you all these years. Let me look after you."

This was exactly what she had been trying to avoid since their reunion in Richmond. She pushed away from him. "Please, don't."

"Your husband isn't worthy of you, Helen. I knew as soon as I met him that he wouldn't understand what happened to you. Not the way I did. You need someone to take care of you, to cherish you, as I would for the rest of our days."

It was extremely tempting. She was in dire need of some cherishing at the moment.

She put her hand on his arm. "Thank you, my dear, dear friend, but I must be on my own for a while to work this all out." She gave him a shaky smile. "I'm not quite the little flower you imagine I am, you know. I can manage by myself."

It was true. She could. She might not choose to be alone, but she would be able to cope if she had to.

Richard looked taken aback. "I'm sure you can, but

will you think about what I said? You don't belong in a
brash, cold country like Canada. I believe your heart is
here, in England with Emma and me."

"I don't mean to be cruel, Richard, but there won't
be an 'Emma and me' for much longer. She'll soon be
moving out, and you will have to make a new life for
yourself."

Behind his glasses, his eyes had a stricken look.

"I'm sorry, Richard, but it happens to us all eventually."

He took off his glasses and turned aside to polish
them with his crisp white handkerchief. "She's the light
of my life." He looked at her. She had never before seen
him without his glasses.

"I know she is," she said very gently. "But you have to
accept the fact that children grow up and leave home."

He put his glasses on again. "Even more reason for
us—"

"I don't want to think about it anymore, if you don't
mind. My head's pounding. I'm going for a walk. On my
own, please," she added as Richard made a move
toward her.

She was not to have her wish. She had just reached
the hazel coppice when she heard Julian hailing her
from the lawn.

Her impulse was to pretend she hadn't heard him,
but she couldn't avoid him all day. Sighing, she turned
to wait for him.

He strode across the lawn, clad in his country costume
of corduroy trousers and thick hunter's-green pullover
and swinging a rustic walking stick.

"I have just had the most amazing confrontation with
your husband," he announced when he reached her.

Helen's heart fell. "I thought Bruce had gone to
bed."

"He was in his room, but not asleep. I thought it was
time he and I had a chat about you, so I went up to see
him."

"Oh, Julian. I did ask you to let me deal with it. Apart from anything else, Bruce is dead tired. He hasn't slept for two nights."

"I applaud your show of wifely concern, although I regret to say I think it is sadly misplaced. The man's a boor, Helen. How could you ever have married him?"

"Perhaps because he wanted to marry me," she said sweetly.

The remark went right over his head.

"He virtually attacked me for having seduced and, as he termed it, 'abandoned' you. I told him you were just as eager as I was to—"

"No need to give me the details. For heaven's sake, Julian, you're both behaving like idiots. You act as if my virtue were some sort of bone to be pulled between you. Besides," she added wearily, "this all happened so long ago, it's a wonder you can even remember that I was eager."

He came closer. "Oh, I can remember it all right. Do you recall that first night, in the lane by the Thames?"

She tried to retreat but found a tree at her back. "No, Julian," she said as he took her face in his hand. "For the love of God, don't complicate matters any further. Someone could see us."

This entire day was taking on all the aspects of a French farce.

He pulled her against him, pressing her spine against the tree trunk. This isn't happening, she thought. It can't be. "For God's sake, Julian. Bruce might be looking out the window."

"Good. Let the bastard see who really loves you." He bent his head and kissed her fiercely. "Let me love you again, Helena." His low, resonant voice throbbed against her throat as he kissed her there, his mouth warm against her cold skin.

For a moment the old magnetism engulfed her.

He kissed her again on the mouth, this time slowly,

sweetly, and she instinctively opened her mouth to him and pressed her body against his.

"We belong together, Helen. We were destined for each other. Come and be the mistress of Marsden Court."

Damn. Why did he have to spoil it all by talking? She had a terrible urge to giggle. She was reminded of the final scene in the old James Mason movie *The Seventh Veil*, with three men vying for the heroine.

Unfortunately, with her it was only two men.

"I was a bloody fool to leave you." This sounded more like the old Julian. "And you were a bloody fool to run away." His hold on her tightened. "But it's not too late, my darling. Let's make up for all these lost years."

She was about to reply when they heard urgent shouts. They seemed to be coming from all over the house.

"Something's wrong," Helen said, breaking away and making for the house.

Martin was running toward her across the lawn, shouting her name.

Emma flung open a window on the upper floor. "Come quickly," she yelled. "It's Aunt Hilary. I think she's had a heart attack."

31

Aunt Hilary was lying on the upstairs landing, her legs crumpled beneath her. Helen fell to her knees beside her. "Oh, my God. Oh, no." She took her aunt's hand in hers. It lay there, limp.

Emma's scared voice came from above her. "I heard her come out onto the landing. She said that she'd heard angry voices and she was afraid someone was hurting you."

Hilary's eyes opened. "Helen?"

Helen squeezed her hand. "Yes, I'm here, darling. Helen's here, beside you."

"So much . . . pain," Hilary gasped.

"I know, I know, but it will soon be gone."

Someone bent down to cover her aunt with a blanket. Helen looked up at the blurred sea of faces above her. Her eyes focused on Bruce. "Isn't there anything we can do?"

He dropped on his knees beside her. "Straighten her legs," he told her. "Very gently. The ambulance is on its way." He looked up. "If someone would fetch some pillows, we could prop her up a little, to make her breathing easier."

Pillows were brought. It was Bruce who lifted Hilary and placed them behind her.

He smiled up at Emma, who was hovering close by. "You must be Emma. Would you support your great-aunt from behind, Emma, so the pillows don't slip?"

Emma looked happy to be given something to do. Helen met her frightened eyes. "Thank you, darling," she mouthed.

Bruce remained kneeling beside her. "I'll stay here, just in case she needs CPR," he said in a low voice. "All we can do now is keep her warm until the ambulance arrives."

Helen was struggling not to cry. If Hilary opened her eyes again, she mustn't be crying.

She felt Bruce's arm around her.

"It's all right, darling," he said, his voice calming her as it had always done. "Everything's going to be okay. The ambulance will be here any minute now."

"Oh, Bruce, I'm sorry. I'm so very sorry," she whispered. "I've hurt you so much."

"Hush, sweetheart. Don't think about it anymore."

"They're on their way," Martin called from below. "The police car is in touch with them. Just two miles to go."

The rest was a blur to Helen, a composite of ambulance men in uniform, a nightmare ride through the sunlit countryside, and then the arrival at the small hospital.

There, Hilary was whisked away and not even Helen was allowed to go with her. "You'll be able to see her soon," the nurse told her.

Not much more than five minutes later, Emma burst in with Alan, Karen, and Martin behind her.

Helen curbed her impulse to rush to Emma and hug her. Emma had Alan. Instead she smiled at Karen. "You made it almost as quickly as the ambulance."

"Martin drove at a hell of a lick," Karen said, giving him an admiring look. "How is she?"

"We don't know yet. The doctor's with her now."

Helen suddenly realized that someone was missing. "Julian didn't come with you, then?"

Martin gave her a wry grin. "My father's not too keen on hospitals. He said someone had to hold down the fort, so he'd stay at home."

Somehow Helen wasn't surprised.

It was a long, agonizing wait, interrupted by a frustrating interview with the doctor, who was amazed that no one in this large group of family members seemed to know anything about Hilary Barstow's medical history.

Eventually he was able to track down her doctor from the name and number in the address book Helen had found in her aunt's handbag.

"Apparently she has a long history of heart problems," he told Helen after he had spoken to him. "Didn't you know that?" he demanded accusingly.

"I'm sorry, but I keep telling you that this is the first time I've visited my aunt in thirty years."

The doctor—who appeared far too young to be a fully qualified doctor—looked at her as if she were a cretin. "She was advised that a bypass operation was necessary, but her doctor tells me she refused even to consider it."

Helen focused on a spot above his shoulder, avoiding the look of censure in his eyes. She couldn't really blame him. Her aunt had been sadly neglected.

Later that afternoon Hilary was moved into a two-bed room. The other bed was unoccupied.

"Isn't there a private room available?" Bruce asked.

"We don't have private rooms here," the doctor told him. "And she wouldn't get any better attention, anyway. Probably not as good."

"Then we'll pay for a private nurse," Bruce told him. "Obviously a rampant socialist," he said to Helen when the doctor stalked away.

Even after the move, they had to wait another hour

before they could see Hilary. By this time a heart specialist had been called in.

The specialist was comfortingly middle-aged. He
confirmed the younger doctor's rather pessimistic view
of Aunt Hilary's chances, only with a far more kindly
manner.

"May we see her?" Helen asked.

"Yes, you may go in now, Mrs. Lawrence. She's very
weak. We'd prefer her to rest, but she insists on speaking
to you. A few minutes only, please."

"Come with me, Bruce."

He nodded. They went into the room together.
Aunt Hilary seemed to have shrunk. There were tubes
everywhere, leading in and out of her body.

Helen sat on the metal chair beside the bed and
gripped the bed rail. "I'm here, darling."

Very slowly, Hilary turned her face toward her. The
muscles twitched about her mouth.

"Husband," she said, her eyes swiveling to Bruce,
who stood behind Helen.

"Yes, darling. This is Bruce."

"Big."

Helen smiled. "Yes, he is big. A big, strong Canadian."
She felt Bruce's hand grip her shoulder.

"Daughter?"

"You mean Emma?"

Hilary shook her head so hard, Helen feared the
tubes would be pulled out. She laid her hand on her
aunt's arm. "Quietly now. Lie still. You mean Karen,
right? She'll be coming in to see you in a minute."

Silence filled the room, broken only by the blip of the
heart monitor. Then a tear stole down her aunt's cheek.

"What is it, dearest? What's wrong?" Helen asked.

"Home. I wanted to die at home."

Helen swallowed. "You're not going to die anywhere.
And we'll get you home to Lansdowne House as soon as
you're better, I promise you."

But her aunt wouldn't meet her eyes, turning her face to the other side of the bed.

Another long pause. "I think she may be sleeping," Helen whispered to Bruce. "Maybe we should leave."

Hilary turned her head back. "Lansdowne . . . House," she said in a loud guttural voice.

"Yes, darling. We'll take you back as—"

Her aunt became agitated again. "Yours. Yours," she said, gray eyes glaring in her gray face.

"Mine?"

"House. Yours."

Bruce bent down. "I think she's trying to tell you that Lansdowne House is yours," he said quietly.

"Oh." Helen leaned forward to make sure her aunt could hear her. "No, dearest. It's not mine. It's yours."

Aunt Hilary became so agitated that Helen was tempted to ring the bell for the nurse. "You must lie quietly," she said, terrified at the increased blip on the monitor.

"Are you trying to say that Lansdowne House will become Helen's when you die?" Bruce asked Hilary directly.

She nodded her head, closing her eyes with relief that someone had the sense to understand her.

"Is it in your will?" Bruce asked.

Helen thought it a trifle callous to talk about dying and ask about wills at such a time, but it seemed to set Hilary's mind at rest, for she managed a tiny smile in response to his question.

"Good," Bruce said, smiling back at Aunt Hilary. "If it's in your will, everything will be as you wish. Lansdowne House will be Helen's."

"No, Bruce, it can't be," Helen whispered to him.

Aunt Hilary frowned. "Wrong?"

"No, nothing's wrong. Except that . . ." Helen hesitated. "It's only that my father will inherit the house, Aunt Hilary. It's his as well."

Her aunt shook her head vehemently, her mouth forming a no.

Helen could have kicked herself for upsetting her again. "It doesn't matter, dearest. It will all work out. I don't really need Lansdowne House."

She knew immediately that she had said the wrong thing. The thin hand, bearing needles and tubes, beat upon the bed in frustration.

"Yours," Hilary said vehemently.

"Let it be," Bruce said quietly. "Better not to upset her."

Hilary tried to struggle up on her elbow. "Yours. Geoffrey gave up—" She fell back on the pillow.

"My father gave up his claim to Lansdowne House, is that what you're trying to say?"

A relieved nod again. "Wants you . . . have it."

Helen was stunned. Her father probably had nothing but his meager pensions from the government and the Anglican church. She had never sent him any money. Yet if Aunt Hilary was right, it seemed he had given up his claim to an extremely valuable house in favor of the daughter he hadn't seen for thirty years.

Hilary was trying to speak again. "Must . . . see him."

Helen sat, staring at her aunt, seeing the strong face waver, to become her father's, weak and ineffectual. Then she came out of her momentary trance. "We'll try to get him here to see you."

"Not me." Hilary's eyes glared at her. "You."

Bruce's hand tightened on Helen's shoulder. "Yes, Helen will go to see her father," he said.

Hilary managed a smile again, clearly directed at Bruce. Her eyes turned to Helen. "Promise."

Helen licked dry lips. "I promise."

Hilary nodded to her to come closer. Helen leaned her head down to her aunt's face.

"Sorry . . . about Julian," Hilary whispered.

Helen knew what she meant. "You mean the phone

calls? Don't be sorry, darling. It all worked out for the best."

"Bruce. I like him. Strong. Depend . . ." She couldn't finish the word.

Helen had to smile. "He is. Very dependable."

Her aunt's eyes closed.

"We'll just bring the family in for a moment and then you can rest."

Hilary said nothing.

"Would you stay with her for a moment?" Bruce nodded. Helen hesitated and then said, "Thank you."

She saw that he knew she was not just thanking him for staying with her aunt.

They were gathered at the end of the hall, drinking coffee from paper cups. Her family: Karen and Emma and—not legally, but in essence—her future son-in-law, Alan.

"Would you mind coming in?"

They moved down the corridor, but Karen hung back. "You in particular, Karen. You are her great-niece, and she has never met you."

"I'd really rather not."

"Please, Karen," Helen said softly. "She particularly asked for you."

"Oh, all right."

Emma and Alan went on ahead of them and waited outside the door.

"I wish you had known Aunt Hilary when she was younger," Helen said to Karen. "You're very alike. You would have got along very well, I think."

Yet one more pleasure I have deprived my family of, she thought, but this wasn't the time for added remorse.

They went in and stood near the bed with the awkwardness always present in a sickroom. Emma went to the bed and bent to kiss her great-aunt's cheek.

Hilary's eyes flew open and panned along the faces, frowning as if she were trying to get them into focus.

"This is my other daughter, Karen," Helen said, leading her forward.

Karen stood by the bed. "Hallo, Aunt Hilary." She hesitated and then stooped to kiss her great-aunt.

"Karen."

"That's right."

"Skater."

Karen looked at her in amazement. "How did you know I used to skate?"

"I sent Aunt Hilary all the news about the family every Christmas," Helen said. "She also has photographs of you and David since you were born."

"David," Hilary repeated. "Give . . . love."

"I will." Karen leaned closer to Hilary. "So you know all about us, your family in Canada?"

Hilary nodded. "Clever lawyer."

Karen grinned at her. "Mothers always think their daughters are clever, don't they?"

But as she moved back to make room for Emma and Alan, she gave her mother a quick smile.

Less than an hour later, Hilary slipped into unconsciousness.

Helen insisted on staying in the hospital and just as firmly insisted that everyone else go back to Marsden Court. Reluctantly they did so.

Bruce remained with her.

At five past ten that night, Aunt Hilary died without regaining consciousness. With Helen's consent they made no attempt to resuscitate her. Her heart was worn out.

For several minutes after her aunt died, Helen sat beside the bed. When they told her they had to remove the tubes and machines, she stood up, groaning from the pain in her knees and back.

Bruce put a steadying arm about her. She took a last look at her aunt, bent to kiss her, and walked from the room.

"It's strange. I don't seem to be able to cry any more," she told Bruce. "I supposed the well's dried up. I just feel numb."

"From the little I saw of your aunt Hilary, I don't think she'd want tears."

"You're right," she said with a faint smile. "She loathed people crying." She felt punchy with weariness. "Oh, Bruce. I feel absolutely shattered. To find her . . . and then lose her again, so soon afterward."

"Let's go home."

"Where's home?"

He grimaced. "God, for a moment I forgot."

"You must be absolutely exhausted. That's three nights' sleep you've lost." Helen looked at the buttons on his crumpled jacket, trying to avoid looking directly at him. "Would you prefer to take a room in a hotel?"

"I don't think we'd get in anywhere at this time," he said with a slight grin. "Might look a bit suspicious."

"Oh, you." She gave him a mock slap on his arm. Then her smile faded. "I don't want to sleep alone tonight."

Silence stretched between them. It lasted so long that Helen grew afraid that she had misread everything that had happened since her aunt's collapse.

Then Bruce said, "Nor do I. Will you do me the honor of sharing your bed with me, Mrs. L.?"

"Yes, please," she whispered. "I very much need to be loved tonight."

A strange look came into his eyes. "I'm not sure I'm . . . capable."

"Of course not," Helen said softly. "How could you possibly be after having had practically no sleep for the past three nights?" She laid her head against his creased, white shirt. "I didn't mean it that way. There are more ways of love than that, as you well know. I just need to be held."

"That, I can do."

"The question is, do you want to do it?" she asked his shirtfront. "I wouldn't blame you at all—"

He laid his fingers on her lips and bent down to look into her eyes. "I want to."

32

Geoffrey Barstow *sat* on the terrace of the nursing home, his wasted legs wrapped in a tartan rug to shield him from the chill October air.

He was a tall, thin man of almost eighty, but practically no one would consider him tall nowadays, for he sat all day on his wheelchair, confined to it by the stroke that had taken away his ability to walk and, worse still, much of his ability to communicate.

Most of the time he sat alone, watching the birds or reading his favorite books, over and over again. Chiefly the books of his childhood, Dickens and Stevenson and Scott.

Occasionally he had difficult conversations with the other inmates. (He liked to call them "inmates." After all, this place was rather like a benevolent prison, wasn't it? And he was there for life.)

The conversations were difficult for two reasons. First, because he had great difficulty in getting his mouth to form the words that came easily into his mind. Second, it was hard to have discussions with clergymen without God coming into them. And he no longer believed in God.

He had lost his belief in God thirty years ago, when

his only child had run away from home. He never talked about her. Indeed, no one in the Anglican home for retired clergy even knew he had a child.

He might as well not have had one. She existed in his mind only, a gentle yet spirited creature with wondrous red hair. She would have been in his heart, had he still a heart, but it had been shattered on the day she had disappeared from his life, leaving him in darkness.

He had never forgiven his wife for her cruelty to Helen. Which meant, of course, that he had never forgiven himself, for he had sided with Jane against his daughter, too weak to stand up for Helen at a time in her life when she most needed him.

For ten years thereafter he had lived as a confidence trickster, ministering to his rapidly dwindling congregation, despite the fact that his belief in his ministry had long since been utterly destroyed.

The death of his wife from bone cancer had been a merciful release for them both. His longing to retire was fulfilled when he was partially paralyzed by a stroke at the age of sixty-three.

The retirement shelter had been his home for almost seventeen years now.

The only person to visit him was his sister, Hilary, and she came only two or three times a year. Her visits were more pain than joy, for she insisted on telling him about Helen and her family, showing him pictures of an attractive woman with growing children. The woman had short red hair but otherwise she bore little resemblance to his daughter.

He might have shown more interest had Hilary not said, when he had asked tentatively for Helen's address one day, "Helen is not one bit interested in communicating with you, Geoffrey. She tells me that, as far as she is concerned, she has no father."

After that, he had no wish to hear any more about the Helen who was a stranger to him.

No one else came to see him. Not one single member of the congregation in Ealing he had served patiently and, he had once thought, well, even bothered to write.

Geoffrey Barstow sighed and took out his gold pocket watch. It had belonged to his father, that ebullient and forthright Yorkshireman whom he so little resembled. Two o'clock on Wednesday afternoon. A popular time for visitors.

He stuffed the well-worn copy of *Little Dorrit* down the side of his wheelchair and wheeled himself down the path, away from the terrace.

"You'll get cold sitting out in the wood, Mr. Barstow," one of the keepers shouted after him.

He ignored her, as he always did.

Once he had reached the grove of trees at the foot of the path, he checked to make sure that no one was nearby. When he saw that the wood—indeed, the whole garden—was deserted, he slid his trembling hand into the breast pocket of his shabby navy blazer with its frayed cuffs and pulled out the old wallet that his sister had given him for his seventieth birthday.

With great difficulty he managed to extricate a small photograph from the wallet. It was creased and bent. The photograph was faded, but he knew that it showed a girl with long red hair and eyes the color of the sea.

With the forefinger of his good hand, he stroked the picture back and forth, back and forth. Then, blinking, he carefully put it away again.

The daily ritual of visiting with his daughter having been performed, he sat listening to the woodland sounds, the squeaks and chatter of the birds.

A sharp breeze cut through his old navy raincoat and the rug, biting into him, but it wasn't yet three o'clock. Visiting hours finished at three o'clock on weekdays.

"Mr. Barstow." The voice hailed him from the terrace. He ignored it. "Not coming in yet," he muttered defiantly. "They can yell until they're blue in the face."

"Mr. Barstow." This time the voice was more urgent. "You've got visitors."

He brightened for a moment. Good old Hilary. It had been at least six months since she had been down to see him. The daffodils had been out, he remembered, their vibrant yellow gilding the green lawn, gladdening the heart. If he'd had a heart.

He wheeled his chair along the path, pausing halfway to peer at the terrace through his metal-rimmed spectacles. There appeared to be several people there. None of them looked anything like his sister.

Wretched keeper must have made a mistake. Weren't his visitors at all.

Bother it! They were walking down the path toward him. He'd have to smile and say, "Good afternoon."

Then he saw her. The girl with red hair. Older, of course, but then Helen would be older now. She was smiling at him with Helen's smile, but somehow not her smile. More confident and self-assured.

"Helen?" he said hesitantly.

Helen had been dreading this visit so much that she had lain awake most of the previous night in her grandmother's bed at Lansdowne House. Bruce had woken several times to ask if she was all right. But she'd told him to go back to sleep. He had a lot of sleep to catch up with.

She had been very quiet on the drive down, staring out the window as the countryside flashed by, admiring the way Bruce had adapted to driving in England.

When they came out onto the lawn, she was a few steps behind Karen and Emma, who had now reached the wheelchair. She heard the frail old man say her name, but he wasn't looking at her. He was looking at Emma.

"No, Grandfather, it's not Helen," Emma said. "I'm Emma." She turned to point out her mother. "That's Helen."

He looked bewildered. "Helen?"

Helen came forward, her legs trembling. "Hallo, Father." She bent to kiss his cheek. His skin was like parchment beneath her lips. "Why don't we go inside, where it's warmer?"

He shook his head. "Too noisy." He spoke from one corner of his mouth, his speech slurred.

"All right," Helen said. "Then we'll sit on the terrace. It's sheltered there."

She could see him looking from her to Emma and back again. The administrator of the home had said he had all his mental faculties, but the shock of seeing her—or, rather, Emma—seemed to have clouded his mind.

Once they were all seated, she introduced her family to him. "This is Karen, my daughter." Karen smiled at him, but Helen could see she was uncomfortable with the entire situation. "Emma—"

He shook his head, bewildered. "I thought you . . . had a son," he said slowly. "David."

"That's right. David is in Canada. I spoke to him this morning on the telephone and told him we were coming to see you. This is Emma," she said proudly, her arm about Emma. "Julian Holbrooke's child."

Her father's eyes widened. "But . . ." For a moment he looked terrified, but Helen was smiling at him.

"Yes, Father. Emma was adopted by Richard Turner, as you know, but she wanted to meet her birth mother. So she searched for me . . . and found me. Just a short time ago, we were reunited after thirty years."

Her eyes suddenly filled with tears. She turned away, scrabbling in her pocket for a tissue.

Emma filled the gap. "Karen and I were delighted to find out we had a grandfather."

Helen caught sight of Bruce coming around the building. "And here's my husband, Bruce. He was just parking the car."

Bruce shook hands with his father-in-law, towering over him. Strange how she used to think her father was tall. Now, in the wheelchair, he seemed tiny and infinitely frail, especially beside Bruce.

Emma was chatting away to her grandfather. He barely spoke at all, but his eyes dwelled on her face as if he wanted to fix it upon his memory forever.

Helen felt a strange little pang of jealousy, which lasted no longer than a second or so.

Bruce exchanged a few stilted words with her father, but neither of them seemed at ease with the other.

"I've brought my camera," Karen announced. "Why don't I take a picture of you all together?"

She took two. Bruce behind the wheelchair, Emma and her mother either side of it.

Emma darted forward. "Now you, Karen."

"No, no. I hate having my picture taken."

"Please," Emma begged. "It's a very special occasion."

"Oh, okay." She took Emma's place beside her grandfather. Bruce put one hand on her shoulder and one on Helen's.

"Now, one of the two sisters with their grandfather," Helen said, and was rewarded by one of Karen's "Don't push it, Mother" looks. But she allowed her to take the photograph.

"That's enough pictures, I think," Karen said.

"No," Bruce said. "Just one more. Your mother and grandfather together, on their own."

Helen drew her chair up close to her father and took his thin hand in hers. "We'll bring you copies of the pictures next time we come," she told him.

"I think we three should go for a short walk," Bruce said once Karen had tucked the camera away in her bag.

This was what they had prearranged.

"Good idea," Helen said. "My father and I will have a little chat."

As she watched Bruce and her two daughters walk away, she felt panicky, her heart galloping.

For the first time since they had arrived, he looked at her properly. "Helen. It really is you, isn't it?"

"Yes, Daddy, it is."

"You've changed."

"Of course I have. I'm thirty years older."

"No, not just in age." Saliva gathered at the corner of his mouth. He dabbed at it with a threadbare handkerchief. "You're . . . more assured."

She smiled. "Motherhood—and middle age—has a way of doing that to women."

"Hard to think of you as . . . middle-aged." His hand moved to his upper pocket, then away again.

"We all get older, Daddy."

"Yes."

Helen drew in a deep breath and released it. She mustn't put this off any longer.

"I'm sorry I haven't been to see you before, Daddy, but this is my first visit to England since I went to Canada." A white lie, but it didn't matter. "I'm also terribly sorry that, on my very first visit, I have to be the bearer of bad news."

He thought for a moment and then said, "Hilary?"

She nodded. "I'm afraid she had a heart attack on Saturday, Daddy. She died a few hours later, without suffering at all." Another white lie. "We were all there with her, though. She wasn't alone."

"Poor Hils. She was a good old thing." He stared out into the garden with watery eyes.

"Oh, Daddy." It was difficult to hug him. The wheelchair got in the way. So she knelt before him and laid her head on his lap. After a moment she felt his hand stroking her hair. She looked up at him. "Aunt Hilary wanted to be cremated. No service, her will said."

"No bloody clergymen."

Helen was shocked. She had never heard her father swear before. Then she realized that he was quoting Hilary directly.

"She wants to have her ashes strewn about the garden at Lansdowne House," she told him. "We thought we'd have a sort of celebration-of-her-life party when we did it. Will you come? It's to be on Saturday."

He looked surprised. "To . . . to . . . Lansdowne House?"

"Yes, it won't be miserable or anything. I think it would be very fitting if you were there. After all, it was your home, the place where you grew up."

"Only in the holidays. I was at boarding school most of the time."

Of course. She had never thought about that. She had always imagined her father and Hilary having ecstatically happy childhoods at Lansdowne House, but it hadn't been so, not for him, at least.

"Weren't you happy at school, Daddy?"

"I hated it. They made fun of me be . . . because my father made biscuits."

She imagined him now, the bespectacled, shy bookworm, wrenched from his home, taunted by the other boys, and unable to fight back.

"Why don't you come back with us?" she said impulsively. "It would be lovely for you to see Lansdowne House again, wouldn't it?"

He looked terrified. "Now, you mean?" His fingers scrabbled in the rug.

"Yes, now. We can drive you there and—"

"No, no." His eyes were wide with fear. "I don't want to leave here."

She scrambled to her feet. "It's all right, Daddy. No one's going to force you to leave." She sat down close to him. "You'd prefer to stay here?"

He nodded.

"I suppose that after all the time you've been here, it's become your home," she said. "You feel comfortable and secure here."

He nodded again, this time with a little smile, grateful that she understood.

"Aunt Hilary has left me Lansdowne House, you know."

He nodded.

"Are you absolutely sure that you want to relinquish your right to it?"

"All done. Signed and sealed."

"Yes, I know that. But Richard said it's worth a lot of money. As much as three hundred thousand pounds. Maybe even more when the recession's over. That's a great deal of money. With that kind of money, you could live in the best nursing home in the country."

His eyes glared at her. "I don't want any of it. It's yours. You must have it." His breathing was fast.

She was terrified that he, too, would have a heart attack. "All right, Daddy. I won't argue with you."

"I like it here. It's my home now."

"I understand. If you really want to stay here, that's fine. But we'll make everything as comfortable as possible for you. We'll bring down some of the furniture from Lansdowne House for your room and make it really cozy."

He smiled. "That would be nice."

"And I'm sure you'd like some new clothes and an account with Hatchards for as many books as you want, and . . ." She saw Bruce approaching. Behind him came Emma and Karen. Her heart lifted when she saw that they were heatedly discussing something, perhaps even arguing.

Arguing was fine. As long as they were communicating. That's all she cared about.

She heard Karen laugh out loud and then Emma join in.

"My father would prefer to stay here," she told Bruce when he reached them.

"Permanently, you mean?" he asked Geoffrey Barstow.

"Yes. I told Helen, it's my home now."

"I understand that." But Bruce's expression showed that he really didn't. "Well, we shall make sure you want for nothing in future."

Geoffrey frowned. "I don't need anything." He grasped Bruce's sleeve. "You're a . . . a lawyer, aren't you?"

"That's right."

"There'll be death duties, you know. Heavy."

"Yes, I suppose there will be. Richard Turner mentioned the inheritance tax."

"House needs repairs, too. We must sell the biscuit shares."

Bruce shook his head. "Sorry. I don't understand."

"I do," Helen said. "You're talking about Barstow's Biscuits, right, Daddy?"

He nodded.

"Aunt Hilary told me you'd had a good offer from an international company for them."

"Sell them," her father said.

"I don't think they're mine to sell. The house was left to me, but not the shares. They're all yours."

"I'll . . . give them to you. Need them to pay death duties."

"Let's not worry about that now. Richard's going to sit down with Bruce and work it all out, before we go back to Canada."

His face clouded over.

"Are you sure you wouldn't like to come on Saturday?" Helen asked him. "One of us could come and fetch you, just for the day."

He shook his head vehemently.

"All right, then." She touched his arm to show him

that she understood. "We'll come back again to see you before we leave, I promise. And I'll be back in England, probably before Christmas, to sort things out, so I'll be coming down often to see you, then."

"But I'm right here in England, Grandfather," Emma reminded him, "and I'll be visiting you every week. Next time I come I'll bring my fiancé, Alan, to meet you."

Geoffrey's face brightened. "Good."

"And don't go thinking you'll avoid coming to our wedding. I expect you to be there, in top hat and tails."

Her grandfather flung back his head in a silent laugh. He patted Emma's cheek as she bent to kiss him. "I'll come to your wedding, dear child."

"Well," said Bruce. "I guess we'd better be going. It's a fair drive back to Richmond." He bent to shake his father-in-law's hand. "It's been great meeting you, sir. We'll meet again at Emma's wedding."

Emma and Karen said their good-byes, and the three of them walked around to the front of the house.

Helen was left standing before her father, not knowing how to leave him.

"Give my love to Hilary," he said.

For a moment she thought he had totally forgotten what she had told him. Then she met his eyes and knew that he hadn't. "I will."

She bent to kiss his cheek. "I'll be back very, very soon, Daddy," she told him brightly.

He caught her hand, holding her. Then he lifted his thin fingers to touch her hair and face.

"God bless you, my dearest child."

33

It was a lovely autumn day. Crisp, but no wind. High, scudding clouds in a pale blue sky. But Helen was beginning to miss the sweep and brilliance of the prairie skies.

She smiled at Alan, who had come early and spent much of the morning examining Lansdowne House from attic to scullery. He was presently inspecting the brickwork at the rear of the house. "Is it in terrible shape?"

"Needs a lot of work, I'm afraid, but at least it hasn't been ruined by inept improvers."

"That's what Emma said."

"Ah, but then she's been well trained."

They exchanged smiles.

"Are you sure you and Emma wouldn't like to live here, in Lansdowne House?" she asked Alan very tentatively, remembering the conversation she'd already had with Emma about it.

"It's really very kind of you, but we—"

"I just wanted to make sure," Helen said hurriedly. "Emma's already told me that you'd both prefer to live in London."

He looked embarrassed. "Of course, we'll be very

happy to supervise the renovations for you. It's just that living here while they were being done would mean we'd really never get away from work. I hope you don't think us ungrateful."

"Not at all. Emma's thanked me already. And while we're talking about gratitude, thank you for making her so happy, Alan."

"I think the shoe should be on the other foot. Thank you for having her. I'm a very lucky man."

"Yes, you are," Helen said quite seriously. "Don't you ever forget it."

"I won't."

They both turned to look across the weed-covered lawn, to where Emma was walking arm in arm with Richard, the brilliant gold of her coat brightening the withered garden.

"She has made such a difference in so many people's lives, mine especially," Helen said. "She deserves great happiness."

"I'll do my best." Alan sounded very serious.

Helen laughed. "Is it going to be that tough?"

"Of course not. Emma's very up-front about everything, isn't she? I'll always know where I stand with her."

"You must thank Richard and Mary for that. Certainly not me. I still have rifts to heal with my family in Canada because I wasn't honest with them."

She was thinking particularly of David, who'd been pretty cool with her during their three phone conversations. She changed the subject quickly. "I'm so glad Emma has you, Alan. It's hard enough to leave her as it is. Of course, she has Richard—"

"And Julian."

Their eyes met. "And Julian. Poor Emma. She may rue the day she went looking for her birth parents."

"I doubt it. She seems to have him pretty well sized up, I think."

"He loves her, that's obvious. She just has to make sure that he doesn't interfere too much in her life."

"Motherly advice?"

She made a face. "Sorry."

"He's already decided she'll be married from Marsden Court. Emma is insisting she'll get married in Richmond."

"Oh, dear."

Alan cleared his throat and put down the trowel he had been using to dig at the mortar around the bricks. "We haven't decided on a wedding date yet."

"That's your business, Alan, not mine."

He looked relieved. "I'd elope today, if Emma would agree, but she wants the works. That takes time to arrange."

"You don't want a big wedding, do you?"

He flushed almost as red as the bricks behind him. "Not really. It's not that I'm ashamed of my family, Helen. It's just that their ways are different. I'm afraid they won't enjoy the day, they'll be so worried about doing the right thing."

She touched his arm, knowing how hard it was for him to talk about his family. "Tell Emma that. Don't let her railroad you into something you feel uncomfortable about."

"Railroad?"

She laughed. "I'm a North American, remember?"

He jumped at the chance to change the subject. "So you are going back to Canada."

"Yes, I am. That's where I'm needed. I've a lot of explaining to do, especially to David. Besides, my home's in Winnipeg now. It's where I feel comfortable."

Her own words reminded her of her father. Aunt Hilary was right. She *was* like him. That had been her problem throughout her life. Always trying to avoid facing up to the truth. Well, that was going to change from now on.

"Don't worry, Alan, you're not getting rid of a mother-in-law that easily. I have to come back to sort things out here. Then we'll all be back for the wedding. I'll fly over early to help Emma. And I've told Bruce that I intend to spend one month each year in England."

"Will he come with you?"

"Sometimes. I'm hoping we can do lots of traveling in Europe together. But I also want to have some space to myself occasionally."

"You intend to keep Lansdowne House, then?"

"That depends, as you well know."

They both turned to look up at the house.

"I still think the ceiling is by Angelica Kauffmann," Alan said. "Robert Adam engaged her to decorate several of his houses. That in itself will probably get you some sort of grant to preserve the house."

"But the ongoing upkeep would still be enormous, wouldn't it? We're comfortably off, but not rich, you know. Income tax is quite high in Canada."

"It would be sad if you had to sell it, when it's the family home and you were so happy here."

She leaned against the back of the wooden bench. "All my life Lansdowne House has been the source of my happiness. My home, my haven. Even in Canada I spent far too much of my time living in the past, drawing on my memories of the house. But now . . ." Helen hesitated, wondering how to put it into words. "Now I feel different. Of course, I would like to keep the house, but not if it were to become a financial burden."

"You know it would have to be occupied for you to get a grant."

"It would have to be anyway. Otherwise it would be an invitation for squatters and vandals. That's another problem I have to work out when I come back. And talking about problems, I'd better go and check on the food and then change. Julian and Martin should soon be here."

*   *   *

She had thought it strange that Julian would even want to come to their little ceremony, but, later, when she saw him standing by the dining room window, looking up at the ceiling, she was glad he had.

They had come full circle.

For a moment she was overwhelmed by sadness. She was making the right choice, wasn't she? Then she realized that the sadness was for Julian, not for herself. He looked so alone standing there.

She went to join him.

"I always loved this house," he said.

"I know you did."

"I hate to see it so neglected."

"So do I. I've been talking to Alan about it."

"So have I. He tells me he thinks Robert Adam designed it. I could afford to bring it back to its original splendor, you know." His eyes were suddenly bright with hope.

"That sounds just a little bit like blackmail," she said, smiling.

He smiled back, the old smile that used to make her feel weak. "More persuasion, I should say." He touched her hair. "You look wonderful. I'm glad you took my advice about your hair."

"I had it colored for Aunt Hilary, not you, Julian."

He chose not to hear her. "Won't you change your mind, darling?" He grasped her hand. "I'm not the same man now as I was when I first met your grandmother and aunt here."

"I know you're not. But I'm not the same woman, either." She drew her hand from his, aware that Bruce was watching them. "I wish you contentment, Julian."

"Christ! Shall I buy a rocking chair for the terrace at Marsden?"

She giggled. "I can't see you in a rocking chair."

"Then stop talking drivel about contentment."

Despite the fact that Bruce was approaching, she grasped Julian's lapel and kissed him. "You must behave yourself now. You have a daughter to be proud of. She wants to be proud of her father."

"Lord, yes. I suppose you're right."

"Perhaps she'll make you a grandfather."

Bruce came up to them, his eyes wary.

"You hear that, Bruce? Your wife is talking about Emma making me a grandfather."

It was Julian's rather heavy-handed attempt at being friendly with Bruce. Helen was grateful. But she knew that the two of them would be glad if their paths never crossed again.

Unfortunately, that was highly unlikely.

"Maybe Martin will surprise you first," Bruce said. All three looked across the room at Martin, who was huddled in a corner, talking to Karen.

"Now, there's an interesting combination," Julian said. "Your daughter and my son." He raised his dark eyebrows at Bruce, his eyes alive with mischief.

Helen almost burst out laughing at the look of horror on Bruce's face.

"Winnipeg's a damned long way from London," Karen was saying gloomily. "Just my luck."

"What?" Martin asked.

"To meet someone . . ." She hesitated, not knowing quite how to put it. "Someone I like, who lives thousands of miles away."

Martin cast his eyes over the group by the window. "Despite the distance dividing our families, I've a feeling we're going to have some interesting family get-togethers."

"Oh, shit!" Karen gave a mock shiver.

"I echo your sentiments. Perhaps we'll need to get together somewhere else just to escape them."

"Like where?"

"Do you ever get to New York?" Martin asked.

"Sometimes. I've got a couple of friends there."

"I go to New York quite often on my father's business and to visit my mother. She lives there."

A slow smile spread across Karen's face. "Then let's make sure we've got business in New York next time there's a family reunion."

"Sorry. No chance on the next one."

"Why not?"

"That'll be Emma's wedding. Can't miss that."

"Right." Karen didn't looked convinced.

"Don't you like Emma?"

Karen sighed. "Of course I like her. Who wouldn't?"

"I suppose it must be tough for you. Favorite daughter supplanted and all that."

"Oh, I was never the favorite daughter."

"Join the club." Martin looked over to where his father stood, now talking animatedly to Emma.

"We should both hate her, shouldn't we? Only, hating Emma would be like saying you hate Julie Andrews."

Martin roared with laughter. "God, Karen, you're priceless."

Helen called everyone back into the drawing room and stood before the Adam fireplace, holding up her hand for silence. "I hate speeches, so I'm not going to make a very long one."

She looked at the faces around her. "We are here today to celebrate Hilary Barstow's life. Although some of you didn't even know her well, all of us are connected in one way or the other. As John Donne said, 'No man is an island.' Thank you for being here with me in the Barstow family home for this little ceremony. Now, let's go outside to the garden. Then we'll come back in and toast Aunt Hilary with champagne, as she asked us to do."

After everyone except Bruce had gone outside, she stayed behind, looking about the high-ceilinged room.

"Are you okay?" he asked anxiously.

"I'm fine. Just memories pouring in."

"Happy ones, I hope."

"In this house? Always happy."

"I'll make damned sure you can keep it," he said, his tone almost violent.

"We'll see. It's not as important as I thought it was." She frowned.

"What's wrong now?"

"I don't know. I was just thinking about what I said about everyone being connected. Then I had this strange feeling that someone wasn't here who should be. It was like seeing a large jigsaw puzzle with one piece missing."

He put his arms around her. "I expect you were thinking about your grandmother and aunt. After all, they were a very important part of your life."

She looked up at him gratefully. "They certainly were. Thank you for being so understanding."

He handed her the cracked Minton bowl. She touched the ashes with her finger. "Hi, Aunt Hilary. You're back home."

Then she went out into the garden.

34

The last piece clicked into the puzzle on the flight to Toronto. Ann. Ann was the missing piece.

Helen stared out the window at the cotton-ball clouds, excitement building. Apart from her father, Ann Sturgis was the most important person from her past who hadn't been there with her at Lansdowne House. She should have been.

No one could have been more loyal, more true a friend, than Ann. She had never been able to repay Ann for what she had done.

Now she could.

Throughout the second flight, from Toronto to Winnipeg, Helen hugged her excitement to herself. This was between her and Ann, not to be shared with anyone else. Not yet, at least.

"I thought you were going to call Ann from the airport," Karen remarked as she drank her third cup of coffee in an attempt to stay awake.

"I decided not to. I'd rather phone her tomorrow from home, when it's quiet. Then we can have a good, long chat."

When Karen got up to go to the washroom, Helen closed her eyes, pretending to be trying to sleep, but her brain was in a turmoil. What if she had to sell Lansdowne House?

That didn't matter. She would then have more than enough money to buy Ann a small house or a flat. Either way she could fulfill Ann's wish to live in Richmond.

Of course, it would be better if she could keep Lansdowne House. Ann had her pride. If she kept the house, she could tell Ann she had to have a reliable caretaker for it, especially if it was to be opened to the public, as Alan had suggested. Richard would be nearby to help her, if she needed help.

Richard and Ann? Was that a possibility? It was an unlikely coupling, but they had become friends—fellow collaborators—when she was expecting Emma. Richard was going to be very lonely when Emma left home. Ann was alone.

Helen grinned to herself at the thought of them together. Ann would certainly stir Richard up. Perhaps she would be just too much for a staid solicitor, even if he did have a good sense of humor.

Well, she had no control over that. Fate could take care of it. For now, Ann's immediate happiness was her priority.

She rehearsed the telephone call in her mind. Just wait until you hear my plan, Ann Sturgis. Your days in that wretched apartment are numbered. In a few weeks' time, we'll fly over to England and you can help me sort out the house.

Her heart was racing as she rehearsed the call. You deserve it, Annie. This is going to give me just as much pleasure in the giving as it will you in the receiving.

"You realize you'll be an independently wealthy woman if you sell Lansdowne House. If the market ever picks up, it could be worth as much as a million Canadian dollars."

Helen's eyes flew open. They'd been married so long, Bruce was beginning to read her mind. "I suppose so. But if I don't sell it, it could cost us a lot of money."

"I doubt it. Richard tells me there are ways of getting grants. He and Alan are going to look into it."

"You sound quite excited about it."

Bruce grinned. "I am. I never realized I'd married an heiress. I certainly didn't marry you for your money."

"That's for sure."

His smile faded. "Helen, before we get home there's something I must tell you. I want to tell you now, while Karen's not here."

Helen swallowed. "I don't think I want to hear it."

"I should have told you before we left England, but . . . I was afraid you might want to stay if I did. I'm sure you had offers." He stared at the chair back ahead of him.

"If I decided to stay in England, Bruce, I can assure you it would be by myself, not with anyone else."

"I want to tell you. You said we must be honest with each other from now on."

"That's true. I think I know already, but I don't want to spoil our homecoming by talking about it now."

"If you do know, then at least let me tell you now that nothing serious happened. I want us to make a fresh start, but this is something you must know before we can do that. It's only fair, considering I got so mad at you for not telling me about Emma."

She felt for his hand and gripped it. "Thank you, darling. I promise we'll talk about it soon. Whatever happened, I can't say I really blame you. I know I've been impossible to live with for a long time." She gave him a wobbly smile. "Actually, I've not really been all here for our entire married life. Part of me was over in England, with my baby and all those unhappy memories."

"God, how I wish you'd told me," he said for about the hundredth time.

"I wish I had, too." She pushed away the thought of what might have been. That was all in the past. "I hope you're ready for the new Helen Lawrence. I've got so many ideas for the future, I'm going to drive you crazy.

You'll be wishing for the old boring, uptight Helen again."

He ran his hand up and down the side of her thigh. "Somehow, I don't think I will."

It was snowing when they landed in Winnipeg, the snowflakes flying past the plane window. Strange to think that only three days ago they had been standing out in the garden at Lansdowne House in light coats.

"It's really deep," Karen said disgustedly, "and we don't have our boots."

David met them at the airport.

"It's wonderful to see you, darling," Helen said, hugging him.

He hugged her back, but she could feel the tension in him. "We've a lot of talking to catch up on," she told him. "That's why I came home as soon as possible."

He turned away to load the bags onto a luggage cart and began talking to Bruce about Toronto winning the World Series.

Helen didn't blame David. Not only had he known nothing about Emma, but he must be feeling very left out of the family reunion. She was sure that Karen would tell him he hadn't missed much, but it would have meant a lot to David.

Well, he'd be at Emma's wedding.

As they drove along the familiar streets, Helen felt exhausted but relaxed. The hypnotic movement of the windshield wipers, the tires hissing on the wet snow . . . everything was quiet and laid back. Nothing hectic. There was a lot to be said for the slower pace of a prairie city as an antidote to the tension of the past weeks.

Even if winter had set in far too early this year.

So much space, Helen thought as they drove down Forest Boulevard. Large, individual houses set on spacious lots. The snow was quite deep, piled up at the sides of driveways. Some houses had their colored Christmas lights turned on already.

"Christmas lights at the end of October. That's absolutely ridiculous," she said, and everyone laughed.

"You say that every year, Mom," Karen said. She had chosen to come home with them tonight, rather than stay in her apartment. "Talk about predictable."

Not any more, Helen thought. Meet the new, improved Helen Lawrence.

"I've got something to tell you all," David said as he turned onto their own wide street.

Helen sat forward, eager to see their house as soon as possible. "What, David?"

"I've been able to switch some of my courses to drama, and I've applied for the National Theatre auditions."

Helen felt Bruce stiffen beside her. Oh, no, David. Rotten timing. Couldn't it have waited until tomorrow?

She waited for the blast. Then she saw that Bruce was looking sideways at her with a quizzical half smile. "Well, David, I guess you come by your acting talent naturally. We can't fight genes, can we?"

"What do you mean?" David said. "What genes?"

"You mean your mother forgot to tell you that part on the phone? You were speaking to each other long enough, I thought she'd filled you in on everything. Before she came to Canada, your mother was an actress."

David looked at her in the mirror. "*You* were an actress, Mom?"

"Don't sound so surprised. I wasn't always just a mother, you know. Actually, your father's exaggerating. I was only an amateur."

Bruce leaned forward. "You've a hard act to follow, son. She was damned good." Helen was amazed to hear pride in his voice. "I was told she could have been a great star."

"Who on earth told you that?" Helen demanded.

"The famous Sir Julian Holbrooke, that's who. And he should know, if anyone should."

Her breath caught in her throat. Oh, Bruce, you darling,

you absolute darling, to bring Julian's name so naturally into the conversation. She sought for Bruce's hand and squeezed it very tightly.

"But you'd also better be sure to get good grades," he told David, "so you've got something to fall back on."

"Don't worry, Dad. I'm doing really well this year."

David slowed the car and turned into the driveway, almost skidding on the slick street. For once Bruce said nothing about driving more carefully.

The house was blazing with light. "I know how you like lights, Mom, so I turned them all on to welcome you home."

"Easy to see you don't pay the bills," Bruce grumbled.

Helen smiled. They were back into the old family rituals, yet somehow everything was different.

When they had brought in the luggage and Bruce had poured them all drinks, she went upstairs to change out of her crumpled clothes—and to be on her own for a few minutes.

"Boy, this room is blah," she said to herself, looking around. "It needs to be brightened up."

There was so much to do. Songs to be sung, life to be lived . . . she couldn't remember the right words, but whatever they were, they suited her mood.

She turned to look at the telephone beside her bed.

Tomorrow she would call Ann and tell her about Lansdowne House.

But, even before that, she must phone Emma to tell her they were safely home.

"Thank you, my darling, for making that first call," she whispered into the snowy darkness.

For a few minutes she stood watching the snow falling, the slanting flakes caught in the beam of the street lamp across the road. Then she drew the curtains.

YESTERDAY'S SHADOWS
by Marianne Willman

Bettany Howard was a young orphan traveling west searching for the father who left her years ago. Wolf Star was a Cheyenne brave who longed to know who abandoned him—a white child with a jeweled talisman. Fate decreed they'd meet and try to seize the passion promised. 0-06-104044-4

MIDNIGHT ROSE by Patricia Hagan

From the rolling plantations of Richmond to the underground slave movement of Philadelphia, Erin Sterling and Ryan Youngblood would pursue their wild, breathless passion and finally surrender to the promise of a bold and unexpected love. 0-06-104023-1

WINTER TAPESTRY
by Kathy Lynn Emerson

Cordell vows to revenge the murder of her father. Roger Allington is honor bound to protect his friend's daughter but has no liking for her reckless ways. Yet his heart tells him he must pursue this beauty through a maze of plots to win her love and ignite their smoldering passion. 0-06-100220-8